The Dream Weavers

Barbara Erskine is the *Sunday Times* bestselling author of over a dozen novels. Her first book, *Lady of Hay*, has sold more than three million copies worldwide and has never been out of print since it was first published over thirty years ago. Her books have been translated into over twenty-five languages and are international bestsellers. Barbara lives near Hay-on-Wye in the Welsh borders.

To find out more about Barbara and her books visit her website, find her on Facebook or follow her on Twitter.

www.barbara-erskine.co.uk
Facebook.com/barbaraerskineofficial
@Barbaraerskine

Also by Barbara Erskine

BARBARA
ERSKINE

The
Dream
Weavers

HarperCollins*Publishers*

HarperCollins*Publishers* Ltd
The News Building
1 London Bridge Street
London SE1 9GF

www.harpercollins.co.uk

HarperCollins*Publishers*
1st Floor, Watermarque Building, Ringsend Road
Dublin 4, Ireland

First published by HarperCollins*Publishers* 2021
This paperback edition 2022
1

A catalogue record for this book
is available from the British Library

ISBN: 978-0-00-819589-2

Typeset in Meridien by Palimpsest Book Production Ltd, Falkirk, Stirlingshire

Printed and bound in the UK using 100% renewable electricity by
CPI Group (UK) Ltd

MIX
Paper from
responsible sources
FSC
www.fsc.org
FSC® C007454

This book is produced from independently certified FSC™ paper
to ensure responsible forest management.

For more information visit: www.harpercollins.co.uk/green

For Sue
wisewoman and house healer

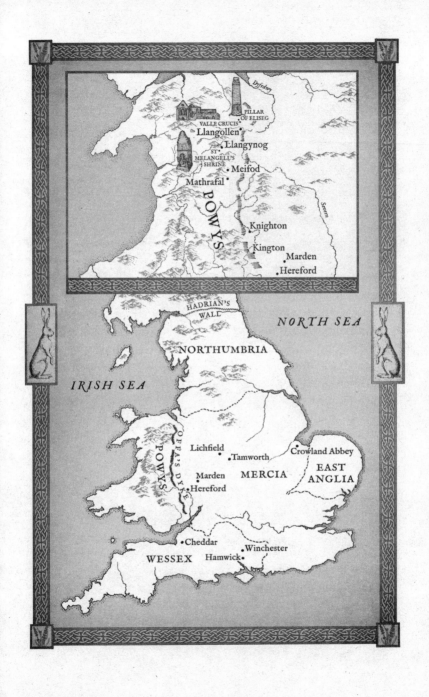

A note on Anglo-Saxon names

These have been transcribed in so many ways from the original script which contained letters unfamiliar to us that there are almost as many variations in spelling as there are authors who write about them. I have selected what I personally consider to be the simplest choice.

The main Anglo-Saxon characters in this book are:

Offa (King of Mercia from AD 757–796)

Cynefryth, Offa's wife, Queen of Mercia

The daughters of Offa:

Ethelfled, in my story, is the eldest

Alfrida is the middle daughter

Eadburh (pronounced Edber) is the youngest

Other historical characters in the story:

King Charles of the Franks, who in AD 800 was crowned as Emperor by the Pope and is better known to us as Charlemagne

Beorhtric, King of Wessex AD 786–802

Ethelbert, King of East Anglia d. AD 794

Ethelred I, King of Northumbria, d. AD 796

Nesta, the herb woman, is fictional

Elisedd, Prince of Powys (pronounced Eleezeth) is also fictional, depicted here as the youngest son of the real King of Powys, Cadell ap Brochfael (c. AD 773–808)

Offa also had a son and heir, Ecgfrith, (d. AD 796) who is only mentioned off stage in the story. In a few sources Offa is shown to have had a fourth daughter, Ethelburh. There is little mention of her and some sources suggest she has been conflated or confused with another woman of the same name, who became an abbess at that period. I have not included her in the story.

For more about the real history behind this story see the Author's Note at the end.

Glossary

Abad	Welsh for Abbot
Calan Mai	Welsh for May Day
Cariad	Welsh for sweetheart, darling
Clas	An early Welsh monastic community
Hafod	Welsh term for a shelter in the high summer pastures
Praefectus	Latin term used by Bede to describe a thegn or prince, next in rank to the king
Scop	Old English for poet or bard
Thegn	Noble retainer of an Anglo-Saxon king
Teulu	Welsh king or prince's household or followers (literally family)
Tylwyth teg	Welsh fairies
Tywysog	Welsh for prince
Witan	Council of the Anglo-Saxon kings

The Story Starts

'Elise!'

There she was again. Wretched woman! Calling. Endlessly calling.

With a sigh, Simon Armstrong slammed down the lid of his laptop and stood up. His train of thought had vanished. He walked across the room and dragged open the front door. He didn't expect to see her. So far he hadn't caught even a glimpse of her, but he had to try. The first time he heard her, he thought it was someone calling their dog out there in the dark, but the more he listened, the more desolate and desperate the cry sounded. He could hardly sit there and ignore it.

The isolated holiday cottage was situated below a high ridge on the border between England and Wales, near part of the overgrown ditch which was all that remained in this part of the world of the famous Offa's Dyke. The house was small and picturesque, stone-built, with roses climbing over the porch, blessed with every modern convenience, everything he had hoped for when he had booked it online. With its huge, solid but slightly crooked stone chimney, the main front windows, two up and two down, and the blue door with its wooden porch, it resembled a child's picture of a little house in a fairy story. Outside, an uneven flagged terrace was bounded by a low stone wall and beyond that a lane led up to what must be one of the most stunning views in Britain. From there he could see the Mid Wales hills of the Radnor Forest, the distinctive outline of the Brecon Beacons, the Black Mountains, and behind him, on the English side of the border, the Malvern Hills and eastwards towards the Shropshire Hills.

But no sign of Elise. Whoever, whatever, she was.

He went back indoors, closed the door and with a shiver walked over to the fireplace. Bending to put a match to the kindling piled in the hearth, he stood and watched as the flames raced across the dry twigs and he felt the first warmth. It was springtime at its most beautiful, glorious during the day, but at night a chill descended on the house, reflecting the fact that it was over a thousand feet up on this lonely, wild hillside. But it wasn't just that making him shiver.

He made it clear to Christine, the cottage's owner, that he had come here to find the peace and seclusion he needed to finish writing his book, ever conscious of his impending deadline, but since the first day he had opened his laptop and, coincidentally, begun work on the chapter about Offa's Dyke, the voice had been there, calling.

That night she came again. He woke with a start, conscious only of the sound of her voice so close outside and of the absolute emptiness of the cottage. Sitting up, he stared round the bedroom in the dark as downstairs she began to bang on the front door. She was sobbing bitterly.

Turning on the lights as he went, he ran down the stairs and dragged the door open. No one. Stepping onto the terrace, he shouted into the cold mist, trying to see her, but there was no sign of anyone there; nothing but the empty swirling whiteness.

He waited until morning to ring his landlady. It wasn't only the physical chill of the place. It was that the cold went right through his bones to his very soul. This had to be sorted.

1

Bea arranged to meet Simon in one of her favourite coffee shops in Church Street, almost in the shadow of the cathedral, round the corner from her home. They had never met before, but she spotted him at once, hesitating in the doorway, looking round. His glance swept over her, moved on, then came back. She wondered what sort of person he was looking for. The one he saw was a woman of middle height, her hair wavy, mid brown, no make-up, but undeniably attractive, with clear skin and large grey-green eyes. She raised a hand and he nodded, threading his way between the tables towards her.

She half expected him to be embarrassed. People usually were when they talked about ghosts; embarrassed or dismissive or scared, but he seemed calm and humorously resigned.

'Mrs Dalloway?'

'Beatrice, please. Or better still, Bea.'

He smiled. 'I'm Simon.'

The waitress brought their coffee and Bea studied him surreptitiously as the girl set out their cups. He was tall – he had had to bend his head beneath the low beams as he crossed the room – with a hearty outdoor complexion, a sturdy tweed jacket, tousled blond hair and hazel eyes. If she hadn't known

3

better, she would have had him down as a local farmer, certainly not the London academic Chris had described. Age: indeterminate. Probably much the same as her.

'I expect Christine has filled you in on my problem,' he said when the waitress had gone. 'When I rented the cottage, she never mentioned a ghost.'

Bea found herself grimacing. 'I don't think, to be fair, she knew there was one.'

Chris, one of Bea's staunchest and best friends, had bought the small tumbledown building several years ago. With the help of her husband, Ray, she had done it up to be the most perfect retreat.

'I have heard a great deal about her tenants over the years, and as far as I can see if they find anything at all to gripe about in what must be one of the loveliest holiday lets in the country, a ghost has never been one of them. So, what makes you think there is one?'

He pushed the milk jug towards her. 'I don't. That was her idea.' He gave a sudden grin. It lit up his hitherto rather solemn face. 'When she couldn't think of any logical explanation for the voice I've been hearing, it was the only thing she could suggest. Being the perfect landlady, she knew at once who to turn to. I could hardly offend her by telling her it was a ludicrous idea. I take it you know the cottage?'

Bea nodded. 'I've been there a few times.' She was trying to suppress her sense of excitement. She was intrigued.

'And you didn't ever feel anything amiss when you were there?'

'No, but then I wouldn't necessarily have done so. I wasn't looking for a problem.' She thought for a minute. 'I'm not sure if you know anything about my rather unusual job, Simon, but presumably Chris filled you in, or you wouldn't be here. I don't walk around the town seeing ghosts wherever I look, all touchy-feely and other-worldly. Nor do I do exorcisms. There is a very competent deliverance team here in the cathedral who will help you if that is what you require. Or there is a psychic Druid who lives over in the Black Mountains beyond Hay who can perform an equally good service if you

4

choose to take that route. I trained with him myself a few years back. I myself work as a freelance practitioner.'

For a moment he looked dumbfounded. 'So, what do you do exactly?' he asked at last.

The touch of amused scepticism in his voice brought her up short. Taking a deep breath, she reined in her enthusiasm. 'I deal with situations that other people consider frightening: the darkest corners of old houses, the sudden banging of doors, the creak of floorboards, the shadows thrown on a wall from an unseen presence. I go to houses that are uncomfortable, find out why and remove the irritant. It may indeed be a ghost,' she glanced up at him with a rueful smile, 'but often it's no more than a draughty corner, or it may be something in the underlying geology of the land; it may be something simply sorted by what people call feng shui; it may be underground water or an unhappy tree or an unfortunate choice of wallpaper, or sometimes merely a difficult neighbour.'

She had spent years training to deal with whatever arose, to rule out the obvious, to produce a screwdriver, to ring a plumber and, occasionally – very occasionally – to speak to lost souls, to reassure the newly departed and guide them gently on their way, to work with shadows and echoes and re-enactments from a past not as long gone as it should be.

He rubbed his face with his hands and stared at her in mock despair. 'Wow! Well, it isn't the wallpaper, I can tell you that much. And I checked with the neighbouring farm this morning and they have no animal, lost or otherwise, of any description, called Elise or indeed anything else. But a ghost?' He heaved a deep sigh. 'Rational people don't actually believe in ghosts, surely?'

So, why on earth had he bothered to come to meet her? This wasn't the first time she found herself regretting the day she had confided her interest in the paranormal to Christine.

'OK.' She paused. 'Well, we'll leave it as something to consider once all the other explanations for your visitor have been ruled out. But I would ask you to be open-minded if you can. Sadly, the response of most people to supernatural happenings they can't or won't accept, or situations they find frightening, is to mock.' She was watching his face, so far

5

studiedly neutral, and was pleased to see him wince as she used the word. 'Let's say, for me these things are real. I am lucky enough to be one of those people who are able to access that world and discern what is causing the imbalance that is making a place uncomfortable, or if something is wrong, contact the beings involved and help them find peace.' She gave him what she hoped was an encouraging smile.

'Well, that's me told! And I thought you looked quite normal.' He reached for his coffee. There was a brief pause. 'Sorry. That wasn't meant to be as rude as it sounded. OK. Here's what's happening. Let's see what you make of it. I rented the cottage to give myself a few months' peace. As I expect Christine told you, I'm an author.'

She nodded. Several would-be authors had found their way to Chris's cottage over the years. Presumably they thought the isolated position, the uncertain internet connection, the dark skies and stunning views would inspire them.

'I am writing a history of the Anglo-Saxons,' he went on. 'The Anglo-Saxon kingdom of Mercia to be exact. I have already written about the kingdoms of East Anglia and Wessex. This is volume three of seven. I have formed a habit of renting a cottage on-site, as it were, when I am on my final draft, to make sure I have an authentic feel of the area I'm writing about and be near local museums and suchlike. I live in London and I have two teenage kids. Peace is at a premium, so that idea works for me. My last two writing retreats were in Suffolk and the New Forest. I saw this cottage online and it seemed ideal. Right on the border between England and Wales – or in my book, between Mercia and Powys – and I was beguiled by the place's charm in the pictures.'

She was studying his face closely and he looked away, uncomfortable under her scrutiny.

'At first I assumed the voice belonged to a real person, obviously,' he hesitated, then went on, 'I still do, to be honest. I assumed Elise was her lost dog, or perhaps a child. But not again and again. If it was a child missing there would be people looking, police, search parties, helicopters . . . but now,' his voice trailed away. 'But now, OK, I admit it, I'm not so sure she, the voice, is real. If it was, I would at least have caught a glimpse of the woman by now. I've tried hard enough. But Christine assures me it isn't the wind or the water pipes or any of your other candidates for weird noises. I rush outside when I hear her, and I call out to her.' He raised his eyes from his cup and held her gaze. 'And,' he hesitated, 'I acknowledge I do feel uncomfortable when I hear her. Cold. And her voice is odd. It comes from far away.' He looked down into his cup again. 'Once or twice she's banged on the door in the night. When I open it, there's no one there.'

There was a short silence, broken only by the sound of soft, murmured conversation at the other tables.

'I'm a rational man,' he went on thoughtfully. 'I do not believe in ghosts, but for the last day or so I have been querying my own sanity. That was why I rang Christine. I asked her if it was possible a previous tenant had lost something, because she kept coming round, calling, and I told her I was finding it distracting. I need her to go away! That's when Christine made this ludicrous suggestion that it might be a ghost. I thought she was joking.' He grinned. 'And then,' he sighed, 'after I ended the call I found myself, only for a nanosecond, you understand, wondering if it actually was a ghost. Or something to do with my writing – perhaps I had somehow conjured her out of my text.'

She saw a touch of embarrassment in his self-deprecating smile as she pondered his words. 'If you have, this would be a first for me. Someone who writes themselves a ghost. I take it this didn't happen in Suffolk or the New Forest?'

'No. It didn't. So, as Christine has brought you in as the cavalry, can you do something?'

This was the time to make her apologies, to say she was no longer doing house cleansing, tell him she was too busy doing other things. Perhaps tell him the truth: that she had virtually promised her husband Mark she would no longer dabble in the supernatural. Anything but arrange to visit the cottage. But already she had felt that faint prickle at the back of her neck, the slight frisson of excitement. There was something here to be followed up, she could sense it already.

2

'He's such a sweetie. Didn't you think?' Chris said later on the phone. She didn't wait for Bea to answer. 'Perhaps it's someone camping locally having a laugh, or someone from the farm. I know you told me never to mention the subject of ghosts in front of Ray or Mark, and that you aren't going to do it any more, but there wouldn't be any harm in looking, would there? He's obviously a bit pissed off, and I'd hate to lose him as a tenant. I've never had a long let like this before.'

In spite of herself, Bea was smiling when she put down her phone. Chris and her husband Ray were darlings. She could visualise the conversation so easily. Chris's remit was sheets and towels and groceries. Ghosts. No. For ghosts, ring Bea. Box ticked.

Mark was in the kitchen preparing supper when Bea finished the call. Behind the elegance of its late Georgian frontage and main rooms their house, the one that came with his job, still clung to medieval roots and the high-ceilinged kitchen came from that much older age. It was large, with ancient flagstones on the floor. The dresser and larder and the huge scrubbed oak table may have come from another century; the cooker, fridge and dishwasher were, thank heaven, modern.

Mark looked up when she walked in and pushed a glass of wine across the table in her direction. 'Was that Chris on the phone? How is she?'

Sitting down, she picked up the glass. 'She's fine.' She hesitated. Should she keep silent or tell him about the ghost? She hated the thought of lying. Hated the thought of being put in this position at all. Better perhaps to prevaricate for now. 'She was telling me that there's a problem with her holiday let. You remember the cottage up on Offa's Ridge? She's rented it to an author for several months, so she's a bit twitchy about everything being perfect for him. I said I would go up there with her tomorrow to take a look.'

He turned back to the chopping board. 'Did she say what kind of problem?'

She shook her head. 'I expect we'll turn it into an excuse for a girls' lunch.'

Simon had slipped the spare key off his key ring and given it to her before they parted. It appeared he was planning to go out next day. 'Better if I'm not there. Go and have a poke around on your own. See if you can sort it.'

On her own.

It had been too late to say no. And after all, how difficult could it be – a wailing voice and a knocking at the door in the night? She had dealt with worse, much worse, before.

Bea loved her husband unreservedly, had done ever since the first time she had laid eyes on him when they were both going to the same sixth form college. Standing in their kitchen, chopping vegetables in his Snoopy T-shirt, a present from their daughter Petra, it was easy to forget that he now gloried in the title of Canon Treasurer at one of England's great cathedrals. Without the dog collar, he was himself.

They had first met going backwards and forwards to college. He was the best-looking boy she had ever seen. Tall, dark hair, scruffy, but not overly so, and with the most charming smile, he had made a beeline for her on the bus on the first day of term and sat down beside her. She only realised how much of a catch he was when she saw the other girls scowling. Their friendship became close and they started to go out together at weekends and sometimes in the evenings to local dances or the pub. No one else had ever had a look in. They confided in each other and told each other their hopes and dreams – and her dreams of the future included Mark. There was only one thing she had kept from him. Her secret life.

When she was a child, it had been her grandmother who listened to her half-excited, half-frightened stories of another world, and told her they were normal. Her grandmother understood, saw as she did, and warned her that not everyone saw these things and that people would tell her that it was all her imagination. In an over-rational, hypercritical world it was easier to keep quiet about her gift than talk about it. Her Nan had also warned her that some people would be afraid of her.

Bea and Mark went on to university together, she to read English, he to do business studies with a view to joining his father's firm in the City. In her secret heart of hearts, she'd imagined that one day they would marry. For two years, life continued according to her plan, but then came his sudden announcement and her world fell apart.

He was going to give up his business course and become a priest. They would still be there at uni together, he assured her, still travel up and down on the same train at the beginning and end of term. But, perhaps inevitably, she realised almost at once that he was becoming a stranger. When her parents moved to London, she went with them. His original plan to join her there was abandoned. After graduation he took a curacy far away in the North of England. They lost touch. She applied for a post as an English teacher close enough to her parents to stay with them until she found her feet.

She had lost Mark, but she had not lost her interests. She began to attend workshops and seminars, meeting people with the same abilities as herself. She studied healing and spiritual development. She studied ghosts. That was when she realised she had found her true calling.

Boyfriends came and went. No one serious. No one who could ever take Mark's place. And then, out of the blue, they met again quite by accident and that had been that. She'd put aside her reservations, swept into the giddy passion that carried them into marriage and through his first two parishes, where she had proved herself remarkably good at being a vicar's wife with two children and a respectable job in a local school.

But her gift never left her, nor did her wish to help the people who needed her services as a healer and a medium. That was a part of her, and she'd told Mark about it before they married. At first he was shocked and incredulous. 'Has it ever occurred to you that this is all in your head? That you're imagining it?'

And she had said, yes, of course it had occurred to her, and perhaps he was right, that was all it was. 'But it is very real to me, Mark. And it works.' They left it at that.

She knew he was uncomfortable with it, but he had reluctantly accepted his wife's strange gifts in the end, what else could he do? She had helped him by keeping that side of her life to herself as far as possible. People came to her through quiet recommendations and mostly she worked alone. She was discreet. She never charged. Her grandmother's advice, to keep schtum, stayed with her; it was the unspoken rule she and Mark both lived by. Most of the time.

Everything changed after it was suggested that his career, his popularity in his parishes, his calm competence and his background in business, had been noticed and that the Dean and Chapter at Hereford Cathedral might view his application for the vacant position as Canon Treasurer with interest. She hadn't been at all sure what it would mean to give up their sprawling rural parish and move into the Cathedral Close; the idea worried her, but Mark had been so certain this was God's calling. These days, clergy partners follow their own lives, he assured her. She could still be a teacher.

She could still be a healer of houses.

As long as no one knew about it.

He accepted the job.

Their daughters, Petra and Anna, viewed the change with tolerant good humour. They were both bright, serious, and remarkably level-headed, as they used to point out, considering their father was a vicar and their mother a psychic. Neither had inherited Bea's gifts, though secretly she saw her own skills as a healer in Petra, who had from a small child wanted to become a vet. It was from Mark that Anna inherited her love of music which led her to want to make it her career. They had settled easily into their new bedrooms, loving the creaky floorboards and the beautiful little cast iron fireplaces and the views, one to the front and one to the back of the house. Both were at university now, Petra studying to be a vet in Edinburgh, Anna in her first year at the Royal Academy of Music in London.

The household had become suddenly very quiet.

Bea gave up her full-time job when they moved. She became a supply teacher instead. The spasmodic routine suited her second job perfectly. As promised, she pursued it with discretion.

Their lives settled down until that day when, a year ago, in an old house deep in the remote countryside of the Welsh Marches, she had encountered her first poltergeist and she and Mark had had their first major row.

The drive had been long and winding, the house at the end of it ancient, hung with creepers, and almost at once Bea felt a twinge of doubt. On the phone the problem had seemed textbook. Ghostly noises. Knocking. Items being moved about in the night.

As she parked her car and climbed out, she had realised at once that she shouldn't have come alone. One of the rules was, if it looks in any way complicated, take someone with you; make sure there is someone there to cover your back. There was something here and it was something bad. But it was too late to turn back. The front door had opened and the couple who had contacted her emerged. Mr and Mrs Hutton were elderly – perhaps late middle age – and they were clinging to one another, their fear and anxiety obvious.

'Are you the ghost hunter?' Ken Hutton had wrenched his arm out of the clutches of the woman at his side and ran down the steps. 'Thank the lord you're here! Go in. Quickly. It's happening now!'

Bea had a routine. Protect herself; surround herself with light. Stay very calm. A quick prayer. Do not show fear. Never show fear. Project unthreatening love and reassurance.

'It's started throwing things.' Daisy Hutton had been visibly shaking. 'I wish we'd never come to this wretched place!'

'We should have known there was a reason the rent was so low,' Ken had muttered. 'We're leaving, I'll tell you that much. We're leaving as soon as we can, and we'll want our deposit back!'

'I'm not going back in.' Daisy was genuinely traumatised.

'Nor me.' Ken had shaken his head violently. 'You go in. First door on your left down the hall. In the library. God help you! We'll be in the garden when you've finished.'

For a moment Bea stared after them before turning back towards the house. She had never felt more alone.

'Christ be with me, Christ within me.' She had repeated the age-old words of the breastplate of St Patrick as she headed towards the front door. The safety net, the all-encompassing, wraparound armour of the prayer, would keep her safe; surround her with light.

The hall was shadowy, with oak floors and panelled walls. Old blistered paintings hung on the walls, and there was a worn Persian rug on the floor. The house had smelt damp, she remembered vividly, and cold, and yes, there was an atmosphere of evil so intense it seemed to drip from the beams. Grasping her pocket-sized Bible and her small carved wooden cross, picturing herself as safe and strong in her protective shield, she took a deep breath and opened the door of the library.

Something huge and black flew at her head. It landed at her feet with a crash and she saw it was a book, its pages torn and splayed. Within seconds several other books were hurtling round the room, a chair toppled over in front of her, a candlestick rolled across the table, the room was filled with a sound like the roaring of the wind and she felt a powerful thrust between her shoulder blades. It sent her reeling.

She had no time to think. Her reactions were automatic. She held out the cross in front of her and addressed the entity as though it were a naughty child. 'Stop it! Now! You can't frighten me.'

The response was a hiss and a demonic shriek from somewhere on the far side of the room. Clutching the cross more tightly, she had ploughed on resolutely. 'I can help you. I can give you a road out of here and guide you towards peace and light.' She dodged again as another book fell at her feet. The room's temperature had fallen several degrees and in the corner she had seen the sudden flicker of flames. It had been a battle of wills. Her opponent was a man, an elderly man, deeply unhappy and beleaguered; at his wits' end. Almost as soon as she sensed his identity, he was there, in the shadows. 'Let me help you.' She didn't plead. She was in control and reassuring. She paused, waiting for the next book to fly at her. Silence. The atmosphere had changed. The flames in the corner died down, leaving the smell of charred wood. He listened to her.

Bea had been able to see him more clearly at the end, stooped with pain, agonising physical pain, lonely, wrapped in a shabby woollen garment like a dressing gown, trimmed with fur. The room had smelt musty, airless. It was so cold that Bea's breath was condensing in front of her as she moved towards him. 'I'm here to help you. I want you to look upwards, towards the light. She was visualising a large double door, opening onto a beautiful landscape. 'It's open, can you see? It leads to somewhere warm and full of sunshine. It's safe there. Step towards it. That's right.' She saw him hesitate, glance round. There was a heavy leather-bound book in his hand and after a moment he leaned forward and put it on the table. She heard him groan as if the slightest movement was painful. 'That's right,' she encouraged. 'Only a few steps more. There is no more pain in the next life. It is bright and full of sunlight. There are friends there. Leave this dark place behind.'

He took a step towards the corner of the room where she pictured the door. Then another. He was almost through when it all went wrong.

'Has it gone?' The voice in the doorway had made her jump. Ken Hutton was staring in, his knuckles white on the doorframe.

Irritated, Bea had tried to ignore the interruption. 'It's beautiful through there. And safe. Angels are waiting for you; can you see them? You are not alone now. Go with God, my friend. Be at peace.'

In her mind's eye, she had reached out to close the door behind him and as she did so a flash had cut across the room. 'Got it!' Ken had been triumphant.

Bea had turned to see the camera in his hand. It was pointing straight at her. 'Don't!' she shouted. 'I do not want photographs. I explained to you, this visit must remain totally private and confidential. You agreed.'

He had lowered the camera reluctantly and she remembered his words clearly. 'It was so incredible. Impressive. I wonder if I got the ghost. Did you see him? I could hear you talking as if he was an ordinary bloke. It was a bloke? He won't come back, will he? Oh bloody hell! Look at the mess. All these old books. I'll clear it up if it's safe now. Chuck them all on the fire.'

The visit to that house had shaken her more than she liked to admit. Still in shock, she hadn't mentioned it to Mark. Then, four days later, there was a headline on the front page of the local paper:

LOCAL GHOSTHUNTER EXORCISES POLTERGEIST,
photos on pp 3, 6 and 7

Mark had been beside himself. 'Have you any idea of the harm this will do? I asked you, I begged you, to be discreet. You're on the front page for heaven's sake!' He had shaken the paper at her.

'Let me see!' She had finally managed to snatch it off him. 'Look. It's all blurry, Mark. No one would recognise me.' The large leather volume, balanced on the edge of the table, was in centre focus. It was actually rather a good picture. She could see herself there in the background, a white face, an arm raised with the cross in her hand. Oh God, that was dramatic, like the poster for a film, but her face was in shadow. Dodging away from Mark, she scrabbled in the paper, looking for the inside pages. There were half a dozen more photos, none of them recognisable, she was pretty sure, and none of the ghostly figure. There was a long article with the pictures. She scanned it quickly, praying her name was not mentioned. It wasn't. The journalist had made a big thing of the absolute anonymity demanded by the exorcist, describing her, rather flatteringly, as an attractive woman with phenomenal powers. Bea dropped the paper, relieved. 'The chances are no one will see it, Mark. It's gutter journalism. And if they do read it, they won't know it's me.'

He had looked at her, his face white. 'It says there that the creature, the ghost, tried to kill you, Bea. It says you wrestled with it, that there was furniture flying round the room and you exorcised it with bell, book and candle and flashing lights.'

'That's complete nonsense,' she had retorted, flustered. 'The flashing lights were from Ken Hutton's own camera. And the poor soul wasn't a creature, Mark. You of all people should know that. He was the shadow of an old man. He was more frightened of me than I was of him. An earthbound spirit who was sick and frightened and lonely. He threw the books at me because there was nothing else there to defend himself with. I prayed with him, Mark. I did not perform any kind of exorcism – how I hate that word – and he left.'

'It says there in the paper that he tried to kill you!'

'That is somebody's imagination.' She had reached out for Mark's hand. 'I knew what to do, darling. I was safe. And I did tell Mr Hutton before I went there that everything I did had to be confidential. He agreed.' She sighed. 'He broke his word. It won't happen again.'

Had she promised not to do it again, something that was as much a part of herself as breathing? No, not as such, but perhaps she had let Mark believe that was what she meant.

But a visit to a holiday cottage on Offa's Ridge was hardly comparable; a ghostly voice, at best a woman hunting for a lost pet, at worst a restless spirit, perhaps, nothing more. She would be able to sense at once what if anything was wrong, deal with it and be home before Mark had returned from evensong.

16

As though reading her mind, Mark paused from his cooking to take a sip from his glass. 'This problem,' he said casually as he reached for the last onion and picked up the knife again. 'Does it involve ghosts?'

She sighed. A straight question deserved a straight answer. 'I don't know. I think it's unlikely. This chap, Simon, is an author. He's been disturbed by some noises. A voice, he said. He complained to Chris and she gave him my name. She didn't realise I haven't done any house clearances lately.' She dropped her gaze, aware she was being disingenuous. 'Obviously she's anxious. She doesn't want to lose him as a tenant. She wants me to set his mind at rest, nothing more. I won't spend long up there. I need to get a feel of the place, that's all. I suspect I shall find a tapping creeper on the wall or, as he suspects, a lady looking for her lost dog.' She glanced at him and caught the anxiety that showed on his face. 'Don't worry, Mark. If I think it's dangerous, I will leave at once.'

He sighed. 'If he's an author, perhaps his characters are haunting him.' His expression was carefully neutral now. He turned to scrape his chopped vegetables into the sizzling pan on the stove.

Bea laughed uncomfortably. 'We thought of that.' She reached for her wine. 'It's probably more that he's not used to living on his own in the country where owls hoot and foxes scream. Do you remember how spooky that sounded when we were in our first rectory? I promise I won't get involved in anything dangerous. I'll just go and see. I know you'll hold me in your prayers, darling. It will all be OK.'

3

There was something here.

It was a presentiment, nothing more, that whisper of cold air at the back of her neck. She recognised the feeling and paused by the gate. Should she stop now? Go home? Forget it? No. Of course not. This was for Chris, and for Simon and his peace of mind. There was nothing here but an unexplained voice. She began her routine of safeguarding herself against whatever might be lurking in the fabric of this pretty place, visualising herself and the cottage and its garden surrounded with light and love, murmuring the prayer of protection. Then, with an almost imperceptible shiver of apprehension, she began to climb the steps towards the front door.

There was only the one main room downstairs at the cottage; Simon had pulled the table over towards the large stone fireplace and there were several books on it, neatly arranged, with a mug holding pencils and half a dozen ballpoints, a stack of A4 paper, presumably a printout of his manuscript, more books – quite a lot of them, she realised, as she looked around – piled on the floor in the corner. She could see his printer sitting on a side table. The hearth was swept clean, the log basket full.

There was no sign of a laptop. Presumably he had taken that with him when he went out.

She paused in the doorway, feeling for an unseen intruder, but there was nothing there. Reassured, she walked slowly across the room and went through into the pretty modern kitchen, built as a lean-to on the back of the building. Breakfast dishes had been rinsed and left to dry on the draining board. There was fruit and a cereal box on the worktop, presumably more food in the fridge. Nothing untoward there, either. When she made her way back into the main room and up the narrow, dark, corner staircase, she found the two bedrooms, one double and one with two narrow single beds, with their matching bedspreads and elegant lamps, were equally tidy. It was barely possible to see which one he had selected as his own. She resisted the temptation to look in the cupboard or chest of drawers. The ghost – if there was a ghost – was hardly likely to be lurking there. What interested her was the atmosphere. Or lack of it. The cottage felt empty. Not only because there was no one there; it was empty of echoes, almost sterile in its silence.

Frowning, she went back downstairs to the front door.

On the terrace outside there was a small wrought-iron table and chairs; beyond the low stone wall the view opened out across a broad valley towards the distant hills. It was breath-takingly beautiful.

The fear hit her suddenly and completely. One moment she was relaxed, lost in the beauty of the hazy distances, the next her stomach had turned over, her heart rate had tripled and she found herself staggering across the terrace to lean against the house wall, barely able to stand.

Hide. She had to hide.

Her instinct was to bolt back into the house, slam the door, and then, what? The car. She had to get back to her car, but she couldn't move.

Closing her eyes, she took several deep breaths. She had been stupid, caught unawares by the stillness of the cottage, the glorious countryside. The world had spun for a second out of time into that weird unnatural silence. But the world was

19

back now. She could hear the song of a skylark, high above the ridge, see the sheep grazing peacefully on the far side of the lane, hear them calling to their lambs.

Elise!

The voice came from the garden behind the cottage.

Elise!

Bea felt the hairs standing up on her arms. It was a woman's voice, but muffled, strange, exactly as Simon had described, coming from far away. Steadying herself, reinforcing her shield of protection, she tiptoed to the corner of the terrace and peered round.

The back garden was small, beyond its wall the open pasture-land of the hillside. She could see no one there, although someone could hide with ease amongst the bushes and trees. Bea took a couple of steps onto the grass. Around her the scent of daphne and viburnum and daffodils filled the air.

'Please, don't be afraid. I only want to talk to you.' Recovering her composure, she spoke out loud, her voice low and steady, unthreatening. 'Where are you? Can you show yourself?' The voice most certainly did not belong to someone from a farm or a campsite, this was someone from another world.

At first the figure didn't register. There was a woman standing there, near the wall, no more than a hazy shape, but already she had gone, if indeed she had ever been more than a shadow amongst the many wind-tossed shadows of the garden.

From the depths of the shrubbery a blackbird let out a cascade of alarm notes as it dived out of the greenery and flew up into the trees. Bea swallowed hard, steadying herself sternly. This was the first time she had confronted something from the other worlds since her experiences in the old house, and she was shocked to find herself trembling.

She took a few steps forward. 'I want to help you,' she called. But the voice and the shadow had gone.

She made herself walk back inside the cottage. There was nothing in there either. No sound. Still no echoes. It was empty. Safe. Wandering over to the table by the window she glanced again at the typescript sitting there. *Kingdoms of the Heptarchy. Volume 3: Mercia*. This was Simon's book. He had wondered, if only jokingly, if he had written his ghost. In the absence of any other signs, did this perhaps contain a clue to what had just happened?

With a final glance round the room to ensure she was alone, she dropped into the chair by the empty fireplace and pulled the manuscript onto her knee. Amongst all the different-coloured sticky markers that bristled from every page she saw one larger than the rest. It was labelled 'Chapter 12: The Offa's Dyke Years', and belatedly she wondered if he had left it there for her to see. She reached over to the lamp, switched it on, and, still wearing her coat, began to read.

We will probably never know whose idea it was to construct a dyke between Mercia and the neighbouring kingdoms of the wild, mountainous country that later came to be called Wales. Modern thinking is that it was the result of discussion and agreement rather than the imposition of a constructed border and that, if only because it has been so definitively named after him, it was the inspiration of King Offa of Mercia (AD 757–796) a man with the ambition, manpower and administrative organisation to achieve such a large and consistent enterprise.

The dyke as it survives today does not stretch the full length of the border between the two countries and only in a few places does it coincide exactly with the modern national boundary. Much of the dyke has been destroyed or lost, but from what remains within the landscape it appears to have been roughly 70 miles in length, though Bishop Asser, in his Life of King Alfred, *written some 100 years after Offa's death, describes it as stretching north–south, 'from sea to sea', that is, it is assumed, from somewhere on the north-facing coast near Prestatyn, overlooking the Irish Sea, down to the cliffs at Sedbury on the Severn Estuary, incorporating ditches and banks from earlier periods, some possibly Roman, implying the idea of an imposed border may not have been quite such an original concept as assumed. The kings of Powys*

*in particular had over the centuries shown considerable
interest in invading their eastern neighbour with its rich and
fertile landscape – they attacked Hereford no less than four
times during Offa's reign alone, the last major attack in his
reign, as far as we know, in the year 760.*

In pencil, Simon had noted here, *also 778?? 784?? 796? Bloody
hell!*

Bea smiled and read on:

*Offa had far more ambitious things to do than protect this
leaky western edge of his kingdom. His main interests faced
north, south and east. He had the kingdoms of East Anglia,
and Wessex, Kent and even Northumbria in his sights; he
would be pleased to ensure peace on his western borders with
the peoples the Anglo-Saxons called the* waelisc, *meaning
foreigner, a word that eventually segued into the word
'Welsh'. The protection was to be achieved by the simple
process of digging a ditch, which would, as part of the
construction process, automatically raise a defensive bank
immediately beyond it. Forts and watchtowers have not
survived, if they ever existed. Even the possible presence of a
palisade of some kind on top of the bank is in contention.
There is much still to be discovered about this famous land-
mark.*

*At some point a meeting must have been convened between
Offa or his representatives and King Cadell ap Brochfael of
Powys, the grandson of the man who had beaten him so
resoundingly in the Battle of Hereford in the year of Our
Lord, 760 . . .*

Drawn into the story, Bea turned the page and settled back
more comfortably into her chair. Without realising it, she
allowed her circle of protection to waver and grow thin.

4

The lofty wooden Saxon hall with its carved roof timbers and luxurious hangings was full of people. The feasting done, Offa had beckoned a group of his followers and guests into a side chamber where the plans for the great dyke had been spread on the long trestle table. The spokesmen for the King of Powys were standing together at the head of the table, looking down at the long roll of parchment. At their head, Prince Elisedd, the King of Powys's youngest son, was looking quizzical. Around them were gathered Offa's scribes and advisers, members of his family, his surveyors, the local shire-reeves and the ealdormen and thanes.

'My youngest daughter, the Princess Eadburh, will represent me on your journey to the site,' Offa announced abruptly. He nodded towards one of the two young women who had seated themselves at the far side of the table. 'She knows my mind on this matter as she and I have ridden the boundary together.'

If he meant it as an insult to select the youngest of his daughters for the job, there was no visible reaction from the men opposite him. He sat down and reached for a horn of mead. He was speaking directly to the prince, scrutinising the young man's face. 'Why did your father, King Cadell, not come? Or one of your brothers?' This lad was still wet behind the ears. He didn't look as if he could lift a sword, never mind negotiate a truce with the man who considered himself the most powerful king on the island of Britain.

Elisedd met his gaze squarely. 'My father has business at our palace at Mathrafal and my brothers have gone with him. I assured him I was more than able to supervise the route of your ditch.' He spoke with confidence, his grasp of the Saxon language fluent.

Offa narrowed his eyes. 'The route has been agreed by both parties.' His voice was harsh.

'And as long as both parties keep to the designated plan, all will be well,' the young man countered. He turned to address the girl. 'I am sure you and I, Princess, young though we both may be, will be able to oversee this stretch of the work without conflict.'

She was watching him with the same narrow-eyed concentration as her father. Her hair, bound into a single heavy plait beneath her headrail, was the colour of sundried hay, he noted, the same as so many of these Saxons, and just like her sister. His gaze shifted to the second girl. Older, he guessed, by a year or two, but softer. There was a third sister as well, or so he had been told, his informant adding that with their mother they formed a nest of vipers, best avoided. He covered his smile with his hand as he realised that Eadburh was still watching him, and judging from her icy expression could read his every thought. He reached for his mead horn and concentrated on the honeyed richness of the local brew, refusing to look at her again. All trace of humour had vanished. That frigid blue-eyed stare had left him frozen to the marrow.

The emissaries from Powys had been accommodated in one the royal guest houses within the palisade. The huge enclosure, on a bluff above the River Lugg, held the great hall of Sutton Palace plus a dozen or so other halls of varying magnificence, together with kitchens, bakeries, workshops, weaving sheds, stables, plus a multitude of smaller buildings, forming what amounted to a small village. Taking two men with him, Elisedd rode out through the heavily guarded gateway, heading along the narrow winding river with its damp meadows and rich carpets of flowers. As the gates swung shut behind them, he breathed a sigh of relief. He had no reason to suspect anyone of treachery, but King Offa's bodyguard, armed at all times, seasoned warriors to a man, filled him with unease. The concept of a recognised boundary between their two nations, putting an end at last to the centuries of invasion and counter-invasion, made sense. Whether or not their neighbour would stick to his own rules was not a matter for him. His father and Offa had drawn up the master plan a decade before, and slowly the digging of the ditch and the erection of its earthen rampart had happened, each local district providing the men and money to undertake the huge enterprise, in some places working with earlier earthworks, in others incorporating natural barriers, hills and rivers, into a boundary that would at least stall any potential infringement of the truce. In the distance the reassuring hills of his homeland rose in a misty barrier against the western horizon.

'So, do I assume we have to remain here?' One of his companions, Morgan ap Cadog, rode up beside him. Elisedd deduced he felt as uncomfortable in the lair of their neighbour as he did himself. He nodded ruefully. 'Once the marker stakes are in place, we can go home. Then all that needs to happen is to send men to keep an occasional check that all is as it should be. There is no reason to assume he will cheat us of land at this stage.'

'And in the meantime you have to ride the planned route with the she-devil daughter,' Morgan responded. 'He chose the youngest for the job, but by the gods, he chose the most feisty!'

Elisedd laughed without humour. 'I would have preferred one of those old warriors, if I'm honest, but I'm sure we can ride side by side without clawing one another's eyes out.'

'And you can write a poem dedicated to those periwinkle eyes!' Roaring with laughter, Morgan leaned forward to rub his horse's neck.

Elisedd smiled. He was used to the ribbing of his followers. It was his experienced soldier brothers who earned the respect and obedience of his father's men. He was the dreamer, the poet – a much-respected calling in his own country, but he knew this mission as a diplomat was his father's way of testing his resolve.

The sound of hooves behind them caused him to rein in and turn to face their pursuers. It was Princess Eadburh with four heavily-armed warriors. She came to a halt beside him, making her horse rear and cavort under the sharp bit. 'If you are riding out to survey the site of the ditch you should have waited for me.'

'I was merely riding out to clear my head after your father's generous feasting, Princess. It's nearly sunset; to ride up to the site tonight will take us too long. We won't see anything in the dark. We'll go tomorrow.' He watched as her horse circled again, tossing its head up and down. He considered telling her to loosen the rein so the poor animal could stand still, but thought better of it. She did not look like someone who would appreciate criticism, real or implied.

As though reading his thoughts, she dropped the reins on the animal's neck. It stopped immediately and she laughed.

Elisedd schooled his face. That was the second time he felt she had read his thoughts. 'I shall look forward to our ride tomorrow then.' His words were studiedly neutral in tone.

She gave him a dazzling smile and without a word turned the horse to gallop back the way she had come, her escort in her wake.

'Phew!' Morgan gave a theatrical wipe of his brow as they watched the riders disappear across the meadow and into the woods. 'I hope you aren't expecting me to ride with you tomorrow.'

'Indeed I am. I expect you all to come.' Elisedd was watching the wind ruffle the long grasses, whisking away the trail left by the princess and her attendants. 'I don't wish to be eaten alive.' And with a shout of laughter he set his own horse at a gallop in the opposite direction.

5

The banging on the front door jerked Bea awake. She looked round, her heart thudding, the pages of the manuscript sliding off her knee and scattering around her feet. The room was ice-cold. She stood up and went cautiously towards the door and put her ear against it, listening. 'Who is it?' She hadn't bolted it when she came in, she realised.

There was no reply.

Taking a deep breath, she pulled it open. There was no one there. Wisps of cloud were drifting up the valley and the sheep on the far side of the fields were calling calmly to one another. Overhead, a red kite circled ever higher in the sunlight until it was out of sight in the glare far above the shadowy fields.

Whoever had knocked with such desperate force was gone.

Turning back, she looked around the room. She had been asleep, dreaming, and her protection, she realised with horror, was no longer in place. The knocking had left the energies around her fractured and the echoes had become jagged, her dream still with her with vivid clarity. She played back the scene in her head: the noisy hall with its smells of cooking and woodsmoke and crowded humanity, the ride across the meadows, the confrontation of the Saxon girl and the Welsh

27

prince. All of it so sharply focused, so intense, it had been almost more than real. And every part of it had been somehow relevant to this house. But it was gone. With a sigh she set about gathering the scattered pages of Simon's manuscript off the floor, the manuscript that held the clues she sought. The strange jump from intense noisy emotion to numb emptiness was a new experience, as was that moment of fear she had felt outside on the terrace. Even when she had confronted the violent poltergeist she hadn't been gripped by fear like that.

Setting the pile of paper down on the table, she was acutely aware that part of her wanted to go back into the dream to find out what happened next. She glanced round the room. It was growing more shadowy now that the sun had moved round. She ought to go home, but if she did, what was she going to say to Simon, or to Chris for that matter? She hadn't been able to interact with the woman in the garden, much less ask her to move on, and they expected answers. And she wanted answers. What, if anything, had Offa's feast and the young handsome prince to do with this cottage? Beyond the name.

This was Offa's Ridge. He must have been here at some point. Or perhaps not. She had never really thought about it. Offa was famous. Perhaps because his name was so easy to remember compared with some of the Welsh names of the villages roundabout, he was everywhere. There were Offa's cafés, Offa's giftshops selling Offa's fudge in the villages round about. And of course the Offa's Dyke footpath that wandered backwards and forwards more or less following the length of the actual dyke and then on from sea to sea, as described by Asser and quoted in Simon's manuscript, the footpath that ran almost past the door of this cottage.

Did the answer lie in the dream world? She glanced back at the manuscript. Was that the woman in the garden's way of communicating her story? Was it Simon's imagination that had triggered this sudden ghostly visitation, as they had joked? This hadn't happened to her before, but then every case she had dealt with had been different. She pictured the young and beautiful princess with her cornflower blue eyes and tried to match the figure to the shadow in the garden. No. That didn't seem to fit, but was that somehow where the answer lay?

'Bea?'

The voice from the terrace made her jump.

'Simon?' she hurried over to the door. 'I didn't hear your car.'

'That surprises me. The poor thing groans in mortal agony every time I drive up the hill in a cloud of smoke.' He stepped inside and she saw him glance round. 'So, have you sorted it?'

'I heard the voice calling. And I felt something.' She hesitated. 'Cold. Fear. Very powerful emotions.'

He gave her a sharp look. 'Did you manage to make it go away?' Reaching into his pocket, he pulled out a box of matches and headed towards the hearth. 'I'll light the fire if you're cold.'

She saw him look over at his manuscript on the table as he squatted down before the hearth.

'I was reading the bit you marked.'

He waited a moment while the flame caught then he straightened. 'I felt it might be relevant. I had read my way through more than half the book without any problem, then every time I began to rework the chapter about the dyke in Herefordshire and the first time we hear of Offa at his palace near Hereford, the knocking started. And that sad, desperate voice.' He grinned cheerfully. 'Was it a figment of my imagination?'

'No, I don't think it's your imagination.'

He raised an eyebrow. 'So, who is Elise?'

'I don't know.' She sat down on the edge of one of the two chairs, wondering how to explain to him what had happened. 'I didn't realise King Offa had a palace near Hereford,' she said at last, focusing on something she assumed he would be able to answer. 'Do you know where it was?'

'You read that bit?' He glanced at the typescript again. 'As I say in there, it was probably four or five miles away from Hereford itself, near an ancient hillfort they call Sutton Walls, Sutton being the Saxon for South Tun, tun meaning town. It would have been Offa's southernmost base in Mercia. They think he may have had a hunting lodge in what is now Hereford as well, but the evidence is all so scant. Archaeologists used to think the hillfort itself was the site of his stronghold, then they did a series of excavations in or near various villages nearby and they've found more signs of Saxon building there. There's nothing to see now above ground, as far as I know, but it's obviously an area with quite a bit of relevance. I'm going follow up forensic studies they've undertaken lately and see if they've reached any conclusions, so my book can include the latest discoveries. We do need to know where he was based.' He perched on the armchair opposite her. 'Sorry. I'm getting carried away. Back to the point in hand.'

She was watching the cold blue flames run up the kindling and spread to the logs. This was when she should say no. Tell him that it was awkward because of Mark's job and direct him to someone else. But she knew she couldn't. She was far too intrigued already by her dream and the echoes it had left in her head.

'Contacting your visitor wasn't quite as easy as I thought it would be,' she said cautiously.

'Ah. I sense there's a no coming. Couldn't you do it?'

'I didn't say that.'

'I'm too sceptical for you?'

'No. You can't be entirely sceptical or I wouldn't be here.'

'OK. Let's compromise. Let's say I'm a pragmatist. I'm prepared cautiously to suspend disbelief in the interests of scientific research. So, where are we so far?'

Sensing that he wanted to spar with her, she responded with a gentle reprimand: 'Scientific and research are dirty words to people like me.'

'Maybe.' He inclined his head. 'I withdraw them. I asked Christine for help, so it would be churlish to dismiss the help she provides.' The fire was already beginning to throw out some heat and he eased his jacket off his shoulders. 'Go on, tell me what you have found out.'

'Normally I find this sort of challenge intriguing and generally it's relatively simple to diagnose the situation. But here . . .'

She paused, suddenly serious again. 'I haven't managed to see the woman as anything other than a shadow, but I heard her clearly and I heard the strange echo to her voice, as you described it. Then' – she stared into the flames, replaying it in her mind – 'you came back and the moment was lost and I failed to make contact with her.' She fell silent again. 'There is something about this that unsettles me.'

'Bloody hell!' He gave a hollow laugh. 'If it unsettles you, what do you think it does to me?'

She looked up at him sharply. 'Are you afraid to stay here alone?'

'No. Certainly not.' He stood up abruptly. 'No so-called ghost is going to chase me away. I don't like being constantly interrupted, that's all.'

'But you're a scientist, being pragmatic,' she reminded him with a grin. 'You shouldn't be distracted by this. You should be thinking in terms of logical explanations.'

'Hang on a minute!' He raised his hands in mock surrender. 'What's this about me being a scientist? I am a historian.'

'But one who draws on archaeology and, as you said, forensic studies.' She leaned back in her chair and closed her eyes. 'Sorry. I'm being over-defensive. But it was you who mentioned the words scientific research.'

There was a brief pause. 'Has anyone investigated you?'

Her eyes flew open. 'No! No, they haven't. They're usually happy that I have got rid of whatever it was.'

'Which brings us full circle. All I asked was that you get rid of my wretched visitor.'

'And I will, but I have to confront your ghost. If she doesn't want to appear to me, I need to find out the full story so I can work out how to approach this.' She levered herself to her feet. 'Leave it with me. When can I come again?'

'Whenever you like. But preferably soon. I have a tight schedule. I need to be able to concentrate.'

'Tomorrow then. I'll ring you first.'

As she made her way across the terrace and down the steps towards her car, she paused, her eye caught by a stone lying almost at her feet. It hadn't been there before or she would have noticed it, she was sure.

She stared down at it thoughtfully, then she bent to pick it up. It was about the size of a hen's egg and fitted neatly into the palm of her hand. The colour of dried blood, streaked with grey and smooth as crystal, it had a gentle warmth to it. She wiped some clinging smears of soil off it carefully and studied it for a few seconds. This was one of those moments she had learned to trust, an intuition, something Simon would never understand. In days gone by it would have been considered a message from the gods. There was something special about the stone; she didn't know what yet, but it had appeared as she was looking for answers.

Slipping it into her pocket, she glanced back at the front door. It was closed. Simon had not waited to wave her off.

Standing quietly in the shadows of the hedge, Nesta, daughter of the forest, herb-wife and sorceress, smiled to herself. She had recognised this woman at once as a kindred spirit, a seeker of truth, a follower of the stars. In picking up the stone, the woman had accepted the challenge, and so was bound now to follow the story to its end.

Mark was in his study when Bea returned home. She paused outside his door. His room had once been the formal dining room of the house, overlooking the Close with its ancient lime trees and the huge squat shape of the cathedral itself filling the view from the windows, and it made a pleasant study with more than enough space for his desk and his books and chairs for when he needed to use it for private meetings. All was silent behind the door. She turned away to tiptoe upstairs without disturbing him.

While he had been a parish priest they had grown used to living in what they liked to call tied cottages, the last, a small modern house built in the corner of a rapidly expanding rural village, a typical new rectory to replace the long-ago-sold Old Rectory. Since they had moved into the Close, however, home had been this wonderful piece of history. It was one of several houses upgraded for the senior clergy in the early nineteenth century from a range of far older buildings. It had the best of both worlds – the back rooms still felt medieval, the front were late Georgian. Bea loved it.

It was on the attic floor at the back, high under the hipped slate roof, that Bea had made her own sanctuary in a room overlooking their small garden. It was her private domain. She called it her study. This was where she felt safe, where she studied the world that meant so much to her, the world with which she didn't want to embarrass her husband.

Going in, she quietly closed the door and leaned against it. Up here she kept her books, her notes, her meditation space. There was a large cushion on the floor, candles, framed hand-coloured Arthur Rackham prints, and pictures of sacred landscapes on the walls. She stood staring out of the window across the walled garden towards the huddled roofs of the old town beyond it for a few long minutes then turned back into the room. She needed to think, and by think she meant meditate and pray. Now she was safely home, on her own ground, she wanted to analyse what had happened.

What should have been a routine visit, a gentle exploration of a situation, a reassuring encounter with a lost soul who needed guidance and love to send him or her on their way, had turned into an unsettling and frightening experience, over almost before it had happened, followed by something that seemed to be a dream but was so lucid and meaningful that it had to be a part of some message from the past.

She pulled the stone out of her pocket. Seeing it suddenly there in front of her outside the cottage, she had subliminally recognised it as a signpost into the narrative into which she had been led by Simon's book. It was part of the story. She didn't know how yet, but she had sensed it strongly.

Lighting a candle, she sat down on the cushion, the stone between her hands. On one of the courses she had been on they had made a study of psychometry, the science – she smiled to herself at the word Simon would have balked at – of conjuring the past through the touch the fingers, by connecting to something tangible, holding an artefact – a piece of jewellery, a comb, a lock of hair – and using it to focus the mind on the person or place to whom the artefact was linked. This was something she had practised instinctively as a child, not realising then that what she did was anything more than her imagination, that the ability was a reality and a very precious gift. She had tried it before with stones from castles and ancient sites, from gardens and ruins, always conscientiously returning them when she had finished with their story. With this stone perhaps she could link to the past of the cottage, safely, here at home without a sceptical historian looming over her. Stones had always been there; stones were brilliant witnesses. They were as old as the ground around them and perhaps if she had found the right one it would provide the link she needed to whatever had so frightened the woman at Simon's house. If she had been guided to the link, she owed it to that lost soul to find out what had happened.

Slowly Bea began to compose herself as she heard the cathedral clock chime the hour.

A nest of vipers.

The phrase leapt out of nowhere. And then,

But that is not how it was.

6

'You know Papa intends me to marry the son of the King of the Franks.' Eadburh's eldest sister, Ethelfled, looked up suddenly from her sewing. Taller than her sisters, she was a powerful young woman, clever and humourless. Her face wore a smug smile. Her sisters froze. They were all of an age where they knew marriage was their destiny and that their destiny was at present foremost in their ambitious father's thoughts. Aggressive and relentlessly acquisitive, Offa of Mercia ruled with ruthless ambition what had become the most powerful of the kingdoms of Britain. Girls of marriageable age were valuable assets, and his three daughters perhaps the most valuable of all.

'Did Mama tell you that?' Eadburh frowned. 'I thought Ecgfrith was going to marry one of King Charles's daughters. He wouldn't want you both over there, surely.' Their only brother, a more powerful bargaining chip even than they were, was still in the mead hall across the courtyard with their father and his advisers. She reached into the basket on the centre of the table for a skein of silk. The sound of music drifted across the compound to the women's bower, together with the rowdy shouts and laughter of the men.

'Mama thinks King Charles is playing politics. He uses his children like pieces on a gaming board just as Papa does, and has no intention of marrying any of them to anyone at present,' Alfrida, the middle sister, put in. She was the most thoughtful of the three girls, quieter and perhaps the cleverest.

'It wasn't Mama. I overheard two of the thanes' wives gossiping.' Ethelfled blushed.

'Well, you can't believe anything they say,' Eadburh retorted. 'He might have chosen any of us. Me, for instance. I may be the youngest, but I'm the prettiest!'

Her sisters both laughed. 'I think we can guess who he has in store for you.' Alfrida fixed Eadburh with a mocking gaze. 'He's obviously got the puppy from Powys lined up for you.'

Eadburh stared at her. 'Who?'

'Prince Elisedd.' Alfrida giggled. 'Why else would he send you off with him to stare at a line of wooden stakes and a thousand men carrying baskets of mud for his wretched rampart when he could have sent one of his surveyors. Marriage is the best way to ensure peace between the kingdoms. He's told us so often enough.'

'So, if you know so much about it, who has he got in line for you?' Ethelfled pushed back her stool and stood up suddenly. 'Has he told you?'

Alfrida shook her head. 'He keeps very close counsel, as we all know.'

'Who keeps close counsel?' Their mother swept into the room, two of her handmaids trailing after her carrying baskets of newly picked herbs. Cynefryth, unlike her daughters who all took their colouring from their father, had dark hair and sallow skin. Her eyes were hazel, and at this moment narrowed as she sent a sharp glance at each of the girls in turn.

'Papa.' Alfrida met her mother's eye defiantly. 'We were discussing our marital fate.' Her voice carried a touch of bitterness. 'I presume that was why he allowed Eadburh to go riding with King Cadell's son this afternoon. At least she gets to lay eyes on her intended husband.'

'I don't know where you get the idea that Offa intends

36

anyone to marry that young man,' their mother said curtly. 'He has mentioned no such thing to me.'

'Thank the Blessed Virgin for that!' Eadburh said fervently. 'Can I help you with your herbs, Mama. Sewing bores me.' She threw down her work. 'And no doubt if we are all to be queens like you, we don't need to excel in that particular skill.' She glared at Alfrida, who loved embroidery.

Cynefryth suppressed a sigh of exasperation and walked back towards the door. 'Come along then. These were picked this morning while the moon was still in the sky; I have to see to their steeping while they still hold the life force of the moonlight, and there are salves to make.' She did not add that there were spells to add and charms to recite, known only to her, which was why she did not leave the task to a local herb-wife.

In the king's royal residence when he was in this part of Mercia there was a great hall, the huge oak beams resplendent with carved beasts, and a royal bedchamber and all the space and outbuildings that the king's vast entourage required. The stillroom, a small reed-thatched building behind the infirmary, was overseen by a local woman, Nesta, not merely a herb-wife, but also a powerful sorceress and a force to be reckoned with, if local gossip was to be believed. Oblivious to Nesta's haughty stare as she and Eadburh walked in, the queen sent her out of the hut as though she were no more than a servant to gather more plants from her list.

As soon as they were alone Eadburh turned on her mother. 'So, is it true? Am I to marry the Prince of Powys?'

Cynefryth was pushing up her sleeves as she reached into the baskets to sort out the leaves she had already gathered. Betony, meadowsweet, hemp and cinquefoil. The study of plants and leechcraft was one of the queen's passions and wherever she and the king went as they toured the kingdom it was made clear that the herb rooms of the various palaces they stayed in on their royal progress were her special territory. Her boxes with their stock of bottles and pots were already arranged on the tables, their lids thrown back.

Cynefryth did not bother to turn to look at her daughter. 'No, you are not. What would be the point of building the great dyke between our countries if we could buy a secure border with your virginity?'

'But Papa does plan to marry us all off?'

Her mother sighed. 'Of course. And soon. But your marriages will be the results of much thought and negotiation. I can promise you that a younger son of one of the British kingdoms would not be worth the trouble. Why would your father want to build his influence over there in a land of mountains and mists and very little else? You are a valuable asset to us. Your brother and your eldest sister will in all probability go to the court of the Franks. You and Alfrida will have glorious matches in kingdoms in Britain your father wants tied in firm alliance.'

'So that much at least is decided?' Eadburh felt oddly deflated. Was she not valuable enough to have had her destiny chosen yet?

'Nothing is decided,' her mother gave a tolerant smile, 'but it won't be long, child. Your turn will come. And in the meantime, I will teach you all I can of my herbal arts. Neither of your sisters has the application to learn or the interest and my plants have their uses in ways you cannot even dream of.'

Behind them the door opened and Nesta came back in, a woven willow basket over her arm. She paused as she saw the queen and her daughter standing by the table, her expression inscrutable.

'Come in, woman.' Cynefryth beckoned her towards them. 'The sisters of Wyrd must have sent you back at this moment. You can start my daughter's lessons in the craft this very day.'

Bea stared at the Saxon worktable, spotlit by a ray of sunlight that streamed in through the doorway onto the wilting herbs and the pile of baskets. In the distance, behind the glare of the sun, she could see the outline of a long low hill rising out of the trees, and in front of it the soaring roof of a vast barn-like building, the mead hall of the king. The stillroom itself appeared to be a simple structure, but built of sturdy beams, the walls of wattle and daub, with tables and shelves stocked with bottles and dishes and jars. Bunches of drying herbs hung from the rafters. There was a fire at one end of the room, over which hung a bronze cauldron. She could smell the exotic scent of the herbs, mixed with the familiar warm aroma of sawn wood and thatch, and she could hear voices shouting in the background, cows bellowing, horses neighing and the sound of hooves, the rattle and bang of hammers, people shouting, dogs baying.

As she grew more aware of the surroundings and the smells and the warmth of the sunlight, she realised the noises, the voices of women had grown distant, fading as she strained to hear them. Soon there was nothing to hear except the song of a robin from the fruit trees in the orchard. She blinked several times. The bird wasn't there in the past, it was here, in their own garden, its evening song echoing in through her window. The scene of the royal palace and its inhabitants had gone.

Gently putting the stone down on the floor in front of her, Bea sat for a long time without moving, deep in thought. She had hoped that, if it worked at all, her meditation with the stone would take her to the past of the cottage on the ridge, to see its origins, the people who had lived there, the scenes of anguish that had led to the loss of Elise, but it had taken her straight back to the story of Offa's daughters. It had continued where her dream had left off.

Elise?

Not a lost pet, not a woman, a man. The puppy from Powys. *Eleezeth*, they had called him. The name came back to her with sudden clarity, as did the strong angry faces of Offa the king, and Eadburh, his daughter, their eyes locked, their body language combative. Is that what this was all about? A Celtic prince, an Anglo-Saxon princess and a modern day historian who had inadvertently conjured up the past? Hardly able to breathe as the full realisation of what she had seen dawned on her, Bea scrambled to her feet and reached for her note-book. Never trust your memory; memory is the most fallible part of what you do. First impressions and recall are vital. Always write things down. She remembered the words she had learned at her first lecture on psychometry, what her teacher had referred to as time travel. Meditation with the stone she had picked up from Simon's front garden had taken her to a royal palace on the flatlands near a river, in the shadow of a long low hill. The stone had taken her back to the presence of Offa and his family, into the heart of the nest of vipers.

7

'So, what happened up at the cottage?' Mark had joined her in the kitchen. He was looking utterly exhausted, sitting down at the table as she pulled the carton of leftover stew out of the freezer. As she reached for a bowl to put in the microwave, he said, 'Sorry, love. I'm not really hungry. Do you mind if I just have coffee? I've got some figures I must sort out in the study. I'll get something to eat later.'

He watched while she made the coffee, took the mug with a grateful smile and carried it out of the room. She hadn't had to answer his question, to lie or prevaricate. Her secret was still her own for now. With a sigh of relief, she put the stew back into the freezer and waited until she heard the door of his study close.

Of course it couldn't be Simon's book alone. The stone proved that. Somehow the scene she had witnessed must have been connected to the cottage on Offa's Ridge, a place named perhaps not because it was so near to Offa's Dyke, but for another and altogether more personal reason.

She reached over to the stack of books on the dresser and found the local road map.

The Iron Age hill fort at Sutton Walls, one of the places

Simon had mentioned, was five and a half miles to the north of Hereford. She stared at the page for several seconds then dropped the book and reached for her iPad. There were several mentions on line of Offa's missing Herefordshire palace and its possible location. She smiled to herself as she swiped her way slowly through the various entries. That long hill she had seen through the door of the herb room was the right shape for a hill fort. The palace, busy and fortified as it was, had been on the flat land below it, where she had seen Eadburh and her Welsh prince riding through lush meadowland in the bend of a gently meandering river towards the line of higher ground. She traced the line of the River Lugg with her finger on the map, then found the dotted line of Offa's Dyke, following it as it veered westwards across the contour lines towards the trig point on Offa's Ridge, and realised her hands were shaking. It was at least twenty miles away, but do-able on a horse, surely?

Twenty minutes later she was back in the attic, sitting in candlelight, nervously holding the stone once more between her hands. Performing her protective rituals, surrounding herself with light and love and muttering her prayer, she emptied her mind to connect with the story again.

She awoke much later as the candle flickered and burned out, leaving her huddled on her cushion in the dark. The cathedral clock was striking midnight. It hadn't worked. There had been no dream, no vision of the past. Nothing but deep exhausted sleep.

'I wanted to thank you. You seem to have fixed my ghost.' Simon rang shortly after nine the next morning, minutes after Mark had left the house with a folder of notes for his finance committee. Bea was standing in her attic, staring out of the window as she held the phone to her ear. 'I'm not sure what you did, but I haven't had a peep out of her since you were here.' He sounded cheery. 'She seems to have decided to leave me in peace. I wanted to catch you before you left to let you know and save you a wasted journey. I got a lot of work done last night, thanks to you.'

His words took her aback. It had never occurred to her that Simon might not want to continue the hunt for the voice.

'I'm so pleased,' she said, a reflexive polite response, her voice flat. 'But to be honest, I didn't do anything.'

He laughed. 'Perhaps she realised she had met her match. Or perhaps you showed her there was nothing here for her. Next time I'm in Hereford, let me buy you a coffee to say thank you.'

Bea gave a rueful smile. 'I would like that. And do contact me if she does return.'

As she switched off the phone and tossed it down onto the windowsill she felt completely deflated.

The stone was lying where she had left it the night before on the sill, next to the phone. Picking it up, she held it thoughtfully, feeling it grow warm between her palms. 'So, have you really gone away?' she murmured. She felt a prickle of excitement as her vivid memory of the women gossiping came back to her, the sorting of herbs, the strong smells of plants, and sawn wood and something else, something indefinable, in the room where they were standing.

Were they haunting the cottage? She realised she wanted to know the answer to that question incredibly badly.

Deep in thought, she walked away from the window. There could be no harm in trying again, surely. She didn't need Simon's permission, after all, to pursue her enquiry. If it worked, she could at least identify the place. The people. Find out if this was more than a dream, and if so, why the owner of the voice was anchored in this world. Mark need never know. She would tell him later that Simon had called off the investigation, which would be true, but meanwhile, the house was quiet, no one was going to disturb her; she had to try one more time to find out what happened next.

The direction the great dyke was to follow was marked out with stakes. To the north the line it followed was clear, near completion, the earth still raw, the deep groove across the land topped to the eastern side by a high bank. Behind them the vast encampments of the workers sprawled through the fields

43

and woods, the neater offices and tents of the supervisors and the king's surveyors in a cluster a short way beyond. Here and there as far as the southern horizon smoke still rose from the systematic burning off of brushwood to clear each section as the next area of work began.

'So, does it meet with your approval?' Eadburh turned to the prince, who was standing near her, his eyes narrowed as he gazed at the massive earthwork.

'It hardly matters if I approve,' he commented quietly. 'As long as it follows the planned route. My father's surveyors and yours have agreed the detail.'

'And it allows your people some rich areas of good border land,' she reminded him.

He nodded. 'It seems the great Offa is tired of being defeated by the armies of Powys.'

'Or that the armies of Powys are defeated, once and for all,' she retorted.

They were both squinting into the setting sun. Glancing across at him when he didn't reply to her barb, she saw he was smiling. Months earlier a raiding army had ridden out of the night to burn some farmsteads near Hereford, threatening yet again its monastery and its minster, and a furious Offa had come south in person with his war band to consolidate this most vulnerable of borders. Even now, Offa's warrior guard, there to protect their princess, were watching this young man's every move, hands on their sword hilts. It occurred to her how brave the prince was, to come alone but for a small group of attendants, relying on Offa's promise of safe conduct. She herself, she realised ruefully, would not trust her father's word further than the far corner of the table, so was Elisedd naïve or stupid or part of some greater plot? She looked back into the dazzle of the sunset. A huge army could be hidden out there in the folds of these hills and they would never know until it was too late.

The kingdoms of the west intrigued her. Britons. The original people of this island. Foreigners, Welsh, as her people called them, speaking a different language, following different laws, living in remote hidden valleys or on mountains with their peaks in the clouds, a land with different legends and myths and stories, tribes who had inhabited the island of Albion long before her own ancestors had settled there, incomprehensible to the Saxon race and frightening. Very frightening. And yet this man, with his handsome features and his quiet ways, did not seem so very scary or so very different, and he spoke her language fluently.

Catching his eye, she felt herself blush. 'We should return to the camp. It will soon be dark.'

He inclined his head. Turning his horse, he set off slowly back towards the encampment, allowing her to follow or not as she pleased. She scowled, savagely holding her own mount back. Was even her horse beguiled by this soft-spoken foreigner, automatically trying to follow him into the shadows of the night.

'We should go too, Princess.' The voice at her elbow came from Burgred, one of the warriors pulled from her father's war band to be her personal guard. He squinted back towards the crimson clouds gathering in the western sky. Any moment the sun would slip below the hills.

'You think the prince would trick us?' She stared after the receding figure as it disappeared into the darkness, his men already gone ahead of him.

Burgred was a tall man, uncomfortable on horseback, his helmet framing a handsome, weathered face, his armour sitting easily on his broad frame, one hand on his reins, the other resting on the hilt of his sword. 'I trust no one, Princess. A hostage, snatched away into the hills yonder, would be a powerful weapon to use against your father.'

Eadburh hid the bitter smile that threatened to betray her opinion of just how little her father would value her. A hostage might prove a bargaining piece, but no more. Offa had other daughters he clearly held of greater worth.

Her horse moved restlessly beneath her and she realised that Burgred had leaned across to put his hand to its bridle, intent on leading her back towards the camp. 'No!' she snapped. She smacked his hand away. 'We go when I say so.'

His face darkened but he bowed his head in acquiescence

and reined back a few paces. Eadburh watched in silence as the sun sank into the bed of cloud and the crimson of the sky darkened to the colour of dried blood. On cue, an owl hooted near them. Then, with a sigh, she kicked her horse into a trot. The men of her escort looked at each other knowingly and fell into place. Only Burgred drew his sword as he glanced over his shoulder towards the west.

As the gates closed behind them and her escort peeled away towards the stables, Eadburh headed towards the queen's hall and their bedchambers. One served the king and queen, and one was for their daughters, the three framed beds furnished with linen sheets and with furs and tapestries. Alfrida was already sitting there in front of her dressing table as one of her women unplaited her hair and began to comb it out. There was no sign of Ethelfled.

Throwing herself down on her bed, Eadburh watched in silence.

Alfrida glanced at her. 'So, how did it go with your handsome prince?' She gestured the girl with the comb to leave her and swung round on her stool to face her sister. 'Do you think he will make a good husband?' She suppressed a giggle.

Eadburh kicked off her leather shoes and pulled her feet up, tucking them under her skirts. She was still wearing her heavy riding cloak against the chill of the evening, which permeated the room even though there was a fire burning in the central hearth. 'He's handsome enough,' she agreed grudgingly. 'But not to my taste. Too thin and,' she hesitated over the word, 'too delicate.'

Alfrida snorted. 'You would prefer a hunk like Burgred? We have all noticed how he dances attendance on you. He has eyes for no other. His hands trail near yours—'

'Be quiet!' Eadburh stood up furiously. 'If he touched me, I would tell Papa to have him killed!'

'Oh, whoa, no!' Alfrida raised both her hands in mock horror. 'You can't afford to lose such a good fighter.'

'We can if he dares to think—'

'He doesn't dare to think anything,' her sister said. 'Can't you take a joke? The man would die for you, but that is his job.'

'Indeed it is.' Eadburh tightened her lips. Looking round for her own maid, she realised they were alone. She stood up and bent to pull off her stockings. She dropped them where they lay and climbed back onto her bed, hugging her knees thoughtfully. 'Mama said Papa would not contemplate a Welsh husband for any of us.'

'I know she did. I was only teasing. So, would you be happy to go to marry a Frankish prince instead?' Alfrida's question was an afterthought.

Eadburh shrugged her shoulders. 'If he was destined to be the greatest king in Christendom I would. But if any of us are offered, it will be Ethelfled, as she's the eldest.' She scowled, then sat forward, reaching across to take her sister's hand. Suddenly she was smiling with excitement. 'Let's make a list of all the eligible men in neighbouring kingdoms we know are seeking wives, then we can choose one each and we can begin to work on Papa.'

'And no one from the British kingdoms of the west,' Eadburh said firmly.

'No, no one from the kingdoms of the west.'

Later that night Eadburh lay awake for a long time, unable to sleep. Alfrida had recruited Ethelfled to help them with their list, and the piece of parchment lay on the table in the centre of the chamber with the inkpot and quill. There were several names on it now, and would be more. The girls had giggled long and delightedly as each new name was produced. The men were familiar to them from the discussions and meetings of their father, though not all had been viewed personally. It didn't matter. What they were evaluating was wealth and power. No one could compete with the son of King Charles of the Franks for Ethelfled, but there were other kings and princes to consider, all of whom, they laughed confidently, would be more than delighted to claim a daughter of the great Offa as bride.

The fire had died low and the lamp in the corner was flickering when Eadburh climbed out of her bed and, snatching a rug to wind round her shoulders, tiptoed to the hearth to throw on more logs. Sitting on a stool close beside it, she watched the flames flare and the shadows race across the walls. From the shadows, the breathing of her sisters and the women on the truckle beds along the far wall formed a gentle backdrop to the crackle of the logs. Her gaze lingered on the parchment on the table. Alfrida had painstakingly copied out the names in her neatest hand, one name beneath the other down the page. All three girls had attended convent schools attached to one or other of her father's palaces. They read and wrote fluently in their own language and in Latin, and were as well read as any. The King of the Franks was insistent, so they had heard, on the women of his family being literate and educated and capable of ruling any province in which they found themselves, should the need arise, and Offa wanted no less for his daughters. His own wife had learned to read and write from her mother and from an abbess of her mother's kin.

Leaning across to the table, Eadburh reached for the parchment, staring at the list of names in the firelight. There were kings and princes there of East Anglia and Northumberland, of Sussex and Wessex and Kent, two were scions of kingdoms far north beyond the great wall of the Roman Emperor Hadrian, but there were none from the west of her father's dyke. Rerolling the parchment, she stared into the fire for a long time before letting it slip through her fingers into the ashes. She watched it crumble and slowly disappear, then, straightening her back and pulling her rug more closely round her shoulders, she turned to face the doorway. She was, Bea realised, looking straight at her.

8

With a cry of fear, Bea dropped the stone. She scrambled to her feet. She had been there in the palace of the king, in the bedchamber with his daughters, an invisible eavesdropper, blatantly watching, as though this was some kind of a film, there but not there. It had never occurred to her that Eadburh or her sisters might be able to see her. With the rattle of the stone on the floor it had all gone, vanished, leaving her disorientated and reeling with shock.

For a while she stood still, deep in thought. Slowly her heartbeat steadied and her fear subsided. Of course it couldn't have been a two-way contact. She may have thought Eadburh was looking straight at her, but nothing had happened. The girl hadn't reacted. Her gaze had been dreamy, preoccupied, thinking about her future and what lay there.

Nevertheless, this had been a warning. Simon had told her the quest was over. She had settled whatever restless spirit there had been in the cottage. She knew better than to persist in an enquiry that was finished. The door was closed. She must leave it at that.

She picked the stone up off the floor and put it on the top of the bookcase, then ran down the two flights of stairs, grabbed her jacket from the pegs in the hall and, opening the front door, let herself out of the gate in the low wrought-iron railings that bordered their narrow strip of front garden and walked out into the Close. It was busy with mid-morning crowds strolling the paths and sitting in the sun on the benches under the trees. It was nice out there. Normal.

She had grown very fond of the cathedral, with its walls and great tower of mottled pinky-brown sandstone. Unlike its soaring Gothic cousins elsewhere in England, it had kept its smaller and more compact shape as an echo of its early Norman origins, reflected inside by the vast squat Norman pillars in the nave. It was crowded today. There were two parties of tourists making their way round, one standing at the back near the modern memorial window to the SAS, staring up at the stunning area of blue glass, and the other between the choir stalls, looking up at the vaulted roof.

'Beatrice!' One of the volunteers who worked there as a part-time guide was standing by the donation box near the north entrance and spotted her at once. There was little that went on in the cathedral that Sandra Bedford missed. 'Have you come to find Mark?' The woman was tall and stick-thin with neat hair and clear brown eyes behind her wire-framed spectacles. Wearing her identifying lanyard and the blue cassock of an official guide, she peered at Bea intently, her smile eager. 'Are you joining us for the tour?' There were several people standing round them now, waiting for it to begin.

'Not today, Sandra.' Bea did not want to engage in conversation with anyone at this moment. With a wave of her hand she turned away from the door, heading towards the north transept. There was a special place in this great building that she thought of as her own. A place where she had found a friend and an adviser.

When they had first moved into the Treasurer's House it had had its own ghosts, terrible, violent memories of a long-past battle, the shouts of men fighting, the clash of iron swords, the scream of horses. Horrified, she had prayed for their souls; she had carried a bowl of burning herbs into every room and she had placed powerful protective crystals, discreetly, so Mark and the girls wouldn't notice. They had heard nothing. She hadn't known then what had caused such mayhem here in the peaceful Cathedral Close, but then she had learnt of the ancient skeletons archaeologists had found working nearby. Whoever those poor men had been, Saxons, Viking, Welsh or English, they had been ghosts from an ancient past, long before the houses round the Close had been built, probably before the cathedral itself was there, and they were at rest now. She had told Mark when it was all over and he had brought her here to the little chantry chapel off the north quire aisle to pray together. And it was here, when she later returned alone, that she had seen for the first time the shade of the wise old man she had come to think of as her mentor.

Finding the chapel empty, she sat down, pulled back the hood of her coat and began cautiously to try to find the silence.

For a long time nothing happened. Away from the crowds, no one had switched on the lights and it was dark in the chapel, scarcely any murky light filtering through the elaborate stained-glass windows, but someone had lit a votive candle and placed it on a stone shelf near the altar. The flame was steady, illuminating a small patch of the delicate vaulted roof, throwing the graceful lines of stone into stark relief.

It was only slowly that Bea became aware that the old priest was in the chapel with her. She gave a half glance under her eyelids and saw the reassuring shape sitting against the wall by the altar, the shadow of his robe barely there in the flickering light, his sparse circle of hair white beneath his cowl, his face indistinct, always indistinct.

He never spoke. Once or twice she had tried to link with him; she knew he could hear her, but his was a vow of silence. And peace.

'What should I do?' she whispered. 'Please tell me.'

A swirl of draught entered the chapel as down in the nave someone opened the main door into the north porch. As the candle smoked the chapel filled with the smell of beeswax and surely, just a little of incense.

'Don't go back, my child.' The voice was soft, barely audible. 'Don't go. There is danger there.'

Her eyes flew open. The old man had vanished but, for a short few seconds, the sound of his words echoed in her head. Her heart thudding uncomfortably, she stared round the chapel. Danger. He had warned her of danger.

The sound of footsteps outside the doorway distracted her momentarily. 'And this,' she heard Sandra's voice clearly above the shuffling of feet, 'is our loveliest chantry chapel. These were specially endowed when they were built as sacred places where a priest would sing masses and say prayers for the soul of the donor and his family. Sadly, during the Reformation they were dismantled and the priests chased away. Nowadays it's reserved for private prayer.'

It took a moment for her to register that Bea was there, sitting in the corner on the furthest of the short row of chairs, and she backed out again, trying to usher the group away, but they didn't want to be ushered. One or two pushed past her, staring eagerly round the tiny space. Bea leaned forward, her hand over her eyes. She could feel them looking at her, curious. Perhaps prayer was something they did not expect. They were tourists, and tourists tended to be, as Mark had once remarked with enormous sadness, unaware of what a cathedral was for.

Silence descended again as the sound of feet finally died away and she closed her eyes, trying to forget the interruption, concentrating on why she had come, trying to calm the shock and apprehension that had flooded through her at the old man's words, silently begging him to come back. To explain.

But he had gone, chased away by the Reformation and by the needs of a secular age. There was no shadow now near the altar.

And already she knew what she must do. He was right. She must leave the cottage to its dreams. She must not get pulled in. There was danger there.

But first she must take back the stone.

To her relief, Simon's car was nowhere in sight. She pulled into the cottage's parking space and picked her handbag off the passenger seat. In it was the stone, wrapped in a silk scarf. She had not allowed herself to touch it again with her bare hands and even now, as she turned towards the gate, she held the strap of the bag at arm's length. She had originally picked up the stone seemingly at random on the steps inside the gate and she stood for a few moments allowing herself to sense the right place to put it back. The flower bed beside the steps seemed best. No one would trip on it there. She thanked it for its communications and allowed it to slide out of the silk wrapping onto the cold damp earth amongst the daffodils without coming into contact with it again. With relief she stepped back, stuffing the silk into the bag and slinging the bag on her shoulder. The sunlight was illuminating the valley below, sucking up the low-lying mist. It was a beautiful spot. She glanced back towards the stone, feeling a stab of regret. The intensity of her visions had been so immediate, so real, she had been intrigued and captivated and entranced. *Don't go back. There is danger there.* The old priest's words echoed for a moment in her head. He was right, the job was done. The voice had gone; to pursue the quest would risk . . . What? Risk contacting the past in a way that was far too intimate and seductive. At the end of a successful delivery from a ghostly manifestation she had been taught to visualise those two great wooden doors closing slowly behind the figures as they walked towards the light. Those doors must never be reopened. She must close the doors on the past and let it go.

She was jolted out of her reverie by the distant sound of a car climbing the hill. It grew closer, the engine straining. Simon pulled in beside her, bringing with him the unedifying smell of burning clutch, and emerged carrying two bags of groceries. He grinned at her. 'I wasn't expecting to see you here.'

'I'm sorry. I know when you rang this morning you said there was no need for me to come up again but I needed to return—' She paused abruptly. She had been about to mention the stone. 'Your key,' she improvised hastily. It was after all still in her pocket.

He nodded. 'You needn't have bothered. There was no hurry. Come and grab a cup of coffee while you're here. As you can see, I've been stocking up.' He led the way up the path and opened the door.

'So, no more signs of your unwelcome visitor?' Following him through into the kitchen, she dropped his key on the table.

'Not a peep.'

'Can I ask you something?' She followed him back into the living room and perched on the edge of one of the two chairs, clutching her mug as he dropped some kindling into the hearth and bent to light the fire. 'Is there any possibility that this cottage was once part of a much more ancient building?'

He glanced at her as he reached into his pocket for his matches. 'You're still on the quest then?'

'I'm still intrigued. I don't want to stir anything up, especially as the problem seems to have gone, but I was wondering – following an idea, no more than that.'

This was not what she had planned to do. She did not want to pursue the story, and yet somehow she could not stop herself asking.

'I suppose Christine might know about this place's antecedents. I'm no architectural historian, but the walls do look older in some places than in others,' he replied as he found a slightly larger log to balance on top of the flames. 'I vaguely assumed it might have started life as a farm building. I think it's been a dwelling of some sort for a hundred years or so. Victorian maybe? I can't quite remember what she said.' He threw himself down opposite her. Like her, he had kept his coat on; the spring sunshine had not yet managed to find its way inside the thick stone walls.

'Not Anglo-Saxon then?'

He shook his head. 'I doubt it. But to be honest, it would be very hard to establish anything for sure. As I said, probably a byre, later converted to a cottage, maybe incorporating some ancient walls. Who knows how old they might be. An archaeologist would probably be able to tell you more.'

'But it wasn't a palace.'

'Oh, good lord, no.' He laughed. 'The footprint of the building is tiny.'

She nodded thoughtfully. 'I thought I might go and see what's left of Offa's stronghold at Sutton Walls,' she said. 'It's so odd that I live near it and yet I never even knew it existed.'

'That's because it doesn't.' He grinned. 'As far as I can ascertain, there is no sign of a stronghold up there from his dates. They have more or less ruled out anything at the Iron Age fort itself, and although archaeological digs have produced Anglo-Saxon stuff in quite a few places around the area, and they did find a couple of Saxon water mills down near the River Lugg, there is nothing to see now.'

'Oh.' She felt let down.

'Sorry.' He glanced at her in some amusement. 'There are lots of places round here you can still see the dyke though.'

Oh yes. The distant hills, the sunset, the tell-tale line of smoke, the armed men on their impatient horses as Elisedd and Eadburh exchanged chippy remarks. Bea could picture them so clearly, she with her red, woven cloak, the hood pulled up over her braided blond hair, he, also cloaked but in a dark checked heavy wool, fastened on the shoulder by a round brooch, sword at his side, hanging down next to his saddle, his horse with its decorated bridle. His head was bare. No hood, no helmet, no restraining circlet as a king or a prince might wear, just wild dark hair, the same colour, she remembered now, as his horse's mane.

And she had been there. The wind had been blowing, snatching her hair too, feeling cold, roaring through the stand of trees behind them in the valley beyond the ridge.

No, that couldn't be right. She hadn't been there. It was a dream.

'Bea?' Simon's voice was sharp. 'Did you hear me? Are you OK?'

She swallowed. 'Sorry, I was remembering something. A picture.' Almost without realising it, she pushed her hair back out of her eyes. 'It must have been some history book from my childhood.'

'Ah. Children's books so often hold evocative memories.' He reached for his coffee and took a gulp. 'I asked if you'd been to the Offa's Dyke Centre. That's the place to go if you want to know what life was like in the time of Offa.'

But I do know!

She managed not to say the words out loud. Hastily swallowing her coffee, she stood up. 'I'll keep that in mind. But I must go now, and you'll be wanting to get back to work. I hope all remains peaceful.'

She hoped her departure had not been too abrupt as she drove down the hill and turned onto the winding road that led back towards civilisation. As she had run down the cottage steps she had glanced towards the flower bed for a last glimpse of the stone. There was nothing to be seen but the tossing heads of the daffodils.

Chris and Ray lived in a lovely old house in the centre of Eardisley, one of the villages on what was known as the Black-and-White Trail, a group of little towns famous for their timber-framed buildings. It was only twenty minutes or so from the cottage.

Bea followed her through into the kitchen.

'So, has the ghost gone?' Chris was sorting laundry and in the next-door utility room, the washing machine and dryer were going full tilt. She was a plump, motherly woman, some twenty years older than Bea. 'Sorry about this. It's change-over day for our B & B guests in the house. What with Easter coming up, we're run off our feet. You have no idea what a relief it is not to have to change the sheets every couple of days in the cottage as well. That's why I couldn't bear the thought of losing my first and only long-term tenant.' She glanced over at Bea. 'The ghost has gone?'

Bea had an irresistible vision of her catching a ghost in a butterfly net and putting it out of the window. 'As far as we can tell. It has only been one day.'

'But you think so, right?'

Bea nodded slowly.

'And it was a real ghost?'

Bea smiled. 'Oh yes, it was a real ghost.'

She watched as Chris sorted through another load of sheets and stacked them on the ironing board. 'I thought you had someone to help you with all that.'

Chris nodded. 'But even ladies who help go on holiday. Usually at the most inconvenient times.' She sat down and ran her fingers through her hair. 'God, I'm knackered. Let's have a glass of wine. Then I'll make us something to eat. Ray has swanned off for the day to play golf.' She slid off the stool to retrieve a couple of glasses from the draining board. She reached for the half-empty bottle of red wine on the worktop and unscrewed the top. 'So, we own a haunted cottage. What a turn-up for the books. I wonder if I need to declare it when I describe the place for the next visitor. Perhaps not. I wouldn't like to see it on TripAdvisor. It's a bit lonely, and not everyone likes a haunted house. You're sure it's gone?'

'I'm almost sure.' Bea grinned.

'But I can see you're not happy about something. Has Mark been beating you again?' She loved teasing Bea's gentle, serious husband.

Bea laughed. 'How did you guess? No, it's nothing to do with Mark, bless him. It's . . .' she hesitated, 'to do with the cottage. Do you happen to know how old it is?'

But even as she asked, she knew how irrelevant the question was and Simon had already answered it. The building itself wasn't old enough to feature in her visions – Offa had lived twelve hundred years ago. But the ground on which it stood, the ground from which she had picked the stone, was a different matter. That stone could have been lying there, parted from its bedrock, for thousands, millions, of years; it could have been part of some old walls. And perhaps, just perhaps, Eadburh herself was the contact. Could she have touched it? Maybe she had picked it up, held it in her hand long enough for it to assimilate something of her emotions. Thrown it at her officious bodyguard.

Chris pushed one of the glasses towards Bea and sat down next to her. 'Sorry, this might be a bit manky. We opened it a couple of days ago. And no, I've no idea how old the cottage is. A hundred years or so, I'd guess. I can't remember what it said on the deeds when we bought it. Nothing very exciting or I would have put it on the website. Come on, darling, spill the beans. What happened when you were up there on your own?'

Bea looked at her friend doubtfully. Chris seemed genuinely concerned, and interested. She had never mocked Bea's unusual talents, unlike some. 'I heard the voice Simon complained about and then I saw her, just vaguely, in the garden at the back.'

'Flipping heck!' Chris reached for the bottle and topped up her own glass. Then, almost as an afterthought, she poured some more into Bea's as well. 'Are you sure?'

Bea gave a rueful nod.

'It was your imagination.' Chris folded her arms. 'It must have been.'

'No,' Bea whispered. 'It wasn't.'

9

'Hello, Mark. Did Bea find you earlier?' Seeing Mark heading purposefully away from the cathedral office in the College Cloisters, a file of papers under his arm, Sandra Bedford hurried to catch up with him. 'I thought she looked very tired,' she said. 'And worried.'

Mark suppressed his irritation. People like Sandra were the backbone of the cathedral. Without them, the place could not run as smoothly as it did, he reminded himself sternly, but this particular woman was a busybody he could well do without. 'I haven't seen her since I left home. I must have missed her. I've been in meetings all morning.'

'Perhaps she left you a message?'

The slight query in the remark seemed to imply he should reach for his phone and then tell her what Bea had wanted. He sighed. His smile was strained and he hoped she didn't notice. 'I'm on my way home anyway.' Already he was on the move again. 'I'll catch her there. Thanks for letting me know.' He missed the look of frustration and disappointment on her face; another group of visitors was arriving, heading towards her, and he was able to escape.

'Bea?' he called as he let himself into the house.

There was no reply. He walked through the hall and glanced into the kitchen. She wasn't making lunch and she wasn't in the snug either. With its cosy open fireplace and a window overlooking the narrow strip of side garden, the snug was their private space, once probably one of the pantries in the days when the house had staff. It was somewhere he and Bea could relax and watch the TV and hide from the world. Turning back into the kitchen, he grabbed an apple from the wooden bowl on the table and headed towards his study.

An hour later she still hadn't appeared. He pushed aside his keyboard and went back to the kitchen to make himself a sandwich. There was still no message on his phone and her own was switched off. Only then did he check to see if she had left a note. Usually she did if she was going out anywhere, in case he needed her urgently. In the past, when he was a parish priest, that had been often, but now with his job change she was far less involved and had more time for her own activities. Sandra had said she looked worried. He sighed, full of misgivings.

He had often wished he didn't disapprove so profoundly of her dabbling, as he couldn't help thinking of it, in the paranormal. He knew it was her passion and, face it, her calling. She had never made a secret of it, and had been clear that she could never give up her interests. They were part of her as much as his own faith was a part of him. It was, in some ways, her profound spiritual beliefs that had attracted him back to her when they had met again after their separation, but in other ways they still slightly repelled him. And since they'd come here to the cathedral, he had found himself begging her, perhaps, if he was honest, almost demanding that she give it up. Not her beliefs. He could not interfere with those; nor her ability to see things beyond the normal, but to stop going to people's houses, stop exorcising spirits. She had been furious when he had used that word. Exorcism had connotations of force and banishment while she dealt in gentleness and understanding and persuasion, but the fact remained he did not want her to go out and deal with other people's problems. Not those sort of problems, the sort that could and had put her in extreme danger. The very thought of what had happened to her in that old house with the poltergeist made him angry and if he was honest with himself, afraid.

She had left no note.

'Bea?' he went to the foot of the stairs. Perhaps she was up in her study.

'Bea, darling?' He headed upstairs, glanced into their bedroom, and out of the window, through the unfurling leaves on the lime trees outside in the Close, towards the bulk of the cathedral with its massive tower, the four Gothic pinnacles rising into the sky, lightning conductors for sacred energies, as she had mischievously pointed out.

He very seldom went up to her private study. It was an understanding between them that this was her retreat. Perhaps he avoided it deliberately, not really wanting to know what went on up here. She had never told him not to come, but he still felt an intruder as he pushed open the door and looked in. The window faced onto their small walled back garden two storeys below, with its gate out into one of the town's hidden courtyards and the alleyway between a cluster of old houses that jostled towards the town centre. There was a vase of tulips on the low table, a couple of colourful cushions on the floor, a bookcase overflowing with volumes. There was a small Celtic cross on the wall. His eye rested on it, reassured. Though she was a Christian, her interests brought her so often into the vicinity of pagan enthusiasts who vociferously loathed the Christian faith that he wondered sometimes just how liberal her beliefs were. The room was comfortable, a little sitting room, a sewing room perhaps. He smiled ruefully to himself. Get real, Mark! Not a stitch of sewing had ever been done in here. Or at least not since the Victorians had left. He had to admit it had a delightful atmosphere, light, friendly, safe. His eyes slid quickly over the tray of tea lights, little bottles of essential oils, jars of dried herbs, crystals and he found himself growing more and more anxious.

Whatever else the room showed, there was nothing to give a clue where she was. But suddenly he knew. She had told him in her own oblique way, sidestepping his questions the night before. Chris had said there was a problem at the cottage. This was not a leaky tap or a rattling window frame. It was a voice. A mysterious knocking at the door. She had gone back there.

With a quick look at his watch, he ran downstairs two at a time. He had no more meetings scheduled for today; he could catch up with his reports later.

He knew where the cottage was. They had been there several times together when Chris and Ray had been doing it up, sharing drinks and picnics with them, listening to the banter between the two women who had been close friends for years. Naturally she had not been able to resist going to help when Chris had asked.

Parking next to a distinctly old, mud-coloured Volvo, Mark climbed out of his car. The view was stunning, the air cool and sweet with grass and that ubiquitous softly pungent smell of sheep dung. There was no sign of Bea's car, so perhaps, please God, he had been wrong about where she was. The car must belong to the author who had rented the cottage, the author who even now was emerging on to the doorstep.

'Hello. I heard a car.'

Mark felt the man's eyes stray to his dog collar, always the first part of him people noticed. He rather wished he had taken time to change into mufti before setting out. 'I'm sorry to call unannounced but I was . . .' Passing? Hardly! 'I was looking for Bea. I thought she might be here, but obviously not.'

'Are you part of her team?' The man looked puzzled. He held out his hand and introduced himself.

So, she hadn't mentioned she was married to the Church. He didn't confirm or deny the team bit. 'The husband. Mark.'

A buzzard was circling overhead and both men looked up as it let out a plaintive call, flying lower across the valley beyond the gate. 'She was here earlier.' Simon was still watching the bird. 'She didn't stay long. She only came to return my key. I'm afraid she didn't say where she was going.'

Elise!

The woman's voice was distant, plaintive, like the cry of the bird.

Mark saw the other man's face blanch. 'Was that – was that someone calling?'

Simon nodded. 'I thought Bea had sorted it.' His lips tightened.

Mark felt himself shiver. 'That was your ghost?'

Simon nodded again. 'Do you want to come in?' He turned abruptly and led the way inside the cottage.

Mark followed him. The man was scared, Mark could see that clearly, and he had to admit he was uneasy himself.

The room was busy, lights on, papers strewn across the table, the laptop switched on, a low fire smouldering in the hearth. There was a half-empty cup beside the laptop.

'I'll make more coffee.' Simon walked straight across the room and led the way through the door in the far wall into the kitchen. As he reached for a jar of instant, Mark saw his hands were shaking.

'Have you actually seen this ghost?' he asked. His voice was calm and he hoped he sounded matter of fact.

Simon shook his head. He screwed the lid back on the jar and slammed it down on the counter. 'I am a rational man. I've been writing history books for fifteen years. I do not get spooked by the subjects of my study. This house is perfect for my needs! I do not believe in ghosts and I will not be chased away!'

Mark swallowed his anger with Bea and concentrated on the man opposite him. There had been more than a touch of desperation in his voice. 'Did Bea suggest you leave?'

'No. No, she didn't. I told her I wasn't afraid, and I'm not. She came to give me the key back because I thought that the problem was sorted, and it seemed to be, 'til a minute ago when you arrived.'

'You think it's something to do with me?' Mark felt unaccountably aggrieved and at last Simon smiled.

'No, sorry. No, it's got nothing to do with you. And what could be so scary about a voice, for goodness' sake?' He picked up his mug and headed back into the sitting room.

Mark gazed thoughtfully after him, then, topping his own drink up from the bottle of milk Simon had left on the table, followed to find him squatting in front of the fire.

'You heard it, didn't you,' Simon went on. 'I'm not imagining it. It's that note of desolation I can't cope with, and that echo. It comes from so far away.'

'She's a lost soul,' Mark said softly. It was the first time he had ever encountered a ghost and he was amazed how certain he was. Strangely he wasn't afraid. All he felt now that he had heard the voice was intense sympathy and the overwhelming need to help. 'I know this is Bea's department, but it's mine as well. Would you mind if I prayed for her?'

'Mind?' Simon looked up. 'Of course I don't bloody mind!' He looked shocked at his own words. 'Sorry. Forget I said that. Please. Pray away. I don't think Bea has done anything yet. At least she told me she hadn't. She seemed to imply sorting this problem was something she needed to go away and think about before she did it. Whatever it is she does. Then I had a night's blessed silence and I thought, well, her coming here must have been enough, the wretched woman has gone. But I obviously spoke too soon.' He threw himself down into the chair and closed his eyes. Distancing himself from whatever was to come next. Mark knew the signs. People uncomfortable with prayer weren't sure how it worked or what they should be doing while it happened.

Putting down his mug, he went to the door. The troubled spirit was outside. He would start there. He noticed he still wasn't feeling scared; uncomfortable perhaps, but not scared. Leaving Simon sitting by the fire, he stepped out onto the terrace.

He thought he could sense her listening, sense that she knew he wanted to help her in her distress. He talked to her gently, as Bea had told him she did, as he would counsel a living person. Then, closing his eyes, he prayed. He used the words of the old prayer book for the sick and dying, then he recited the words of the *Nunc Dimittis*: 'Lord, now lettest thou thy servant depart in peace' and then he switched to Latin, sensing it might be more appropriate. A modern Church of England man, he didn't know many Latin prayers, but he had heard enough sacred music in the cathedral to know this one. '*Requiem aeterna, domine.*' When he opened his eyes at last he saw she was standing there near him on the terrace, an indistinct figure, a plait of silvery hair slipping from beneath a black veil, her dress long and homespun, a wooden cross hanging from her girdle.

She was a nun; an elderly nun.

Raising his right hand, he made the sign of the cross. '*Requiescat in pace, domina*,' he whispered.

He didn't move for a long time after she disappeared. The terrace was totally silent. The birds had gone. Even the sheep were quiet. The only sound was the soft moan of the wind soughing through the trees on the sides of the valley below them.

'You addressed her as *domina*. Lady.'

Mark turned to see Simon standing in the doorway. 'It seemed appropriate somehow.' He wondered how long Simon had been there watching.

'Poor woman. She's at rest now?'

'I hope so.'

Mark sat in the car for several minutes before he reached forward to turn on the ignition. He had seen a ghost, spoken to a ghost, prayed for a ghost. Suddenly what Bea did made more sense. He had always kept an open mind about her stories, believed that she believed in what she did, but always he had had that niggling kernel of doubt. Up to now. But even so, the fact remained that she had lied to him; or if not lied, at least let him believe she was not going to get involved with Simon and his ghost.

Simon, having watched him walk down the path and get into his car, had gone back indoors and closed the door. He too had seemed thoughtful.

'*Requiescat in pace*,' Mark murmured again as he let off the handbrake at last. 'Rest in peace.'

Now he needed to find his wife.

10

'Don't be silly! Of course I'm not drunk!'

Ray had insisted on driving Bea home that evening after he found his wife and Bea giggling in front of a TV sitcom.

'No, I can see you're not drunk, Beatrice,' Ray persevered patiently, 'but I don't think you should drive. You can fetch your car tomorrow!' he added firmly as she protested. 'You will have to get Mark to bring you over to collect it.'

'We only had a couple of glasses each at lunchtime!' She was feeling thoroughly ashamed of herself.

Ray had been quite shocked when he returned home from the golf club. Chris and Bea had finished the bottle and then opened another.

'It was my fault, Ray,' his wife called out. 'Being washer-women is hard work.' They had finished the laundry between them and made up the B & B beds in the house ready for Chris's next influx of visitors.

Ray had shaken his head tolerantly as he dropped Bea off in Hereford.

Mark was not finding it quite so easy to be understanding. 'You could at least have left me a note. I was worried sick not knowing where you were. After Sandra's message this morning I thought there was something really wrong.'

'I didn't leave any message with Sandra. I barely spoke to the woman!'

'She said you were looking for me. She was concerned.'

'No, it was her idea that I was looking for you. I was looking for someone else.'

'Who?'

Bea was silent for a moment. This was not an interrogation she wanted pursued. 'Look, I only wanted to be alone for a few minutes and the wretched woman pounced on me. It was none of her business!'

'I'm sure she thought she was being helpful,' he reprimanded. He was finding it difficult to contain his anger. 'I know where you've been.'

'With Chris.'

'Before that. I went up to the cottage. I met Simon Armstrong.'

Her mouth fell open. 'Mark, I—'

'You promised me you would give up doing it!' Suddenly he was shouting.

'I didn't make any promises! I just didn't tell you everything, and that was only because you weren't in the house long enough for us to have a proper conversation! You seldom are, these days!' She pushed past him into the kitchen. 'Back off, Mark! If you remember, you promised not to interfere! Chris asked me to go up there to help, you know she did. I told you. I didn't lie!' She faced him defiantly, her eyes sparking with anger. 'You had no right to ask me to give this up. I know I agreed to stop, but I can't stop being me. I'm not going to make a habit of going to people's houses, I know that would reflect on you if anyone found out, but this was different. Very different!'

'Different in what way?' He had followed her. He sat down at the kitchen table and folded his arms.

'It wasn't in Hereford, and it involved a stranger. No one was going to find out.'

'And when you got there you couldn't do it.'

She stared at him, dumbfounded. 'What do you mean I couldn't do it?'

'You didn't remove the ghost.'

'I did. Simon told me it was sorted and I needn't go back. Mark, I was—'

'I saw her.'

It was a full second before his words sank in. 'What do you mean you saw her?'

'While I was talking to Simon, we both heard the voice calling. I prayed and she appeared. She was an elderly nun.'

'You *saw* her?'

'I saw her.'

'That doesn't make sense,' she said at last. She sat down opposite him. 'She's a young woman. A girl. She wasn't a nun.'

'I thought you said you hadn't seen her.'

'I didn't. At least,' she added quickly, 'only a shadow in the garden. And the voice is a young woman's voice.'

'No. Not the voice I heard.'

'Then we didn't hear the same person.'

They stared at each other in silence.

'The main thing is,' Mark said at last, 'I saw her and spoke to her, and I prayed with her and she's gone, Bea. She seemed at peace.' His tone had changed.

She nodded.

'And Simon can get on with his book.'

'He'll be relieved.'

'And thank God, you won't have to go up there again.' He took a deep breath, swallowing his anger. 'Bea, I had no right to ask you not to do this, but please, in future, if there is another case, at least be discreet. And don't whatever you do say anything again that could be misconstrued by Sandra Bedford.'

There was a long pause. 'Why did you go up there?' she asked. She was not ready to let this go yet. 'Were you spying on me?'

'No! When I couldn't find you, I was worried. I guessed that was where you were.'

'And now you've seen a real ghost you're probably even more worried.'

He nodded slowly. 'My first ghost. But she wasn't scary. She was . . .' he hesitated, trying to find the right word, 'not quite real, but more than a shadow. I thought she was very sad.'

'And you think she was a nun?'

'She certainly looked like one.'

'Are you sure she wasn't just wearing medieval costume?' She was thinking back to Eadburh and her prince. If the ghost was an elderly nun, it wasn't Eadburh. The thought was half comforting, half disappointing. There was a long silence. 'I know we joked about it,' she went on at last, 'but I wonder if Simon's book really has stirred up something from the past.' She glanced across at him. She knew that expression, carefully schooled, mildly interested, the face, she always teased him, that he would reserve for hearing really shocking confessions if he ever did such a thing. 'He's writing about Anglo-Saxon Mercia. King Offa. She – your nun – wouldn't fit, would she? I don't suppose they were even Christian at that period.'

'Offa was a Christian, Bea.' He sighed. 'The minster here in Hereford had already been going a couple of hundred years by the time he became king.'

'How do you know?'

He laughed. 'In case you hadn't noticed, Bea, I work in a cathedral dedicated to St Mary the Virgin and to St Ethelbert the King, the latter having been foully done to death by none other than your King Offa.'

'Really?' That caught her attention. For a moment she forgot her anger. It occurred to her that she had never once wondered who St Ethelbert was, let alone connected him to King Offa. 'Offa can't have been a very good Christian if he was a murderer.'

'Possibly not. The original cathedral is said to have been built over Ethelbert's tomb.'

'You would think that would hold him down all right,' she said drily. 'When you say original cathedral, do you mean this one isn't original? What happened to the first one?'

'I'll give you three guesses.'

'The Reformation? Cromwell?'

He shook his head. 'Long before Cromwell. No, the Welsh.' He smiled tolerantly. 'I gather they were always popping across the border to burn Hereford.'

That was what Simon had said. 'But wasn't that why Offa built his dyke?'

'Indeed. But it didn't work. If your guy Simon is writing a book about it, he must know.' He stood up. Technically it was her turn to cook, but one look at her exhausted face made him realise that was probably not going to happen. He went over to the freezer and after some rummaging triumphantly produced a pizza. It was his way of apologising. He hated it when they quarrelled. Time to forget about ghosts, at least for now.

When she looked up at him again it was with another question. 'Mark.' She hesitated. 'Have you ever heard of there being ghosts in the cathedral?'

He groaned. 'Not as far as I know. That's your department, darling. I'm not sure I'm qualified to comment.' He switched on the oven.

'But you're a priest! You of all people should believe in ghosts. We've talked about this before. But now you've seen one.' Now that they had broached it she wasn't going to let the subject drop.

'Officially I don't believe in them. You know what we believe officially. It's all in the Creed.'

'But unofficially?'

'I keep an open mind. I don't believe they wander round causing trouble. At least' – he hesitated – 'I didn't until you were attacked by a poltergeist.'

'Forget the poltergeist,' she snapped. 'After all these years with me, you must realise—'

'Yes. Yes, I do believe some spirits wander the earth, inconsolable, and I do believe you can help them, Bea. I also believe they can be dangerous – demonic, even – as you found out in that old house. And if we're talking about the ghost of Offa of Mercia, who had the most awful reputation as a murdering thug, I would very much rather you never get close enough to find out. If Simon is some kind of a link to him, then I'm begging you, I'm begging you, Bea, to have nothing more to do with this.'

'But Simon's ghost is a woman,' she said softly. 'A nun. You said so yourself. She would not be demonic.'

She hadn't been thinking of Simon's ghost. She had been thinking of the gentle old priest who sat in the side chapel and who had told her not to go to the cottage on the ridge because there was danger there.

Bea lay for a long time that night, aware that Mark was still awake beside her. It wasn't until at last she felt him relax into sleep that she slid out of bed. Staring at him in the dim light thrown through the bedroom door by the lamp on the table on the landing, she felt a wave of affection. Sleep had wiped the care lines from his face; his hair was tousled by the pillow, making him look young again. They had come very near to having a major row this evening. She sighed. She knew how difficult it was for him, but she was not going to stop her enquiries.

Climbing up to her attic, holding her breath as the stairs creaked under her cautious footsteps, she paused in the doorway. She sensed at once that Mark had been up there. She didn't really mind – she knew now that he had been searching for her, but still, he had left a raw anxiety in the air. Normally she would light some incense, waft it quickly round the space to soothe it, but she couldn't do that now. The smell might drift down the stairs and wake him up. Tightly wrapped in her dressing gown, she lit the candle and sat down on the cushion. She had returned the stone. She had decided not to follow up on Eadburh's story. The priest in the cathedral had warned her against it. Mark had warned her against it. She must turn her back on the three sisters and their dreams of the future. That door was closed. The past was in the past where it belonged. All she could do now was pray that Mark had laid the unhappy spirit to rest and that the cottage was at peace.

*

As the flame of her candle flickered and died, she found herself nodding off to sleep. Waking up in the small hours, stiff and cramped, she crept back downstairs to bed. If she dreamt about Eadburh she didn't remember it. Her sleep was deep and undisturbed.

The next thing she knew was that it was morning and Mark was calling to her from the bottom of the stairs. He had returned from morning prayer. 'We've got to go to collect your car, remember? I have wall-to-wall meetings later.'

He waved her goodbye outside Chris and Ray's house before heading down the road back to Hereford. She stood and watched his car disappear, deep in thought. Was it all over? Had it really been that easy?

By the time she had shared a quick coffee with Chris, collected her keys and climbed into her own car, Bea knew what she was going to do. She couldn't leave it there. She had to go and check out the cottage. She would know at once if Mark's prayers had worked. If so, then well and good. She could drive away and forget about it. But what if the ghost was still there? Who was this nun who had so meekly vanished after a few priestly prayers? There was only one way to discover the answer to that. She would have to find the stone again. Without it, she was not going to be able to go back to Offa's court, and she realised, she had to know what happened next to the three sisters. Only then could she put the poor woman's soul to rest and find out what if anything she had had to do with Eadburh and her prince.

It was a relief when she saw no sign of Simon's car at the cottage. Wondering briefly where he had gone so early in the morning, she stood by the gate for a while looking round, surrounding herself with protective light. It was very cold up here, high on the hillside, the morning still with that new-minted feel. Birds were singing and a lamb somewhere on the hillside was bleating for its mother.

Slowly climbing the front steps she stood for several minutes on the terrace, putting out cautious feelers, but there was nothing there. No voice, no shadows, no nun. Mark was right.

She had gone, whoever she was. She felt an unexpected pang of disappointment, and, if she was honest, a tiny bit of resentment. Mark's prayers had worked when her own methods had failed.

She stood looking thoughtfully out across the valley.

She didn't sense the shadowed figure standing by the hedgerow. It wasn't a nun, nor was it a blue-eyed Saxon princess. The woman was tall, her figure concealed by a dark, roughly woven cloak, her hair stirring in a gentle breeze that had nothing to do with this mountainside, in her hand a spray of fern leaves, her gaze fixed on Bea.

Bea spent a long time surveying the flower bed. Squatting down she allowed her fingers to trail through the daffodils, sure she would feel the stone when it was close, half concentrating, half listening to a thrush singing from the tall birch tree that overhung the terrace. Looking up towards the bird at last, her eye was caught by several stones that lay on the low wall that bounded the lane. There it was. 'So, someone moved it?' she breathed. And maybe, in the strange way of things, the bird was showing her where it was. She stood staring down, not touching anything, trying to feel her way, wanting to be sure. But she was sure. She recognised the flecks of crystal on the surface of the pebble, the strange burnished colour, the streaks of dull red, the slight polish from the warmth of her own hands.

The bird was still singing. She looked up and smiled, mouthing a quiet thank you before picking up the stone and slipping it into her coat pocket. She hesitated as her gaze strayed towards the hedge, her attention caught by something she couldn't quite see, then giving a slight shake of her head she turned away.

There was still no sign of Simon when she pulled out of the lay-by and set off down the hill.

She was very tense as she sat down on her cushion and took the stone into her hands, breathing in the sweet smell of lavender wafting round the room from the incense stick. She had once again surrounded herself with the protective shield of light and was confident in her own strength and yet she

73

was nervous. Whoever it was Mark had banished from the cottage, it was not her blue-eyed princess, of that she was sure. The job was done, the cottage freed of its troubling presence, but she hadn't been able to get the picture of the young woman's face out of her mind, the intense reality of her vision, and the heart-stopping moment when Eadburh had looked in her direction. That connection had been too intense to ignore. She had to go back. Just once. After all, Mark had more or less said he knew she would. He had acknowledged that he had no right to stop her doing it; all he had said was, be discreet.

She sat for a long time, the stone between her palms, her protection in place, her mind a receptive blank. Nothing happened. In its holder the incense stick turned to ash and the smoke gently dissipated round her. The room grew cold as outside the sky clouded over and a soft drizzle began to streak the window panes. A sharp cramp in one of her legs brought her back to herself and she scrambled to her feet, bitterly disappointed. Leaving the stone on the table, she went downstairs. Her phone was lying on the kitchen table. She had missed calls from Mark and Chris and Simon.

'Simon?'

He picked up almost at once. 'Good morning.' He sounded cheerful. She had been afraid he might have seen her when she came up to the cottage, but he made no mention of her visit. 'Did Mark tell you he came up to see me yesterday?'

'He did. And he told me he managed to persuade your lost soul to leave you alone.'

'He did indeed. Or at least, so far so good. You make quite a team between you.'

Team? Is that what Mark had told him? 'Good. I'm glad you can get on with your writing now.'

'It's going well. But I hadn't forgotten that I've promised you a coffee next time I'm in town. I wondered whether tomorrow might be a good time? I have arranged to meet one of the archivists from the cathedral library. Perhaps we could get together afterwards?'

*

74

Bea arrived at the café at four, as they'd agreed, but Simon was late. She had almost given up when he appeared at last. He was looking very pleased with himself. 'Sorry to keep you waiting. I was talking to the most fascinating woman. Quite an expert on Mercia in her own right, as it happens. I think I'm going to have to rewrite a huge chunk of the middle of my book.'

'And that pleases you?' She would have thought he'd be upset.

'Oh yes. It's exciting. I know it's extra work, but she pointed me in the direction of material I had completely missed. I could have got it all so wrong. Coffee and cake, please.' He looked up as the waitress hovered alongside them. 'And for you?' He threw a glance at Bea as he levered some notebooks out of his bag. 'Please. Join me in cake. This is a celebration.'

She found his excitement infectious. 'OK. Thank you. So, what is it you've discovered?'

'Archaeology for this period is rare in this part of the world and written documentation even rarer. So far. I knew there were Early English books in the cathedral library that I wanted to see, and that in itself is wonderful, but Jane was telling me about a house out in the sticks with a newly discovered collection of ancient books and documents with, she thinks, a very exciting provenance. She said she can get me in to have a look, and she can arrange for me to have access to the documents provided I don't tell anyone where I've seen them as their existence is all very hush-hush at present.'

'That sounds marvellous. Is this Jane Luxton you're talking about? I know her. She's very knowledgeable.'

He grinned happily.

'I suppose I might have guessed you'd know her. If you both live in Hereford, you would run into each other at some point.'

'Well, the cathedral is certainly a tight community.' She saw his puzzled expression. 'Did Mark not mention that he works there?'

'Oh, I saw the dog collar, but I didn't like to ask him where he was vicar of.'

'He's a canon in the cathedral.'

'Is he indeed.' He seemed impressed.

'So, Jane has found out about these documents?' She steered him away from the subject of Mark.

'The owners of the house were given an introduction to her and she went to see them. She thinks one book in particular would interest me. It's written in Old English and there are references to Mercia. She showed me some photos she's taken of one or two pages and they are exquisite. They had the most beautiful handwriting in those days. Have you seen reproductions of Bede's History, or the Anglo-Saxon Chronicle? Then you can guess what I'm talking about.'

'And it couldn't be a forgery?'

His face clouded and she felt sorry she had suggested such a thing, but already he was turning the pages of his notebook. 'It could. I'm not sure I am knowledgeable enough to be able to tell, but I read Old English – the language of the Anglo-Saxons – and I've seen a great many genuine documents in my time. I'm prepared to suspend disbelief for now.'

'What are the documents about? Could she tell you?' The waitress had brought their coffee and two slices of lemon drizzle cake.

'History, she said. And there are entries about Offa and his family. Oh, bad luck. Don't worry. I'll get you another one.' She had dropped her fork on the floor. Her hand was shaking.

'Offa's family?' she echoed.

He nodded. 'He had at least four children. Three daughters that we know about, and one son. All well documented.'

'And a wife called Cynefryth.'

'That's right.' He nodded vigorously. 'Did you see her mentioned in the draft of my book? Thank you.' The waitress had seen Bea's mishap and brought her another fork.

'The nest of vipers,' Bea whispered thoughtfully.

Simon stared at her doubtfully. 'Ah, that sounds more like historical novel territory.'

'It does, doesn't it.'

Was that what had happened? What she had seen wasn't a moment out of time, a shiver in the matrix after all. It had merely been a rehash of some historical bodice-ripper she had read as a teenager and completely forgotten. Crestfallen, she stared down at her plate, lost in thought.

If only there was someone she could talk to about all this. If only Meryn was here. She had first met Meryn Jones, the man she called her Druid guru, after she realised she wanted to pursue her esoteric studies and take them to a more serious level and she had gone to a centre in Scotland where he was a teacher. She had fallen in love with his Celtic spirituality, and he had encouraged her to trust herself. She had even come, one summer holiday, to the Black Mountains in Wales, to work with him. If he had been around, she would have referred Simon and his ghost to him in the first place, and not tried to sort the situation out herself. But Meryn steered a path between his career as a psychic Druid at home in Wales and another as a visiting professor of esoteric studies at a college in the States, and that was where he was at the moment, far away. He would have known at once whether she could have faith in her story. He would have told her to listen to her instincts.

Bea realised that Simon was staring at her. 'Penny for them,' he said. He dug into his piece of cake.

'I was thinking how exciting it must be to hear about a never before discovered source of material.'

'I can't wait.' He nodded vigorously.

'Will you tell me if there's anything—' She stopped in mid-sentence as he frowned.

'I can't tell you where it is. I don't know myself. And you must not breathe a word about this to anyone.'

And that was that. She could not ask him anything further. He had no idea about her sudden interest in the family of Offa of Mercia, and she didn't want to tell him why she wanted to know, not when it might be no more than memories of a novel she had read years ago, or of a film she had seen on TV or at the cinema, or even some remnant of a history lesson from her school days, rehashed in her imagination. She could imagine his reaction if she did. Her street cred, what there was of it, would be gone forever so far as he was concerned. If she ever convinced herself her experience was real, then she would tell him, ask him to confirm things, but not yet. Not now.

His admonition to keep the discovery quiet reminded her of something Mark had said. 'By the way, please, Simon, can you make sure you don't say a word to anyone about the reason for Mark's and my visits to the cottage? Protocol, you know.'

He grinned. 'I remember. You said. Confidentiality clause.'

She laughed. 'I couldn't have put it better myself.'

Twenty minutes later they said goodbye and she stood watching him walk away to retrieve his car. 'I'll let you know next time I'm in town,' he said as he left. 'Perhaps we can have coffee again, and I may be able to tell you something about my adventure. It's good to have someone to talk to from time to time when I'm on my own all day.'

I'm on my own all day too, she thought as she made her way home. For once the thought didn't depress her.

The house was deserted as she expected, silent but for the occasional tapping sounds of chisel on stone, which carried across the grass from the masons' yard tucked against the cathedral wall on the far side of the Close. When she checked her phone she found a message from Mark saying he had been coerced into standing in for the dean at a local event and would be home late.

With a smile, she headed for the stairs.

The sun was setting and the attic room was full of shadows. There was a faint smell of lavender in the air and she found herself wondering suddenly if that was what had blocked her vision? It was the standard cleansing herb today, but in Eadburh's time what would they have used?

She turned to her bookshelf for inspiration. There were books here she almost knew by heart, and some she needed to read again. *The Leechbook of Bald*, *The Nine Herb Charm*, *The Physicians of Myddfai*, *Aspects of Anglo-Saxon Magic* . . . her books, collected over the years, waiting to be used. There was information here about Celtic and Anglo-Saxon herbs and charms and runes. She thought back to what she knew of the

Anglo-Saxon world. Their gods, their magic, their belief in Wyrd, the working of destiny. Her eyes strayed to her jars of crushed herbs, passed over the labels, stopped. Came back. Mugwort. Of course. She had picked some last summer on the banks of the River Wye, dried it and put it there in one of her pretty pottery jars ready to be used as incense. The herb of dreams and divination. She dried her own burning herbs, following the ancient Scots and Welsh traditions that her grandmother and then Meryn had taught her. Cynefryth's herb-wife would have known what to use, done the same. What was her name? Nesta.

As she lit a piece of charcoal and sprinkled on a pinch of dried leaves, Bea didn't notice she was no longer alone in the room. The shadow of a woman was standing behind her.

Bea stood for a while looking out of the window at the clustered medieval roofs of the city beyond their garden until she could smell the pungent fragrance of the herb spiralling around her. She turned at last to light her candle, then, sitting down, she picked up the stone.

This time it worked.

11

The first time his hand had touched hers it had been an accident. A quick brush of the fingers as they both reached for the bridle of the nervous horse, but the touch had been like the spark of summer lightning. Their eyes met and Eadburh felt a jolt in her chest that left her breathless. Elisedd felt it too. She could see from the shock on his face. His gaze lingered just that bit too long, as though he were seeing her for the first time, before he bowed and stepped away as she soothed the horse and passed the rein to one of her bodyguards. The next time they met they were standing on the edge of the great ditch watching the serfs pass the baskets of soil hand to hand up the slope to build the rampart ever higher. By some unspoken signal they had turned their horses to walk slowly north along the line of the ditch, both concentrating on the work going on around them. The third time they were alone together they turned south towards the sun, drawing further away from their escort, talking of inconsequential things, once or twice laughing at nothing at all. The next time, heading alone towards the site, she told him it was almost time to say goodbye.

'My father plans to move the household north after Easter. We are to spend a few days at our palace at Lichfield while he holds meetings with his archbishop, then we go on to Tamworth.' She had meant it as a way of breaking the almost tangible silence between them but her voice carried a desperation she had not intended. This strange foreign prince with his silver eyes and his dark wild hair had become fixed in her thoughts in the day and in her dreams at night. Without realising it, she found ways of talking about him to her sisters and to her mother as they worked with the herb-wife in the stillroom, enjoying the sound of his name, wanting to hear them say how handsome he was, how charming. Her mother had begun to frown at the all too frequent mention of the young man's name. Eadburh had flown off into a rage when her sisters had teased her that he might be a potential husband. Perhaps she had protested too much. Cynefryth glanced across at Nesta, the herb-wife, and saw she too was watching the girl with a speculative frown between her eyes as if seeing danger there. Thoughtfully she turned back to the parchment on which she had copied a charm she wished to use to bring a favourite mare into season. Next time she saw the king she would mention her suspicion. This youngest child of theirs was a strong-minded young woman given to outbursts of temper when she didn't get her own way. He needed to have a stern word with her.

'Why did your father choose you and not one of your elder brothers to come to see this stage of the work through?' Eadburh pulled her horse alongside the prince's mount and turned to face him at last. Behind them their attendants huddled back out of the wind as another shower of rain rattled out of the west.

'I'm the only one who speaks your language.' He had strong white teeth, she realised. His smile was warm in the handsome face, a contrast to the grim expressions of the men who followed him everywhere. Like her own escort, they were constantly watchful and suspicious.

'Is your father's kingdom large?' It had not occurred to her to be interested up until now in the land he came from. All she knew was that Powys stretched out beyond the hills to the west and north into the misty distances.

He nodded. 'I can show you.' There was mischief in his eyes now. 'Ride with me to the top of that ridge.' He pointed across the ditch that was forming at their feet. 'In a few days we won't be able to cross this any more. We would have to travel to one of the guarded crossing points. From the top of the ridge we can see for miles.'

'You've been up there?' She looked at him curiously.

'Of course. I need to see that all is well at home.'

'And you can see that all is well from there?' She didn't hide her disbelief.

'Come, and I'll show you.'

It was too exciting a thought to resist. 'We have secret matters to discuss as emissaries of our respective fathers,' she bade Burgred sternly. She saw the suspicion and even rebellion in his face as he realised she was ordering him to stay behind, but already she was on her horse and following the prince down the steep, slippery side of the ditch and up its western flank.

It was further than it looked. As the two horses galloped through the woodland, she felt a moment of fear. They were on the far side of the ditch now, in the kingdom of Powys, where the people spoke the strange language they called Cymraeg, still believed in fearsome ancient gods, and fought like demons, swooping down from their mountains and disappearing again as suddenly, wrapped in mist. She gave a delicious shiver of excitement as she looked round. But there were no people here. The woods appeared deserted and already the trees were thinning as the track began to climb.

The open hillside rose high above the surrounding country. As they pulled the horses up, blowing heavily, Eadburh looked round. She could see in every direction, back the way they had come down into the flatlands of Mercia with the Malvern Hills in the far distance. In front she could see mile upon mile of mountains, stretching as far as she could see. As the clouds raced across the land from the west she saw dark shadows skimming the hillsides, and then the sunlight illuminating first one spot then another. 'It's beautiful,' she breathed. 'But very wild. Where are your cities?'

He laughed. 'We have no cities. You are looking at the land of dragons. Over there,' he pointed northwest, 'the dragons sleep, guarded by the saints. And over here,' he pointed away towards the southwest, 'you can see the peaks of the snowy beacons and the land of eagles.' He slipped from his horse and looped its rein over his arm, then he came over to help her dismount. 'So, what do you think of my father's kingdom?'

'I can see why he would want to raid the rich lands of Mercia!' she commented crisply. She was trying to ignore the wild beating of her heart as he stood so close beside her. She had never felt this way about a man before. The power of the attraction was overwhelming her.

He laughed. 'I suspect there is truth in that. But we have rich lands too, verdant valleys, rivers full of salmon, forests teeming with game.'

'You know my father plans for you and me to marry,' she said suddenly. She hadn't meant to say it; it wasn't true, she knew that.

He was barely taller than she and slender, but she could see the ridged muscles of his arms. He wore gold bracelets and a circular decorated brooch of gold held his cloak in place.

She saw the shock of surprise in his face at her words.

'No mention has been made of that to me,' he said guardedly.

'It is a secret, between your father and mine.'

'And does the idea please you?' The wind was tearing at his hair; his eyes were on hers now, amused, teasing.

She looked away hastily. 'I'll consider it, certainly, as I will consider the other princes my father is offering for my consideration.'

'Oh, there are other princes?'

'Naturally. The son of the King of the Franks.'

'I had heard he was to marry your sister.'

'Possibly.' Her eyes flashed. She had been caught out. She stepped away from him sharply.

He reached out and grabbed her wrist. 'I would hope that, given the choice, you would prefer me.'

She looked down at his hand, strong and muscular, weathered against her pale skin and she felt a strange stab of excitement. 'I think I might,' she whispered. She took a step closer to him and caught her breath as his arm went round her shoulders.

They kissed for only a second and then he pulled back. 'We can see the world from here, Princess, but don't forget that means the world can see us. I doubt but that your escort are somewhere close behind in the fold of the hills over there, guarding their princess for their king, and my men too, if they are doing their job, will not be far away. We must go back.'

'Not yet.' She held his gaze. 'It's too soon. We must find somewhere they can't see us.' She turned away to scan the hillsides around them. 'There, where the ground dips down into the valley.'

They led the horses down the hillside into the lee of the slope and there they found a summer shelter, built for shepherds, a roofless enclosure of stones, sufficient to keep the weather at bay. And the wolves. Elisedd tied the horses to a stunted thorn tree near the entrance and taking her hand he led her inside the walls out of the wind. He unfastened his cloak and spread it on the ground so they could sit down. 'So, when did your father tell you we were to marry?'

She bit her lip. It was too late to withdraw her rash words. She couldn't admit it was a lie. And she wanted him to kiss her again. Her blood was on fire. Besides, she thought wildly, perhaps she could persuade her father that the marriage made sense. It did, after all. This ditch would never be enough to prevent raids across the border and a marriage alliance would seal the peace once and for all. Her hand was in his, lying on the warm wool of the cloak, and her blood was racing and they were alone. As she leaned towards him, all her common sense and training had long since flown out of her head.

'No.' It was Elisedd who drew back. 'We mustn't. Not without the blessing of the Church.'

'We are blessed here by your dragons and your old gods of the mountains.' She threw herself against him, scarcely able to breathe. 'What can it matter if we test ourselves to make sure we are suited. Your blood runs as hot as mine. I can feel it.' She put her hand over his heart, feeling its steady beat under her palm through his tunic. She pressed her lips against his, and then she was in his arms.

When they pulled apart at last, exhausted, the sun had slipped round in the sky and the shadows were lengthening. Sitting up, peering out over the drystone wall they could see overhead two birds tumbling in the clear air, black silhouettes high in the sunlight. Elisedd laughed. 'Look. Ravens. The messengers of Branwen, daughter of Llyr. She was our ancient goddess of love.'

Eadburh caught her breath. 'Then she has witnessed our exchanged vows and we are already married in her eyes. We will go before the bishop later. Look, there are hares out there too. All nature is making love.'

They sat for a while, watching the two hares leaping round the clearing, oblivious to their audience. 'We in Powys have a patron saint of hares,' Elisedd murmured. 'She's called Melangell. Many centuries ago one of my ancestors was hunting a hare, and the hare saw a beautiful woman watching the hunt and it fled to hide from the dogs in her skirts. She pleaded for the hare's life, and because she was so beautiful the king granted her wish. He fell in love with her on the spot and wanted to marry her, but she refused, saying she had come to Powys to live the life of a holy virgin, so he gave her land to build a convent there.'

'That's a lovely story.' Eadburh gave a wistful smile.

'One day I promise I will take you to her shrine. But now we must go back! It grows late.' He reached for his tunic, then he helped her to her feet. The two horses were grazing quietly outside, and there was no sign of anyone around, but suddenly he sensed danger. 'Get dressed. Quickly. We've been up here much too long. Our guards will long ago have grown suspicious.'

She pulled on her gown and quickly began to rebraid her hair. 'They wouldn't dare come up here.'

'They would if they were worried. Come, let me help you mount. If we ride back openly, there is nothing they can do.

If they followed us, they will have disobeyed our orders, if they admitted they didn't follow us, they would have disobeyed your father. So long as we get back before dark, all will be well.' He vaulted onto his pony. 'Follow me.'

From his hiding place in the edge of the wood, Burgred watched the two figures emerge from the sheepfold, retrieve their horses from the shelter of the old thorn and ride towards him eastwards down the spine of the ridge. He waited a while for them to disappear over the edge of the hill then he ducked back through the trees to where he had left his own horse grazing. Behind him the ravens cried out their warning unheeded.

The sound echoed through the attic room and died away. As Bea opened her eyes she saw the candle flame flicker and die. Only a trail of smoke was left to remind her of what she had seen. And now she knew where they had been. Elisedd, Prince of Powys and Eadburh, daughter of Offa, had been making love on the ridge where Simon was writing his book. That original tumbled stone wall had been part of what in Wales they call a *hafod*, a place of refuge for the beasts up on the mountain for the summer grazing. Until the beginning of May, the ancient time of *Calan Mai*, it would have been deserted.

She sat staring into space for a long time. There was only the faintest ray of light in the sky now above the rooftops and she watched as it faded. Outside in the town the street lights came on one by one and she could hear the swish of tyres on the wet road in the distance. It must have rained while she was there on the open hill in the early spring sunshine. Was she riding too? She had no sense of how she had seen everything, how she had watched the events unfold. She looked down. The stone had fallen from her fingers and lay on the carpet. She reached forward and picked it up. Had Eadburh held it at some point, left her emotions and her dreams imprinted on the surface of this small smooth lump of rock?

She felt a sudden wave of excitement. What she had seen

was amazing; unbelievable. She had been privileged and blessed by her experience. She pictured the two young people in one another's arms. Was she being voyeuristic, watching two young people make love? But she had been unable to look away. Thank goodness Eadburh had not noticed her watching. She did not think the girl would have been pleased to see a stranger hovering in the shadows of the shepherds' summer retreat. The thought of those cold angry eyes made her shiver. Better to think instead about the hares boxing in the grasses, the sound of the wind in the thorn tree, and the ravens calling a desperate warning.

A warning. The man in the trees. A grizzled warrior in leather breastplate and helmet, his eyes angry as he spied on his king's daughter and her lover, his hand on his sword as he rode after them into the darkness.

The insistent knocking on the front door two floors below dragged Bea back to reality. Unwillingly, she stood up and made her way downstairs. The house was still deserted. Turning on the kitchen lights, she stood staring into space for several minutes, still there, on the hillside in her head, unable to drag herself back to the present, then she heard the knocking again. The last person she expected to see standing on the step was Sandra Bedford. Outside the rain was pouring down. The air in the Close smelled of wet grass and flowers.

'My dear, I am so sorry!' The woman propped her dripping umbrella against the wall, and stepped past her into the hall. 'I've been so worried. It never occurred to me I might be embarrassing you by telling Mark you were looking for him. I made assumptions and I shouldn't have. It was none of my business who you were meeting in the cathedral and none of my business if you were there to pray.'

She walked uninvited towards the drawing room, pushing the door open, pausing only for a second to reach for the light switch as she realised the room was in darkness. Behind her, Bea watched her open-mouthed. This room, overlooking the front of the house, mostly furnished courtesy of Bea's mother-in-law, was very formal, the furniture beautiful – rejected by

Mark's brothers' families as too big for their London flats – but austere. Mark and Bea kept it for the formal entertaining that was part of his job and as the perfect place for Anna's piano. 'Don't worry,' Sandra beamed, 'I'm not stopping. I just wanted to make sure you weren't cross with me. Where is the dear canon? Is he here? No, of course not. He's gone to the mayor's reception hasn't he, to represent the dean. Good! So, we can have a nice chat.'

It seemed to dawn on her at last that the room was cold, the curtains open onto the darkness. 'Ah. Are we in the kitchen?'

Already she was backing out of the room again. In the parish, the kitchen was common property. Everyone would head in that direction, offering to help, making sandwiches and cauldrons of tea. Cursing herself for opening the front door in the first place, Bea followed. At last she was beginning to pull herself together. 'Sandra, I'm so sorry. I was about to go out. It's sweet of you to call in, and there is absolutely no need to apologise about Mark. It was all a misunderstanding.'

'Are you sure, dear?'

Bea saw the woman was wistfully looking at the kettle. 'Absolutely sure. Look, you must come round another time and have tea, but I really do need to get on now. You know what it's like. Never a moment to oneself.' As hints went, that was as direct as she could make it, but it still took another few minutes to usher Sandra back to the front door. Finally closing it behind her, Bea leant against it with a sigh of relief.

Outside, Sandra put up her umbrella and frowned. The canon's wife had been deliberately disingenuous. Otherwise, surely, she would have told her who she was meeting and why. And there was something odd about her tonight. She looked guilty, almost as though there was someone there with her, someone she didn't want Sandra to see. She shivered. It felt as though a black shadow had settled over the Treasurer's House. As she headed across the Close she glanced back over her shoulder. The fanlight above the Dalloways' door, a semi-circle of light in the darkness, suddenly disappeared. Bea had turned off the hall light.

*

'I thought it best you know, sir.' Burgred looked up under his eyebrows at the king. 'They did not have long together alone, but if they plan further encounters . . .' He was trying to guess the king's reaction. He had been charged with keeping the king's daughter under his surveillance, a simple enough task, but he had allowed Eadburh out of his sight and failed to keep her safe. Brave man though he was, he had seen men killed for less and he felt himself quaking with fear. He had no intention of admitting that the two had spent an afternoon together before he had tracked them up to the ridge.

He saw Offa's face redden with fury and felt his throat contract with terror. 'Do you wish me to kill him, sire?'

'No!' Offa's roar of anger could be heard beyond the heavy curtain in the great hall itself, where men and women stopped abruptly in what they were doing and looked fearfully in the direction of the king's private chamber. 'You cannot kill the wretched boy. I am trying to make peace with his father! If they had only minutes together' – he paused and glared at Burgred, lowering his voice – 'no harm was done. Were it long enough to endanger my daughter's reputation, you would pay with your life.' There was a heavy silence in the room. Cynefryth had warned him that the girl was besotted. He should have listened.

'Your daughter's virtue is safe, sire.' Burgred breathed a prayer to Woden that this was true. 'I will swear it on the bones of St Chad.' Double surety.

Offa saw the man's fingers tighten on the hilt of his sword to stop them trembling and his eyes narrowed, but he let it go at that for now. If no harm had been done, then all could be resolved naturally. Already the enormous cavalcade of wagons and packhorses was being readied and assembled so the king's court could return to his favourite palace at Tamworth for Easter. Distance would effectively solve the problem.

He sent for Prince Elisedd the next morning, presented him with generous gifts and messages for his father and bade him farewell. It was left to Burgred to ensure that the young man would have no chance to say goodbye to Eadburh, escorting him and his party with a guard of honour back towards the dyke, across it and on his way towards the distant mountains in the west.

Eadburh had been thinking about Elisedd all night, her body alive with longing, planning how they would ride up once more to see the site of the dyke and be alone together again, but first, with the small part of her that still clung to her mother's cold, analytical training, she wanted to ensure that the plan for her future was in place.

'When will you announce our betrothal, Papa?' It had been hard to find a moment with her father, but at last she managed to corner him in the solar, commanding his astonished house-carls to leave them alone. 'You have not said a word about my forthcoming marriage and we are about to set off for Tamworth.'

She had managed to sweet-talk her father before, after all, when she had wanted a particular silky-coated white pony that he planned to give to her eldest sister. One pleading look from her wide blue eyes had won his doting agreement in seconds. She had no doubt at all that acquiring a husband who was a royal prince would be as easy.

'Your marriage?' Offa narrowed his eyes suspiciously, well aware that she was playing him with those big cornflower eyes and wheedling tone. 'I have made no plans to announce your marriage, child. If any betrothal is at the forefront of my mind it is your eldest sister's.'

'But surely, you should do it here. Now. Before we go. While the prince is here.' Her heart was thudding with sudden fear as she stared at her father's implacable face. She had convinced herself that the engagement was as good as arranged. It made sense, it was everything she wanted and dreamed of.

'What prince?' Offa sat back in his chair by the fire. 'Surely you don't mean that boy from Powys?'

'Of course I mean Elisedd.' Her eyes were hard now, holding her father's gaze.

He studied her thoughtfully for several seconds, then he

threw back his head and roared with laughter. 'Your mother told me she suspected you nursed such foolish dreams, and she assured me she had made it clear to you that it would be impossible. I would not waste an opportunity for alliance on any Welsh kingdom. Why do you think we are building our dyke? I want to keep them at a safe distance, you stupid child. Forget him. Forget this godforsaken corner of my kingdom! We will be leaving for home tomorrow, stopping to celebrate Easter at Lichfield along the way. You will not see him again. He's already gone. I have sent him on his way with golden gifts for his father. That should keep them happy.' He leaned across to the table and picked up a horn of mead, raising it to his lips with an expression of intense enjoyment. As he set it down on its stand he looked back at his daughter. 'Are you still here?'

Her face was white with anger. For a moment he felt a jolt of unease. She was so like her strong-minded mother, this youngest child of his, and as such he should not underestimate her. 'I will consider finding a husband for you as soon as we are settled back at Tamworth,' he conceded. 'There are useful connections to be made. I need steady alliances with Northumberland. Or perhaps Kent. Leave it with me, sweetheart, and I will choose you a fine stallion.' He roared with laughter, coughed, then called for his attendants. She was dismissed.

Prince Elisedd left his followers to wait for him at the foot of the ridge. He rode up the long trackway alone, climbing to the summit, threading his way between rocks and trees, and dismounting at the entrance to the fold. Leaving his horse with its rein looped over the gatepost, he wandered in.

Bea strained forward. She watched him stand looking round and she saw him sigh. He was every inch a prince today; he wore gold ornaments at his wrists and the heavy, ornately carved brooch to fasten his cloak. His horse stamped its hoof and pawed at the ground impatiently as he took a step into the shadow of the low stone walls and then another. He knew she wouldn't be there. Bea could feel his resignation and his

91

despair. He had lost her and as a poignant farewell he had come to revisit the magic of that encounter. She saw him turn away and again he sighed. He was looking straight at Bea, but if he saw her, he gave no sign.

Walking back, he unhitched his horse and led it slowly along the track. As the hill opened up he could see the countryside for miles in every direction. To the east the line of Offa's great ditch ran up and down over the hills, a raw scar on the landscape, a clear message that here the Border March between Powys and Mercia was forever fixed.

He narrowed his gaze, staring east towards the triple peaks of the Malvern Hills, shrugging themselves into the evening haze. He knew deep in his heart that she could never have married him. She was destined for marriage to a king. She was not free to marry where her heart led, any more than her sisters were. His few short hours with her had been no more than a dream of what might have been. He hoped she would be happy. Mounting his horse with a heavy heart, he turned it back towards the west and began the long ride towards his own destiny.

'What is it? What's happened?'

Alfrida was watching her sister pace up and down the gardens, her face set with fury.

'Papa has sent him away?' Eadburh stopped abruptly. 'He's gone!'

'Who's gone?'

'Elisedd!'

'But why do you care? You've told us often enough that you despise him.'

'I changed my mind. He's a king's son. He's handsome and . . .' Eadburh paused. 'I like him. And you and Ethelfled told me you thought Papa intended him for me. You said we were as good as betrothed!'

'I did not!' Alfrida was indignant. 'I never said any such thing. And Mama confirmed it. She said no way would Papa even consider it.' She caught her sister's arm. 'Stop walking about and talk to me.'

Both girls were swathed in cloaks as a sharp cold wind swept in from the north. Ox-carts were being loaded in the courtyards, their beds dismantled, boxes packed. They were used to this regular change of residence as the peripatetic court of the king moved from palace to palace round his kingdom. As servants ran frantically here and there, the daughters of the king found it expedient to keep well out of the way. 'I thought Papa had changed his mind. I was expecting the announcement.' Eadburh knew she was being disingenuous. 'It made sense for me to marry him.' She turned desperately away to hide her tears. 'I love him.'

Alfrida frowned. 'Don't be silly, you only think you do! You've scarcely talked to him.' Her fingers tightened on Eadburh's wrist. 'Have you?'

Eadburh nodded. 'Of course I've talked to him! We rode together. We . . . we talked a lot when we went to inspect Papa's ditch.' She felt Alfrida's sharp eyes on her face and she turned away abruptly. 'He's gentle and kind. He told me stories of the dragons that live in the hills, and the saint who saved the life of a hare.'

Alfrida let out a scornful gurgle of mirth. 'They told us he was a poet! He doesn't sound like much of a man to me! I want to marry someone who's a warrior! And preferably a king.'

'Which will mean going far away from Mercia.'

'So!' Alfrida raised her chin defiantly. 'That will be an adventure.'

'And you would go to him without ever having set eyes on him? Supposing he's ugly! And cruel!'

'He won't be. Papa would not send me to someone I couldn't love.' Alfrida's confident tone faltered.

'Have you ever kissed a man?' Eadburh asked suddenly.

Alfrida shook her head.

'Well, I have.' Eadburh couldn't hide her sudden smile. 'It was so exciting! And wonderful! It makes your heart race, and—' She stopped abruptly. She had been about to confide in her sister about what had happened and she realised, just in time, she could never do that.

But already Alfrida's eyes had narrowed speculatively. 'Does Mama know how you feel?'

'No. No one knows.'

The sight of their mother walking towards them silenced Eadburh abruptly and both girls turned meekly as the woman beckoned them over.

Eadburh hung back and peered over her shoulder as her sister and mother disappeared into the hall. For a long moment she stood there as the rain began to fall and scanned the garden as though searching for someone.

Bea caught her breath as the girl looked straight at her and the air seemed to crackle and grow thin. 'Who are you?' Eadburh breathed. 'What is it you want? You who watch me so carefully from the shadows. Do you think I haven't seen you there, eavesdropping on my secrets?' Her blue eyes were hard as agate as she met Bea's gaze and held it. She raised her hand and made the sign of the cross. 'Angel or demon, you are not wanted here.'

Then the rain clouds closed around her and she was gone.

The stone slipped from Bea's fingers with a crash. She sat, not daring to move, her heart thudding under her ribs. The gardens and the shadowy figure of the princess had vanished and with her the scent of woodsmoke that hung over the settlement, the splash of rain and the distant barking of a dog.

Bea's mouth was dry as she stared round the room, her own room, lit by the flickering candle. Outside, street lights from the town were casting shadows across the gardens behind the canons' houses. She could hear the rain on the trees and on the rooftops. She stared down at the stone lying on the floor at her feet. Eadburh, daughter of Offa, King of Mercia had seen her, locked eyes with her and spoken to her.

She sat immobile for some time, hardly breathing, frozen with fear. That wasn't supposed to happen. She should have been protected by her cocoon of light. She should have been safe.

When at last she stood up she stepped shakily over the stone without touching it; leaving it lying where it was and made her way to the door. They had gone. All those people in the past had gone, but even so, she had to get out of the room, had to distance herself from the memory of those angry blue eyes.

12

The house was nestled at the head of a hidden valley. As the car drew to a halt, Simon peered through the windscreen at the grey stone façade. Around them the gardens lay sprawled and tangled in a mass of unruly colour, daffodils everywhere, peering defiantly through collapsed mossy pergolas, stone balustrades, lichen-draped trees and on what might have once been a lawn around the edge of a grey stone fountain, long ago run dry. Simon had been afraid Jane would insist on blindfolding him, the woman's paranoia about secrecy had been so intense, but now he saw why there had been no need. He hadn't a clue where they were, whether they were in England or Wales, or Narnia itself.

'What a fabulous place,' he breathed. 'What are they going to do with it?'

'I don't think they know themselves.' Jane switched off the engine. 'There are quite a few places like this around here in the Marches. Lost in time. Forgotten. Magical.' She smiled at her companion. 'It would need a fortune to put it right and I doubt if the young couple who have inherited it had any idea what they had been saddled with.'

That assumption was soon proved wrong. They had heard

the car and the massive oak door had opened before Jane and Simon had reached the flagstone steps. They were, Simon reckoned, in their mid-thirties, Kate, obviously pregnant, was tall, with long dark hair, knotted back in a ponytail, framing an aquiline, attractive face with intense brown eyes. Her husband, Phil, was also tall. Slim and wiry, he wore glasses that gave him the look of an academic completely out of his comfort zone. Which he clearly wasn't. Simon and Jane followed them into an enormous kitchen at the back of the house that looked as though it had last been modernised sometime in the early 1800s. There was however electricity, a small cooker and a kettle and a sink that had modern-day taps.

'I don't know if Jane has explained,' Phil said to Simon as they sat down with cups of coffee. 'Kate's great aunt left her this place.'

'I've been coming here every year since I was a child,' Kate interrupted gently. 'She knew how much I loved it. I was her only relative. My parents were killed in a car crash several years ago.' Her voice shook slightly but she swallowed hard and carried on, 'and I have no brothers or sisters, so it's up to me to try and look after it.'

'The snag is, there's no money,' her husband went on bluntly. 'So it's a choice. Keep the stuff and sell the house, or sell the stuff and try and run the house in a way that will pay for itself, as a B & B or a retreat or for glamping, something like that.'

'I'd never been into the library. It was always kept locked. I didn't even know it existed.' Kate took over the story again. 'We contacted Jane in the hope that some of the old books in there might be valuable.'

'And I,' Jane looked over at Simon, 'found what I suspect are treasures beyond imagining.' She grinned. 'I was wondering what to do. Ideally, I should take them back to the cathedral, where we have a strong room with the correct humidity and climate control, although, to be fair, they seem to have been safe here for a very long time. I was going to arrange to consult someone about a valuation when you walked into my office, and suddenly I had someone on the spot who can read Old English far more fluently than I can, which I suspect is what this one particular book is. Kate and Phil would love it if you could take a look and hopefully confirm my suspicions.'

Their coffee drunk, and their hands thoroughly washed on Jane's instructions, Simon followed the others back up the broad oak staircase to a shadowy landing on the first floor. As they walked down it, the sun broke through outside, shining through the window at the far end of the corridor, illuminating the dust that rose from the wooden floorboards as they walked. He smiled. There was something about dust motes dancing in the sunlight that spelled magic. They were making their way towards what must have been one of the main bedrooms in the house. He had been expecting to see the library itself, but instead he found himself in an empty room, with nothing more than a large trestle table on which lay a selection of old – very old – books, with a few mismatched dining chairs scattered round the walls.

'We brought them in here so we could see them properly,' Phil put in. 'The library itself has no tables or chairs. Most of the furniture in the house is rotten, to be frank, and we've been warned that the lovely old oak pieces that have survived probably have no value these days anyway, so we are counting on the books.'

There was an Anglepoise lamp on the table, attached to a trailing lead. Phil leaned forward to switch it on.

'That's an old Welsh Bible,' Jane explained to Simon, pointing at a huge vellum bound volume, and these are diaries of some kind; judging by the writing, they could be fifteenth or sixteenth century.' Her finger pointed along the line of books. 'One or two of these have bookworm and need urgent conservation, but most are in reasonable condition, considering their age. There is an early Shakespeare here. That on its own, if it's a first folio, is probably worth a million or two, I would guess.' She paused for effect, glancing from one to the other with a delighted grin. 'But this is our pièce de résistance.' She stopped to pull some foam supports from her bag and arranged them on the table, then she carefully lifted a volume towards them into the pool of light from the lamp and, cushioning it on the rests, she opened it at the first page. It was fairly large and heavy, and as Jane opened it, Simon saw the neatly inscribed writing on the pages, the coloured initials.

He stared down at it in awe. Pulling forward a chair, he sat down and stared at the page.

'Yes, that's Old English,' he breathed.

'What does it say?' Kate whispered. 'Can you read it?'

'In the year of Christ's Nativity, 494, Cerdic and Cynric, his son, landed at Cerdicessora with five ships.' He looked up. 'It's a copy of the Anglo-Saxon Chronicle.'

'A copy?' Kate looked devastated.

He smiled at her. 'Everything was a copy, don't forget, until the invention of printing. There are various surviving versions of the chronicle. They are histories of the island of Britain. It's believed that the original version was written for King Alfred and then copies were sent around the country to various monasteries, where they were kept. Each monastery then continued to keep the chronicles up to date by adding to their own version. The closest one in this part of the world that I can think of offhand is the Worcester Chronicle, but these chronicles would have been copied and distributed all over the place. Which doesn't,' he added hastily, seeing Kate's continuing disappointment, 'detract from the value. To be honest, I haven't a clue how much it would be worth. You would need a writing expert to date it, but it's obviously a very early copy, and it's written in Old English. Some of the marginally later copies – and I'm talking perhaps twelfth century rather than eleventh – were written in Middle English.'

He desperately wanted them to go away and let him read it. His fingers were quite literally itching to turn the pages.

He turned to Jane. 'Are you going to advise sending it to London?'

Jane nodded. 'I think that's what Kate and Phil will probably decide to do. I have suggested we might invite someone here from one of the auction houses to have a look.'

'Would you allow me to transcribe some of this into modern English first?' Simon was carefully turning the pages. He looked up at Kate. 'I wouldn't take it away. I would come and do it here. As I think Jane told you, I am writing a history of Mercia, and this is the nearest thing I will ever come to first-hand reporting of what I am writing about. It might be a different version to the one I know. It might have extra bits we don't know about. Local bits.' He reached out and laid his fingers gently on the page. He was gabbling, he knew it, but he couldn't stop himself.

Kate glanced at her husband. 'I don't see why not.'

'And with your permission, I will meanwhile contact one or two people I know who deal in medieval manuscripts,' Jane said. 'I won't tell anyone where you are, and neither will Simon, until you have had a chance to make a decision about what to do and who we should show them to. In the meantime, I do advise you to keep these under lock and key.'

As Simon climbed back into Jane's car he could feel himself shaking. 'I don't think I had let myself believe you. If that is genuine, they're sitting on a fortune that would probably make a Shakespeare first folio look cheap.'

'I hope so, for their sake.' Jane reversed the car and headed back up the overgrown drive. 'And in the meantime you can go back tomorrow and start copying. So you are hoping for something that isn't in the other versions?'

Simon lowered his window and took a deep breath of cold air. 'You mentioned Offa and his family?'

Jane nodded. 'One of the pages I looked at when I first came over seemed to contain his name a great deal, with some women's names. And there are pages that have been scratched out. You'll see when you go through it.'

Simon felt his stomach tighten with excitement. 'It's unlikely there will be anything new, but as you say, I won't know till I read it. The narrative stopped, I noticed, in 1055. Some versions went on into the twelfth century. Just touching it was something so special, and with a bit of luck a local monk might have inserted something extra. That's the joy of the chronicles. Mostly they are annals, as you know, a year-by-year account of the most important things that happened, but occasionally a flash of personal opinion breaks through. Or even better, gossip.'

Jane laughed. 'All historians are romantics at heart in my opinion, and us librarians are more so than most. I saw you stroke the page. I wanted to do the same. Those books have almost certainly sat there unread for centuries. They showed me the library downstairs. Very dark and musty. The books must have been collected at some point by an antiquarian ancestor of Kate's, but I suppose they're now destined for a glass case somewhere.' She sighed. 'I wish we could acquire that chronicle for the cathedral, but Phil and Kate need the money and we could never afford it.' The car bumped over the cattle grid at the end of the drive and turned onto the road. 'You think you'll find your way back here?'

Simon laughed. 'Or will it disappear into the mist like Brigadoon and we'll never find the house again.'

'Or the people in it.' Jane shivered. 'Did that place strike you as haunted?'

Simon looked across at her sharply. 'No,' he said firmly. 'No, it didn't.'

It wasn't Mark who had given Bea the little cross, but her mother's cousin. 'I thought it apt, dear, as you're marrying a vicar,' the old lady had said, pressing the small velvet-lined box into her hand. Bea had never worn it, but now she sat on the bed, the closed box in her hand, staring down at it. Last night, Mark had returned after she had finally gone to bed and he had taken care not to wake her. This morning he finally left at about ten o'clock, kissing her on the top of her head as she sat, still in her dressing gown, over the last dregs of her coffee.

She had awoken late, with a splitting headache, and he had offered to cancel his appointments for the day to look after her, but she'd insisted she would manage without him. 'I think I might go back to bed for a bit, catch up on some sleep. Don't worry about me. I will be fine.'

She pressed the little button on the velvet-lined box and opened the lid. The gold cross was about three centimetres high, a proper crucifix with a tiny slim figure of Christ on a twisted, strangely arboreal cross, beautifully engraved in minute detail. She picked it up, the chain slipping through her fingers, and studied it critically. Some of the house healers she knew made a point of wearing a cross when they worked, on the grounds that the predominant culture of this country had been Christian for two thousand years and even for non-believers it was part of a common reference point from which to work. She always took her small hand-held wooden cross with her, but she had never felt the need to actually wear one, conflicted as always between her reluctance to label herself in any way and her loyalty to Mark and the Church she had been brought up in. But now. Now, she felt oddly at a loss. She sat for a long time, the gold cross in her hands, staring across the room towards the window. Eadburh had thought her an evil demon and invoked the cross of Christ against her. Would it put the woman at ease to see her wearing the symbol of their mutual faith, or was that the most awful hypocrisy on her part? And what was she thinking even contemplating the idea that she might encounter Eadburh again, that she would defy common sense and do the very thing Mark had begged her not to do.

Putting the cross down on the bedside table, she began to dress. Jeans and sweater. She was not planning on going out. She made the bed and went to the door, hesitated, turned back and, grabbing the cross, slipped the chain over her head, tucking it inside her sweater, then she headed for the attic stairs. She couldn't leave the story there, she just couldn't. If Eadburh was prepared to tell her more, then she needed to find out what happened next. However scared she felt, she believed the cross would give her courage to go on with her quest and use the knowledge she gained to help the woman's soul find peace. She was fully prepared this time. It wouldn't be dangerous and Mark would never know, unless she told him herself, and she had no plans to do that.

13

Cynefryth had insisted that Nesta ride close to them on the long journey through the kingdom of Mercia, back to the most spacious and the grandest of Offa's royal palaces, his base at Tamworth. The herb-wife, brighter than most, she had grudgingly to admit, and a source of knowledge derived from Celtic roots as well as life at the Saxon court, seemed to have formed some kind of friendship with her unruly youngest daughter as they worked together over the herbs in the stillroom, and the queen hoped that she would be able to deflect some of Eadburh's tantrums which were beginning to upset the entire household. She was not accustomed to enquiring about the serfs and peasants who served her, and was not sure what Nesta's background was; for all she knew the woman was the daughter of some local ealdorman, but she was intelligent, literate and experienced, and in spite of her relative youthfulness she had a certain confidence about her that occasionally called for respect and a certain wariness. She knew the women of the household thought she was a sorceress, a witch. So much the better. She was happy to wash her hands of Eadburh and leave her to Nesta.

Nesta watched and waited.

*

Eadburh had missed her monthly flow and she felt sick and tired and aware of an increasing sense of panic. It could not be that she was with child. It had to be because of the exhaustion of the ride back to Tamworth. Settled once more into the comfort of the women's bower, she would soon recover her spirits, of that she was sure. She demanded restorative drinks from Nesta and sat dreaming in the spring sunshine. And she wrote Elisedd a letter. 'I would like to see your dragons and the beauty of your mountains and hear the songs of your heart.' It was romantic foolishness, and she dared not say more. If they could but meet, she would tell him everything and they could be wed. Her father need not know where she had gone. Even in her most optimistic dreams she realised that to run away with the Prince of Powys would probably cause a war, all plans for the dyke forgotten. She didn't care. All she wanted was to feel the strong arms of the prince around her, telling her all would be well.

She entrusted the letter to Burgred, confident that he could not read, promising him riches beyond his comprehension when he brought her back a response from the royal court at Mathrafal, and threatening him with dire consequences if he spoke of this to anyone.

Then she waited.

Burgred took the letter straight to the king. Offa read it then threw it on the fire. He turned to Burgred, his face contorted with anger. 'How many times did she meet with this man alone?'

Burgred met the king's gaze defiantly. 'Only the once.'

'Are you sure?' Offa's eyes, the colour of a jay's wing-flash, were hard as iron.

Burgred felt himself quail. 'Only the once, great king, and for no time at all.'

For barely a heartbeat Offa thought, then he looked up, his decision made. 'You will return to Sutton and stay there. The princess will think you are on your way to deliver her letter and no more will be said of the matter.'

Burgred set out the same day, relieved to have got off so lightly, raising his hand in farewell to the guards at the gate, riding fast, zigzagging towards the west before giving up all pretence of heading towards Powys and turning south as instructed by the king to join one of the old Roman roads that would take him towards Worcester and beyond it Hereford. After a while he turned his horse off the road to follow a drovers' trail across a lonely windswept hill and it was there, with no witnesses beyond the curlews, that Offa's men caught up with him and cut his throat. Once the ravens and kites had finished with the body thrown into the rushes that bordered the lonely pool nearby, there was no trace that Burgred, the guardian of Princess Eadburh's honour and the king's messenger, had ever passed that way.

At the royal palace Eadburh waited in ever-growing despair. Why did Elisedd not reply to her letter? In her most secret dreams she had pictured him riding in from the west to claim her hand. In the end there was nothing for it but to tell her mother. Her mouth dry with fear, she waved Nesta away and drew the older woman to the far end of the herb garden. Making sure none of the weeding women were within earshot, mother and daughter set down their baskets and sat on the bench in the sheltered corner. 'I have missed my courses for two months. I need a tincture to bring them on and I'm not sure which herbs to use.' She tried to sound casual, to keep the desperation out of her voice.

She darted a glance sideways at her mother's face. It was not reassuring. Cynefryth turned to look at her, and she saw the woman's gaze drop to her stomach. 'You are with child.' The fury in her voice cut like a dagger bladed with ice.

'No! No, I can't be,' she stammered. 'It is some ailment. I have been feeling ill for several days. Vomiting . . .' her voice died away.

'You are with child,' her mother repeated stonily. 'If your father finds out he will kill you. I take it, it was that little Welsh snake.' It seemed impossible that so few words could contain such hatred. 'We sent him on his way too late; we gave him gifts instead of slicing off his manhood and garrotting him for the traitor spy he was!'

'It wasn't his fault, Mama. I thought we were to be married.' Eadburh raised her chin defiantly.

'You lie! You knew there was to be no marriage! And even had we considered it for a single instant, you couldn't wait for a treaty to be signed? You dragged him into the bracken like a cottar's whore?'

'I love him.'

'No. You were full of lust! You are a princess of the royal house of Pybba. You could have said no.'

Eadburh wanted to stamp her foot, but she forced herself to lower her eyes meekly. 'It was my fault and it was for me to say yes or no. And I . . .' she faltered, 'I wanted it. I admit it. If Papa had arranged the marriage, there would have been no harm. It is his fault, not mine.' A quick flash of defiance.

'But there was no plan to marry you,' her mother repeated angrily. 'None. We told you so. Your eldest sister will be married first and only then will your father decide on suitable husbands for you and your sister.'

'Then you must tell me what to do.' Eadburh waited, as always wary of a mother whose temper was legendary.

Cynefryth tightened her lips. Her face was white and drawn. 'I will procure the right ingredients from Nesta and make you a drink.' She spoke so quietly that Eadburh had to lean closer to hear her words. 'Have you confided in her?'

'No, Mama.'

Cynefryth scanned her face then nodded, satisfied. Eadburh realised with sudden horror that her mother would allow no one to find out about this and live. 'The mixture will make you sick and you will take to your bed, confiding in only one of your women to help you with what will follow. The silence of that woman afterwards must be ensured.' She held Eadburh's gaze. 'You understand me?'

Eadburh understood only too well. 'I will not kill one of my maidens for sharing my secret,' she retorted. 'I will choose someone I can trust.'

'Indeed you will.' Cynefryth stood up, pulling her cloak around her tightly. 'Go to your bed now and let it be known that you are unwell.'

Eadburh watched her mother walk across the garden, her skirts trailing against the edges of the herb beds. As her ladies fell in step behind her, Cynefryth beckoned Nesta to her. The two women talked briefly, then moved on, pausing here and there to pick a sprig of this and a few leaves of that, dropping them into Nesta's basket.

Eadburh shivered miserably as a cold breeze blew across the garden. She knew what her mother would use. Pennyroyal and rue, mugwort, marjoram . . . There would be other ingredients, too, to make sure, and spells, of that she was certain. But maybe, just maybe, even now Burgred might return with a letter for her, offering her a route out of her dilemma, a way to certain happiness.

Burgred did not come.

The drink when it arrived was bitter and made her gag. Her mother stood over her while she drank it, then summoned her ladies to pull screens around her bed before leaving the chamber. She beckoned one woman to remain with her daughter. Brona, the eldest of the group, who generally served food to her young mistress. 'Do not leave the princess, do you hear me? This medicine will clear away the evil spirits that have made her ill, but anything she passes must be thrown on a fire outside. You will fetch no one else and care for my daughter yourself, alone.' The queen glared at the woman. 'Have I made myself clear?' Brona bobbed a curtsy. 'Very clear, lady.' She pursed her lips. Eadburh's women were a close group and observant. They knew what was wrong with their young mistress, though none would have dared comment. As soon as the queen had appeared with her jug in her hand, they had guessed what was going to occur. None of them wanted to be there when it did.

Cynefryth left a second goblet of the drink on the table beside the bed. 'If nothing happens before the candle burns down, give her this second dose,' she said, then she swept out of the chamber without a backward glance.

Eadburh groaned. 'It's disgusting. The taste of it makes me want to vomit.' She lay back on the pillow. She was very scared.

The candle had only half burned down when the first cramps began. The pain grew worse and worse. She was drenched in sweat, doubled up with pain and had vomited twice when at last the blood came. It was a long time before Brona scuttled out of the chamber, carrying a bowl covered with a cloth, leaving Eadburh, white as a sheet and exhausted, lying on the bed. 'Come straight back,' she gasped as the woman disappeared through the screens. 'Please, don't leave me.'

She slept at last, awoke and slept again. There was no one there to answer her calls and when, as it grew dark, her mother came, it was to remove the unneeded second dose, pull her covers straight, and briefly put her hand on her daughter's hot, damp forehead.

When Eadburh awoke next morning the screens had been removed, the fire was burning cheerfully and her ladies were chatting in subdued tones as they went about their business as usual. She never saw Brona again.

14

Bea sat at the kitchen table shivering. She couldn't get the scenes she had witnessed out of her head, or the smell of blood and vomit. She took several deep breaths and stood up, going to switch on the kettle. She had been there, watching a man die swiftly and silently on the lonely track amongst the hills, and she had been there in the shadowy candlelit chamber, watching the girl writhe, sobbing, on the bed. Whatever had been in the mixture her mother had administered had been pretty near lethal. And the woman, Brona. What had happened to her? It was obvious she had not come out of the situation well. Bea dropped her head into her hands, rubbing her face hard to dispel the picture of the servant hurrying through the screens and out of the building into the night, carrying the cloth-covered bowl before her. Thankfully Eadburh had shown no signs this time of realising she was being watched from a distant time and place. She had been far too preoccupied with her own troubles, and when at last someone had come to look after her it was one of her other attendants who, grim-faced, had sponged her face and hands and brought her a bowl of what looked like bread and milk. She had taken only a couple of sips from the horn spoon and then lain back on the pillow, her eyes closed.

Bea reached up and clutched the gold cross hidden under her sweater. It was a long time before she staggered to her feet and headed across the kitchen to retrieve the jar of instant coffee from the cupboard. The strong-and-black, that was what Mark called it when there was no time to make the real thing. It was their private code. It meant something truly awful or stressful or complicated had happened at work and he was trying to contain his exhaustion or frustration or both. As she drew the mug towards her and took a sip, she found herself longing to confide in him about what she had seen, but she knew she couldn't. Not about this. He wouldn't understand why she had deliberately gone back to the cottage again and he would be distraught and furious when he realised she had once more deliberately put herself in danger. But was it danger? Or was she just being voyeuristic, watching other people's dramas as one would watch a TV box set? With a sigh she finished the coffee.

Upstairs she had wrapped the stone in the silk scarf and put it in a wooden box on the top shelf of the bookcase. It could stay there for now. She somehow doubted if she would need it again.

It felt ridiculous, creeping across the cathedral transept, waiting for a group of visitors to arrive and trying to hide herself amongst their number in order to avoid Sandra's eagle eye. In the event, the woman was nowhere to be seen and Bea was able to make her way up towards the quire without being observed.

To her relief, the chantry chapel was empty and she could slide into the safety of her corner seat unseen. No one had lit a candle today; the rack was empty save for a few burned-down stubs. After a few minutes she stood up restlessly and went over to select a fresh candle and reach for the lighter, then she knelt down. He wasn't here, and he wasn't going to appear. She sensed it with absolute certainty. Why? Why would he abandon her now? And where was he? For the first time she wondered if her gentle, praying priest had an existence away from the chapel. Did his life of prayer and devotion carry on in a different place, on a different plane? Somehow she had assumed he was anchored here, that this had been his whole world, but perhaps not, perhaps he was a travelling adviser, busily shuttling between different customers, as she did when she was working, whether it was at school or in the healing of a house, dropping in, being helpful and moving on.

But I still need you!

Fearing she had cried the words out loud, she shot a quick look towards the doorway, embarrassed, but the chapel stayed empty of enquiring faces. After ten minutes she climbed to her feet and retraced her steps, planning to go home. But that, she realised, was the last place she ought to be because she might not be able to resist going upstairs, and reaching for the stone, and plunging once more into the past. The thought terrified her. She must not lose control. But the lure of what she had seen was like a drug, dragging her back. What had happened to Eadburh after she lost the baby?

She needed to know.

'Bea? Are you OK?' Bea was saved by her friend Heather Fawcett, who caught up with her in the middle of the Close. 'Bea, love, what's wrong? You look as though you'd seen a ghost!' Heather was a small woman with neatly waved grey hair and beautiful azure eyes that had been a lethal lure to the young men she had encountered earlier in life. At this moment her eyes were full of sympathy.

Bea and Heather had known and liked each other for many years, since their husbands found themselves in neighbouring parishes in the north of the county at the start of their careers. To have found themselves neighbours had been a serendipitous bonus to their friendship, Bea in the Close and Heather, sadly now widowed and alone but full of energy and optimism, living round the corner in a narrow winding terrace of little Victorian cottages, just outside the cathedral gates. Heather was the only person in the cathedral community to whom Bea had confided her interest in the supernatural and her self-appointed job. She had to talk to someone and Heather, a volunteer and something of a mother figure to the huge number of selfless people who helped keep the cathedral going, would understand.

Shortly after her experience with the poltergeist they had been sitting over a coffee at an outdoor table in the market square, watching the crowds hurrying between the stalls around them, and Bea had poured out the whole story.

'It was a strange place. That library must have been incredibly old; there were some lovely books there. I don't know who actually owned that house, but I have to say I wouldn't have chosen Ken Hutton as my tenant. He wanted to burn all the books afterwards. I begged him not to, but God knows what he did in the end.'

It had been a relief to talk to someone about it and even more of a relief when the lurid headlines had appeared in the paper and she was living in terror of someone finding out it was about her. Heather's was a voice of steady reassurance.

'So, did you get rid of the ghost?' she had asked.

Bea had nodded. 'I think so. I would have loved to know his story, where he came from, when he lived, what pushed him over the edge like that, but I have to leave it there. That's one of the rules. I have to leave him in peace now. I don't want there to be a risk of accidentally calling him back.'

They hadn't talked about it again.

They sat opposite each other now at Bea's kitchen table. Bea hesitated for several seconds then she plunged into her tale.

'I was asked to go up to a cottage on Offa's Ridge – you know, that wild area up beyond Kington on the border with Wales. It's being haunted by a wailing voice. A lost soul. I thought I could contact it – you know how I work – and I thought I would be safe. But now,' she paused, grasping for the right words. 'Now, I think I've got myself in too deep and I don't know how I'm going to get myself out of it. I don't want to get myself out of it.'

Heather reached across the table and took her hand. 'I thought you told me you'd learnt from that experience with the poltergeist.'

Bea gave a wry smile. 'I'm not proud of the way I've handled this. I should have known better.'

'Indeed you should. Bea, darling, if you're worried, why don't you contact one of the deliverance team?'

The deliverance ministry consisted of a group of men and women who responded to reports of ghostly occurrences in the diocese from local parish clergy or people who came to them through their website. They were a dedicated and experienced group of people and Bea had met and liked most of them, but she shook her head vehemently.

'No! No, Heather. Absolutely not! Mark would have a fit! I did suggest them to Simon at the very beginning, but he didn't go for that idea. Please, you must promise me you won't tell a soul. Mark knows about it but I let him think it was sorted. He went up there and prayed and the ghost went away.' Bea pulled her hand away and stood up. 'I haven't told you the half of it. I did something so stupid,' she went on, pacing up and down the kitchen. She didn't dare look at Heather. 'When Simon told me it was dealt with, I deliberately tried to follow it up anyway, to go back into the past. The story was intriguing, somehow it got under my skin and I was curious. I didn't want to leave it as some kind of unfinished episode. And,' she turned back to face Heather, 'I brought it home with me.'

Heather frowned. 'You always told me you knew how to handle this sort of thing. You said there was no danger.'

'There isn't any danger! At least . . .' Bea looked away again, unable to meet her friend's shrewd gaze. 'If there is, it's of my own making. It was so exciting, Heather! I've never had an experience like this before. I was actually there in the past, in the court of King Offa! I know what I should have done. I should have shut it down, surrounded the whole scene with love and light, explained to the people there that they needn't be earthbound, that they should let go of their story and move on to another world and the next stage of their journey, but . . .' she fell silent.

'But you didn't,' Heather put in softly.

'No. I didn't. Just now, upstairs at home, I was in the women's chamber, watching one of Offa's daughters miscarry her baby. That's why I was upset. Oh, Heather, it was awful.' She flung herself back down on her chair. 'It was deliberate.

An abortion. She had taken some kind of herbal drug to make it happen. I could see it all, hear it, smell it!' She only realised there were tears pouring down her face when Heather stood up and went to tear a piece off the kitchen roll standing beside the sink, then handed it to her before putting her arms round Bea's shoulders and giving her a gentle hug.

'Poor Eadburh. She was barely more than a child and her own mother made her get rid of it. I know it happens. It's happened throughout history. But I was there with her. I felt all her pain.' Bea was rubbing her face with the palms of her hands, too exhausted to go on.

'You mustn't do this again, Bea. You know that, don't you,' Heather put in at last.

'I know.'

'Can you keep it under control?'

'I don't know.' It was a whisper. 'Oh, Heather, I'm sorry. I didn't mean to pour all this out to you. You showed up when I was feeling so upset by the whole thing. You were on your way somewhere, weren't you, and I've delayed you.'

Heather stood up. 'Will you be OK if I leave you for a few moments? I'm so sorry, but I was on my way to the cathedral shop. They'll be waiting for me to take my turn behind the counter, but I can tell them I'll be a bit late starting and then I'll come straight back.'

Bea sniffed. She blew her nose on the tissue. 'No, no. Don't be silly. You don't have to come back. I'll be all right. I'm sorry. I shouldn't have lumbered you with my antics. I needed someone to talk to, that's all. I'm not going to go back there. Not now. And I'm sorry I've made you late. You go. I'll be fine.'

'You're sure?'

Bea nodded.

'I'll ring you later. And don't worry, I won't say anything to anyone.' Heather smiled reassuringly as she headed for the door. 'Be strong, darling.'

Chris's phone call came as Heather left. 'I'm popping up to the cottage to drop off some stuff for Simon. Do you want to

114

go with me? I'm heading into Hereford to go to Waitrose first, so I can collect you.'

Bea hesitated. She should say no. Cut off all contact with the cottage and Simon and whatever it was that was happening in her head. She was stressed and exhausted, and her mind was still whirling. She would be mad to go. She had promised Heather. She had promised herself.

Chris picked her up on the corner of the car park. 'The cottage isn't really equipped for a long let and his children are coming up for part of the Easter holidays, so there are a few things I told him I'd drop off. He's out today and it suits him quite well, I think, for me to go when he's not there. It will give you a chance to suss the place out and make sure the ghost hasn't returned.' She glanced across at her friend. 'Have you spoken to him again?'

'We had a coffee, as it happens, when he came into Hereford for a meeting.' Bea took a deep breath. 'He seemed happy about the cottage. He didn't seem to have had any more strange voices calling.' She was not going to tell Chris about Mark's part in what had happened or about what had happened earlier, or about her conversation with Heather.

'But you'd like to check, yes?' Chris negotiated the tricky turn onto Eign Street.

Bea gave a grim smile. 'You know I would.'

The cottage was less tidy than last time Bea had been there. There were books and papers scattered all over the living space, unwashed mugs and a cereal bowl in the sink in the kitchen and a couple of shirts hanging on the line in the garden at the back.

'It looks as though he's making himself at home,' Chris said as she unloaded her shopping bags. She had brought cleaning materials and spare linen and a couple of extra saucepans. 'I didn't suppose he was going to have any massive parties, though he did mention that his wife and kids might come for the odd weekend,' she said as she stuffed a packet of dusters and some surface cleaner into the cupboard under the sink. 'Somehow I got the impression he hoped they wouldn't. At least he's got everything he might need now.'

'He mentioned he had a couple of teenagers,' Bea put in. She was standing gazing out of the window into the garden.

'He wasn't sure they would even want to come.' Chris straightened, her face red from bending down to the cupboard. 'Frankly, I'm amazed he would want them here. That'll be the end of his peace and quiet.'

'Perhaps they are students of Zen.' Bea smiled.

'I don't think so. That's why he looks for isolated places to do his writing. Good,' Chris looked round. 'That should sort him out if they come. There are two beds in the second bedroom anyway and a couple of blow-up mattresses in the cupboard under the stairs. They can't expect the Ritz. So, are you going to go all crystal-ball on me and check if your ghost has really gone? I'll sit out on the terrace and contemplate the view while you do your thing.'

Her thing. It was the last thing Bea wanted to do. She was exhausted and stressed, but at the same time it would be interesting to have a feel of the atmosphere. Leaving Chris seated at the small table outside the front door, she wandered round to the back garden, trying to spot anything that reminded her of the sheepfold in her vision. This was the place, she was almost certain. The outline of the hills was the same, the angle of the ground, the lie of the land on the far side of the wall. The garden was uneven, hidden now beneath shrubs and drifts of daffodils. She walked over to the wall, the stones sprouting ferns and clumps of moss, liberally dotted with patches of yellow lichen. Had this wall witnessed Eadburh and her prince making love? She checked her watch. She probably had no more than ten minutes before Chris began to wonder where she had got to. She rested her hands lightly on the topmost stones and emptied her mind, waiting.

But there was no trace of any echoes outside or inside the cottage, of the nun or the fear she had felt, nor of the passion that had so briefly flared and died within the walls of that sheepfold so very long ago. The drama, the intense moments of love or lust, then the loss and sorrow were gone. Bea had sensed rather than seen the prince ride into the sunset, quite literally a silhouette against the glowing sky as the sun slid behind the mountains. She gave a wistful smile. The passion between the two had been so strong, but she guessed he had had a lucky escape. She doubted if Offa would have been a comfortable father-in-law.

She made her way back to Chris. 'Is everything put away and neat?' She knew that was important to the landlady in Chris's soul.

Her friend nodded. Growing bored with the view she had gone back inside to do a bit of surreptitious tidying. She had even remade the bed and twitched the covers straight. Everything had been tucked into the rightful places in the cupboards and she had looked round the living room, obviously itching to pick up the scattered papers and straighten the cushions on the armchairs by the fire, but managing to resist the urge.

Locking up behind them, the two women made their way down the path and back to the car.

'No ghosts now?' Chris looked across at Bea as they climbed in.

'No ghosts now,' Bea confirmed. 'The cottage feels at peace.'

'Well, let's hope Simon doesn't stir anything else up,' was Chris's crisp comment as she backed the car round to drive back down the hill.

'Can you really read it?' Kate was standing watching as Simon made himself comfortable at the table and switched on the Anglepoise. He had brought his notebook, and a pencil – no ink of any kind must come near this sort of treasure – and they had agreed that it made sense if he were to take photos of the pages that referred to the kingdom of Mercia so that he could pore over them at home. But in the meantime he would allow himself this one day with the actual thing.

'I'll leave you alone then,' Kate whispered when she realised he wasn't listening. Already he was there, deep in the text.

In this same year of Our Lord 757, Ethelbald, King of Mercia, was murdered at Repton . . . Offa seized the kingdom of Mercia . . . Offa, the son of Thingfrith, the son of Eanwulf, the son of Osmod, the son of Eawa, the son of Pybba, and so on back to the last, or in fact the first, name on the list, *the son of Woden.*

That was so cool. To be descended from the gods. He loved this stuff and knew a lot of it by heart from the printed versions of the main surviving chronicles. The births and deaths of the successive kings of the kingdoms of what was to become England, and their bishops and the kings of the Franks and the popes: the men – and they were nearly all men – who mattered, the battles between them and the laconically reported appearances, as first rare and then more and more frequently, of 'the heathen', the Vikings, who were to ravage and conquer so much of the country over the next centuries.

This was pretty much a faithful copy of other versions of the chronicle, and as far as he could see contained nothing particularly new. The beautiful script was neat and careful, the occasional red capital letter at the head of a page, exquisite. He could imagine the monk who had copied it sitting in his candlelit cell working tirelessly day in, day out, copying out his version, only the later parts varying from the original as history became actual reportage. He turned the page and skimmed down the lines of script. The copyist had changed here, the new scribe not quite so neat. There were several places where mistakes had been made and scraped off, leaving the vellum rough, and once or twice an empty leaf had been left in between the others presumably to be filled in later. Perhaps by now the author was sitting in a scriptorium, other men around him, all working intently at their tasks. Simon leaned closer, screwing up his eyes, cursing the fact that he didn't have a magnifying glass. Were the pages actually empty or had they been erased? He stood up abruptly and went to the door.

Kate and Phil were downstairs in the kitchen. 'I don't think I've ever seen a magnifying glass here. You could try my aunt's desk in the library,' Kate said in answer to his request.

He followed her directions along the main hall, letting himself into the large book-lined room. So, this was the library Jane had mentioned. It was shadowy, the shutters closed, and very cold. He looked round, shivering, at hundreds, probably thousands of books, innumerable treasures spanning centuries lining the walls, library steps, a small table, several carved chairs and more books, everywhere he looked. How on earth had she managed to filter out the few she thought the most valuable? He walked over to the large roll-top desk which sat by the window and, pulling open one of the shutters to give himself some light, he gazed down at the dusty papers and pens lying on the blotter in front of him. There were cubbyholes filled with old ink bottles, seals, little boxes of rusty paperclips, papers, envelopes, what looked like old bills, but no magnifying glass. No. All this felt too much like spying. He would rather get hold of one in Hereford next time he was there, and that would give him an excuse to come back. Leaving the desk untouched, he pushed the shutters closed as he had found them and went back to the door. There was something about this room he didn't like.

It was a relief to be seated again at the table upstairs. Leaning forward, his phone in his hand to photograph the text, he turned another page, and there it was, the extract Jane must have been thinking of when she said there was a section all about Offa's family. Reaching for his notebook, he picked up his pencil and copied down the words, transcribing them into modern English as he read.

784 Offa the king defeated the men of Powys and took the lands of Pengwern and began to build his great ditch between Mercia and the tribes of the west. In the following year Egbert, son of Eahmund fled from Wessex, then to exile in the court of King Charlemagne.
787 The son of Offa, Ecgfrith was consecrated king by Archbishop Hygeberht of Lichfield while his father still lived. At his consecration was the king's wife Cynefryth and his daughters, Ethelfled, Alfrida and Eadburh. In that same year the heathen raided the coast of Wessex.

The next two pages were blank.

His heart thudding with excitement, Simon picked up his phone and took careful photos of each page, the empty leaves as well as those covered in writing. In one place a whole page had been cut out, leaving the smallest ragged traces that it had ever been there.

He read on. The story progressed haphazardly. Again this was stuff he knew. And then it stopped. Abruptly, halfway down a page. He screwed up his eyes. There was more, but the writing had been erased. He turned over two pages. The next entry was for the year 806.

And also in this same year, on 4 June, the sign of the holy cross appeared on the moon one Wednesday at dawn; and again this year on 30 August, a marvellous ring appeared around the sun.

He continued photographing every page, concentrating hard, making sure nothing was omitted. There was no time to read it all, but he could do that later once the pictures were safely on his laptop. He turned to the last page. The entry was scribbled. No neat lines pricked here. It was the final entry and it was for the year 1055.

King Gruffydd is harrying Herefordshire. He has laid waste to Leominster and the convent of the nuns there. We fear he may turn next towards us. Only by the Grace of God can we be saved. We pray for our own Blessed Saint Cuthbert whose festival we celebrate in two days' time, to be with us here and protect this holy——

And that was it. A dash as though the scribe had stopped mid-sentence, a blot of ink and then – nothing.

He shivered. Had King Gruffydd arrived? He would have to see if he could check from other sources. In his imagination he pictured the scribe throwing down his quill pen and the little knife he used to sharpen his pens and erase his mistakes, pushing away his inkhorn and standing up, moving away from his writing slope and, for whatever reason, never coming back. From his name, Gruffydd was Welsh. Obviously he was Welsh. And what had happened in those missing years? He bent closer. Why go to the trouble of scraping them away, why not just cut them out?

He looked down at his scribbled notes. Most of the chronicle was as he remembered from the general translation in his own much-thumbed Everyman edition, which was up at the cottage. But there were extra bits, bits he didn't recognise, bits that referred only to Mercia. This was definitely a local version. He ran through a list of possibilities in his head. Priories which would have had a scriptorium. Leominster, perhaps – although the final entry seemed to contradict that. Or St Guthlac's in Hereford. Or perhaps Hereford minster– the earliest version of which probably dated, if he remembered right, from the mid seventh century. Most copies of the chronicle that still existed had been saved during the Reformation by local antiquarians and scholars when the monasteries and their precious scriptoria and libraries had been so cruelly and viciously dismantled. This house was easily Tudor, probably earlier. Perhaps this book had languished here, lost, but safe since the sixteenth century. Simon reined in his imagination sternly. The experts would find out. Guesswork had no place in serious history. And yet . . .

'Will studying the book help with your work?' Kate was alone in the kitchen when later that evening he put his head round the door to say goodbye.

'I'm not sure whether there is any new information. As Phil suggested, I have taken pictures of the pages that refer to Mercia and I will read them more carefully when I have them on my computer screen at home.' He paused. She was peeling potatoes, rhythmically dropping them one by one into a bowl on the table. 'I can't thank you enough for letting me see this treasure. The feeling of actually touching something so very special is beyond words. I felt as though I was in the same room as the guy writing that document, a thousand years ago. I could picture him, with his pen and inks. Almost hear the silence; perhaps the echo of plainsong around him as he worked.'

She nodded. 'I sometimes feel that here, in this house. When Phil is out, like now. The echoes of the past come back. He's too practical to feel it, which is probably just as well, as someone needs to be hands-on here, but there is something very special about an old building.' She shivered. 'My great aunt left me the house. For her last few years she was in a home and it was rented out to various people. They didn't always look after it very well, but at least they didn't steal anything. Those books were still there and her jewellery was still in the drawer in her bedroom.' She smiled. 'Nothing all that valuable, sadly, but still I was amazed no one had taken it. Some time before she died, I gather there was a bit of an incident with one couple. They said the house was haunted and made a huge fuss about it. They seem to have left very suddenly, but I never heard any more about it. It was empty at the time she died, and I've never sensed a ghost here, but there are all sorts of legends about the place.'

'Do you know when it was built?'

She shook her head. 'I expect there are records in the library. We do have a bit of Offa's Dyke in the garden. Do you want to see?' She put down her knife and dried her hands on a dishcloth. 'More hands-on history.'

He followed her out and across the back lawn towards the shrubbery.

'Wales's answer to Hadrian's Wall,' he said ruefully as they stood together looking down into the brambles.

She laughed. 'This is one of the lesser known bits. I'll show you on the map.'

Back in the kitchen, they pored over a much folded and refolded Ordnance Survey map. The house was circled in red. 'Otherwise we can't find it ourselves! It's here. See. There are other bits of the dyke marked on the map. We've traced its route through the fields here, but they were ploughed up during the war and it's mostly been lost.' Kate stared down at the map in silence. 'It's sad, isn't it. But there is still a bit of it left.' She sighed. 'Jane phoned, by the way, to say she is bringing someone over to look through the books. I hate the idea of selling anything, but if we are going to save the house we need the money, and I suspect it would be better for them to be somewhere safe, away from the damp and spiders.'

'That's true.'

'If you would like to come back and have another look before the guy comes, you would be welcome.' A twinge of pain crossed her face and he saw her hand go to the bump under her shirt.

'When is it due?'

'Not long now. Have you got children?'

He nodded. 'That's why I need a retreat to do my writing. The patter of tiny feet all over the house can be a tad distracting. But in a big place like this it will be wonderful. Exactly what it needs.'

He smiled to himself as he climbed into his car. Tiny feet indeed! Two teenagers and a wife who heartily detested the Anglo-Saxons and everything to do with them.

The house was empty when Chris dropped Bea off outside the cathedral gates in Broad Street. She couldn't remember where Mark had said he was going that afternoon, but she remembered him saying it was his turn to take evensong so he wouldn't be back until after the service. She shivered. She wished he was there. Solid dependable Mark. He would keep her safe. Stop her being tempted by something she knew she must resist.

Wandering through into the sitting room she stopped in front of the piano, lifted the lid and played a note. She was missing the girls more than she could say. The sound of Anna's music had filled the house, as had their voices, their arguments. Their laughter. Their noisy presence was everywhere when they were at home. If they were there, she wouldn't need to go upstairs. She struck the key again. Middle C sounded gently round the room and faded to silence.

Heather's voice floated into her mind.

You mustn't do this again, Bea. You know that, don't you.

Of course she mustn't. It would be insane. She could not risk being seen, really seen, by those ice-blue eyes from the past. She felt again the sudden frisson of fear, a tiptoe of cold across her back and, for a second, she seemed to hear her teacher, Meryn's, voice at the back of her head.

Possession and obsession, Bea. Remember the two most dangerous parts of this job. Don't let either touch you. Protect yourself. Close the doors against the past. Never be tempted to go through them. Never go back.

But if she was completely in control, there would be no danger. The doors were closed. She wasn't planning to go through them. She was interested, yes, curious as to how the story would progress, yes. But obsessed? No. Obsession would be too dangerous.

'I have arranged your marriage.' Offa never spoke to any of his daughters with affection in his voice. He had summoned Eadburh to his private office, behind the great hall at Tamworth. Outside, the autumn winds were racing through the trees in the great forest beyond the palisade, she could hear the roar in their branches but here it was strangely still, the king and queen seated side by side by the brazier that warmed the room, in unaccustomed alliance as they confronted their rebellious daughter. At her father's words, Eadburh had clenched her fists, hanging at her sides hidden in the folds of her gown. She shivered, her head high, and waited.

'I have decided to give you the highest honour. You will be married to King Beorhtric of Wessex. We will ride back to Sutton to celebrate Christ's Mass in the minster at Hereford and meet him to seal the agreements, then the marriage blessing will take place. The marriage will confirm our alliance and ensure peace between our kingdoms and his friendship and support for your father.'

Eadburh opened her mouth to object, to argue, to ask what kind of man it was she was to go to, but her mother was staring into the fire and refused to meet her eye, and already her father had reached for another scroll, his attention focused elsewhere. 'Oh,' he looked up again. 'You should know. The King of Powys's youngest son, Elisedd. He met with an accident and died.'

She gasped. 'No!'

But already he had looked away again, calling to his scribe, reaching for another document. There was to be no further explanation, no argument, no further discussion for her.

She stared at her father, her eyes wide with shock, unable to assimilate what he had said. Then she turned to her mother, but Cynefryth was still staring into the fire.

Her shoulders slumped and she turned away, refusing to give way to tears. That was why Elisedd had never answered her letter. He was dead. She found she had stopped breathing as she dashed the unshed tears from her eyes. Was this not, after all, what she had wanted: to marry, to be away from her father's court and all the memories of what had happened, her dreams of a baby that never was, a tiny soul out there in the darkness crying for a mother who had never held him, she always thought of him as a boy, never had the chance to love him, never wanted to acknowledge he had ever existed. Her dreams that one day Elisedd would come back for her, whisk her away from Mercia into his distant mountains where they could have a dozen more children, had shattered like a piece of glass dropped on a tiled floor.

She shivered. So, she was to marry a king, not a mere prince; and she, the youngest, was to be married before either of her sisters. Taking a deep breath, she straightened her back and raised her chin. Elisedd was gone. Dead. With an effort she put the thought behind her. Dreams were for children. She would never see him again. Had it been an accident or had her father had him murdered? She would never know, but she would find out. One day she would discover what had happened to him. But for now, this marriage must be triumph enough.

The royal household set off down the old Roman road south before the snows came. She was not part of the discussions between the two kingdoms; she remained loftily aloof. Marriage to a king was the summit of a royal daughter's ambition. Her sisters were insanely jealous that she should have been chosen as the first of their father's daughters to marry. She pretended she was pleased. She had never set eyes on King Beorhtric. Nor did she wish to.

She did not see Bea hovering at the periphery of her vision watching from a different world.

15

Transferring the photographs to his laptop, Simon examined the pages of the chronicle, zooming in on each page and studying the text with meticulous care. The first scribe had made very few mistakes and his initial letters were beautifully executed, his writing exquisite. His successors were not so careful. More and more mistakes crept in over the years, most scraped away and rewritten on the rough surface. In a few places trouble had been taken to polish the vellum smooth again before the corrections were inserted, but some of the later mistakes were merely crossed out and the new word written in over the top; as though the scribe was careless or in a hurry. Simon sat back, wondering about this last man. Was there no one to oversee his work? A senior monk perhaps, or the abbot himself? And what had happened to stop him working so abruptly and irrevocably?

Going back to his study of the photographed pages, Simon came to one that was blank and he could see now clearly that several dates with their appropriate entry had been scraped off. Again, it had been carelessly done, almost tearing holes in the vellum in places. The lack of care meant the missing words had not been removed without trace. There was a chance he would be able to read them. He reached for his own copy of the chronicle.

In the year of Our Lord 789 Offa gave his daughter Eadburh to Beorhtric of Wessex, much against her wishes, to make certain that the kingdom of Wessex remained within his alliance, and in those days came for the first time three ships . . . these were the first ships of the Danes to come to England.

And in a footnote another scribe had added in a different hand that the ships landed at Portland, on the south coast. Poor old Eadburh. Wessex, her new kingdom, had been the first part of England to be hit by the Vikings. He enlarged the page until it was nothing but a moonscape of faded dots. Slowly and carefully he refocussed and as he did so one of the scrubbed-out sentences became clear: *And King Beorhtric's marriage was attended by lightning and fiery dragons were seen flying in the air and the people saw this as portents of evil attending the arrival of the Mercian lady.*

Simon sat back. That comment was not in any of the other versions.

He leaned forward again eagerly. What else had the chronicler put into his record? The screen was blank. He screwed up his eyes in frustration. In his excitement he must have leaned on the keyboard.

He had been concentrating so hard he hadn't noticed the sound of the wind in the trees outside. Rain was rattling against the window and in the distance he heard a low rumble of thunder. He looked back at the laptop and at that exact moment all the lights went out. Only the pale rectangle of the blank screen illuminated the room.

Standing up, he made his way to the door and dragged it open. It was eerily dark outside, the sky boiling with black cloud. As he stood on the doorstep he saw a zigzag of lightning slice over the hills of Wales. He gave a rueful smile. So, the King of Wessex's marriage to Eadburh had been attended by lightning and fiery dragons, and here they were again to frustrate his attempts to read more.

Behind him, the lights in the house came on for a brief second, echoing the flash in the sky, then they went off again. He reached for the switch by the door. Nothing. Going back to the laptop, he powered it down to save the battery and then returned to the door. If the ancient gods of the Mercians were prepared to put on a show for him, it would be churlish not to watch.

'Bea, are you up there?' It seemed only minutes after she had retreated up to her attic room that Bea heard Mark's voice from the bottom of the stairs. She frowned crossly, and levering herself up from her cushion on the floor she went to the door. 'Yes, I'm here.'

She heard the thud of his footsteps, running two at a time up the steep narrow flight. She saw his eyes register the candle, the incense in its burner.

She thought he was going to be angry, but all he said was, 'I've got a couple of hours before I take the service. I thought maybe we could do something together. Go out for a walk, perhaps.'

'Mark, it's pouring with rain.' The storm had drifted in over the rooftops from the west and as she spoke a gentle rumble of thunder echoed round the room.

She saw his shoulders slump.

Eadburh's grief at the news of Elisedd's death had been overwhelming. Momentarily as she turned away from her parents, Bea had seen the look on her face, the fact that she was to marry a king, completely overtaken by her shock and devastation. She never knew, as Bea knew, that before he rode to his death Elisedd had returned to their trysting place. Though he realised their marriage was never going to happen, never had been going to happen, that she had always been and always would be out of his reach, he had ridden up there to say goodbye. Had he had any presentiment that he was going to die? Bea would never know that. She realised suddenly that she was almost in tears.

'Bea?' Mark was staring at her strangely. 'Did you hear what I said?'

'Sorry,' she reached for a tissue and surreptitiously dabbed her eyes. 'It's the storm. You know they always give me a headache.'

'I said, let's go for a walk in the rain. Defy the elements.'

Another rumble in the distance reminded Bea of a dog growling threateningly in its throat. 'Are you serious?' She laughed in spite of herself.

'Yes, I'm serious. I love being out in storms. You know I do.'

'But we might get struck by lightning.'

'Not here. Not in town.'

She gave in. They headed for Castle Green and then under the lime trees down towards the river. Standing on the footbridge with its iron lacework they paused, staring down at the mud-coloured water of the Wye as it flowed beneath their feet.

The rain was pattering down on Mark's umbrella. 'What did you get up to this morning after I left?' he said at last. 'Anything exciting?' It was a casual question.

'Chris picked me up and we went up to the cottage to leave some spare sheets and cleaning stuff for Simon. I gather his family are coming to stay with him for a few days over Easter.'

'No sign of the ghost?' Again the enquiry was casual.

She tensed and too late realised he must have felt her reaction as she held his arm beneath the umbrella.

'No. I did wonder if there was still something in the garden, an echo, but there was nothing there.' Elise had ridden into the sunset like a lovelorn hero in some romantic movie. Riding, did he but know it, to his death. 'No nun this time, and no wailing voice.' She kept her tone light. She let go of his arm.

'You have to drop this, Bea.' He glanced at her and then looked away, leaning on the rail, studying the river with exaggerated care. 'There is too much going on in that cottage. If Simon is satisfied that you, that we, have sorted it between us, then leave it at that.' He was pleading with her.

Too much going on? He too had sensed there was more to uncover.

'I'll leave it when I'm ready, Mark!' she retorted crossly.

It was not up to him to tell her to leave it. She thought she had made that clear. She sighed. 'In any case, it sounds as if he will be preoccupied with his family for a while. I expect that will distract him and help clear the atmosphere. I've no reason to go there again.'

She looked up at him and found he was staring at her. 'You're wearing your cousin's cross,' he said.

Her hand flew to her neck. She had thought it safely concealed under her sweater. 'I put it on when I realised she thought I was a heathen,' she stammered without thinking. 'I wanted her to trust me.'

'You wanted who to trust you?'

There was a moment of silence broken only by the sound of the rain.

'Offa's daughter,' she whispered.

She saw him close his eyes as if in pain. 'Bea—'

She was furious with herself for letting the name slip. 'I can take it off now. I won't be seeing her again.'

'Don't!' His reaction was sharp. 'Don't take it off, please.'

Bea let go of his arm and stepped away from him. Without the shelter of his umbrella, she was soaked in seconds. The storm was coming closer. The huge black thunder clouds were growing if anything blacker and more threatening.

'Mark—'

'Promise me you won't summon her again. You are summoning her, aren't you, she's not just appearing.' He stretched out his arm to shelter her under the umbrella, but she moved further away, her back to him.

'I don't summon her, Mark. She appears when she chooses.' That was a lie. She watched as a branch torn from a tree by the storm appeared from beneath the bridge, carried downstream on the current. 'Don't ask me to promise anything. We agreed you would not interfere with what I do.'

'But it's dangerous, Bea. Don't you understand?'

Obsession and possession.

'It's not dangerous, Mark. I know what I'm doing.' Rain was seeping down her neck and she wasn't sure if the wet on her cheeks was from the rain or from the angry tears she felt were very close. She gazed up at the sky, clenching her fists. If there was a clap of thunder now, she would probably lose it. Shout at him. Argue. Whose side were the wretched elements on, anyway? Was Thor a Saxon god, or was he a Viking? She huddled into her raincoat, trying to decide whether or not to turn and walk away.

'Sorry.' His voice was penitent, so quiet she almost failed to hear it because of the rain. 'Can we start again? Go and get some tea?'

She nodded. Ducking under his umbrella again felt like a concession, but it was only a small one.

It took a while to get used to the idea that she was queen, that hers were the keys to the household, indeed of the whole kingdom, that her mother was not going to appear with her face set hard as rock and her eyes as daggers as she surveyed her daughters' latest assumed transgressions, that Alfrida and Ethelfled had remained in Mercia to satisfy her mother's need for control while she was free of her at last. The wedding in Hereford had been rich and splendid, Eadburh's sisters attending as their sister was raised to the status of queen. Eadburh waited with glee for them to curtsy to her, but then when the moment came for her to part from them she found her eyes full of tears and the three girls hugged one another for a long time, all too aware that fate, in the shape of their father, was sending them in different directions and they might never meet again.

Locking away her thoughts of Elisedd as best she could, Eadburh resigned herself to her future as a queen. After all, how bad could that be? She had brought four women with her to her marriage, one of them her closest companion, Hilde, and one the herb-wife, Nesta, with whom her mother had parted with reluctance. She set off with her new husband south to Wessex followed by cartloads of gifts, her dower and her morning gift, the riches presented by the satisfied husband on the day after their marriage. Part of that gift had been the horse she rode, a silky-maned, prancing mare named Mona for the moon.

Beorhtric was some ten years younger than her father, a

fine figure of a man, strong, upright, hair brown, his eyes hazel. At first sight she had been pleased to find he did not repel her. Her sisters had spent long jealous hours gleefully explaining to her that even if she hated her prospective husband and he looked like Grendel, she could not refuse him. She was not some common housecarl's wife; she was a princess, a peace weaver, and part of her father's plan.

It had not occurred to her that her husband would know at once that she was not a virgin, that perhaps he would be angry and send her back as soiled goods. It was only when she saw him looking sideways at the sheets of their bed after their first night together that she realised she should have listened to her mother, who had advised her to make sure there was a smear of blood on the heavy linen. Perhaps it did not matter, for he made no comment. Her whole body had tensed against him as he took her and she had found it hard not to struggle and turn away, for his kisses left her cold. She hoped he would assume that her resistance was natural in a maiden.

As the long procession wound its way south, the rains set in. They stopped at various royal palaces along the way, none of them as prosperous and well appointed as Tamworth or Sutton, but they would do. She refused to allow herself to think of the riches which would greet her eldest sister if she married the son of the great King Charlemagne. She, Eadburh, was now a queen. It was up to her to guide her husband to greatness as her father's obedient ally.

Within the first weeks of their marriage she discovered that her husband intended to leave her to her own devices; at night in the royal bed he demanded her obedience and submission, crowing that he was a stallion, a rutting stag. She gritted her teeth and bore it all in silence. In the daytime he was like her father, constantly overseeing his vast and sprawling kingdom, dictating letters, meeting with the ealdormen and thanes who ruled it for him, distracted by the shocking raid of three heathen longboats on the most southern part of his kingdom and the slaughter that ensued before the raiders put back to sea.

She began to assert herself slowly, tentatively at first, asking whether she could appoint her own ladies of the household. He waved her away and told her to do what she thought best; he was preoccupied with matters of state. Slowly, cautiously, she increased the range of her influence. The wives of her husband's thanes were her companions. She disliked most of them and knew the feeling was mutual. She was seen as an outsider, a symbol of Mercia's perceived aggression, but she quickly became more confident, realising that the women were afraid of her. Once, in a fury at the clumsiness of one woman who had dropped her spindle, she swore she would have the woman's hand chopped off. That same night Beorhtric arrived in their bedchamber white with anger. One of his most senior thanes had complained to the king that his wife had been threatened and he had left the court not only with his wife but his entire retinue and his war band.

'I only shouted at her because she was so careless!' Eadburh was full of righteous indignation. 'The woman is a fool.'

'The woman is the wife of one of my most valued thanes. Why was she spinning like a serf?'

'We all spin, Husband.' She was genuinely astonished at his anger. 'In her case, badly. If her husband cannot control her outpourings, he is weak and you are better off without him!'

The king had stared at her in silence. She could read his thoughts so easily she was actually sorry for a man who could not dissemble. He was shocked, he was angry, but above all he was full of admiration. She met his gaze unflinchingly. 'I understand people, Husband,' she said quietly. 'I learned from my father.'

She saw the muscles of his jaw tighten and she suppressed a smile. She understood Beorhtric himself well enough by now to know that any mention of Offa would stop him in his tracks and remind him that his was now in every sense a client kingdom.

Push and pull. Demand and give. She was working out her own way of controlling him. Before he had time to process her words, she reached for her girdle and began to slip out of her gown. She knew by now he was not a man who could resist the lure of flesh. As he shouted his climax loudly enough to alert the whole hall of his triumph, he would forget any doubts he had about this forceful young woman who was sharing his kingdom and his bed. He would never know that as he mated with her she closed her eyes and, grasping for a modicum of comfort, pictured her dead prince.

It had not been part of the arrangement that Val would arrive a day early at the cottage on Offa's Ridge, drop the children off and then go. Simon stared at his two offspring in sheer bewilderment, trying to process his wife's reaction to the cottage, the rain, the mess of papers and books, his own scruffy, unshaven work attire. She, as usual, was immaculate, even in casual clothes, chosen no doubt to look good in her role of elegant, relaxed chauffeur arriving at a country cottage: slim-line jeans, designer trainers, expensive sweater that had somehow managed to survive a 150-mile drive uncreased, her ash blond hair as always softly waved, seemingly untouched by the Welsh wind and rain that had assaulted them on their way up the path from the car. He couldn't help comparing her with Bea in her functional but slightly arty attire, woven tops and dresses, linen trousers, beads and scarves and the little cross she had taken to wearing.

Val's look of barely disguised dismay registered with him only too painfully. 'I had already guessed this place would be too small for all of us, Sime, so I made a back-up plan.' She gave him a hug. 'I'm going to leave the kids with you and then go and stay with the Fords in Worcester. I didn't think you'd mind. They'll be revising a lot of the time anyway so you can still work, and you don't want me kicking around here getting in your way.' She wandered into the kitchen, which thanks to his landlady was spotless, and he could hear her voice as she talked urgently into her phone. He looked ruefully from his son to his daughter and back. They avoided his gaze, both standing uncomfortably near the front door as though they too might change their minds about spending the Easter holidays with him. Val returned after a full five minutes. 'OK. That's fixed. I can do my own thing while you entertain the children for a few days. I am sure you will all have a wonderful time without me. But don't forget they've both got revision.'

She hadn't even stayed long enough for a cup of tea.

'It's OK, Dad. Chill. We won't get in your way.' Fifteen-year-old Felix threw himself down in the armchair by the fire, his phone already in his hand, his eyes glued to the screen.

Emma was still standing at the door, looking wistfully after her mother. As the sound of Val's car died away, she turned and surveyed the room. 'I like it here,' she announced. 'It's cool. Kinda magical.'

Simon felt a surge of gratitude. 'That's a good word for it. Sorry about the rain.'

'It'll clear – I checked the weather app.' Felix glanced up. 'We brought all our gear. Mum said it always rains in Wales.' They had dropped their belongings in a heap of rucksacks and boots and anoraks just inside the door.

'And you've brought your books?' Simon scanned the luggage for signs of study. Felix was about to take his GCSEs, and his sister her A levels.

'I'm having the spare room, if there is one,' Emma announced, ignoring his question. 'Felix can sleep on the sofa. Where is the sofa?' she added, casting a suspicious eye over the cottage.

'No sofa.' Simon felt it was a personal failure. 'There is a spare room and I gather there are blow-up beds.'

Felix greeted this news with surprising equanimity. He was once more engrossed in his screen. The internet signal was apparently having one of its better days.

They were so alike these two that sometimes people took them for twins in spite of the two-year age gap. Both were tall and slim with mid blond hair, Emma's very long, Felix's very short; both had grey-blue eyes and fair skin. There the resemblance ended. In character they were completely different, and it soon became clear that Emma, the eldest, was as usual in charge. She lugged her stuff up the stairs and into the smaller of the two bedrooms, establishing possession of both beds, one to sleep on and one to put her stuff on, before her brother could change his mind and argue, then she came downstairs again to investigate the kitchen. 'What on earth are we supposed to eat, Dad?' The question floated through the door as Simon tried to heave a bag containing what he assumed to be one of the beds out of the cupboard under the stairs.

He sighed. 'I haven't stocked up for you lot yet, I'm afraid. I wasn't expecting you 'til tomorrow. We'll go out for supper, OK?'

Behind him, Felix had put down his phone and moved over Simon's worktable. He opened the laptop. 'What on earth is all this?'

'Be careful!' His father rounded on him sharply. 'I'm deciphering a manuscript. It's part of my work. It wouldn't interest you. Don't touch, please.'

'It's OK, Dad. I'm not going to do anything.' But he was, his hands already busy over the keys. 'Is this language Anglo-Saxon?'

'Old English. Photos of an ancient volume. I'm transcribing it into English.'

'It's beautiful writing.'

'It is, isn't it.' Simon found himself smiling. 'Imagine, all done with a quill pen and ink made from crushed oak galls.'

'Let's see.' Emma was there now, peering over her brother's shoulder.

'You saw this actual book?' Felix was swiping gently through the pages. 'Look at the lovely way this guy has decorated some of the letters. They're not illuminated, are they? If they were, they would be covered in gold. We saw them at the British Library – do you remember when you took us? But he's put them in red with some little twiddly bits. He's taken so much trouble.'

'I didn't know you were interested in this sort of thing,' Simon said quietly.

'You don't know much about us, Dad, be fair,' Felix retorted. It was said with tolerant humour. 'You're always locked away in your study and Mum never lets us near you on pain of death.'

That was a gross exaggeration, but he let it pass.

'You've obviously forgotten I'm studying history, so I'm supposed to be keen on this sort of stuff,' Emma put in, glaring at her brother. 'Hey, look at this bit.' They had arrived at a blank page, shaded with scratchings out and shadowy deleted words. 'Why did he do that? What does it say?'

'That's what I'm trying to find out.' Simon felt an unexpected warmth towards these two beings who were supposed to have sprung from his loins, but who he had always assumed to have come from some distant planet. 'It's a bit like a detective story. The scribe has written something he, or someone else, doesn't want to be read by other people. I'm not sure why he didn't cut out the page, which he has done elsewhere. I would love to be able to work out what it was he'd written.'

'Can we help?'

Had his son actually said those words? Simon grinned at him. 'I would love you to, if you can. Your eyes would be much better than mine.'

'But we don't speak Old English,' Emma put in. Simon heard an echo of his wife's voice there; the cold light of reason.

'Dad does.' Felix was leaning in, tapping at the keys. 'Your phone camera isn't all that good, but we can use the software on Dad's laptop to enhance what's here.' His voice had lost its note of perpetual boredom. 'And then Dad will be able to read it as it floats up off the page.'

16

When Mark returned home after evensong, Bea was in the kitchen preparing supper. She looked up. 'I've heard from Petra and Anna.'

'How are they?' He reached gratefully for the glass of wine she pushed towards him.

'It doesn't look as though either of them will be home for Easter.' She turned to slide a roasting tin into the oven, hiding her expression. The disappointment of not seeing their daughters had hit her hard. She hadn't realised quite how much she had been looking forward to their visit. 'Supper will be ready in half an hour.'

'They both rang?'

Bea nodded. 'They know we miss them, and they'd obviously been discussing it, but it can't be helped. They're busy young women now, with their own lives. It's our own fault for having such talented kids.'

Mark laughed. 'When I was a student, my mum always used to say that I only came home when I ran out of clean clothes.'

'That's boys for you!' Bea retorted. 'It didn't apply to me. I loved my parents and wanted to see them.'

'And the girls love us, darling. You know they do,' Mark said gently.

She nodded. And if the girls were there, she wouldn't have time to be tempted. She wouldn't have to fight the longing to go back, to see what was happening to Eadburh. Instead she could concentrate on them.

'I've given myself an admin day tomorrow.' She realised that Mark was talking to her. 'So I'll be home all day – perhaps we can nip out to lunch as a treat. But don't worry if you've got anything planned.'

'No. Nothing.' If he was there she would have to abandon any plan she might have had to spy on the Queen of Wessex. She gave a wry smile.

'Something amusing?' He had seen her fleeting expression.
'No. I was still thinking about the girls.'

'I suppose we'll get used to them not being around much.' He sounded wistful. 'But as you say, they're both talented and we are so lucky that they are driven by those talents. Please. God, they don't waste them.'

They were finishing their supper when there was a knock at the front door. With a groan, Mark climbed to his feet, just as Bea's phone announced she had a text. It was from Heather. **You OK?**

Bea smiled as she typed her reply: ⌐ xx

As she looked up, Mark reappeared with Sandra Bedford in tow.

'My dear, I am so sorry to intrude again. I know how precious your time is in the evenings.'

Bea felt a prickle of unease. She sighed. 'Can we give you some coffee, Sandra?' She was beginning to dislike this woman intensely, with her busy darting eyes and her ingratiating smile. 'Why don't you and Mark go to the study and I'll bring it in.'

'No. No, my dear, this isn't a cathedral matter. I happened to be passing and I saw the lights were on and' – Sandra paused dramatically – 'I wanted to check on you both. I sensed last time I came over that there was some family crisis going on and I wanted to offer my help. I know how hard it is when the canon is so busy and I wanted to assure you that I am there for you, if you need me. We all need someone to confide in, don't we?' She paused, looking from one to the other expectantly.

Bea shivered. The cold breath on the back of her neck was a suspicion, no more. A warning. The woman spelt trouble. Mark, who was looking perplexed and irritated in equal measure, managed to reply, 'That's so kind of you, Sandra.'

'And very thoughtful,' Bea put in. 'But there is nothing happening that you need to worry about, I assure you. I expect I was tired and rushing about as usual. I'm so sorry if I gave you the impression there was something wrong.'

'Perhaps you're doing too much. I heard that you have taken on a job that fills a lot of your time.' Sandra pulled a chair towards the table and sat down. She was still wearing her coat. 'That must be very difficult, what with taking care of the dear canon as well.'

Bea opened her mouth to reply, but Mark stepped in. 'Bea is very busy in her job as a supply teacher, but she looks after me beautifully, Sandra, I assure you.'

'Oh, I didn't mean to imply that she doesn't.' Sandra looked hurt. 'You know, perhaps I will have that cup of coffee.' She began to unbutton her coat. 'How are your children? They're both at university, aren't they? I suppose we all feel the need to fill that empty nest when they go off to study.'

'They are doing very well.' Mark walked over to the worktop and switched on the kettle. 'Our eldest is training to be a vet. I'm so sorry, Sandra. I'm afraid I know nothing about your own family. Do you have children yourself?'

There was a moment of silence. 'No,' she replied eventually.

'I'm sorry. I thought you implied . . .' Mark looked at Bea desperately for support.

'I've seen you with children in the cathedral,' Bea put in. 'You're so good with them. And you're right. We do miss the girls very much. But on the plus side, it is blessedly peaceful in the house now.'

It was a full fifteen minutes before Sandra finished her coffee and at last stood up to go.

Closing the door behind her, Mark turned to Bea. 'That was a fishing expedition. The woman is impossible!'

'She's obviously very lonely.'

Lonely and malicious.

Malicious and dangerous. Bea put the thought out of her head.

'And I am being unchristian,' Mark was saying. 'I'm sorry, if so. I will have a word with someone tomorrow about her circumstances. But even so, to call uninvited at this time of night. It's too much. And why is she so interested in you? What was all this about you having a job that takes up so much of your time?'

'I do have a job. I'm a teacher, as you told her.'

But they weren't talking about teaching, were they?

'A proper job.' He sighed. 'No, sorry. I didn't mean that to come out like that. I'm obviously having an attack of tactless idiocy. Of course you have a proper job, it's just that it's a bit on and off, isn't it? And it's holidays now.' He was silent for a moment. 'OK. I'm going to say it. Supposing she's got wind of your ghost hunting? There's no way someone could have told her, is there?'

'Certainly not through me,' Bea said indignantly. 'She's being nosy, Mark, and ironically she's right, we were talking about missing the girls.' She gave a hollow groan. 'You don't think she's got this place bugged, do you?'

He laughed. 'I wouldn't put it past her. Every institution has a Sandra somewhere. But darling, please be careful. If word got out, it could prove so awkward for me. You do see that.'

'I do. And I have always been discreet. Chris is the only person who knows and she is aware she mustn't say anything. And Simon has promised. And so had Heather. It was only that one wretched man and if Sandra knew about that she would have let us know ages ago. I don't see how she could have picked up anything, I really don't.' She paused. 'I'd like to think she came over because she has a kind heart and means well, but could you keep reminding her I'm a teacher? Perhaps drop a few hints that I do some tutoring as well in the holidays. Anything to put her off the scent.'

'I can't lie, Bea.'

She sighed. 'Dear old George Washington! Of course you can't lie, but you could imply.' They looked at one another and after a moment's hesitation they both burst into laughter.

Much later Bea slid quietly out of bed and tiptoed across to the window, looking down into the Close. The half-moon was casting the hard shadow of the roof across the grass. There was no sound from Mark as she made her way to the door.

Sitting down in the candlelight upstairs she took several long quiet breaths, seeking into the silence for a sign from Eadburh, whose story had moved down to the kingdom of Wessex, far from home and from her sisters, far from Offa's Ridge and the cottage on the hill. There was no danger in watching the queen as she rode, no chance of her seeing Bea. She had remembered to control the scene, to protect herself.

Eadburh was riding along a winding track with high cliffs towering above her, followed by a party of her husband's warriors. There were two women with her: Hilde, who had accompanied her from home on her first long ride from Mercia, and another who had become her preferred companion among the thanes' wives who surrounded her. The countryside was spectacular, wild, a land of eagles and wolves.

The messenger caught them up at a bend in the track where the grasses blew gently in the wind. He dived into his bag of letters and found one for her, and she dismounted, then made her way to a fallen lump of limestone that formed a natural bench in the sunlight while her ladies talked and giggled with the messenger as he rested his sweating horse.

The letter was from her elder sister, Ethelfled.

I am married, and in Northumbria, and father's reach spreads ever further across the island of Britannia. Tell me you still think of me, sister mine, for I am lonely among strangers here. My hope of marrying the son of Charles, King of the Franks, came to nothing. Instead I reign beside my new husband, the king in this wild country. Father was angry beyond measure that his careful plans to ally with the Franks did not succeed, and although Charles's sons remain without wives he announced he would no longer seek a marriage for me there. Within months I was on my way to wed Ethelred at a place called Catterick on the great road north, and now I live in a savage distant place among the hills.

Eadburh gazed up at the towering grey cliffs above her with a rueful smile. After the gentle landscapes of her homeland she too was in a wild setting, though the palace itself at Cheddar, not two miles from here, was in the flatlands below the Mendip hills, on the banks of the River Yeo. She had been drawn to this wild gorge; it reminded her of the landscape that might have been hers had she married a prince of Powys. She batted away the sudden sharp pain of the memory and turned back to the letter in her hand. For Ethelfled to reach out to her with this homesick missive must mean she was lonely indeed.

I expect our first child and my husband needs a son to grow tall and strong as we live here amongst his enemies who jostle always for position, ever looking for the chance to depose him.

Eadburh dropped the letter on her knee, once more looking up towards the cliff where a peregrine falcon swooped down through the cloud. There was a wild goat up there on the cliffs, balancing on a narrow ledge, its curved horns a sudden silhouette against the sky. So, her sister was pregnant. Unconsciously her hand strayed to her own stomach, which was still stubbornly flat. She had wondered more and more often if her mother's remedy to rid her of Elisedd's child, the baby she still mourned so bitterly in some locked away part of her heart, had rendered her unable to bear more children. The time had come, she realised, to seek help in that regard; she needed amulets and charms. With a sigh she refolded the letter and tucked it into the embroidered pouch at her girdle. The messenger had further bulky missives for Beorhtric from Ethelfled's husband and already he was remounting.

As his horse disappeared round the bend in track, the sound of its hooves echoing off the high crags, Eadburh looked up and with a sudden jolt of fear she crossed herself.

Bea froze. In her fascination with the scene before her she had drifted closer without realising it. The woman's eyes locked on hers. 'Demon! Witch! Why do you follow me? I banish you three times three and still you return!'

Her women clustered round their frightened mistress as she leapt to her feet, and Bea saw two of the warriors from their escort reach for their swords, staring round in terror. She clutched her little crucifix, holding it out it in front of her. 'I am not a witch!' she heard her own voice, thin and scared in the silence of her room. 'I'm not . . .'

But they had gone. The Queen of Wessex and the people anxiously surrounding her had faded into the past and Bea could only imagine them there, on the track, staring round in confusion as the cry of the falcon echoed from the cliffs above them and died away into the silence.

The sound of the front door quietly opening and closing had woken Simon. He reached for his phone and stared at it groggily. It was 2.30 in the morning. With a groan he climbed out of bed and went to peer out of his bedroom window. He could see the faint outline of his daughter sitting on the wall outside in the dark. She was smoking a cigarette.

Grabbing a heavy sweater, he tiptoed downstairs past the recumbent form of his snoring son and let himself out into the cold night air.

'Emma? What is it, darling? Can't you sleep?'

Hearing the door open, Emma had hastily stubbed out the cigarette and tossed it over the wall. 'I thought there was someone out here, Dad.'

'Felix is asleep.'

'Obviously.' There was enough light from the stars to see her smile. They could both hear his snores through the door.

'It's a beautiful night.' Pulling his sweater more tightly round himself with a shiver, he sat down beside her. Above them the stars were a brilliant carpet across the sky, the half-moon low on the horizon. After their urban sky at home in London where one could see even the biggest constellations only occasionally, he had been stunned by the sheer number of stars out here.

'There was a woman out here, shouting. I'm surprised you didn't hear her. She'd gone by the time I came downstairs.'

He sighed. 'Was she calling for Elise?'

'So you did hear her?'

'Not this time. I was asleep. I had hoped she'd gone.'

'Who is she? Who is Elise?'

'I don't know.'

'Dad?'

He sighed. 'No one knows who she is. When we look for her, she disappears.' He sighed. 'We're beginning to think she's a ghost. Christine, the woman who owns this place, asked the local ghostbuster to come by and see if she could get her to leave. At first I thought it had worked, but obviously not.' He could feel Emma's gaze fixed on his face and he waited for an explosion of laughter. It didn't come.

'A real ghost?' She sounded impressed.

'A local vicar was up here as well, and he said she was a nun.'

'A nun!' It was an incredulous squeak. 'What was a nun doing up here?'

He grinned. 'Good question. But she's not a scary ghost.'

'I'm not scared.' Emma was looking at him with something like awe. 'That's so cool. A real ghost! Wait till I tell Felix! Vicars and nuns!' She gave a gurgle of glee. 'Better not tell Mum. She would think you'd gone mad – or kinky.'

'She already thinks I'm mad.' Simon couldn't stop himself.

Emma reached over and put her hand on his for a second. 'She does love you, Dad. You do know that, don't you? It's this weird job you do. She would much rather you were an accountant.'

Simon let out a splutter of indignation. 'An accountant! Where on earth did you get that idea?'

'I heard her say so. She was on the phone to one of her friends. She didn't mean it. She's very proud of you really. But it is a bit weird, going away every couple of years or so and locking yourself away in remote places for months at a time to get away from us. It's kind of rejecting everything we stand for.'

Simon was silent. Was that really how his family saw him? He had thought Val understood.

'I'm not rejecting you, Em. Never that. You know how much I love you all,' he said at last. 'But I have to get my head round so many facts when I'm putting my books together, and I need silence to concentrate, not just for an hour or two but for weeks at a time.'

'And you've ended up in a cottage with a ghost who yells at you!'

'Ironic, isn't it.'

'Can we get your exorcist back?'

'For goodness' sake! How am I supposed to sleep?' The front door opened so suddenly they both jumped. 'Nattering out here at three in the morning!' Felix appeared, clad in only a T-shirt and shorts, his hair standing on end. He stood on the doorstep, his feet bare. 'You've been smoking, Em. I can smell it.'

How, Simon found himself thinking, can he smell it out here with all this glorious fresh air?

'I haven't. I don't smoke!' she denied it automatically. 'And as for us talking, you should hear yourself snoring. Neither of us could sleep a wink. You were making the whole place rattle!'

'I wasn't. I don't snore.'

'Kids!' Simon stood up wearily. 'This is why I need peace to write. Can we adjourn the argument until morning? Please?'

17

Bea heard the clock strike the half hour from the cathedral. It was 2.30 in the morning. She must stand up, put away the stone, go back down to bed.

Soon.

But first she must repeat her protective ritual. Make sure she was safe. With or without the protection of her cross, she never wanted to feel Eadburh's icy gaze on her again. She shuddered at the memory.

Eadburh had always known Nesta for what she was. Though modestly dressed, and with downcast eyes as the queen approached her, she gave off an aura of confidence and power, and at her girdle she wore the tools of her trade, one of them a tiny ball of rock crystal set in a silver mount. She and Eadburh had formed a strange bond long ago, perhaps strengthened by the knowledge that although it had never been mentioned between them, she knew about Eadburh's pregnancy and had probably helped concoct the mixture that had led to the miscarriage, though Eadburh had no doubt in her own mind that the idea and that particular charm had been entirely of her mother's making. Eadburh beckoned her away from the throng and led the way through the palisade and out into the gardens.

'I need your special help.' She held Nesta's gaze, expecting her to look away. She didn't. 'I need certain medicinal plants I don't see growing here.' Her glance swept the windblown herb beds. 'And charms I don't know myself. I need to have a child.'

'There can be no child as long as your womb is elfshot.' The woman stated it as a fact.

Eadburh took a step back. She had not expected such frankness.

'I can give you charms to help you conceive and we will make a potion to make your woman's parts soften to your husband. At present the spirit of your dead child fights for its place in your affections. It must not be allowed to win.' The woman was taller than Eadburh and older by at least a dozen years. For the first time in her life, Eadburh could feel another's power reducing her to obedience. This was, she realised with sudden apprehension, someone stronger even than her mother. She felt a shiver of fear. 'You speak nonsense! What dead child?' She pulled her veil round her face.

'The child I see clinging to your spirit shield, begging to be let in.'

Eadburh staggered back a step, her eyes filling with tears. 'You lie!'

'You loved it and you wanted it; you knew what your mother's potion would do and you still drank it. You killed the child in your womb. You must send it on its way with your blessing. Every woman has love enough for dead children as well as living.' The woman's eyes softened momentarily, then they were once more cold and calculating. 'I will give you what you need. Follow me.'

Nesta's workroom was on the far side of the palace grounds, a small wooden hut with a sturdy roof. Around it she had planted a new garden of herbs, surrounded by a wattle fence to protect it from the weather. She pulled open the gate and led the way in. 'These plants are more sheltered in here. They are grown with the blessing of the sun and rain. If we walk the path together, I will sense what you need and pick them for you when the moon and stars are in the right places in the firmament.' She turned sharply, so she and Eadburh were face to face, no more than a foot apart. 'Once this magic is in train you will not be able to step back from it. You are certain you want a child by Beorhtric?'

'Of course.' Eadburh's mouth was dry. 'He is my husband.'

'By treaty, maybe, and by the blessing of a Christian bishop, but you do not love him in your heart and the stars decree you are destined to be his downfall.'

Eadburh looked at her askance. For a moment she couldn't speak. 'You know nothing,' she said at last. 'My father sent me here to seal an alliance between our kingdoms. For our marriage to be blessed, I need a son.'

Nesta grunted. 'Then you must put aside your love for another. If you are eaten with grief and the need for revenge, there is no place for a new soul to come in.' She walked on and stopped again, facing the line of carefully tended plants. 'You know your herbs. You know as well as I do what is needed to make you conceive. Send your women away.'

'What women?' Eadburh turned in time to see Hilde and two other ladies standing uncertainly by the gate. They had followed her from the king's hall. One angry command from her and they fled.

'You will need to know who are your friends in this country,' Nesta commented tartly. 'That is, after all, why you insisted that Hilde and I accompany you to Wessex. You are sleep-walking, queen, and what you require of me is dangerous. Take care.' She stooped and picked a sprig of mugwort. 'Tuck this into your gown and I will give you a pouch of fern seed. It will hide you and your thoughts from those sent to spy on you by your husband. He uses guile with you, but you can use a far more powerful magic against him.' She gave a grim smile. 'Ideally, we need a stone from a lapwing's nest to hide you from him, but for now this will do.'

Eadburh held out her hand for the leaves. 'You serve the old gods,' she said flatly. 'But so do many. Their ways are strong and their magic works. Do you want a reward of gold for this special service?'

She saw the look of disdain on the woman's face, but her words contradicted her expression. 'We all want gold, lady.'

'Then you shall have it.' She hesitated as she tucked the herb into her bodice. 'Where did you learn your craft, Nesta? I suspect your magic is stronger even than my mother's.'

'My family came from the forest.' The woman seemed to feel that was answer enough. Eadburh looked past her, peering into the dark shadow beyond the palace's wooden ramparts that signalled the miles of wildwood with its lonely empty tracks and hidden patches of moorland, forest that stretched east and northwards, unbroken as far as Mercia and beyond. She shivered. Turning away, she walked slowly back to the gate. As she let herself out of the herb garden she glanced round, the wind catching her veil, her eyes narrowed in the sunlight.

Bea jumped back out of the way, feeling herself brush against a bush of rosemary by the gate.

For several seconds Eadburh paused, and as her gaze hardened, Bea felt herself grow cold. 'So, you watch me still.' She was speaking directly to her. 'You are not my husband's spy and you do not come from my father, so who has sent you?' The power of her gaze and the force of her anger made Bea quail. 'Come near me again and you will die!'

She didn't realise she had cried out loud until she heard Mark running up the stairs, and then he was there, his arms around her, holding her close. 'Bea! What is it, darling? What's happened? I heard you shouting—'

'I . . . I'm sorry. I must have been asleep. Dreaming.'

'You're shivering.' Helping her to her feet, he guided her to the door and down the stairs into their bedroom. Reaching for her dressing gown, he wrapped it around her shoulders, then he sat down on the end of the bed beside her and put his arm round her again. 'I came back late and the house was in darkness, so I assumed you'd gone to bed. I was working in the study and I must have fallen asleep.'

Her teeth were chattering. 'I . . . went upstairs to meditate.'

'Bea!' He stood up. 'You must realise how dangerous this is.'

'And I've told you, I'm being careful.' But however careful she was being, her safety ritual hadn't worked. She shuddered. 'I'm cold, that's all. I didn't realise how late it is.'

'Then why did you scream?'

'I didn't scream.' She stared at him, astonished.

'Oh believe me, you did.' His voice betrayed how frightened he was. 'Come on, let's go downstairs. It's warm in there and we need to talk.'

According to the bedside clock it was ten past three in the morning, but she got up and led the way down the stairs. Mark, sensing her tension as she peered into the corners of the hall and through open doorways into the darkened rooms beyond, sat her down at the kitchen table and put off any further conversation for a few minutes while he made them both a mug of hot chocolate.

'So.' He sat down beside her at last. 'What really happened? Why did you scream?'

'I'm sorry for waking you.'

'Bea!'

'I was dreaming about the kingdom of Wessex. About a wise woman called Nesta who makes herbal potions. She said she came from the forest.'

'That doesn't sound so frightening.' He was trying hard to keep his voice calm.

'No.'

'What happened next?' He could read her so easily. He put his arm round her shoulders again.

She took a deep breath. 'OK. I was back in the past. It's so vivid. So real. And she was there. Offa's daughter.'

She felt him freeze. Literally. His arms had grown rigid and she sensed a chill run through him. She saw his lips move and she waited for an explosion of fury. Then she realised he was praying for her.

'Whoever it was, it was a dream,' he said at last.

'She saw me, Mark. She looked at me, out of the past and saw me. It wasn't a dream. I saw her make the sign of the cross. She thought I was evil.' She could hear the disbelief in her own voice. 'And she wasn't scared of me, Mark. She was angry.'

'Dear God!'

She wasn't clear whether that was his prayer or an expression of horror.

'I was scared. I admit it. Very scared.' She took a deep breath. 'My fault. I obviously didn't do things properly, I didn't protect myself, I didn't shut the door behind me.'

'It doesn't sound as though she would have much of a problem with doors.' His face was ashen.

'Not that kind of door.' She gave a wistful smile. 'It's never happened before. I'm experienced enough to know better.'

But it has happened before, hasn't it? He didn't say it out loud. 'Have you shut the door now?'

She nodded.

'And she won't come back.'

'No.'

'Are you sure?'

'Yes.' She took a deep breath. 'I'm sure.'

He heaved a deep sigh. 'Bea, you can't go on like this.'

'I know. I'm sorry.'

'Can you stop?'

She gave a hesitant smile, reaching for her mug. 'Of course. I don't know why I cried out. I didn't mean to wake you.' As she lifted the mug to her mouth, she smelt a sharp herbal smell on her fingers and remembered the rosemary bush. Only then did she remember to visualise the doors between that world and hers and slam them tightly shut.

'I wanted to make sure you were OK.' It was Heather, on the phone next morning. 'Have you got time to come over for a chat?'

Heather led Bea into her cosy living room looking out onto a narrow garden full of spring flowers.

'So, has anything else happened?' Heather sat down opposite her friend and studied her face.

'It happened again. Last night. I was in the past with Offa's daughter and the wise woman who seems to be advising her.'

'Was that where you wanted to be?'

'Yes. Yes, it was!' At first hesitant, suddenly Bea was full of enthusiasm. 'It was amazing, Heather! I was there with them.'

'Actually there?'

'Yes. I could see every detail and, more to the point, they could see me!' She stopped abruptly. 'Swear this won't go any further. I could put out my hand and feel the plants in the hedge around the herb garden. I touched a bush of rosemary and rubbed it with my fingers, and when it was over and I was awake again, I could smell the rosemary on my fingers.'

Heather stared at her. 'Are you saying you were really truly there? As in, not here any more. Gone.'

'I don't know. Mark came up and found me and I was there in my study, so no, I hadn't disappeared.' She was silent for a few seconds. 'He said I called out.'

'So, Mark knows.' Heather breathed an audible sigh of relief. 'Thank God for that! I don't know how all this works, but it seems very dangerous to me.'

Bea shook her head. 'It's not dangerous. We may be able to see each other, but if they are ghosts to me, I must be a ghost to them, surely.'

'A ghost from the future?'

'A shadow. A ghost they can't touch. Or hurt.'

'You touched the rosemary, Bea.'

For a moment both women were silent.

'What did Mark say about all this?' Heather asked cautiously.

'He was upset,' Bea admitted. 'He wanted to believe it was a nightmare. Then he asked me if I could stop it happening. I told him I could.'

The morning went well. Simon drove the kids to the small town of Knighton where they explored the Offa's Dyke Centre, followed the path along the River Teme, standing with huge embarrassment at the appointed place on the national border, with one foot in England and one in Wales, for a photo for their mother, and then walked a surprisingly long way along the footpath before returning to Knighton to devour a huge lunch and supervise the shopping at the local supermarket. By the time they got back to the cottage, both children were suffering from phone withdrawal symptoms, but to Simon's delight, while Emma retired to the garden to sit in the sun and catch up with her friends online – not revising, he noticed – Felix, having looked up some links, pocketed his own phone and headed for his father's laptop and the photos of the chronicle. It appeared he had been thinking all morning about the task of enhancing those blank pages.

Simon watched over the boy's shoulder, holding his breath as he saw the texture of the vellum on the first page swimming into focus on the screen, the tiny dots where the scribe had pricked guidelines on the page before beginning to write, and then there it was: a page of text, faint but just about readable. 'I looked up the inks they used,' Felix muttered. 'Some of them bonded with the skins and are much more durable than others. I think you're in luck here, Dad.' He looked up at his father, trying to hide the triumph in his eyes. 'The guy tried to scrape it off, but the marks are indelible. Shall I spell it out for you?'

Simon was aching to get back to his chair in front of the screen, but he sensed this was something he needed to allow Felix to do. He reached for his notebook and nodded. 'Your eyes are better than mine. Spell away.'

There was a long silence, then Felix pushed back his chair. 'I can't read it. The letters are all different. It's in Anglo-Saxon.'

'Old English,' Simon automatically corrected him. 'But I will still need your help. Perhaps, if I get stuck, you can draw the letters out for me.'

Between them they began to decipher the story.

In the year 793 the heathen raided the Holy Isle of Lindisfarne and slaughtered those monks who could not flee, much to the distress of King Ethelred, newly married to Ethelfled, daughter of our king. In her terror and weakness, the lady miscarried of a son.

'Weakness!' Emma looked up indignantly from her phone. Obviously she had been listening with half an ear. 'The woman had witnessed a massacre!'

154

'Or at least heard about it from men who were there. I'm afraid monks didn't have much time for women,' her father replied. 'And he is writing as a historian.'

'Historians being famously insensitive.' His daughter's muttered retort did not register with Simon, who hadn't raised his eyes from the screen.

The following year Offa the king promised his daughter Alfrida to Ethelbert, King of East Anglia. When Ethelbert came here to collect his bride, Cynefryth the queen was consumed with jealousy that her daughter should be wed to such a godly man, and at her command Ethelbert was foully done to death, his head struck from his body . . .

'Wow, Dad! This is awesome! He was murdered!' Felix was leaning over his father's shoulder as Simon read the words out loud.

'It's a well-known story.' Simon's eyes were fixed on the screen. 'But this is special. This is written by someone local and it gives a motive, or at least what the local gossip gave as a motive for the murder.'

By the Grace of God, Ethelbert wrought miracles wheresoever his head lay and it was borne at last here to the priory of St Guthlac and hence on to the minster . . .

He looked up. 'Do you know the most important word on this page? It's "here". This chronicle was written in Hereford!' He could barely contain his excitement. 'You're a genius, Felix! And now the end date of the last entry in this particular chronicle, 1055, makes sense. It was the year the Welsh invaded Mercia yet again.'

'So, Offa's Dyke didn't work?' Felix stared at the screen, fascinated.

'No, it didn't. In that splodge of ink at the end, Felix, if I'm right, perhaps you can see history happening.'

'Can we go and see where it all happened?' Emma looked up again. It appeared she had been listening after all. 'Like the murder of the king. I'd like to see where the miracles took place.'

Simon nodded. 'Let me find my book about the history of Hereford. I believe the modern hospital is built on the site of the old priory, so there's nothing to see now. But we can go to the place where, according to legend, Ethelbert was murdered; a sacred spring was said to have gushed up from the ground after he was killed, and they built a church on the site. Then we can go to Hereford itself to see the cathedral which is dedicated to him – because obviously he became a saint and there is a holy well there somewhere dedicated to him which we can see.'

'What did they do with his head? How gross!'

'According to the records, it was eventually taken to Westminster.'

'Why?'

Simon looked up at his children and beamed. 'Why don't we try and find out?'

Emma went back to her phone with a sigh then she looked up again with a shiver. 'There is the most awful draught in here,' she complained loudly. 'When are we going to get supper?'

Simon looked up. He hadn't noticed that it was already growing dark outside. 'Now,' he replied, reluctantly closing the laptop. 'We can go on with this tomorrow.' She was right. It had become cold in the room. In the fireplace the logs had burned down to ash.

The following afternoon, after consulting his map, Simon drove his children over to the village of Marden, near the Iron Age fort of Sutton Walls, and down a long lane towards the church. Besides being the scene of Ethelred's muder, this was one of the places, he explained, where they had found archaeological traces of Anglo-Saxon habitation, making the fields round here a potential site for Offa's palace.

Emma stood at the back, just inside the door of the church, watching her father and her brother as they wandered up the aisle to stand in front of the chancel, staring up at the high windows. Normally she was the one to poke around old churches while her brother scoffed about the stupidity of people believing the garbage that was religion when it was nothing but mind control over the masses, fading him out with the ease of long practice, quietly enjoying the beauty of old stone and ancient art, but there was something about this church that made her uncomfortable. The Church of St Mary the Virgin was very large, almost as broad as it was long, airy and friendly. Or at least it should feel friendly. Behind her, someone had turned a corner of the nave into a library and there were masses of books there, lots of notices on a board, kids' toys, but there was also a huge amount of dark wood here at the back. So, where was the gushing spring her father had mentioned?

There was a door in the panelling at the rear of the church with St Ethelbert's Room written on it. She tiptoed across and pushed it open. It led into a dark, empty room lined with chairs. There, standing rather forlornly in the middle of the floor, was a narrow wooden structure, looking more like a plant stand than anything else, with a brass plate labelling it as St Ethelbert's Well. She studied it, puzzled, then knelt and lifted the small wooden lid at its base. A circular hole, dry at the bottom, was all there was to see of the sacred spring. She felt a massive jolt of disappointment. She had, she realised, been expecting something much more spectacular: bubbling water, or at least a magical pool. Not Lourdes perhaps, but not this. She gazed down it for several seconds, then slowly replaced the lid and stood up, glancing back through the door.

Up at the east end of the church, Simon and Felix had stepped up into the polygonal apse with its huge network of roof beams. Walking back into the nave Emma felt her stomach suddenly churning uncomfortably. Her pulse was racing. She wondered if she was going to be sick. Clutching the back of the pew nearest to her, she closed her eyes and tried to breathe deeply and slowly. After a minute she opened her eyes again and saw a young man, no, a boy, much the same age as Felix, standing there, between her and the porch. Tall, wrapped in a long cloak, his eyes were wide, scared, pleading as they sought her face, his mouth open as if in protest as her ears were filled with the sound of a long agonised scream.

The next thing she knew, she was running through the churchyard, dodging between the graves, heading through the long grass as fast as she could, twisting her ankle on the uneven ground.

'Emma! Wait!' Her father's voice, behind her.

Get away. She had to get away.

She came to a stop on the bank of the river that flowed along the edge of the churchyard, staring desperately down into the water. Somewhere she could hear a bell ringing.

'Emma, what is it?' She flinched as Simon put his hands on her shoulders. She was shaking violently as she subsided onto her knees on the muddy ground.

'Bloody hell, Em!' Felix appeared at her father's side. 'What on earth's the matter?'

She was gasping, unable to speak, her heart still thundering in her chest. Simon slipped off his jacket and wrapped her in it, then he squatted down beside her, his arms round her. 'It's all right,' he murmured. 'You're safe. You're OK now.'

They stayed like that for several minutes. Felix opened his mouth, about to make a facetious remark, then he thought better of it. He leaned against a tombstone nearby, watching his sister as her colour began to return.

'I'm sorry,' she said at last. It came out as a whisper. 'I don't know what happened.'

'That's all right, darling.' Simon gently pulled her against him, feeling her body relax a little.

'Can you hear the bell?' She put her hands over her ears.

That was too much for Felix. 'The bells; the bells!' he intoned in a voice full of mock horror.

'Stop it, Felix!' His father rounded on him. 'What bell, Em? I can't hear a bell.'

She swallowed hard. 'It's stopped.'

'Can you stand up?' Simon straightened painfully. The ground was damp and cold, and a bitter wind was finding its way into his bones now he had given up his jacket.

Emma nodded. She scrambled to her feet and stood forlornly looking down into the river. 'What happened to that boy?'

'What boy, darling?'

'The boy in the church. The boy who screamed.'

'It was you that screamed, Em!' Felix put in. 'I've never heard anything like it. They pay women who can scream like that, you know, for film soundtracks.'

Emma ignored him. 'His face was so kind; and it was filled with so much horror.'

'Excuse me!'

They hadn't noticed the elderly man approaching across the churchyard. 'Are you all right?' He was bent, his face weathered. As he reached them, he was pulling off a pair of gardening gloves. Simon looked up to see where he'd come from and noticed a wheelbarrow, fork and spade under a tree. 'I couldn't help seeing the young lady was upset.'

'She's fine, now. Thank you.' Simon gave him an apologetic smile.

'Did you see the ghost?' The old man addressed Emma with a twinkle in his eye. 'It takes some people like that. There is a ghost of a cavalier who was killed by the roundheads in the church tower, but if you were in the church itself, then you saw the ghost of our young king. If you saw him, it's a blessing, my dear. More than a blessing; you will never go blind, so they say.'

'Your young king?' Emma repeated shakily.

'King Ethelbert. His holy well is in the church. Did you see it? In the vestry? It's here by the river the great man was murdered, and they buried him in secret. But his ghost appeared and Offa, who was king in this part of the world, was forced to go on his knees to the Pope of Rome to ask for forgiveness. Then the pope made Ethelbert a saint. This is a doubly sacred place. You've no reason to be afraid. They had to dig him up to give him a proper burial, and when they took his body away on a cart to Hereford, his head, that had been cut off, fell off the cart and bounced across the road, and it hit a blind man who could immediately see again.' He had obviously told this story before and was thoroughly enjoying himself. 'See the two stone heads, one on either side of the porch door over there? That's King Ethelbert and the pope.'

'It wasn't a man,' Emma said when the old man finally stopped talking. 'It was a boy. Like my brother.'

There was an awkward silence.

'So why,' Felix put in at last, 'is the church not dedicated to St Ethelbert? Like the cathedral?'

'Because the Pope of Rome told King Offa to dedicate it to the Blessed Virgin Mary.' The old man was back on track. 'She keeps a special eye on our Border March, you see. She's even come over here, you know, from heaven, over there into the Black Mountains, to make sure we were all right.' He waved his arm vaguely towards the west. 'You'll find an inordinate number of churches in the March dedicated to the Blessed Virgin.'

'My sister heard a bell as well,' Felix went on.

The old man looked impressed. 'Ah, that's a whole 'nother story. We have lots of stories here. That's the mermaid's bell. It fell off the tower and she dragged it down into the depths of the River Lugg here, and she lives in it, so they say. And there's another bell, the pilgrim's bell. They found that one in the river and all. That's in the museum in Hereford.' He sighed. 'I've got to go. You go back inside, my dear, and say a prayer for the soul of our king. He didn't mean you to be afeared of him.'

They watched as the old man plodded back to his wheelbarrow, collected a thermos from under a yew tree and trundled his way slowly out of sight.

'Do you think he was a ghost?' Felix said after a moment or two.

'I think it's time we went home,' Simon said firmly.

'No.' Emma bit her lip, then she went on. 'He's right. I should go in and say a prayer.'

'You don't pray!' Felix sounded incredulous.

'Maybe I should.' She glared at him.

Emma pulled off her father's jacket and, pushing it into his arms, headed back towards the path to the church door. Pushing it open, she peered in.

Behind her, Simon caught Felix's arm and held him back. 'Let her do it alone,' he whispered.

Emma stood close inside the door and held her breath. The church was empty and quiet. 'Are you there?' she whispered. There was no reply.

She forced herself to walk past the spot where the figure had stood, moving steadily up the central aisle towards the altar.

She stood still for a long time, her eyes closed, trying to form a prayer, but she didn't know how, or what to say, and at last she turned away.

Simon and Felix had come in quietly after her and were seated side by side in the back pew.

'I want to light a candle for him. There aren't any here.'

Simon stood up. 'We could do that at the cathedral. They have a shrine to St Ethelbert there. Why don't we go there tomorrow?'

And perhaps tomorrow he could contact Bea or her husband to ask what to do about a teenage daughter who had seen a ghost. Not the ghost of the powerful king she had expected to see, but the ghost of the teenager from East Anglia who had been lured to Mercia on the promise of a royal marriage, who had been treacherously murdered and at whose shrine Emma now wanted to light a candle.

18

The magic had worked. At last, after two miscarriages of the sons her husband longed for, Eadburh had conceived again and carried a child to term. It was a girl. She gazed down at the little thing, lying in its crib, and saw to her dismay in the wide dark eyes an echo of her husband. Although she knew Beorhtric was disappointed it was not a boy, she smiled. Nothing would spoil her sense of triumph. This was her child and she would no longer feel so alone. She named her Eathswith.

For a while she was content. Her dreams of Elisedd had faded, and with them her plans to avenge his death. She only thought occasionally about Elisedd's baby, whom she still pictured as a little boy, and with him the two lost children that had followed him into the dark. As Nesta had advised she had prayed for each child in turn, promised each her love, kissed each on the forehead in her dreams and pushed them gently away, back into the world of spirits.

She scarcely thought about her family at all. Her sisters seemed content with their lot and she seldom heard from them, Ethelfled in faraway Northumbria and Alfrida, as far as she knew, still in Mercia awaiting her father's decision about whom she should marry. She had not really expected to hear from them. Their worlds were different now. She did not hear from her mother at all, beyond a baptismal gift for the child. The little girl was strong and bawled lustily, and life had settled into a routine with her nurses as slowly they travelled around her husband's kingdom, feasting, hunting, in winter spinning and weaving, playing board games and listening to the tales of the *scops*, the travelling singers and poets who arrived from across the land. Besides those activities Eadburh joined more and more often in her husband's meetings, enjoying the political thrust of court life, discussing politics with his ealdormen and thanes and at times calling discussions of her own, feeling more and more empowered as she pushed the limits of her influence to see how much free rein the king would give her, sensing the resentment of the men around her, but ignoring it with lofty disdain. The kingdom was at peace. There had been no further sightings of the heathen ships in the channel. All was well.

It was a shock when the letter came. She stared down at it, the words jumping in the candlelight, seeming to wriggle and writhe upon the page like a basket of snakes. Her husband had handed it to her when he found it amongst a bundle of letters in Offa's messenger's bag. She had been sitting by the fire playing with their little daughter. The letter was from Alfrida.

I was betrothed to a king at last. A boy king, some years younger than me, but I was assured good looking and already lusty. And he came from his kingdom of East Anglia, to our court at Sutton for the treaties and the wedding vows. And he was young but he was tall, and so handsome and gracious, sister mine, and kind and good and rich and strong amongst kings, and our mother saw him and she was bitterly jealous that I was to wed such a handsome lad, and she had him slain! Murdered! They cut off his head! Our father claims Mama had discovered a plot to assassinate him, but that is untrue. I know her and her insatiable lusts. She could not bear for me to be happy and free!

Alfrida had written with such force the nib of the quill had torn through the parchment.

I am no longer a daughter of Offa and our mother is as dirt beneath my feet. Beware lest they betray you too. I am going to my promised husband's kingdom and there I will give myself to God. I will no longer be a piece on my father's gaming board.

Bless you, my sister and may God give his protection to you and to my little niece. You will not hear from me again.

Eadburh's hands were shaking as she read the last words. 'What is it, Wife?' She hadn't realised that Beorhtric was watching her. He threw down the document he was reading and reached out for her letter. She handed it to him without protest, too shocked to speak.

He read it twice then put it down on the table. 'I trust she cut the throat of the scribe who wrote these words for her,' he said coldly. He paused then he went on, 'I have a missive from your father on the same matter. His version of the story speaks of East Anglian treachery and betrayal.'

'And who do you believe?' She did not tell him that Alfrida's letter had not been written by a scribe. She recognised her sister's hand, with her anguish and fury portrayed in every line.

He sat back in his chair looking thoughtful. 'I am your father's ally.'

Eadburh beckoned the nurse who was hovering in the background and handed the baby to her, dismissing her curtly. 'And so you are as ever bound to him hand and foot!' She saw his expression darken. 'Is it not true? You were, after all, given my hand as a bribe to keep you trotting at his heels.'

'As your sister Ethelfled was given to the King of Northumbria. It is the way of kings.' His voice was surprisingly gentle. 'You knew why you and I were bound together. You and your sisters are peace weavers. I suspect your father's version is the true one. He saw your sister as another link to a kingdom he saw as his ally, then he discovered treason.'

'So he admits it? He admits murder? He didn't send the boy king home, he had him executed in cold blood!'

'It was the boy king who planned murder, Eadburh, and

the queen who uncovered the treason. It is written here, plain.'

'No!' Her anguished denial rang out over the crackle and hiss of the logs in the central firepit. Silence fell in the mead hall as faces looked towards them and hastily looked away again. She was still holding the string of corals she had been dangling before her little daughter's fascinated gaze. As the baby pulled at them the string broke and the beads rolled away onto the floor. She watched them as they came to rest. The boy who had arrived with a basket of logs for the fire put them down and bent to gather up the beads, but she gestured sharply that he leave them lying in the ashes.

'My sister was in anguish when she wrote that letter,' she cried.

'King Offa will find her another mate.'

She looked up at him, her eyes narrowed. 'So that's it. We are mated like mares to a stallion. One mate does not suit so its throat is cut and another chosen.' Elisedd too had been unsuitable and so had had to die. She fell silent as the flood of bitter memories overwhelmed her.

He smiled. 'You are more than a mare, my queen. You advise me; you sign my charters as one of my council. You rule at my side as my equal.'

'And I thought I did so in my own right, not merely as my father's deputy.'

'Can you not be both?' He sighed.

She studied his face in the shifting firelight. He was a weak man, she knew that. He had allowed her to have more and more influence in the running of the kingdom. Was that what had doomed her sister's marriage? Had Ethelbert of East Anglia, young as he was, proved too strong an option, so he had been swatted away like a hoverfly that turns out to be a wasp, to be disposed of before it stings.

One of the coral beads was beginning to blacken in the ash. She gazed down at it. What would her father do to a daughter who disobeyed him? If Alfrida did as she promised and tried to leave for a distant convent, would he stop her? Or was God the one person with whom the great King Offa would not dare pick a fight?

Beorhtric had turned away to extract another letter from the pile, unfolding it, holding it to the candlelight. As she watched him, she saw his eyes widen in horror. She waited while he read it, then sharply demanded. 'Further news from Mercia?'

He turned to look at her. 'This is from the archbishop's hall in Lichfield. The ghost of King Ethelbert has appeared to the people of Sutton and to King Offa himself, demanding retribution,' he said softly. 'It seems the king feels guilty, even if the murder was done by another hand.' She saw his hand was shaking. 'He has sent to Rome through his archbishop to ask Pope Adrian what he should do.' He sighed. 'The good king, your father, is, it appears, much troubled by the thought of ghosts.'

Eadburh shuddered. Unable to stop herself, she glanced over her shoulder. The huge hall with its carved and painted beams high above them in the smoky darkness above the reach of candlelight was crowded and noisy, with the *scop* in one corner tuning his lute to sing to the throng, and in another a group of men laughing loudly at the antics of a tumbler juggling his coloured batons, but in the darkest shadows, the places the candles could not reach, that was where her own ghost lurked, the strange woman who watched her, silent, terrifying.

Bea jerked back, as though by moving she could hide from the woman's gaze. The smoke from the hall and the smell of sawn timbers and roast meats, dogs and horses and human sweat, dissipated in a swirl of cold air and she realised suddenly that she was outside, at home in the little back garden in Hereford, sitting on the stone seat in the corner under the mulberry tree. It was bitterly cold, and strangely silent after the roar of the Anglo-Saxon hall.

'Bea? Are you out there?' Mark was standing at the back door, looking for her.

She scrambled to her feet. She hadn't meant to go back.

Not again. Not so soon. Not out here, spontaneously. Without the stone in her hand.

Mark was waiting for her in the kitchen.

'Did you get Simon's message?' He had opened the fridge and was looking inside. 'What are we having for supper?'

'There's some smoked trout and salad. What did Simon want?' She was still disorientated and chilled to the bone.

'He seemed troubled. He said he had been trying to reach you all afternoon and phoned me in the end instead.'

'Not his wailing nun again?' She tried to make light of it as she shrugged off her jacket. She hadn't intended to dream. She had not had the stone out there with her, or incense, or even a thought of Eadburh and the past. She had gone out to cut some late daffodils, she remembered now, and then sat down to enjoy the sunlight by their little fountain with its shroud of emerald moss. She had left the scissors lying on the seat beside her.

'No, this was his daughter. He took his kids to the church at Marden this afternoon to give them a bit of insight into the story of St Ethelbert and Emma, I think her name is, freaked out. What? What is it?'

Bea was staring at him in horror. Beorhtric's hall; the parchment letter in a woman's hand.

'She saw a figure in the church,' Mark went on, 'and is convinced it was the saint. She wanted to light a candle, only there weren't any apparently, so she wants to come to the cathedral tomorrow to visit the shrine. Simon is a bit concerned that his happy, atheist, solidly fact-based family is disintegrating before his eyes into a superstitious bunch of hysterics, and he is above all terrified that the children's mother, who has apparently retreated to Worcester to get away from his obsession with the Anglo-Saxon world, will get wind of it.'

'Poor Simon.' She hooked a chair out from the table with her foot and sat down. 'Are we allowed a drink today?' They had agreed that giving up alcohol for Lent was a step too far this year, but they would try and do it three days a week.

He gave a wry smile. 'I think we might. It has been a stressful day. I encountered Sandra on my way home this evening. She is still very concerned for your welfare.'

Bea sighed. She stood up and went to the cupboards in the dresser to find a bottle of red wine and two glasses. 'Jesus will forgive you,' she said firmly as she poured him one.

'Jesus forgives everything.' He sounded almost too fervent. 'Even Sandra Bedford.'

'What did you say to Simon?'

'That I would meet them tomorrow so we could go to the shrine together to pray for the soul of St Ethelbert.

'Wow. This is two teenagers?' She took a sip from her glass. She was still trying to banish the picture of Beorhtric's hall from her mind.

'It doesn't necessarily make them bad people. It would be nice if you came too.'

'I would like that. I'm sorry I didn't get Simon's call. I left my phone on charge.' It was still there plugged in on the dresser. She dragged her attention back to the present with an effort. 'I haven't met his children.'

She did so next day as she followed Mark into the Chapter House garden behind the cathedral café. They found them seated at a table, Simon with a cup of black coffee, Felix and Emma with bottles of juice, both young people looking a little self-conscious. Introductions made, Mark and Bea sat down with them.

'So, you're a real ghost hunter.' Felix obviously did not believe in the subtle approach. He fixed Bea with a stare that was half admiring, half accusatory.

With a quick apologetic glance at Mark, she gave a small nod. 'I'm sorry I didn't pick up your calls yesterday,' she said to Simon. She had switched on her phone at last, her eye as always automatically scanning down the list of missed calls in case there was something from Anna or Petra, then skipping on to play back with increasing concern Simon's series of messages. He had obviously been very worried about his daughter. Emma was sitting at the table now, studying her drink with exaggerated care. 'Can you tell me what you saw?' Bea asked.

Emma shrugged her shoulders. 'The king.'

'With his head on,' put in her brother with a grin.

'When you're ready, we can go to the shrine.' Mark was wearing his dog collar, from time to time acknowledging the greetings of people walking past.

Emma looked scared at the prospect. 'What do we have to do?'

'You don't have to do anything, Emma. It's up to you.' He waited for a response, then when she didn't look at him, stood up. 'Shall we go and see?'

He led the way back into the cathedral and towards the Lady Chapel where the brightly coloured pillar shrine to Ethelbert, king and martyr, stood in the middle of the floor, surrounded by a swirl of tourists. Emma stared at it and he saw the dismay on her face.

'I thought it would be old, with ancient carved stone.'

'I'm afraid not.' Mark sighed.

'What happened to the original one?'

'I expect Henry VIII had it demolished,' her brother put in. 'Remember the Reformation?'

'It's too modern,' she said at last. 'I wanted to light a candle. I wanted to pray for him quietly.'

Bea traded glances with Mark, then stepped forward and touched Emma's arm. 'Come with me.'

The chantry chapel was empty of people, two votive candles already lit on the shelf beside the altar. 'This is one of the places set aside for private prayer,' Bea whispered. 'I'll wait for you outside.' There was no sign of her priest in the shadowed corner where he so often sat. Pulling the heavy door with its ancient grille half closed behind her, she tiptoed out, leaving Emma alone.

'I'm not sure I know what I was expecting a shrine to look like,' Simon said later when they returned to the café for lunch, carrying their trays back into the garden. 'But not that. I understand it's a memorial and modern and tells the story of the poor man's murder, but I agree with Em, it's not a place designed to encourage you to contemplate and pray for his soul.'

'Different times,' Bea said apologetically.

'And our main shrine these days is to St Thomas Cantilupe,' Mark put in. 'In medieval times his name became more famous than that of St Ethelbert, I'm afraid, and although the cathedral is still dedicated to St Ethelbert, Thomas has rather taken over. There is a splendid shrine to him over there in the north transept with a place to light a candle to his memory and to pray.' Mark stood up. 'Forgive me, folks, but I have things to do. I'll leave Bea to look after you and show you Thomas's shrine, and perhaps some of our other treasures. The Mappa Mundi and the chained library are world famous.'

'Nice guy,' Felix commented as Mark made his way out of the café.

Bea smiled. 'I'm glad you approve.'

'Talking of the library, I haven't told you yet about that wonderful old book I went to see,' Simon put in. It took some time. As she listened, Bea watched the interaction of Simon with his two offspring, both of whom seemed fully engaged with his enthusiasm.

As the story unfolded between elaborate explanations from Felix about multispectral imaging techniques and the possibilities of finding an infra-red microscope, she began to feel a whisper of unease.

'You say the house was down a long drive; the library was on the ground floor?'

He nodded.

'This house. I know you have to keep its whereabouts secret, but it isn't by any chance called Coedmawr, is it?'

The shock on his face confirmed it without him having to say anything else. 'You know it? You know Phil and Kate?'

'I don't know them, no, but I went there once, a while ago. There was an elderly couple living there. The Huttons. They were tenants.'

'Ah, before Kate's aunt died and Kate inherited.' He gave an abrupt laugh. 'Jane asked me if I thought it was haunted and I said no. But what do I know?'

'And you were right. It isn't anymore.' Bea shivered.

Felix looked up eagerly. 'You went there to deal with a ghost?'

'I went there to deal with a poltergeist.'

'Oh good grief!' Simon glared at his son. 'Well thank God Kate and Phil don't know about it. At least they've never mentioned it.'

'And we won't mention it either.' She waved her hand dismissively. 'We'll talk about it some other time. Go on about the chronicle.' The chronicle which was perhaps one of the books Ken Hutton had threatened to burn. She had begged him not to. Perhaps she had saved the library with that last impassioned plea.

She listened enthralled as Simon related the local version of St Ethelbert's demise, and the amazing relics that were destined to lie for a while under the roof of the local priory.

'So, Offa admitted the murder and repented?' she said when he finished. Her voice was husky. Surely it could not be coincidence that the story should emerge now. 'But why did he admit blame when your chronicle says it was his wife who did the murder?'

Alfrida herself had said it was her mother, consumed with jealousy, in her letter to Eadburh, a source about which Simon knew nothing.

'Offa was scared of the ghost,' Emma put in. 'Imagine murdering a saint; even if it was his wife who actually did it. He would've had to take the blame – he couldn't let people think she would do something like that without his knowledge. And on his own doorstep. They think his palace was right there, you know, across the river from the church.'

'But Ethelbert wasn't a saint then, Em,' her father pointed out. 'It was the murder, or martyrdom, that led to him being created a saint.'

'It was the miracles he performed, Dad,' his daughter corrected. 'I've googled him.' She had cheered up with a plate of food in front of her. 'The pope told Offa to build the cathedral or be damned.'

'It wasn't quite like that. He told him to build the church at Marden first, and then yes, a great cathedral where the saint could finally rest.'

Bea listened quietly. She could feel her heart beating unsteadily as they skirted round the story, the story she already knew. 'So, what happened to Offa's daughter, widowed before she was even married?' she asked Simon at last. 'Do you know?'

He nodded. 'I mention all this in my book on East Anglia, but I felt it deserved at least a footnote in the present volume as well. It was all so dramatic. She fled to Ethelbert's kingdom of East Anglia and made her way to Crowland Abbey in the Lincolnshire Fens, which was dedicated, interestingly, to the same St Guthlac as the minster here, where our chronicle was written. The story goes that she had herself walled up in a cell as an anchorite, or anchoress – that is someone who devotes their life to God and is declared dead to the world. She spent the rest of her life there.'

'Grim.' Felix licked his lips ghoulishly.

'And how long did she live?' Bea whispered.

'I don't suppose anyone knows for sure, but one version says she might have lived another forty years or so. Can you imagine!' Simon gave a theatrical shudder. 'It's generally assumed her tomb was lost when the Vikings attacked the abbey. She too was made a saint.'

Bea was tempted to tell them about the letter, about Alfrida's angry and heartbroken vow to her sister, but how could she? If she ever told Simon about her secret peephole into the past it would be in private, without his children or Mark there. And if she told him any more about her visit to Coedmawr, that too would be very private and on condition he never told Kate and Phil. There must be no mention of poltergeists unless they mentioned them first.

She was shaken out of her thoughts by the sound of her name. 'Bea, dear!' Sandra Bedford had made her way through the crowds unnoticed and was hovering over their table, a mug of tea in her hand. She interrupted Felix's next question, which was about the practicalities of being walled up; food, and sanitation. Her gaze swept over Emma and Felix to Simon, and rested on him speculatively. 'I saw the dear canon leaving you just now. How nice to be able to sit here in the sun with your friends.'

Bea's heart sank. 'Sandra. Simon, this is one of our invaluable volunteers. They run the cathedral for us.'

Simon stood up and held out his hand. 'How nice to meet you. This is a wonderful place.'

'May I join you?' Sandra was already sitting down. 'I saw you earlier at the shrine of St Ethelbert. Such a sad story, but such an inspiration.'

'I saw his ghost,' Emma put in. Bea looked away. This was the last direction she wanted the conversation to go.

'Indeed?' Sandra smiled, reaching forward to put her hand over Emma's. 'Then you were indeed blessed, my dear. Was that here, in the cathedral?'

Felix took a swig of juice from his bottle. 'Dad took us to see the church where the murder happened.'

'Indeed. That is interesting. You are teaching your children to love history.' She smiled at Simon again. 'I'm sure I know your face. You've been here before, I think? I'm sorry, I didn't catch your name.' Bea saw the sideways glance, the eager way she sat forward.

'I'm Simon Armstrong. I'm a historian specialising in the Anglo-Saxon period, so we are spending some of the Easter holidays doing some research on the hoof, as it were.'

Please, don't mention the ghost in the cottage. Bea's fervent plea was so loud in her head she was sure that the others must have heard it. Hurry up! Drink your drinks and let's get out of here. But it was too late.

'So, how do you come to know Mark and Bea?' Sandra's attention was directed at Simon with what Bea was beginning to think of as her gimlet smile.

Simon hesitated. 'We have a mutual friend in the owner of the holiday cottage I'm staying in.'

'Bea is helping Dad with the ghost in the cottage.' Felix stepped in with both feet. His self-mocking grin, designed to show he wasn't entirely serious, escaped Sandra completely.

She swivelled on her seat to face Bea, her gaze avid. 'You help with ghosts? Surely that's the canon's job, dear.'

'And Mark sorted it for them,' Bea said firmly. 'He went up to the cottage and prayed.'

'But you're the actual ghostbuster, right?' Felix persisted. 'I wanted to ask you about that. That's the coolest job!'

For a moment Bea was speechless and Simon must have seen her panic for he stood up suddenly. 'Listen, I'm so sorry, but we are going to have to go. Come on, kids. I'll ring you, Bea.'

Emma was glaring at her brother as she stood up. 'You berk! Do you want to tell everyone!' Her whisper carried clearly across the garden as the three of them hurried away.

Bea was left staring helplessly at Sandra. 'Nice people,' she said. 'But it makes me realise how pleased I am my girls are grown up now.'

'What did he mean, you are the actual ghostbuster?' Sandra's voice was icy.

'He's confused. The owner of the cottage Simon is staying at is, as Simon said, a friend of mine. The daughter, Emma, is a bit flaky as you saw, and Mark suggested they come here so he could pray with them at the shrine.'

Sandra nodded. 'She's a pretty girl.'

Bea breathed a sigh of relief. 'Isn't she? Poor Simon. As he said, he's a historian. I don't think he realised his wife was going to deliver the kids to the cottage and leave them with him for a few days. He had come up here to write in peace and he has been trying to think of ways to keep them engaged with what he does.'

'It sounds as though the girl is entering into the spirit of it.' Sandra took a sip from her cup and grimaced; obviously her tea was cold. 'Talking about ghosts is so dangerous, I always think.' Her gaze was speculative once more. 'Such stupid superstitious nonsense,' she added with fervour. 'I'm surprised the canon encouraged her.'

'She wanted to light a candle and pray,' Bea said reproachfully. 'I think we can trust Mark to have made the right decision about what to do.'

Sandra looked taken aback. 'Of course. You're right.'

Bea pushed her plate aside and stood up. 'I am sorry, Sandra, but I must get on. I have a whole lot of things to do this afternoon. It was lovely to run into you. It's such a peaceful place, isn't it, this garden?'

Before the woman could respond, Bea turned and hurried away, oblivious to the expression on Sandra's face as she watched her go.

'Why did we have to leave?' Felix was still grumbling as Simon unlocked the car.

'Because Bea was uncomfortable talking about ghosts in front of that woman.' Simon climbed into the driver's seat. 'She specifically asked me not to mention that part of her life to anyone else.'

'Well, you should have told us.'

Simon sighed. 'I didn't think the subject was going to come up in public like that.'

'She was a nosy old bat,' Emma put in. 'For goodness' sake, Felix! You dropped Bea right in it.'

'Why? I thought you said it's her job. Why would she not want anyone to know about it? She's not embarrassed about it, is she?'

'She might be, in front of her husband's colleagues.' Simon pulled out into the traffic. 'She might well be.'

'That woman did look a bit creepy. Pushing her way into someone else's conversation like that.' Felix was finally getting the point. 'Why don't you ask Bea and Mark up to the cottage again, Dad? I for one would like to go on with that particular conversation.'

'As long as Mum never finds out,' Emma chipped in from the back seat. 'That wouldn't go down well either.'

Sandra sat still for a long time after Bea disappeared. One of the girls from the café came and cleared the table with a cheerful greeting. Sandra didn't hear her. Her instincts had been right. Beatrice Dalloway was a psychic.

Her mouth had gone dry, her heart was beating unnaturally fast and she could feel a pain in her stomach as the memories came flooding back. The excitement, the ability to inflict terror, the intense thrill of power and control, then at the last, the loss of that control and the utter, blind fear that had swept over her in an overwhelming tide. She had made a lot of money from her psychic readings. She had manipulated her clients, hooking them with her promises of dreams to come, then gradually drawing them in with warnings and cautions and threats until they didn't know how to escape. She read their body language – cold reading, she had discovered it was called, and she was good at it, too good. It had taken some time but eventually she had begun to suspect she was genuinely in touch with something beyond herself, that she was genuinely able to predict the future, that what she did was real. For a while it was glorious. She advertised in a local paper and more and more people came to see her, then one day she had foreseen a death. A real, hideous death, and she had not known how to deal with it. She had messed up, her customer had run away in tears and had told people, lots of people, what Sandra had said. What was written in the stars could not be altered; not long after that the woman was killed by her abusive partner. The police came and interviewed Sandra. She was terribly afraid they would think she was involved, but in the end she was written off as a crank who had made a lucky guess. That had hurt.

She turned in the end to the Church for reassurance and help and security. She never looked at the cards or her crystal ball again. She had never told anyone what had happened. She had been lucky. She had escaped. The past was behind her, but her intuition was still there.

That evening she pulled a file labelled LOCAL GHOSTS from the bottom drawer of the desk in her sitting room and carried it over to the table. It was full of newspaper cuttings. Slowly and methodically she picked her way through them. There it was: LOCAL GHOSTHUNTER EXORCISES POLTERGEIST. She read the article carefully. They did not name the house or give its exact address, but there were four pages packed with lurid details. The nameless exorcist was described as *an attractive woman with phenomenal powers*. Sandra snorted. It emphasised the fact that the exorcist had demanded anonymity. Well, she would, wouldn't she, if her husband was a canon at the cathedral. The woman's face was nowhere clear in the shadowy pictures, but there was enough detail for her to be fairly sure it was

Bea. She put the clippings back in the file and sat for a long time, staring into space.

So, Beatrice Dalloway had a dangerous secret. Her instinct that the woman was trying to hide something from her was right. Not only that, she could tell when someone else was being shadowed by something evil as clearly as she had known it for herself – and Beatrice was being overshadowed by something very evil indeed.

19

'Should I wish to consign someone to the place of demons forever after watching them die in agony,' Eadburh whispered, 'would you be able to teach me the charms I need?'

Bea shivered. Though Eadburh was whispering, the meaning of what she said was perfectly clear. She crept closer.

Eadburh had grown to rely on Nesta more and more over the last two years and, as far as such a thing were possible, they had become friends. Nesta and Hilde were still the only people in the Wessex court who Eadburh fully trusted. Bea saw a flicker of doubt in the woman's clear grey eyes. 'What you ask is very wrong.'

'What these men did was very wrong.' Eadburh clenched her teeth. 'Both are murderers. I have discovered the name of one, and the other is for the future to reveal. I have someone who will take the potion to them.'

'And it is not for anyone at this court?'

'No.' Eadburh's eyes were burning with hate. 'No one here, and no one will ever know where the death blows came from.'

'Then why do you need poison? Why not send your "someone" to do the deed honourably with a sword in the open? Poison is a secret remedy.' Nesta stood her ground.

'That is for me to know. I am avenging great wrongs, and I am the only one who knows the name of the man who committed one of them.' She had seen it in a bowl of spring water under the light of the full moon, the face of the murderer of Alfrida's intended husband, swimming and flickering as he turned towards her, his helmet framing a strong broad brow and flint-dark eyes. She had recognised him immediately. He worked for her mother.

'The man's name?'

'If I tell you, then there will be two of us here who know.'

'I do not kill strangers. If I have to answer before the gods of my people and the God of yours, I must know why I did what I did and to whom I gave the death blow.'

Eadburh considered this, then nodded. 'Very well. His name is Grimbert. He came to my father's court as a murderer seeking sanctuary and my father gave it to him. He has worked to climb in their esteem and is now my mother's chancellor and, I sometimes think, her lover, though that is not his crime. The man he has killed by foul murder was a king, little more than a boy, by treaty about to become the husband of my sister. The murder has gone unavenged and uninvestigated, and that cannot be allowed to be the verdict of history. He had the young king's escort slaughtered with him and their bodies thrown in a rubbish pit on the side of the hill near my father's palace, and then killed with his own hands the men who had helped him do the deed. Now he sits at my mother's table, preening and enjoying her favours, knowing he has her in his power because he holds her secrets. The other killer murdered a prince; a prince who was my friend. When I know his name, I will tell my messenger to act.' She tightened her lips. She had said all she was prepared to say.

'And to hold secrets does indeed give people power,' Nesta said thoughtfully. 'So you now have power over me. And I over you.'

Eadburh reached into the scrip hanging from her girdle. Her hand, when she withdrew it, clasped two fine gold belt chains, a tiny gold distaff to hang from one of the chains and some small exquisitely enamelled trinkets. She held them out to Nesta, who took them without enthusiasm.

'So we are friends.' There was no warmth in Eadburh's statement.

'Indeed we are.' Nesta nodded slowly. She sighed. 'Come to my garden tomorrow and I will guide you to the ingredients you need and give you the charm to be said over them, but you must make the spell yourself and you must wait for the waning moon.' She turned away and walked slowly across the garden, her gown trailing against the beds of lavender and rosemary, releasing their scents into the night air.

Bea shrank back into the darkness. Eadburh had stopped and was looking round sharply, as though suspecting that there was someone there, watching. She must never guess that this conversation had been overheard. For a second Bea felt a wave of real terror grip her. The shot of adrenaline in her stomach shocked her out of her trance, bringing her back to the present and the attic room and the realisation that downstairs someone was knocking at the front door.

Sandra followed Bea into the kitchen and watched as she plugged in the kettle. She sat down at the kitchen table.

Bea lifted the biscuit tin down from its shelf and pulled off the lid. She put it down in front of her guest. 'I'm not sure when Mark will be back, if you've come to see him.' She could hear the hostility in her own voice.

'No, dear, it was you I wanted a word with.' Sandra reached for a piece of home-made shortbread. Bea stared at it, unsure where it had come from. Made by some kind person no doubt for one of the finance meetings, where they were trying to raise millions of pounds for the cathedral fabric fund. She pushed a plate towards Sandra and then as an afterthought took one for herself.

'Such a nice family you were talking to in the Chapter House garden. It was so reassuring to see that they were taking an interest in the cathedral.'

'Indeed.' Bea turned away to replace the biscuit tin on its shelf.

'How long have you known them?'

'Not long. I thought I told you about them. Simon is staying in a holiday cottage belonging to a friend of ours.' Bea sat down opposite her, braced for the inquisition.

'I am worried by something that boy said.'

'Oh?' Bea took a deep breath, trying to control her anger. Silently she began to count to ten.

'He mentioned ghosts.' Sandra raised her eyes from her biscuit and looked Bea directly in the eye.

'It was a door banging in the cottage, Sandra. Christine had asked me to go with her to deliver some extra blankets and so forth. It's a tiny place and Simon wasn't expecting his children to join him for the holidays. Chris wasn't sure he had everything he needed. Felix must have heard us joking about the creaks and groans of the timbers in an old place like that.' She saw the woman's expression veer from relief to disappointment, then doubt. 'You surely didn't think he was talking about a real ghost?'

'But you said the dear canon went up there to pray.'

'They asked him to bless the cottage.'

'Because the girl thought she had seen the ghost of St Ethelbert.'

'Exactly.' Bea took a deep breath. 'Teenagers, Sandra. They are very susceptible. Some are over-imaginative, like poor Emma, and some are just a pain, like Felix. I think, and fervently hope that, having had Mark's reassurance, both of them will settle down now to enjoy the countryside. I promise you there is nothing for you to concern yourself about.'

Sandra took a sip of her tea. 'People who talk about ghosts have such a lot to answer for. As if any such thing could exist.' Her voice hardened. 'I'm amazed the canon would have anything to do with it.'

'It's part of his pastoral duty to reassure people and pray with them, Sandra.'

'I suppose so.' Sandra heaved a deep sigh. She looked up sharply. 'So, you didn't have to go to a meeting this afternoon after all?'

Oh heavens, what had she said to this bloody woman? Bea

181

couldn't remember. She had been far too distracted. She forced her most charming smile. 'I had a conference call on the phone earlier and in about half an hour' – she looked at her wrist-watch – 'I have to go to see someone in the town. It's never-ending, isn't it? I know you understand how busy we all are.'

Sandra nodded. 'Are your children coming home for Easter? They are both at university, aren't they?'

She knew they were. Bea distinctly remembered telling her. She stood up, deliberately ignoring the question. 'It was good of you to call round, Sandra. I appreciate you feeling you had to clear up the truth behind Felix's remark. I do hope I've set your mind at rest.'

Sandra remained seated for several seconds then she drained her cup and set it down. As she walked towards the door, Bea found it very hard not to wish that she could command some Anglo-Saxon binding charm to silence nosy neighbours.

The two women met secretly in the herb-wife's small stone-built hut. Much like the workshops Nesta had created at every palace they visited with the king's entourage, it was meticu-lously neat, with shelves of glass bottles, pottery containers, pouches of herbs and boxes labelled with intricate runes. There was a table in the centre and drying herbs hung from hooks in the rafters above their heads. Outside the night was falling and a huge full moon was rising above the hills, throwing a warm buttery light across the fields and forests, and in through the door of the hut.

Bea held her breath as she crept closer. She was there with them in the moonlight, but she was aware that she cast no shadow against the wall as she tiptoed towards the door and peered in.

'This is for you to take outside under the moon as it rises on the first night of its waning. We use no fire for this; it is a woman's charm. You have gathered the worts I specified with your own hand?'

Eadburh nodded. She had a cloth bag with her and she put it on the table. 'Don't open it here,' Nesta ordered peremptorily.

'This is between you and the angels of death. I have here a powder I have made to add to your mixture and two hollow pins. Do not touch them with your hands.' She had the tiny silver objects wrapped in leaves. 'Dedicate them outside to the work you plan, then throw the leaves into the river. Dip the pins into the potion you make, as I told you, seal them with beeswax and wrap them again first in new leaves, then in this piece of parchment. Then only your messenger will ever touch them again.' She looked up at Eadburh, and held her gaze. 'I will whisper what he is to do. The words should not be spoken out loud.'

Bea leant forward, but she couldn't hear anything now but the gentle ripple of water from the river nearby and the rustle of leaves in the night. She saw Eadburh pick up a basket and tiptoe out of the hut, Nesta staying behind, tidying away the scraps of leaf and parchment, throwing a box of something onto the embers of her fire. The moon was rising higher now, the light stronger, turning cold, the scarcely visible bite from its side showing more clearly now as it lifted clear of the hills. Eadburh had disappeared between the willows that lined the riverbank, one moment there in the moonlight, the next vanished. Bea did not dare go after her. She stayed where she was, watching Nesta as she put away the last of her bottles.

The woman turned round slowly and with a shiver Bea felt her gaze. 'I see you watching,' she said softly. 'You who stand at the door so silently in the light of the silver moon, but I sense you mean no harm and will keep our secrets.' There was a long pause. Bea stared at her, transfixed. 'That was why I showed you the way into the realm of the Wyrd sisters with a pebble to guide you. You heard my call and you answered it. You are stronger than I expected. But you must beware. The queen did not see you this time and I shall not tell her, for she will not be so understanding if she knows you were there, be you ghost or spirit or witch from a distant land. Beware. What happened here is done and written in the chronicles of time. It cannot now be undone.'

*

'What happened next?' Simon and Emma were peering over Felix's shoulder as he fiddled with the adjustments. The page on the screen flipped sideways. 'Look, see here?' He moved the cursor arrow as a pointer. 'Someone has written lots of extra stuff down the side of this page. I don't think it's been rubbed out like the previous section, but it's faded a lot. It's written in a different ink.'

Simon bit his lip, trying to curb his impatience. Part of the deal was listening to his son's detailed description of the methods he was using to decipher this stuff. All Simon wanted to know was the contents of the text.

'That red bit—' Emma was leaning forward, her finger dabbing at the screen.

'Don't touch!' Felix let out a shout.

'Sorry, but I thought it might be blood. Maybe that's the moment the Vikings broke in.'

'Or the Welsh.' Felix didn't look up. 'Didn't Dad say they were Welsh? The Vikings were an awfully long way away unless they sailed up the River Wye in their great boats with prows carved like dragons.' He leaned forward a little, fiddled with the onscreen tools as he tried to enhance the blob his sister had pointed to.

'If it was blood it would be brown,' Simon put in. 'I don't think it's that – maybe another ink that was on the desk and got knocked over.'

'By the invaders.'

Felix was obviously taken with his father's theory about the untidy ending on the last page of the manuscript. 'The Vikings did sail up both the Wye and the Severn,' Simon said absent-mindedly. 'The chronicles were initially distributed throughout the land sometime in the tenth century, after King Alfred came up with the idea. They covered very early history, going back to the fabled ancestors of the royal line of Wessex, long before the Vikings made their first raids on Britain. Then slowly they bring events up to date and that's where they shift to being more of a journal with the history as it happens. But the raid in 1055 was the Welsh again, I was right; I looked it up to check. Right, now let's concentrate on what this says about the murder of Ethelbert.

'*The ghost of the dead king*' – he screwed up his eyes as Emma picked up her notebook and scribbled the words down as he spoke them out loud – '*was not laid by prayer but by revenge. Offa did not sleep again, nor did his queen.*' He turned to Emma. 'There is a theory that the murder was instigated by Queen Cynefryth out of jealousy that her daughter was to marry such a handsome and gifted young man, and that seems to be the version our chronicler subscribes to.'

'She was obviously a cow,' Emma put in.

'That I think is an understatement. But we will never know for sure.'

'Unless our friend here has written it down,' Felix put in. 'There is lots of stuff here. Go on, Dad, what does it say next?'

'*Our King Offa made many gifts of land and money to the Holy Church and built a shrine to the saint, in a church dedicated to the Holy Virgin that he set up by the river near his palace.*'

'Like you did, Em,' Felix put in.

'I only put two quid in the box. It was all I had.'

'I meant you prayed. But the fact that you saw the ghost means he was not laid at all, he is still not a happy bunny. Go on, Dad.'

'*The sword that took off the head of the saint was found in the river and was brought to the minster to be blessed with the saint's holy blood still hardened upon the blade.*' He frowned and looked up again. 'Unlikely, I would say. Surely the river water would have washed it off.'

'Not if it was magic blood. He was a saint, don't forget.'

'I think the word you're looking for might be sanctified, not magic.' Simon went back to studying the page. '*Our King Offa would not believe that the queen had wielded that sword, though many thought hers was the hand that guided it.* There you are! It was gossip even then.'

'Will this be useful for your book, Dad?' Felix was looking extremely pleased with himself.

'It will indeed. Let's see what else it says.' There was a long pause as Simon studied the band of calligraphy that had grown ever smaller and more compacted as it reached the edge of the page.

'*Many thought the queen should die for her actions, but none dared a . . . a . . .*' he hesitated. 'I think this word must be accost – accuse? – her. I should think not. She sounds as vicious as her husband. *And still the ghost of the king walked the March.*'

'Ooh.' Emma shivered. 'And still does today. So he was never revenged.'

'Avenged,' her father corrected her automatically. 'But our friend the chronicler says he was.'

'Isn't there anything else?' Felix was staring at the page on the computer. 'Let's see if there are any other bits written in.' He moved to the next page of text. This one was blank but as he zoomed in, enhancing the image until they could see the pores on the calfskin, faint shadows of writing began to appear. Again it was cramped. 'This is difficult,' Felix muttered. 'You might have to go somewhere that specialises in this sort of thing. Universities have much more powerful systems.'

'You're not doing badly, considering,' his father encouraged. 'I can't make out anything, but maybe you can if you relax your eyes. See if you can guess the shapes.'

The screen was wavering, growing darker then lighter as Felix fiddled with the settings, the faint strokes of the quill growing thicker then thinner as he made minute adjustments. Three words suddenly floated up off the page, the queen's lover . . . the Old English script clear to Simon. 'My God!' he whispered.

Both children leaned forward, Felix almost afraid to touch the keyboard in case he lost the words again. He stood up and moved back. 'Sit here, Dad, see if you can read it. Don't alter anything. I think this is as good as we're going to get it.'

Simon slid into his chair. '*The queen's lover died from the sting of a bee, in his . . . . in his ear . . . sent by God, to avenge the holy saint,*' he read slowly. '*All men knew the murderer had at last been taken to Hell to pay the price of his deed.*' He sat back in the chair. 'He was killed by a bee sting.'

There was a moment of intense silence in the room, then, 'So God revenged him,' Emma whispered.

'Looks like it,' said Felix.

'I'd love to know who our chronicler was,' Simon said after a bit. 'I can picture him, sitting there at his high desk with his quills and his little pots of ink, silence all around him, scribbling down the local gossip, then realising he should not have included it in the priory's official chronicle and scrubbing furiously at the page to rub it out, not daring to cut out any more pages perhaps because vellum is costly.' He pushed back his chair and stretched his arms above his head. Outside the windows the garden was growing dark. 'Perhaps his interest in the murder of the saint waned after the murderer died. Other things happened. The Vikings came back. But much further north this time. They raided Iona, which was far away, but word of such a terrible thing must have spread very fast. Their attacks became more frequent and more and more terrifying, with new incursions each year. Then the following year it all kicked off again locally when the Welsh raided Herefordshire and sacked Leominster and Hereford.'

'So Offa's Dyke wasn't working,' Emma put in.

'Maybe it was never finished. The records, as far as they go, put the year as 796 when work on it stopped, presumably with Offa's death. Hopefully archaeology will tell us one day what actually happened—' He was interrupted by a sound outside the door.

Simon felt his stomach lurch. Not now. Not with Emma here.

'What about a coffee break?' he said firmly.

'Who's that?' Felix was already heading across the room.

'Leave it!' Simon said sharply, but it was too late. Felix had grabbed the door handle and dragged it open. It was nearly dark outside, the creepers on the cottage wall thrashing against the windows as the wind rose from the west. 'Hello?' He stepped outside. 'Who's there?'

Elise!

The voice was far away, lonely, despairing.

Simon noticed Emma's expression. She looked like a rabbit caught in the headlights.

'Take no notice, Em. Come in, Felix. She'll go away.'

'Who is it?' said Felix, looking over his shoulder at them. 'Not that woman from the cathedral? She sounds weird. She sounds lost.'

'She is lost.' Emma stood up. 'It's not the woman from the cathedral. Who is it, Dad? She sounds frightened and sad.' She headed towards the doorway and peered outside over Felix's shoulder.

'Emma! No!' Simon said sharply.

'But she needs help.'

'If she needs anyone I will ring Bea and Mark. But you do not go out there, do you hear me?'

'You can't stop me.'

'Actually, we can, Em.' With a glance back at his father, Felix pushed Emma away and stepping back indoors closed the door behind him. He stood with his back to it and glared at her defiantly. 'Is this your ghost, Dad? Presumably she will go away by herself.' He sniggered. 'If she's there at all. I think it's more likely it's the wind. It howls. It seems to blow all the time up here and it's spooky and it does sound a bit like a human voice, but it isn't.'

'You sound like you're trying to convince yourself,' Emma retorted.

'No, I'm being rational.'

She looked at her father and then back at her brother before subsiding into her chair. There were tears trickling down her cheeks. 'She sounds so unhappy.'

'I know.' Simon went over to her and crouched down at her side. 'Try not to take any notice, Em. I think Felix might be right. It could be the wind. It does sound eerie sometimes. I tell you what.' He stood up. 'Let's go and make ourselves some supper. What about one of Dad's curries?'

Mark's message on Bea's phone, which was as usual lying forgotten on the kitchen table, had been brief.

Been trying to ring you. Forgot to tell you, have to be late this evening. Sorry. 😧 CU later xxx

Bea read it twice, then she put down the phone. She turned off the downstairs lights, all except the lamp on the table by the front door, then climbed once more the two flights to the attic.

Nesta's words had been a shock. They were so immediate; so personal. None of this was chance. Once she had followed Simon to the cottage, she had been chosen. But why? Why did Nesta want her to hear this story? She shivered. Whatever the reason, Nesta had recognised her as a kindred spirit and was watching over her.

Lighting her candle, Bea sat for a long moment, thinking. Eadburh was a dangerous, calculating woman, capable of cold-bloodedly planning murder. Life had not been kind to her; she had lost the man she loved, she had been forced to abort his baby, she had found herself in a land of strangers with a man she could never love as a husband, and given birth to his child who, though she played with her now and then with what appeared to be an offhand sense of duty, was being brought up by nurses, as had happened presumably in royal households everywhere for generation after generation. Her relationship with her own parents had veered from distant to outright hostility, and now she was planning to murder her mother's lover, a mother who had orchestrated the slaying of her daughter's intended. Her life had been a Shakespearean tragedy. She was impossible to like, and yet Bea found she could not look away. Was this obsession? Maybe. But she had it under control and she needed to know what happened next. And she wanted to talk to Nesta again.

Slowly and carefully she picked up her stone and closed her eyes.

Eadburh sent Hilde with the king's messenger back to her father's court at Sutton. The messenger carried letters for Offa and for Cynefryth, respectful greetings from their dutiful daughter in Wessex with no comments or questions about Alfrida's fate. And for her sister herself Hilde carried a private, more impassioned missive, begging her not to go, though Eadburh knew deep in her heart as she was writing it that it was probably too late. By the time Hilde arrived Alfrida would be long gone. Hilde carried something else as well. Sewn into the hem of her gown were two tiny hidden packets, and these were secret.

Bea settled back on her cushion, watching Hilde riding through the summer countryside with a small escort of warriors from Beorhtric's personal bodyguard, staying at night in the guest houses of monasteries and convents as she rode steadily northwards over the Wessex border into the kingdom of Mercia and back to the court of the king at Sutton.

She delivered the letter to the queen at last, and greeted the women who had been her friends in the household of the princesses and who now served their mother, and she settled in to gossip and exchange news. The second letter, to Alfrida, she burned as instructed when she learned that Alfrida had left the court at dead of night, only three days after her betrothed had been killed. Her tears and anger had swept through the king's hall like a raging fire, according to the women who had witnessed her grief. They made no mention of accusations or blame, and only spoke of unknown outlaws who had attacked in the night and who had never been caught. They all knew where Alfrida had gone – to the heart of the kingdom of which she should have been queen, to the lonely abbey at a place called Crowland, on a fearsome lonely marsh deep in the reeds, under a huge unrelenting sky amongst the birds and otters and beavers, and there she had dedicated her life to God. Her father had not dared send after her.

As Hilde sat with her companions by the fire in the great hall of the king late in the evening, her gaze passed thoughtfully over the assembled company. Queen Cynefryth was seated a little apart, a man at her side, a tall good-looking man, richly attired with gold buckles and armlets, a man some fifteen years or more younger than the king. The man was leaning towards her, his eyes fixed on her face, a little too close beside her for propriety.

'Who is that with the queen?' she whispered to the woman seated next to her, who was lost in thought, toying with her spindle. The woman raised her eyes briefly and Hilde saw her eyebrow rise, merely a flicker. 'Grimbert. He is the queen's adviser. He oversees the lands and rents of the convents of which she is benefactor.' The woman bent back to her spindle, wrenching a hank of soft sheep's wool from her distaff, her fingers tightening momentarily on the frail thread until it broke.

'And the king allows this?' Hilde's murmur was barely audible.

'The king is preoccupied with his penance from the pope. He pores over plans to build a new church over the holy well that sprang from the ground where the body of the boy was first hidden. He sees nothing and says nothing.'

Hilde watched the queen in silence, surprised that her companion dared speak out so frankly. Her eyes strayed to the king, a strong man still, though in his sixties now, his grizzled hair and weathered skin belying the intense force of his eyes. 'And the king's son?'

'Ecgfrith is seldom here. He keeps his own household at Tamworth, so we hear. He does not frequent his mother's presence.'

Hilde stared at her, again startled to hear such frank speech. Cautiously she turned back to the couple sitting there so brazenly near the king. Cynefryth was still very beautiful. Her hair, long and heavy, streaked now with silver, was only partially covered by her headrail which was held in place by a coronet of enamelled gold set with amethysts. Her face was unlined, her eyes fixed on the face of the man next to her, but the hardness was still there. Hilde remembered how the queen had treated Eadburh, how she had had Brona killed – the women all guessed it, though nothing had ever been proved or even hinted at. She was a vicious, dangerous woman and nothing and no one, not even her husband, could ever control her. Hilde smiled a little to herself. Only, perhaps, another equally dangerous woman. She could feel the slight weight of the two little pouches in her hem dragging on the rushes of the floor, and she turned away from the queen and Grimbert. She had been told to wait for the bees.

20

Mark missed being a parish priest more than he had expected. The promotion to canon in the cathedral had been a temptation he could not resist. He knew there were other equally good candidates for the vacancy and it surprised him how much he wanted the job once his application had gone in. It was the perfect position, with his family background in the world of finance and an aptitude he had firmly turned his back on but which he still possessed. It had not occurred to him that Bea would be uncomfortable with his decision. He discussed it with her, of course, again and again before he had accepted the position, but they agreed they would be happy with whatever God decided and as Mark proceeded through the interviews and discussions that preceded his appointment, they hardly spoke about it at all. He had perhaps assumed an enthusiasm in his wife which was not actually there.

The house in the Close with its Georgian façade and secluded walled garden was a huge bonus and they both loved it, but neither of them had quite realised how much of their privacy would be sacrificed, how close to the job it was, how easily they could be watched. Not all the partners of the clergy were involved with the Church. Some kept their distance completely and their decision was respected. Mark had promised her that that was the case. Bea thought it should apply to her as well. It appeared not.

'I am so sorry to insist on this meeting, Canon, but I felt it was my duty to tell you what is being said.' Sandra had cornered Mark as he was leaving the cathedral office. The cathedral itself was closing to the public for the night and they made their way slowly back along St John's Walk and out into the Close. 'It's just that people talk and, as you know, gossip can do such damage. In a tightly knit community like ours there is bound to be speculation.' She sat down on a bench beneath one of the lime trees and patted the seat beside her.

Mark knew Bea would laugh if she could see him. He was conscious of his attentive face and the tightly controlled calm it displayed. She would not be laughing after Sandra's next words.

'It's about Beatrice. People are asking questions. I thought it important you know.'

'Questions?'

'Her job. I take it she is actually a teacher?' Sandra's smile reminded him of a cat, watching a bird hop closer, oblivious to the hidden threat.

He looked at her with concern, his irritation carefully masked. 'You know she is. And if she is at home at present, that's because it's the school holidays. I'm sorry, Sandra, but I really don't see what business it is of other people what Bea does. It's fully understood within the Chapter that the life of the partners of our clergy are their own affair. Who is it who's asking these questions?'

'Ah, that's not for me to say. I respect their confidence.' She looked smug.

'Then please respect mine. If people ask you, you now know what to tell them.'

Fury and frustration flashed across her face. She was not nearly so good at dissembling as him. 'They need to know something more than that.'

'No, they don't.' He gave her a benign smile. 'And I know I can rely on you to remind them of the discretion we all give one another. It's what makes the Chapter run smoothly.' For a moment he found himself envying Heather Fawcett, who, like Sandra, worked with the volunteers, in her case, helping to run the cathedral shop, her status as a clergy widow recognised and above suspicion. He stood up abruptly. 'And now, I'm afraid, Sandra, I must get on. Please, don't concern yourself any more about Bea.'

There was nothing she could do but stand up too and return his smile. She watched as he walked away from her across the grass, disappearing behind another of the great lime trees that shaded the Close. There was no point in following him. Besides, it was Bea she was interested in. She hadn't been able to get the boy's phrase out of her head. Ghostbuster. And the newspaper clippings had given her all the proof she needed.

Why could the annoying woman not let it go? Mark had agreed to take evensong at a church some miles from Hereford and, climbing into his car, he headed north out of the city, following winding country lanes through tunnels of white blossom. The church he was going to was a favourite of his and he had volunteered to take more than his share of services there while its priest in charge was in hospital. It was a small church, ancient and beautiful, redolent with history. Bea would love it. The thought of Bea reminded him yet again of his encounter with Sandra, and a mile or two before he reached his destination he pulled into a field gateway and reached for his mobile. As usual, Bea's phone was off. 'Darling, I thought I should warn you. Sandra is after you in full cry. Wretched woman! I suggest that if you don't want her to give you the third degree again you lie low and don't answer the door. I shouldn't be too late. The service should be over by about eight and I will come straight home after that. Love you.'

He switched off his phone and put it down on the seat beside him, then he sat for several minutes in prayer. He was praying for the priest, an old man, struggling so bravely against cancer, for the man's congregation, for the village that missed their pastor so much, for the world, so riven with evil on every side. Lowering the window, he closed his eyes as the scent of flowers and grass filled the car. The evening was completely silent, save for the cry of a lamb for its mother and the answering reassuring bleat, and in the distance the eerie call of a curlew from the hills above the village. This was all so far from the hatred of human beings for each other, the pollution of the land and sea, the carelessness with which humanity had treated the sacredness of the planet with which they had been entrusted. He sighed. 'Please God,' he murmured as an afterthought, 'as well as having all that to keep you busy, help Sandra to mind her own business and please, please, keep a special eye on Bea.' Bea, who was straying into such a dangerous place and who would never listen to him when he begged her to take care.

The service was beautiful, the congregation friendly and anxious to talk to him and it was nearly nine before he was able to leave at last, turning the car for home.

Putting his key in the door, he pushed it open and went in. 'Bea?'

The lights downstairs were off except for the lamp on the hall table. 'Bea, I'm back.'

He ran up the stairs two at a time and, turning on the light, looked quickly into their bedroom, wondering – hoping – she might have gone to bed early. There was no sign of her there. With only a second's hesitation he ran up the second flight of stairs, hearing them creak beneath his feet as he knocked on the door of her study. There was no reply. He opened the door and looked in. There was no one there, only a faint smoky essence in the air from a recently extinguished candle.

His heart thudding with apprehension, he turned back downstairs, heading for the kitchen. Bea's phone lay on the table where as so often she must have put it down and then forgotten it. He picked it up. The battery was almost dead. Plugging it in, he checked to see if she had picked up his message. The last message wasn't from him, it was from Simon, sent less than an hour before. 'Bea, I'm so sorry to call you at this hour but I'm worried sick. Emma's disappeared. She heard the voice and got very upset. While Felix and I were in the kitchen she seems to have gone out – we found the front door open – and there is no sign of her. She can't have gone far. The car is still here and anyway she doesn't drive yet. We've called and called and searched the immediate fields. I'm not sure what to do next. The woman, the voice, can't hurt her, can she? Or lure her somewhere? I can't believe I'm saying this—'

'Just ask Bea and Mark to come, Dad!' Mark heard Felix's voice in the distance. He sounded very young and very frightened.

Mark switched off the phone and turned for the front door.

Bea's car was parked outside the cottage beside Simon's; every light in the cottage was on as Mark grabbed a torch from his glove box and ran up the steep path to the front door where Simon was waiting. 'I heard your car. Bea's gone to look for Em,' he called. 'I don't know where she went, but she seemed to know what to do.'

Mark saw Simon give him a sideways glance and belatedly realised he was still wearing his cassock after the service. He took a deep breath, trying to calm himself. 'I'm sure there is no need to worry. They can't have gone far.'

'We should ring the police,' Felix put in. He appeared in the doorway behind his father and Mark wondered if the boy had been crying.

'And we will if we can't find them,' Mark said gently. 'But first let's have another look outside. Has Emma got a phone on her?'

'No, she left it behind in her bedroom.' Felix was shaking his head violently. 'It was the first thing I checked.'

'OK. How long has Emma been gone? You think Bea knew where to look for her? I don't know this area, I'm afraid. So, do you have an Ordnance Survey map? Perhaps we could look at the terrain and see where Emma could have got lost. Are there any hidden valleys and streams where she could slip and fall? Luckily it's not raining and it's not too cold. She couldn't have gone far, surely?'

Already Felix was at the laptop, bringing up a map, focusing in on the contour lines. Simon sat down abruptly. 'I'm behaving like an idiot,' he said, rubbing his face with the palms of his hands. 'I thought – I know it's impossible and stupid and crazy but, with all this talk of ghosts, I thought somehow she might have disappeared through some portal into the past. I'm being an irrational fool. I panicked. I'm sorry.'

'Anyone would panic,' Mark went to stand behind Felix, looking at the screen. 'I think we can assume Bea and Em are still in the present day, Simon.' He gave the man a quizzical look, then leaned closer to the screen. 'You're pretty much at the top of the ridge here and the hill seems to go down in every direction, but there are woods here' – he pointed at the screen – 'and this part here looks like a narrow valley. If it's rocky, it would be easy to slip over and turn one's ankle.'

He looked up as Felix let out a small yelp of distress. 'We have to be realistic, Felix,' he said sternly. 'Emma has not disappeared into thin air and she cannot have gone far. I'm sure Bea will find her, but if she doesn't we'll ring the police, who will probably call out the mountain rescue. Don't worry. She'll be OK.'

'Your dad is looking for us, Em.' Bea could see the torchlight moving in the trees in the distance. 'I'm going to leave you for a minute while I go and call him.'

The girl was huddled, shivering, against the tumbled stone wall that bordered the wood. Bea had already wrapped her in her jacket and tucked her scarf round the girl's shoulders, but Emma clutched at her with a cry of fear. 'Don't go.'

'I have to go, Em. We can't stay out here any longer.'

'Can't you phone?'

'I'm afraid I left my phone at home. If I stand up on the bank there, I can shout. He'll be outside looking for you and he'll hear me.'

'Where is he?'

'I told you, your dad is coming.'

'No, not Dad, Elise. I saw him. She was calling him and I came out and I saw him and I followed him. He was here.' Tears were coursing down her face.

Bea froze. She didn't know what to say, then she recovered herself. 'He's gone, sweetheart.' How was it possible that Emma had seen Elisedd? Plenty of time to work that out later. Bea gave her a quick hug, then she tore herself away. They were in a grassy hollow out of the wind. The track nearby was barely visible in the starlight, but Emma had followed it at a run, only stopping at last when her breath gave out and she had no choice but to pull up, gasping for air. When Bea had found her, she was sobbing desperately, not knowing which way to turn.

Bea set off towards the light she had seen in the trees. Someone out there was flashing a torch. She kept looking over her shoulder, terrified she would lose Emma in the dark. The girl was no more than a dark hump huddled at the base of the wall amongst the fallen stones, too exhausted and frightened to move.

'Simon!' Bea shouted. 'Simon, we're here!' She waved her arms above her head, hoping he could see her silhouette against the stars. Her voice sounded thin and reedy in the darkness as she headed towards the torchlight.

The horse was on her without warning, the sudden thunder of hooves on the turf making the ground shake. She stopped with a cry of fright and faced it, her arms in front of her face to try and protect herself as it raced towards her. She threw herself sideways as with a furious scream the horse half reared. She glimpsed the rider wrenching the reins to pull it away from her, his face a blur in the starlight as he hesitated, looking down at her, then he kicked the animal on, missing her by inches, galloping away along the track towards the west.

'Bea?' She heard a man's voice in the distance: Mark's voice. 'Bea, I'm coming!' Frozen with shock, she couldn't move. Then she saw them: three figures running along the track towards her.

'There!' She was shaking so much she could hardly speak. 'Emma's there. By the wall. She's OK.'

She watched as they ran across the grass and through the heather, following her pointing finger. She saw them stop then she saw the tallest figure, Simon, stoop and pull Emma to her feet, folding her in his arms. Already Felix, ever practical, was dragging off his fleece and tenderly wrapping it round his sister's shoulders. With a sob, Bea subsided to her knees, shaking so much she couldn't stand. The third figure with them was Mark.

'Bea? Bea, darling, are you all right?' He left the group and ran towards her.

'Did you see the horseman? It was Elisedd. He nearly ran me down.'

'Horseman?' Mark crouched, his arm round her shoulders. 'What horseman?'

She found she was sobbing. 'Emma saw him. She tried to follow him.' She looked up. 'She's terrified, Mark.'

'She'll be all right. Simon and Felix are taking her back to the cottage. It's only a few hundred yards away.' In the dark it was almost impossible to make out the building, sheltered below the ridge. Behind them the vast emptiness of the hills was part of the night. He helped her to her feet and hugged her to him. 'Darling, I thought I'd lost you.'

She managed a smile. 'Whisked into the past by Emma's handsome prince.'

'Something like that,' he confirmed drily. 'Can you walk? Let's get you inside.'

He couldn't quite explain even to himself the sudden extra apprehension that had gripped him, the cold breath that was nothing to do with the wind that touched his back.

Pulling the door closed behind them, Simon drew the bolt across and leaned back with a sigh of relief. Emma was unhurt. Apart from being very cold and frightened, she seemed remarkably unfazed by her ordeal. Wrapped in a rug by the fire, her colour had returned and she was beginning to talk. 'I heard the voice like before, but it sounded even more sad this time. I didn't mean to follow it, but it seemed to be so near. I couldn't see her in the dark but I knew she was there, close to me. I opened the gate and walked out onto the hill, and she kept moving further and further away in front of me. And then I saw him; Elise. He's the one she's been calling. I'm sorry, Dad. I didn't mean to scare you.'

Simon didn't know whether to be angry or happy and opted instead for tight-lipped silence.

Felix had vanished into the kitchen to reappear with a tray of mugs. Hot chocolate for Emma. Tea for the rest of them. They all moved closer to the fire, Felix sitting on the rush matting of the floor and Mark perched on a stool. Bea was huddled in the chair opposite Emma. She was trying to conceal the fact that she was still shaking.

'So, who was Elise?' Felix asked at last.

'He's the one she's been calling. She's lost him, and I had to find him for her,' Emma said. She broke into a fresh torrent of sobs.

'I ought to ring your mum and tell her what happened,' Simon said at last as the silence threatened to stretch out too long.

'No!' Emma looked up in horror. 'You mustn't tell her!'

'She needs to know, Em.'

'No, she doesn't. She will only make us go back home.' Felix's expression echoed his sister's. 'She's enjoying her stay in Worcester, Dad. Leave her be. Nothing has happened here. Emma is fine and she won't do it again.'

'No, I won't,' Emma echoed.

'But what if you hear this voice again?' Simon was still leaning against the closed front door as if holding the world at bay.

'If I do, I will ignore it.'

'How did you know where she had gone?' Simon fired the question at Bea.

She swallowed. Clutching the hot mug between her hands more tightly, she held it against her chest. 'It was guesswork. I followed the track towards the west. Always towards the west.'

'Can't you make all this go away?' There was a touch of desperation in his voice.

'I will try. I'm sorry I've not been much use so far. This is all part of a far larger story than I realised. There is so much going on here.' She looked at Mark and he read a whole volume of messages in her eyes. Don't tell them I saw a horse. Don't mention anything. Say a prayer for them to bring peace to the cottage and allow them to sleep well and suggest we

200

come back when it's daylight. And then again: don't mention the horse and rider, please . . .

Mark found he was shivering too. He could still feel that eerie tiptoe of the mountain wind across his shoulder blades. Clearing his throat, he stood up. 'It's late. I suggest we leave you three to get some sleep. I'm sure there'll be no more disturbance tonight. If you will allow me, I will bless the cottage and then' – he couldn't believe he was about to say this – 'Bea will set guardians at each corner, north, south, east and west. Angels to keep you safe. And tomorrow we will return and see if this can be sorted out once and for all.'

He glanced round. No one smiled or flinched or sniggered at the mention of angels, so, raising his right hand, he made the sign of the cross before giving his blessing. It was followed by a long silence. He sighed and, beckoning to Bea, he turned towards the door. Simon stood aside, leaving him to unbolt it.

Outside the cloud had blown away and the sky was ablaze with stars.

21

They drove back in convoy in their separate cars. It was after two when they at last got home, parking side by side in their allotted spaces outside the school and tiptoed past the sleeping cathedral across the grass towards their front door.

'You called him Elisedd.' Mark sat down at the kitchen table, exhausted. 'The man on the horse. You knew Elise was a man.'

Sitting opposite him she nodded slowly. 'I've seen him before, in my dreams.' She took a deep breath. 'I think the voice up there at the cottage belongs to Eadburh. She fell in love with a Welsh prince and they made love up there on the ridge in a sheepfold which I assume was later incorporated into the cottage. Her father banished him and had him murdered, and Eadburh was forced to marry someone else. I believe her spirit is searching for him still.' There was a long pause. 'And perhaps he is looking for her. That horseman. It was Elisedd, I'm sure it was.' The black horse, the flying cloak, the wild-eyed rider. 'I'm afraid for Emma. She's sensitive and she's picked up on the story.'

'Presumably you've told Simon your theory?'

'I didn't think he would believe me.'

'No. I don't suppose he would.' Mark sighed. 'Let me get

this straight. You're telling me that one of Offa's daughters – Offa, the King of Mercia, Offa of Offa's Dyke, Offa who died over a thousand years ago – his daughter, is roaming the hills out there, wailing for her lost lover?'

'You've seen her, Mark. You're the only other person who has!'

'I saw a nun! A nun, Bea. Not a wailing Anglo-Saxon!'

'And who's to say she didn't become a nun?' She looked up at him defiantly. 'You're the one who told me they were Christians.'

With another sigh he stood up, went over to the window and raised the blind to look out into the darkness of the garden. 'You know, I'm too tired to think about all this now, but you have to tell Simon. I think he needs to get Emma out of that house. Whatever you think is happening, whatever you believe, a child is in danger. If she rushes off into the dark again they might not find her so easily next time. All this talk of ghosts and the murder of St Ethelbert, galloping horses and knocking on doors, and the fact that her father is quite obviously scared stiff, has got to her, and we can't risk anything happening to her, Bea.'

She nodded. 'We'll talk to Simon tomorrow.'

Mark slept at once; she used to tease him about the sleep of the righteous as night after night he was snoring almost as soon as his head hit the pillow while she would lie awake, worrying about the day gone by and the day to come, Anna and Petra, the parish and, from time to time, the people who had come to her with their problems from another world and another time. And now, as she lay beside him, she couldn't get the vision of the horse rearing above her out of her head, the man in the saddle, leaning forward, dragging the horse's head sideways so it would avoid hitting her with its hooves. He wore no head covering, she realised now as she pictured him behind her closing eyes, his hair blowing across his face, dressed in dark clothes, a cloak of some kind streaming behind him, caught at the shoulder with a round silver disc. The horse was black but there was the echoing glint of metal on the headband of its bridle. She could smell the horse even now, feel its hot breath on her face, and again she was aware of the ground shaking beneath the thunder of its hooves.

She slept and the scene changed. She was once more at the court of Offa at Sutton. It was daylight. Eadburh's confidante, Hilde, had slipped outside and in the queen's herb garden the flowers were alive with bees. There was a basket on her arm, pruning shears lying amidst a scatter of cuttings, but she wasn't looking at the plants, her eyes were fixed on the gate in the palisade which opened onto a path through the orchard that led to the river. She had to hurry. There were bees everywhere, their hum urgent beneath the song of the blackbird high in the apple blossom behind the hedge. There was no one else in sight. The bell had rung for the meal in the hall and everyone from the king down to the lowest serf was there awaiting the feast. Almost everyone. She had seen Grimbert slip out of the hall after a barely perceptible nod from the queen. She had seen his secret smile.

Their trysting place was down on the riverbank hidden by a stand of alder trees. Grimbert spread his cloak on the ground and sat down, waiting, watching a kingfisher perched on the stump of a fallen willow as it peered down into the water. The water played its part, rippling, flickering, mesmerising. Still the queen did not come. Grimbert lay back, his arm over his eyes against the sunlight as it danced through the pale green leaves of the willow. A bee buzzed near his face and he brushed it away, sending it veering angrily into the air. Another bee joined it and they homed in on a patch of dandelions near his head.

Bea's dream shifted back to the great hall. She watched as the queen leaned over to whisper to Offa and saw his nod, the flash of anger in his eyes followed by the slightest of shrugs as his wife stood up and left the table to slip through the curtain into the private area behind.

Hilde crept closer. She had anointed her wrists with the essence of rose favoured by the queen. When Grimbert smelt it, he smiled.

The agonising pain in his ear made him lash out, but the

poison was instant. When they found his body, there was a dead bee lying on his chest.

Hilde slipped back into the banquet and took her place amongst the queen's ladies. If she had been missed, she would have used an urgent trip to the latrines as an excuse, but no one had noticed her absence and no one had noticed that Grimbert had gone. When the queen returned to the hall, white and trembling, some time later, Hilde suppressed a smile. She knew the queen could make no fuss, raise no alarm, for how could she explain what she was doing down there on the bank of the river when she should have been by the king's side at his feast?

Hilde stayed several more days at the court – to have hurried away too soon in the uproar and mourning after Grimbert's untimely death and the queen's furious grief might have roused suspicion – then she went on her way. But this time she was alone and on foot, her escort sent back to Wessex, while she took the road north and then west towards the cloud-shrouded mountains and deep valleys and passes of Powys on the second part of her quest.

'Jane?' Simon struggled to place the woman's voice on the other end of the phone line.

'Jane Luxton. From the cathedral library.'

'Of course. I'm sorry.'

'Listen, I've persuaded Kate and Phil to let me bring the chronicle, the folio, and one or two other books in their collection here to the cathedral where they can be stored in our underground archive. We have temperature and humidity control here, and our conservator can have a look at them. I've also had a word with an expert from the Bodleian, who has promised to come over and advise us. After that, it will probably be a valuation by Sotheby's or Christie's. Kate thought you might like a heads-up. One last chance to see your chronicle before we lock it away.'

'Yes. Please.' Simon didn't need to think about it.

'It will have to be today, I'm afraid.'

He glanced at Felix, who was once more at the keyboard. Emma hadn't surfaced yet. He had left a cup of tea by her bedside an hour ago and stood beside her looking down with a strange feeling of tenderness such as he didn't recall feeling since she was a toddler with golden curls and huge dark blue eyes. 'No problem. I'll be there.'

'Let Kate know you're coming.'

It was a no-brainer that he would take Emma and Felix. They should both have been studying, but he didn't think that was going to happen and he didn't want to leave them alone. It would be good to get them out of the cottage for a few hours. He left a message on Bea's phone before they left. 'I thought a change of scene might be in order. Can we talk tomorrow instead?'

They were a little subdued as he retraced his carefully memorised route, but the long winding drive and the overgrown parking space with its mossy gravel in front of the ancient house woke them up. They sat in stunned silence as he drew up and put on the handbrake. 'This is well cool, Dad,' Felix breathed at last.

'Sleeping Beauty's palace,' Emma whispered.

Simon climbed out of the car. 'Come and meet Kate and Phil.'

'Let me take some pictures, Dad. My phone has a much better camera than your old thing. I reckon we could do even better than the ones you've taken,' Felix announced when his father queried the need for more pictures as they gathered upstairs in front of the long table and as his father turned the pages of the ancient book with a careful hand while his son took a fresh sequence of photos. It was as they were finishing that Emma stepped forward and laid her hand flat on the last page.

'Don't touch, Em!' Simon shouted.

Emma didn't move. 'I can hear him,' she said suddenly. 'I can hear him talking. He has a pen in his hand and he is looking at his work and someone has walked in and is standing behind him. The old man has dropped his pen and now the inkpot has fallen on the floor, splashing his robe. They can hear shouting in the distance and the old man has climbed off his stool. He's terrified. He has pushed away the desk and is looking round for somewhere to hide—'

'Emma! Stop it!'

She took no notice.

'—it's the enemy. They've broken into the church and now they're in the scriptorium. The two men are running to the door. They run down a dark passage and out into the garden. I can hear their sandals flapping on the stone path and behind them the book has fallen off the desk and into the dark place behind it. The enemy are there, with drawn swords, the blades covered in blood—' Her voice was rising, the words coming more and more quickly.

'Emma!' Simon shouted. Felix had put down his phone. He lunged forward and wrenched his sister's hand off the page as Kate ran into the room. 'What is it?' she cried. 'What's wrong?'

Emma let out a sob. Pushing past Kate, she ran out of the door. They could hear her footsteps thudding along the landing and then down the stairs.

'Em had some sort of vision.' Felix looked down at the open page of the book as if he was trying to see the scene his sister had described. The page was exactly as it had been before. There was no mark from her hand, only that strangely powerful dash of ink at the end of the passage, and then nothing.

'I'm sorry, Kate.' Simon looked up in despair. 'Let her go. We had a bad night; she had nightmares and she was sleep-walking. I think this place has got to her. It's so . . .' He failed to find the right word.

'Old?' Felix filled in helpfully.

Simon gave a grim smile and nodded. 'That about covers it.'

Kate smiled. 'Don't worry. Let me go and speak to her. You boys go on with your photography.'

'That sounded a bit patronising,' Felix whispered as Kate disappeared.

Simon smiled. 'Good idea though. Let her go and speak to Em. I have a feeling she might be quite good at it.'

Kate found Emma in the garden. She was standing amongst the ancient pear trees perfectly still, her arms hanging at her sides, tears pouring down her face.

'Come with me.' She took Emma's hand and led her across the lawn to a pergola, heavy with budding creepers. There was a weathered wooden bench under it and she pulled Emma down beside her.

For a long time neither spoke, then Kate said, 'Phil has gone out and your father and your brother are busy. There's no one here. Do you want to tell me what happened?'

The sympathy in her voice, the sense that she understood, maybe the simple fact that she was another woman seemed to get through to Emma. Once she started talking, she couldn't stop. The experiences at the cottage. The strange feelings. The bad dreams. Things that had happened at school that no one at home knew about, last night's inexplicable race out into the dark, finding herself outside and not quite knowing why and now the chronicle. 'I had to touch it. I had to. I knew I mustn't. I knew Dad would be furious because it's so precious, but I couldn't stop myself. I couldn't.' The tears were still pouring down her face. 'And I could feel it; hear it; see it through my fingers, like electricity! The swords had blood on their blades. And those two old men were running for their lives and the men saw them and they were chasing them and then Felix pulled my hand away and it all stopped. Just like that. Switched off. Gone. Finished.'

Kate sat still. When you don't know what on earth to say, silence is the best option. She didn't look at Emma, her attention fixed instead on the scattering of pear blossom on the lawn. A bee settled on a flower nearby and paused in its foraging, sitting completely still almost as though it was listening.

'Please don't tell my mum.' Emma sounded like a little girl now. A frightened, guilty little girl.

'I don't know your mum,' Kate responded briskly. 'And I certainly wouldn't tell her if I did. I won't tell anyone anything unless you would like me to.' She hesitated. 'But I think your dad would want to know.'

She glanced across at Emma to see she was shaking her head vigorously.

'Has this been happening to you for a long time?' Kate's question was cautious.

Emma nodded. 'I hate it. I never know when it's going to come over me. It happened in school once and it was awful. Everyone teased me. They said I was mad. They said I should see the psych.'

'That's tough.' A movement at the edge of the lawn caught her eye and she saw Simon and Felix standing hesitantly outside the house. She gestured them away sharply.

'Something like this, Emma, is too much for one person to bear alone. I'm not sure I've ever known anyone who can see what you're seeing, but you do need to talk to someone. Perhaps your friends were right in a way. Perhaps a school counsellor or someone like that?'

'They'd lock me up!'

'No. No they wouldn't. But they might be able to tell you how to cope with it.'

It. Kate knew it was an inadequate response, but what was it? Some kind of epilepsy, caused by an over-stimulated imagination?

'I tell you what. Why don't you all stay and have lunch with us. Perhaps a sandwich or something. I think some food will make you feel better, and I promise I won't say anything to your dad.'

'Felix knows.' Emma looked up suddenly. 'It's happened in front of him once.'

'And he's kept your secret?'

Emma shrugged her shoulders. 'I s'pose.'

He hadn't. And Simon did the only thing he could think of. He dropped Emma off at the cathedral gates on the way home.

This time Simon's message had been urgent. 'Please, Bea, I need you to talk to Emma now. Today. It was a huge mistake taking her to that house. She's in an awful state.'

Hilde was dressed very simply. Swathed in a woollen tunic, her hair covered in a veil, with no jewels or money and no possessions at all save a pilgrim's scrip carrying a comb and spare linen and a letter for a king, she walked slowly along the track up and over the first high ridge and down into the

209

foreign land of her people's enemies. She had discussed the disguise she would adopt with her mistress and a pilgrim had seemed an obvious choice. The people of Powys were a God-fearing race, they had followed Christ from time immemorial, or so Eadburh told her, far longer than the people of Mercia, and they would respect a woman alone if she were protected by her service to God.

Hilde's shoes grew dusty and soon wore thin. At first the people, accustomed to border raids, were suspicious of a fair-haired Saxon, even if she was a lone woman, as she asked her way, begging food and a place to sleep from shepherds and swineherds and cottars as she passed. Most were generous in the end. It had been a good harvest, there was bread to spare. Dogs were sometimes her enemy, appearing to suspect she was not what she seemed, but if she had to, she diverted out of their way, heading always towards the setting sun. On the first night at a tiny farmstead, a farmer cut her a thumb stick to help her on her way. Two days later, at a *clas*, a small church community isolated in a deep valley, the gentle old abbot gave her a carved wooden cross to hang around her neck on a thong. Everywhere, scattered through the lonely country she found there were churches and chapels and cross-roads marked by high crosses of intricately laced stonework, every one a place of refuge.

She walked west to start with, anxious to put Mercia behind her, afraid that they might come after her, but there was never any sign of pursuit and the further she walked the more she fell into her role as a woman of God and the more the role settled on her, the more she began to think about the terrible thing she had done. Every heather bell and every bloom on the gorse bushes where a bee paused to suck the nectar, reminded her of the bee upon the bank of the river and the sting which was inflicted by her hand.

When there was nowhere to stay, she curled under a hedge or in a dry ditch, swathed in her cloak and she prayed. She was lost but she no longer cared. When she found her desti-nation, she was instructed to find out who had killed the man Eadburh had loved, and then, armed with the truth, go back all that long way into Mercia to find him. In her hem was the remaining small package, another lethal bee sting to inflict, another vengeful death to take the man who had killed a prince to Hell, another weight upon her conscience.

As she penetrated further into the kingdom of Powys following a barely defined track that led northwards now through valleys between the mountains, the people greeted her almost everywhere with courtesy and friendship. By now she had learned a few words of their language and the inhabitants of the small lonely cottages grew even more hospitable, sharing their dry bracken beds, piles of woollen blankets and sheepskins to give her warmth as summer declined into autumn, pottage to eat and stories to tell by the fireside at night even though she understood only a few words. She was puzzled that there seemed to be no villages on the road, which wound its way more and more deeply into the mountains, where she heard wolves howling at night and eagles calling in the day as they swept high amongst the cloud-covered peaks. She passed lonely steadings and on the tops of some of the mountains she saw castles and palisades and she would feel a ray of hope, but again and again people shook their heads when she asked for the king's court and again they pointed her onward.

Time passed. She learned to hide her loneliness, always hoping that soon she would reach her destination, wondering now if she was walking round in circles. Then at last puzzled faces and eloquent signs of incomprehension were replaced by nods of encouragement. Soon she would be there, they seemed to say. She prayed to the Blessed Virgin to watch over her and learned the names of new and unknown saints to add to her list of protectors.

One day, as the track descended into a broad river valley she saw signs of a larger church, surrounded by dry stone walls and buildings with fields around them and there she stayed for several weeks as a guest of the abbess, regaining her strength and her resolve. This lady spoke her language and was kind, welcoming a new face and inviting her to stay as the cold winds swept in, carrying ice and snow, screaming through the rounded arches of the abbey. She thought some-times of Eadburh waiting for news, always waiting for news as she had when she was a young princess, and she wavered, but Eadburh was safe and warm by the fires of the palaces of Wessex, and here in the frost dusted valleys the abbess cautioned her to wait until the weather cleared and then go on to find news of Prince Elisedd. When she spoke of him, the abbess looked doubtful and sad and said she did not know anything about what happened to the king's younger son or how he had died. She had not even known he was dead.

Simon and Emma were standing by the gate to the Cathedral Close, while Felix waited for his father in the car by the kerb. The girl was wan and tired and tearful. 'She insisted she wanted to speak to you,' Simon said in an undertone as Emma began to hurry away from them towards the cathedral. 'She needs you to calm her down. Reassure her. Tell her she's not a freak!' He looked distraught. 'Let me explain what happened—'

'Let her tell me herself, Simon,' Bea said firmly. 'She is not a freak, I can assure you. She is a perfectly normal young lady who needs some reassurance, that's all. You go and get your-selves some coffee. I'll text you when we've talked.' Bea was watching Emma who had stopped, scuffing the path with her toe, waiting for her. 'Try not to worry. Go. Look after Felix.' She had seen the boy's anxious face peering at them from the car.

Bea led Emma back towards her house, skirting the cathe-dral's great west door and crossing the grass with its crowds of people enjoying the spring sunshine, and, mindful of the likelihood of Sandra's beady eyes spotting them, ducked into Church Street, past its inevitable busker, then down the narrow alley between two shops where the back gate into their garden was hidden in a small private courtyard. Going in that way, no one was going to spot them.

She listened to Emma's story in the kitchen over tea and cake, coaxing her to eat and drink, drawing out the story the girl had told Kate, and as she listened she felt a strange dawning affinity with this sensitive, lost, frightened girl.

'It's nothing to be afraid of. I do it too,' she explained at last. 'It's a gift: the ability to read an object's past through touch. It's called psychometry, and it's an amazing thing to be able to do. Some people are born with the ability, and other people spend hours trying to teach themselves how. You are blessed. And so am I. We can do it naturally.'

She watched Emma's face change from misery to interest and at last to a slow dawning hope. 'You do it too?'

Bea nodded, thinking of the stone upstairs. 'You were sensing something that happened in the scriptorium where the book was being written. The intense emotions of the people there, the scribe, the other monk, the invading army, their feelings were so strong they have embedded in the fabric of the pages so that centuries later they can still be felt by someone who has the gift.'

Emma's expression morphed again, this time into one of complete incredulity. 'That's not possible.'

Bea smiled. 'It is.'

'But that's garbage. It's not real. It was my imagination.'

Bea sighed. 'You can look at it that way, of course you can. Emma, what you do with your gift is up to you. I can show you how to control it. To switch it off, if that's what you want. How to ignore it whenever you feel it beginning to filter into your consciousness. It's not easy to live with and I understand you may not want to. You may prefer to think of it as an over-active imagination. That's up to you.'

'Have you switched yours off?' Emma looked at her intently.

'I have learned to control it, yes. Sometimes I feel I need it to explain things that are happening round me, or round other people, and then I use it. It's another sense we possess like touch and smell and taste.'

And, for want of something else, I deliberately look for a stone to anchor me to the place. That was not something she intended to tell Emma.

'But you couldn't deal with the voice at the cottage. The ghosts.'

'No. That was something different. What your father calls a ghost is an echo from the past.' Bea hesitated. 'But I am going to use every method at my disposal to help understand

213

what is going on up there. There are layers of memories there that are particularly intense and your father's book has somehow brought them into focus.'

'So, it's his fault.'

'It's no one's fault. It just is. Like an echo in a huge dark cave.'

Emma shivered. She looked round. 'Has this house got ghosts?'

Bea smiled. 'It did. I asked them to go away.'

'It's very old.' Emma was looking up at the beams in the kitchen ceiling.

'Parts of it are. It's part of the cathedral estate. There were buildings here for centuries before the Church dignitaries decided to refashion them into beautiful houses for the dean and Chapter. Mark and I love it here.'

'Tell me how to switch it off!' Emma's desperate cry interrupted her.

Bea sighed. 'All right. I think we should go upstairs to my study, where I keep my books and candles and herbs, things that create a calm atmosphere and will help set the mood for what we want to do.'

She led the way up the broad staircase with its elegant handrail and bannisters curving up to the first floor, then on up the narrower flight, conscious of Emma so close behind her she could feel the warmth from the girl's body.

It was peaceful in Bea's sanctuary, and it felt safe. Hilde and Eadburh were for now locked away in the past. She turned to Emma. 'I want you to sit down on the big cushion there and relax. You're so full of tension and stress you won't be able to think straight until you feel more comfortable.' She searched through the music list on her phone and found a quiet tune to play, then she sat down too, in the corner, not watching, not too close; there in case she was needed. The girl needed healing before anything else could happen.

Slowly the window grew dark. Below on the far side of the high garden wall the town lights came on one by one. Emma's eyes had closed. Quietly Bea stood up and lit a piece of charcoal in the little brass dish she kept for the purpose, then she reached for a bottle of dried herbs and scattered a pinch onto the glowing embers. A wisp of fragrant smoke drifted up into the still air. She reached for her phone and quietly tapped in a message to Simon. Don't wait. This may take some time. I'll bring her back to the cottage later. Then she pulled out a second cushion, sat down, leant back against the wall and she too closed her eyes.

22

In the Hampshire palace of King Beorhtric, Eadburh was once more with child. She was sick and miserable and lonely, begging Nesta for tisanes to ease her nausea. At last she had received a letter from Hilde and she sat up and pulled a cloak around her shoulders as she read it. It had been brought back by the king's bodyguard when they returned from Sutton and delivered into her own hand, and she smiled as, tucked amongst the other news, she read the one phrase she was looking for. *And the thane Grimbert was killed by the sting of a bee in his ear.* That was all. She gave a grim smile. She would wait for Hilde to return to hear the further detail, but she was not expecting the woman for a while. She had another errand to perform. Somewhere else to go. Another death to avenge.

The women's bower was draughty and the fire had burned low. There was no sign of any of her maidens or indeed any servants at all. She wasn't surprised. They all seemed to hate her, resenting her manner, still resenting the fact that she was Mercian, resenting the fact that she ordered the court and took over so much of its running from her husband. She guessed where they all were. There was a new minstrel in the great hall of the king and they had crept out of her chamber while she slept to listen to him. She walked down the roofed walkway that had been built between the hall of the queen and the mead hall, towards the sound of shouting and clapping, and stood for a while in the doorway looking in. The guards had uncrossed their spears at her approach. No one else noticed her. They were all concentrating on the young man standing on the dais at the far end. The sound of shouting and applause had died now, and there was intense silence. He was playing a lute and his voice was particularly sweet. She listened for a while, feeling herself relax for the first time in weeks, her hand on her belly where the child was quickening at last, a tiny flutter beneath her ribs. That was another source of resentment in the court, that she hadn't given Beorhtric a son. Well, God willing, she would soon rectify that failing at least. This child would be a boy. She was certain of it.

It was then she looked round for Beorhtric. He wasn't there. With a frown she made her way through the crowded hall, seeing the men and women shrink away from her as she pushed her way towards the doorway into the private royal chamber behind the dais and pulled the curtain aside.

Beorhtric was there, sprawled on his great chair, and there was someone sitting on his lap. He was kissing her, fondling her body as he sat with his back to the door. Eadburh watched for several seconds, stunned into silence before the wave of fury and jealousy hit her. While she languished, sick and heavy and ugly with the misery of carrying her husband's child, he was playing with another woman against all the laws of God and the Church!

'Husband!' Her cry made him jump violently and the woman on his knee almost fell to the ground, recovering herself, spinning round to face her queen.

His queen.

The person on her husband's lap was a man and he was naked.

Bea opened her eyes with a start, reeling with shock and sat not daring to move, her heart thumping, completely disorientated. The room had grown dark and Emma was fast asleep, curled on her cushion. It was several minutes before Bea stood up and groped her way to the bookshelf, turning on the lamp. The room filled with a gentle ivory light as the music of the lute, a twenty-first century lute, played on. She checked her phone. The battery was very low. As she tiptoed towards the door she heard footsteps on the stairs. Mark must be home. She pulled the door open, meeting him on the landing and put her finger to her lips. 'Emma's here. She's asleep,' she whispered.

He nodded and turned away. 'Poor kid. She must be in a bad way after last night,' he said as she followed him into the kitchen.

'She is. And it's worse than that. She's been having nightmares and visions, which explains why she ran off the way she did. She sees, Mark. She's a natural. She has to be shown how to control it all or she'll be destroyed by it.'

'She sees?' He grimaced.

'Sees. The past; perhaps the future. She is a sensitive, Mark.'

He sighed. 'Are you sure? It sounds a bit improbable.'

'Why?

He hesitated. 'Her parents aren't exactly . . .'

He stopped, groping for a word.

'Wacky? Hippy?' Bea supplied it for him. 'Neither were mine. It's not hereditary, Mark. Look at our two. They have a vicar and a weirdo like me for parents and they both ended up normal!' She had, perhaps conveniently, forgotten about her grandmother.

'Sorry!' Mark raised his hands in surrender. 'I was I suppose a bit worried you were reading more into her . . .' He groped again. '. . . her teenage angst, than was actually there.'

Bea stared at him. 'No. I'm not,' she said shortly.

He gave an apologetic grimace. 'No. I'm sorry, darling. I should know better than to question you. You know what you're talking about. Can you cope?'

'I hope so. Yes, I'm sure I can, but first I wanted her to rest. I didn't realise it was so late. I told Simon I would drive her back to the cottage.'

He nodded gravely. 'Why not keep her here tonight? Then

at least we'll know she's safe. She can have Anna's room. I've got to go out briefly. The churchwarden at St Mary's last night told me they normally do a Tenebrae service on Maundy Thursday and he's asked me to take it for them. I have to run it past the bishop. He said I can pop round for half an hour now.' He checked his wristwatch. 'Can you cope with her on your own?'

'Of course I can. I should be used by now to you popping off to have sherry with the bishop.' She smiled.

'Who said anything about sherry?' And he was gone.

Bea texted Simon and then turned to the cooker. Like Kate, she believed food was a great healer, and above all else it was grounding.

'There are some other bits here and there in the margins.' Felix and Simon had picked up some fish and chips to take back to the cottage, then settled once more in front of the laptop. Felix had uploaded his new pictures. 'He hasn't rubbed it out. This is in Latin, even I can see that. And this . . .'

He slid off the chair to let his father sit down. 'They are records of legal agreements,' Simon said after a moment. 'I've seen that before in manuscripts. Almost notes about something they were going to deal with later. Such an odd thing to do when they were taking such care with writing up their chronicle.'

'Perhaps he meant to rub it out when he'd copied it up somewhere else.' Felix watched with interest as his father's mobile pinged and Simon reached for it to read the message.

'It's from Bea. She's going to keep Emma overnight and bring her back in the morning.'

Felix wandered away from the desk restlessly and then walked back, his hands shoved down in the pockets of his jeans. 'What do you make of Emma's freak-out, Dad?'

They hadn't really discussed it, even when they were seated in the kitchen, eating their supper. Simon sighed. 'To be honest I don't know what to think.'

'But you trust Bea?'

'Yes. I do.'

Felix nodded. He squatted down in front of the fire and

219

threw on another log. 'Bea knows what she's talking about, doesn't she?'

Simon nodded. Bea came over as genuine and knowledgeable. Some of the stuff she talked about was truly weird and would be laughed out of court by every rational person he knew, and yet obviously for her it was true and because of that she was taking Emma seriously. As he must. He remembered suddenly Bea's admission that she had been to Coedmawr, that she had dealt with a poltergeist there. He hadn't even queried the coincidence.

He swivelled in the chair to face his son. 'You said Em has told you before about the things she sees?' he asked.

Felix looked sheepish. He nodded. 'She tried once or twice, but to be honest' – he stopped, chewing his lip – 'well, to be honest, I took the mick.'

'You mocked her?' Simon remembered the word Bea had used. It seemed so apt now.

Felix looked away.

'Well, I might have done the same,' Simon conceded. 'If I hadn't seen what happened. Has she told Mum about all this?'

'No!' Felix was horrified. 'Mum wouldn't understand. You know she wouldn't, Dad. If she found out she would rush back here and force us to go back to London whether we wanted to or not. Then she would either forbid Em to talk about this and Em would internalise it, or she'd take her to see a shrink. Far better Em discusses it with someone who knows what she's talking about. Bea is not going to turn her into some kind of weird side show; she will help Em come to terms with whatever this is and deal with it.'

'You sound very certain.' Simon smiled at his son; he had seldom seen Felix look so intense.

Felix nodded. 'She can help Em. Em trusts her.'

The two sat in silence for a while, staring into the fire.

'Are you going to go on staying here, Dad, in spite of the ghosts. For the rest of the summer?' Felix's question came out of left field.

Simon stood up and walked over to the front door. He

opened it and looked out into the darkness. 'This is a good place to work. Perfect,' he said over his shoulder. 'Most of the time I can concentrate really well.' He gave a wistful smile.

'Until you were pestered by your children and a ghostly nun.'

'The children will be going back to school soon.'

'Oh great! You had to remind me!'

'And just as well. You don't seem to be doing any revision at all. How come?'

Felix grinned. 'If one learns a subject properly in the first place, there's no need to revise.'

'So you're going to get top marks in every subject?'

'Probably. Honestly, Dad. There's no point in going over everything. It's all in here.' Felix tapped his temple. 'After all, I knew all about the Reformation and Henry VIII destroying shrines when Em didn't. And she's doing history for A level.'

'Good point. I suppose.'

'The best. Let's forget about it. I'm cool.'

Simon shook his head in despair. 'OK.' He changed the subject hastily. 'Let's go out and look at the stars. They're amazing up here. So many! There is almost no sky left between them.'

He felt Felix behind him. 'Dark skies, they call them, don't they?' the boy said thoughtfully. 'And they are anything but. OK, Dad, so your children are going home soon, but what about the nun?'

Simon smiled. 'Ghosts can't hurt one, can they? I'll get used to her. I'm staying.'

Emma sat and watched while Bea chopped vegetables. When she had at last appeared downstairs, the girl had admitted to being very hungry. 'So, what you're saying is that I can switch this off when I want to.'

Bea nodded. 'I'm not saying it's easy. What you see is seductive, however horrible it is, and of course when you're swept into the story it's hard to keep one foot on the ground of your real life.' She was talking about herself, talking about something that had never happened to her before, not like this, not so insistently, but if the same thing was happening to Emma, then she had to find a way to help her. 'That's the bit you have to learn. But once you know it's possible to step back, you're halfway there.'

'Is this to do with reincarnation?'

'I don't think so. Not in this case. That feeling that you have been somewhere before, that you know the people you encounter, in real life or in your dreams perhaps, is a different thing. Here you are a witness rather than a participant.'

Was that true? Yes, even though Eadburh and Nesta could see her, she wasn't there, with them.

But she was, wasn't she? Eadburh had seen her and Nesta had drawn her in.

'Bea?' Emma was staring at her. 'What is it?'

'Sorry, I was thinking about something that happened to me recently.' Why not be honest with this girl? Think of her as an apprentice rather than a victim. But don't tell her everything. That would only terrify her more. 'I had seen something spontaneously, and I came out of it spontaneously. I wanted to know what happened next because it was relevant to a haunting I was dealing with, and that was when I used a touchstone. I picked it up from the site of the haunting; in this case it was literally a stone, and I formed the intention that I could only see the story when I had the thing in my hand. If the story gets too upsetting, I drop it.'

'And that wakes you up?'

'Yes.' She said it firmly.

It wasn't always true, of course. Surely Emma would see through the over-simplification.

'Hello, I'm back.'

Mark's voice in the hall saved her from the tangle of her own thoughts. 'So, how was the bishop?'

'Amenable. If they want the Tenebrae, he's fine with that. I'd better ring the churchwarden and tell him.'

'What's the Tenebrae?' Emma watched as Mark disappeared towards his study.

'A rather lovely late-night service. Part of the Easter story.

They are going to have it on Maundy Thursday – that's the Thursday before Easter Day. The church is candlelit, with no electric lights on, and they will blow out the candles one at a time until the church is completely dark, then someone will slam the door loudly. The sound symbolises the rock being rolled across the entrance to Jesus's tomb. It's very dramatic. Then they will meditate on Jesus's death.'

Emma grimaced. 'I don't go for that stuff. And' – she leaned forward on her elbows – 'I'm surprised you do. I suppose you have to, if you're married to a vicar.'

'I don't have to do anything because I'm married to a vicar,' Bea said gently. She brought out a loaf and the butter dish and began to lay the table. 'But obviously we talk about things. We have interesting discussions.'

'In our family, "interesting discussions" usually means blazing rows.' Emma folded her arms.

'That's sad.' Mark returned in time to hear her remark.

'I hate it. Mum is a bit fierce sometimes. She doesn't really like the same things as Dad. She wishes he had a proper job.'

'Our children had the same problem, I fear.' Mark smiled. 'It's not very cool, having a clergyman for a father. We're generally regarded as wimps.'

'But you're not a wimp.' Emma spoke with feeling.

Bea turned away to hide a smile. She gave the pan of soup on the stove a quick stir. 'Indeed he isn't,' she said.

'And you believe in ghosts. You must do,' Emma went on earnestly. 'Dad said you dealt with his ghost.'

'Not very effectively, sadly.' Mark sat down opposite her at the table. 'Strictly speaking, the Church doesn't believe in ghosts.'

'What about the Holy Ghost?' Emma knew that much at least.

He nodded. 'I'm always asked that, and the answer is complex. I'll tell you what we do believe in, and that is demons.'

'Really?' Her eyes widened.

Bea turned to glare at him. 'Mark, I think poor Emma has enough to deal with right now without an added layer of mystical obfuscation.' She searched for the soup bowls.

'What is a demon then?' Emma persisted. 'The actual definition.'

Mark threw Bea a quick apologetic look. 'From the Christian's point of view, it's a fallen angel who has chosen to serve Satan.'

'Is Dad's ghost a demon then?'

'No!' Mark responded sharply. 'I personally think she's a lost soul. If she returns, either Bea or I will speak to her and comfort her and send her on her way to God and thus give her, and your father, peace.'

'And can you teach me to do that?' Emma turned back to Bea.

'I can certainly give you some pointers,' Bea said guardedly. 'It takes a long time, Em, to learn all about this, and a lot of experience, but I will give you a list of books you can read and give you some starting points. Enough to deal with your own stuff, at least. It's like studying psychology. You have to analyse yourself before you can start on other people. Later, if you're still interested in taking this further, we can talk some more.'

As Bea began to dish up, Mark caught her eye. 'I think tonight we might have a quick blessing before we eat. To clear the air.'

'Because you think there are demons here?' Emma caught on at once. 'Round me?'

'Because it will give us peace.'

It was very late when they finally went to bed. Bea lay still a long time before she was sure that Mark was asleep, then she slid out of bed and, grabbing her dressing gown, she climbed up to her attic room. Mark had been right. There was something – someone – clinging to Emma and it had to be sorted without frightening the girl. It had gone for now, but she had seen the shadow, wound tightly around the girl's torso, covering her heart and her solar plexus. They had given her Anna's room next to their own and Mark had prayed for her outside the door after she had disappeared inside.

And now it was Bea's turn to pray. 'Please don't let it be Eadburh.' Her prayer was fervent. 'Or Cynefryth, Eadburh's mother.' Emma was obsessed with Ethelbert's murder, but she doubted if Cynefryth had ever been to Offa's Ridge, whereas Eadburh was still there, obsessed, yearning, unshriven and vengeful. Neither woman appeared to balk at killing anyone who got in their way; presumably neither would hesitate to possess an unguarded spirit now.

Bea could feel the residues all around her in the attic. She searched her jars of dried herbs for mugwort and vervain and added some dried rowan berries. With the protective herbs smoking in the small dish, she walked slowly round the room, blowing the smoke into each corner and murmuring a blessing, and suddenly she wondered if she would need Mark up here too. Whoever was here was evil and she – for it was a she – was powerful and she was a dealer in death.

And intuitively she knew for certain now. It was Eadburh.

She left the dish of burning herbs on the table and went out, making a sign of the cross on the door as she closed it to seal whatever it was inside. She was confident that it, she, could be contained and that Emma would be safe at least for now.

Mark was still asleep and she hadn't the heart to wake him. He was so tired even the gently drifting smoke from the burning herbs hadn't reached him. Bea tiptoed downstairs and silently she opened the back door.

Letting herself out, she went to stand by their little fountain, listening to the gentle trickle of the water. Contained within the high stone walls, the smell of spring flowers and grass was all around her. She let it seep into her bones, comforting, gentle. This garden, she was sure, in the shadow of the cathedral as it was, had been used before as a place for prayer and her prayer would be heard. 'Please, help me to be strong enough to deal with this and please help me to keep Emma safe.' She almost expected to see her chantry priest out here, praying in the dark, but if he was here she couldn't see him. It was a long time before, shivering, she went back indoors, bolted the back door and climbed the stairs then crawled into bed.

In his sleep, Mark shifted and groaned as she brought the chill of the garden with her under the duvet.

Hilde knelt before the priest on the cold floor of the stone church in the valley and confessed to him and through him to God that she had killed a man. The penance was harsh. She was ordered to give up the rest of her life to God and to serve for the rest of her days here in this small community as a sister under the rule of the abbess. She bowed her head and accepted the judgement without complaint, and when she asked that Eadburh's letter be delivered to King Cadell by someone else, gave it trustingly into the hands of the priest. The small packet in her hem she took out into the gardens at dead of night and buried deep in the ground. The priest took the letter and gave it to the abbess. She threw it on the fire in the kitchen without reading it. It was never mentioned again.

'I must warn her.' In her sleep, Bea stirred anxiously. Eadburh would never know that her letter was lost. She was still there in Wessex, alone in so many ways, immersed in her own misery and fury and disgust at what she had seen, and she was holding on to that one slender thread. That Hilde would return with the news that Elisedd's death had been avenged. And now that would never happen. Bea, and Bea alone, knew it. Unless Nesta— Before the question was fully formed, Bea had slipped once more back into her dreams.

Eadburh had fled from the king's chamber, through the mead hall, across the courtyard and into the queen's bower and threw herself full length upon her bed, wracked with angry sobs. Her women clustered round anxiously and like fire through dried summer grass the word spread of what had happened. They had known, the women had all known, of the king's preferences. They could not believe that the queen did not know too. But no one had told her.

Slowly Bea crept towards the bed. Without knowing why they did it, the women moved aside to let her pass and without seeing her, closed ranks again behind her. She was there now, standing beside the sobbing queen, looking down at the disordered coverlets, the woven blankets, the sheet torn to shreds between the queen's clutching fingers. And as she watched,

Bea saw the first stains of blood seeping from beneath the woman's hips.

The queen's attendants noticed at last as her first cramps began and sent for Nesta. The herb-wife immediately sent servants scurrying to boil water for tisanes, to remove the queen's gown and change the sheets, and did her best to soothe the distraught woman. And all the time the women scurrying to and fro across the room and around the queen's bed avoided the space where Bea stood, frozen with horror, watching. Only when Nesta glanced her way did Bea realise that the woman knew she was there.

At dawn when it was clear that nothing could be done to save the baby, the midwife came. Issuing reassurances that there would soon be another to replace it, she delivered the child, a tiny boy. He never breathed.

Eadburh slept at last and Bea still stood by the bed, looking down at her exhausted, pale face, at peace for now, as one by one the women crept away to their own beds. At last only Nesta remained. 'So, you are full of pity now for the woman who orchestrated the murder of her mother's lover.'

Bea put her hand up to the cross around her neck. 'I suppose she believed it was justice,' she whispered. 'He was a murderer.'

Nesta inclined her head. 'Then so am I. We were both obeying the orders of a queen.'

'Will she recover from this?' Bea looked back at the sleeping woman.

Nesta stepped away from the bed. 'The answer to that is written in the annals of time.' Her voice had grown distant. 'She will not see the king again for many months. As his son was being born I am told Beorhtric rode out with his war band, heading for the coast where once more heathen warships with their dragon prows are sailing down the Channel. He did not ask about his wife and does not know that she has miscarried. When he is told, I expect he will be sad. A man needs a son.'

The shadows were closing round the bed. Nesta stooped and pulled the bedcover straight then she turned away. Bea stared after her, but the scene was dissolving into cold white mist as the palace shrugged back into an icy dawn.

Bea stirred uncomfortably, pulling the duvet round her, and again Mark groaned. Outside in the garden wisps of mist were drifting through the branches of the mulberry tree by the wall as the first streaks of dawn appeared in the eastern sky.

'Bea? Bea, didn't you hear the alarm? It's time to get up.' Mark put a mug of tea down beside the bed. He was fully dressed. 'I'm off to morning prayer. I'll be back for breakfast.'

Confused and befuddled with sleep, it took Bea a moment to remember they had a guest. 'Any sign of Emma?'

'I imagine she's still asleep. It's early yet.'

And then he was gone, closing the door softly behind him.

It was Emma's turn to dream.

Eadburh was inside her head and the woman, in a haze of pain and delirium, was dreaming in turn that she was a girl again at Sutton in her father's hall. The evening was in full swing, with music and dancing and drink as she snatched up a cloak to cover her finery, evaded her father's guards and rode out alone across the meadows and through the woods towards the west. Drawing rein at last, she paused, staring into the distance, waiting. He was there, she knew he was there somewhere. Urging the tired horse onwards she set off up the winding track towards the summit of the ridge where the prince was waiting for her, his handsome profile catching the rays of the rising sun, the planes of his face accentuated, half in shadow as he turned towards her and held out his arms.

Emma smiled and stretched out willingly towards him, welcoming him into her arms, smelling the scent of sweat and horse and heather on him as he kissed her, feeling his strong hands pulling at her gown, losing herself in the strength and heat of his body.

Bea was making some toast for breakfast when Emma appeared downstairs at last. She sat down at the table and reached for the coffee pot. The girl looked rested. Perhaps a little flushed.

'How are you feeling?' Bea put butter and marmalade on the table in front of her.

'Tired.' Emma blushed scarlet. 'I dreamed about a man and a woman. There were horses and we, they, were up on the top of a hill and it was sunrise.' Her voice faded. Bea turned away to rescue the toast and put it in the rack. She took her time turning back and by the time she did, Emma had recovered. 'It was all very vivid and real.'

Bea smiled. 'He made love to her?'

She had noted the hasty change of pronoun. She had been there too. At the start of her dreams, she had seen Elisedd and Eadburh and the tenderness and passion between them as they made love, but this was different. She bit her lip, worried, trying to see if the dark shadow was still there clinging to Emma, but she could see nothing.

Emma nodded. 'It was me. He made love to me. In my dream.' She darted a quick embarrassed glance at Bea and giggled. 'What am I like!'

Bea hid her anxiety. 'Like a teenage girl. There's nothing to be embarrassed about. All I can say is, lucky you.' She topped up her own coffee mug and gave Emma few seconds to compose herself.

Emma was about to speak when her phone pinged. 'It's Dad. He's coming to collect me later.'

23

As she handed leaflets about the cathedral to a group of visiting tourists, Sandra saw Bea walking through the nave with the girl from yesterday. She had her arm around the girl's shoulders and as Sandra watched she guided her out of sight towards the north aisle. They were going to the chantry chapel.

Another group of visitors were heading her way. Sandra turned away from them, pulling her identity tag over her head and slipping it into her pocket, then she hurried after Bea and the girl. Close to the chapel entrance she slowed up, checking behind her to make sure there was no one in sight. She tiptoed close to the doorway and peered in. They were sitting in the shadows and Bea still had her arm around the girl's shoulders. Sandra took a step closer.

'Can you see him, there by the altar?' Bea said quietly. 'He was a chantry priest here when the chapel was first built. He is my mentor.'

Sandra crept closer. She could hear footsteps approaching; a couple were walking towards her from the transept, heading for the nearby exquisitely carved alabaster monument to Bishop Stanbury, with cameras slung round their necks. She moved slightly to block the entrance to the chapel and when she saw them frown, groped in her pocket for her lanyard and name tag. It obviously gave her a semblance of authority because they immediately veered away, walking on towards the Lady Chapel. Turning back, Sandra was in time to hear Bea's voice, quiet but clearly audible: 'Please tell us what to do, Father. I should have listened to you, but I'm involved now and Emma needs you.'

Sandra froze. She could actually feel the hairs on the back of her neck moving. Almost too scared to look, she scanned the tiny chapel to see who Bea was talking to. There were only the four chairs in there in front of the prayer desk. The floor was covered in matting, the altar bare. No cross. No candles. There was no one else there. Emma had her eyes tightly shut and Sandra could see the girl's hands shaking as she clasped them on her knee.

Bea was quiet now. Her eyes were open, fixed on the altar – slightly to the left of the altar – which was bathed in coloured light filtering through the stained-glass windows. She nodded, as if she was listening, then Emma's eyes flew open. 'No!' she cried loudly. 'I won't do that!'

'Em, darling. If he thinks it best—'

'No! Never! Dad will be here by now. I want to go and find him. Take me out of this horrible place!' Emma jumped to her feet and Sandra turned away hastily. She hurried down the aisle and round the corner into the transept as the girl appeared in the doorway.

Bea and Emma had headed for the café and Sandra followed at a discreet distance. Simon was indeed there, sitting at a table in the far corner. Seeing him, Emma broke into a run and threw herself down opposite him. She looked distraught. Bea followed more slowly and slipped into the seat next to her. 'Give us a moment to calm down,' she said. She sounded completely in control.

Sandra turned to the counter and ordered herself a cup of tea, then, cup in hand, she walked quietly to the table behind them and sat down. She was just within earshot and no one at the table noticed her; Bea had her back to her and in any case the two adults were concentrating on Emma.

'It was creepy. This old man was sitting there, as real as you or me, and he looked at me and he had such a kind face.' Tears spilled over and ran down Emma's face. 'But what he said—'

'What he said was that there was a demon clinging to her and that Emma must pray and that Our Lady and all the angels would keep her safe.' Bea's words, though very quiet, were clearly audible.

'A demon?' Simon echoed the word out loud, and several people turned to look. Bea glanced over her shoulder nervously and to her horror saw Sandra sitting only feet away from her.

Sandra smiled. 'Tea break,' she said weakly.

Bea stood up. 'Simon, I think we should leave. We need to talk. In private.'

Sandra watched as the three of them walked out of the door. She didn't follow. She was too shocked.

Mark was sitting in the snug, deep in thought, when Bea got home. 'Darling, can we have a chat?'

She threw herself down onto the sofa. 'I'm exhausted. But I think we're through the worst with Emma.' She sat forward again and looked at him, worried by his expression. 'What's wrong?'

'Sandra went to the dean.'

Bea felt herself grow cold. 'She was there this morning, in the café. She was listening.'

Mark gave a slow nod. 'He said she's been watching you, following you. For your own good, naturally, and she felt she could no longer keep quiet. Also for your own good. And mine.'

'And what could she not keep quiet about?'

'I think you know.'

'No, I don't! What business is it of hers where I go and what I do? Or of the dean, for that matter. She has never seen me at work. She has never seen me gazing into crystal balls or invoking the spirits of the dead, or whatever it is she thinks I do! And what your wife does as a hobby or as a job is absolutely her own affair and nothing to do with the cathedral!' She stood up, furious. 'That bloody woman!'

'She saw the article in the paper.'

There was a long moment of horrified silence. 'But that was months ago,' Bea said at last.

'Apparently she has a file of cuttings.' Mark sighed. 'She showed the dean. And she told him she saw you conjuring spirits.'

Bea opened her mouth to retort, then she subsided back onto the sofa again. 'She was there, outside the chantry?'

A look of genuine pain crossed her husband's face. 'I don't know where all this happened exactly. What did you do in the chantry?'

'The old priest is there sometimes. I don't conjure him!' she almost spat out the word. 'He sits by the altar and he prays for the souls of the dead, as he was charged to do hundreds of years ago. I go there sometimes to pray quietly on my own and sometimes he's there and sometimes he isn't.'

'And Sandra saw him?'

'I've no idea what she thinks she saw.'

'You took Emma there.'

'You know I did! It was a quiet place for her to pray for the soul of the murdered king. Oh, come on, Mark. This is what the church is for! Sandra is so busy and bossy with her self-importance and her tourists, she's forgotten that people come here to pray!'

He sighed. 'The dean is no fool. He recognises that she's obviously got some kind of an agenda with you, and yes, he knows it's the cathedral's policy to allow partners their own life completely outside the place if they so choose, but he has warned me to ask you to be discreet. You know what a lovely man he is, but he said that she had the light of zeal in her eyes. He has told her he expects her discretion in anything that worries her and that, if anything does, she is to go to him or someone in the deliverance team. And, Bea, you and I know that she will. She will be on the lookout every second to try and catch you out.'

'So, you're telling me I can't go and pray in the chapel any more.'

'I wouldn't dream of it. I'm only saying be careful. And

perhaps choose somewhere less public for your meetings with Simon and his family. The café in the middle of the cathedral is not the place to discuss demonic possession.'

'I would have thought it was absolutely the place!'

'Bea, please.'

'Sorry.' Her anger subsided as she saw the utter weariness in his face. 'I'm putting you in an intolerable position, aren't I?'

'Nothing about my wife is ever intolerable. Tricky, perhaps.'

'I will avoid her. I promise.'

'I think you may find that very hard, given that we live on the premises.' He levered himself to his feet. 'Darling, do you think it's possible you are too invested in this family? Especially in Emma. I know how much you miss Anna and Petra, do you think you are perhaps becoming a little bit over-protective?'

'How can it be over-protective to want to help her?' Bea stared at him, aghast. 'If Meryn was here, I would send her to him, but he isn't. I'm the only one there for her.'

She stood up and walked over to the window and stood staring out. 'Yes, I miss Petra and Anna, you know I do, but neither of them have inherited this ability so it was something we didn't have to deal with. Perhaps it's more that I can see myself in her, Mark. I remember what it feels like to have all these frightening experiences and know that other people don't understand what's happening. I was lucky. My grandmother was there for me, but Emma has no one. Simon can't cope with her, and it doesn't sound as if her mother would be sympathetic.'

'Was she all right when they went home?' Mark asked after a pause.

'Yes, she'd recovered her composure. She was excited if anything. Couldn't wait to tell Simon and Felix what happened.'

'And will you be seeing her again?'

'Of course. If that's what she wants.'

Mark came over and put his arm around her shoulders. He sighed. 'Can we talk about this some more later? I've got to go out again. I've got to do some parish visiting.'

'Plans for Tenebrae?'

'Exactly.'

'I bet Sandra wouldn't approve of that. Candles and ritual and darkness and meditation. All very suspect activities.'

'Well, luckily it's not her parish.' He bent and kissed her on the top of her head.

She stood there without moving for a long time after he had gone. He was right. It was strange that she and Emma seemed to share this ability, but the link was so much stronger than Mark could ever understand. Emma had dreamt Eadburh's dream. The clinging shadow had attached itself to the girl who reminded her of her earlier self and was using her to remember Elisedd and somehow re-enact the intensity of their lost love.

A beam of sunlight strayed through the window, crept across the rug near her feet, then disappeared. From outside she heard the bronze note of the cathedral clock chime the hour.

It was at night that Eadburh thought about her lost baby. The ache of emptiness, the longing for the little boy who had never drawn breath, brought tears in the darkness, but in her dreams he was confused with another child, the son of her long-lost prince. She had convinced herself that it too had been a boy, a boy who would have loved her had Cynefryth not killed him.

Nesta had concocted the potions that had destroyed him, but she did not blame the woman. The sisters of Wyrd had killed both children, as they had caused her to miscarry two other children by her husband. All that was left to her now was her little girl, Eathswith, the little girl she knew she could never fully love because she looked at her mother with Beorhtric's eyes.

No one at court mentioned what Eadburh had seen. Now that Hilde had gone, there was no one but Nesta in whom she felt she could confide, and Nesta had set off on one of her plant-collecting trips into the forest. As always, Eadburh wondered how many people had known, had kept her husband's secret, had laughed behind their hands at her confidence.

When her husband returned to the palace with his warrior

band, life went on as before, but now she watched him and she realised that he had always had favourites. Her father had enjoyed women; her mother seemed to accept it and dismiss them as a part of life, like flies to be swatted away if they grew too persistent, though belatedly she realised that her mother's way of dealing with the situation was to take lovers herself. If Offa knew or suspected what was going on, he would, she was fairly sure, have been reluctant to cross his wife. Cynefryth was the strongest personality in the court. Eadburh gave a grim smile as she sat spinning by the fire, listening to a *scop* who had ridden into Corfe from far-off Canterbury. Lovers were one thing; lovers prepared to murder the man promised to her sister could not be tolerated. She wondered if her mother guessed what had really happened to Grimbert. If she did, would she ever suspect who had done it and from whom that person had learnt her skills? She doubted it very much.

If Beorhtric had ever had mistresses, she did not care. She had assumed he had, to assuage his lust while she was absent from his bed, but matters had changed. This was different. These favourites she was not prepared to tolerate. She watched and waited.

He came back to her side at last when he returned to the court with his war band, and the shocking news he brought with him put all other matters out of her head. Her eldest sister's husband, the King of Northumbria, had been murdered by a group of his own nobles.

'And Ethelfled?' she cried. 'My sister? What of her?'

Beorhtric gave a shrug. 'I was given no news of her.'

Eadburh stamped her foot. 'You must send to ask my father! I have to know if she still lives.'

'We will hear in good time,' Beorhtric said with a sigh. Nevertheless, he sent messengers into Mercia to consult Offa and another to ride north and seek out news of the Queen of Northumbria.

The royal court was at Winchester again, the great wooden hall with its soaring beams and carved dragons rearing to meet one another over the doorway, built in the ruins of the Roman city. The Wessex people did not like the ruins; they lived in fear of ghosts. But the place was a centre with a great stone-built minster and it was here that Beorhtric had chosen to spend the summer. When no word came from the north, Eadburh commanded her own scribe to write to her sister and sent copies of the letter by two separate messengers and, while she waited for news, Eadburh spent her time hunting in the forest, flying her hawks and wondering, ever wondering, why she had not heard from Hilde. Beorhtric had not once mentioned his wife's lost baby, nor did he come to her bed. She was left in peace to worry about her sister's fate and to dream her dreams of lost love.

Bea followed her as she wandered in the gardens and the orchards; she saw her ride away on her milk-white mare and she watched as she dismounted and handed the animal to a groom. Bea walked slowly after her through the trees, somehow drifting in her wake on silent feet.

'Why do you still follow me?'

Bea shrank back as Eadburh swung round, her eyes blazing. Bea had not seen her so close before. Her face was hard, framed in her headrail, strings of garnets set in gold hanging from the brooches that held her gown in place on her shoulders, her fists clenched. The woman was near enough for her to feel the heat coming off her body, to smell the musky scent of amber on her skin and to see her reach for the small knife that hung at her belt and pull it from its leather sheath. Her gown was soft, light, crimson silk. Bea stepped back, reaching with one hand for her cross and with the other instinctively warding the woman off, pushing her away, but her fingers brushed through air without contacting anything solid. Her heart was thudding with fright. The woman's body shimmered and faded as if it was a mirage.

At that moment someone else appeared. A man, solid-looking and heavily built, with a leather jerkin. Bea could smell his sweat as he approached and bowed to the shadowy figure, his heavy features tense. 'Come quickly, oh queen,' he called. 'The king has royal messengers with him in the hall. The king your father is dead.'

The word reverberated through the distances. 'Dead! Dead, dead . . .'

Bea heard Eadburh repeat the word as she turned to run after him. As she disappeared from sight, the scene faded into wisps of smoke and darkness closed in.

Bea clutched at a cushion and hugged it tightly, burying her face in it. The room was dark but faint light leaked through the door from the kitchen. There was no one there. She was in the quiet snug with its comfy sofa and the two old armchairs that had belonged to her father, the pictures and the coffee table, all were familiar and reassuring. Her gaze went to the picture of Jesus surrounded by children. Her husband was a clergyman, she had to expect some signs of his calling in the room and it was a beautiful oil painting they had found in a trawl through one of the antique shops in Leominster. Over the fireplace there was a large mirror. A house-warming gift from Mark's uncle. Climbing to her feet, she went over and stared at herself. How on earth did she appear to Eadburh? She was dressed in navy linen trousers with a loose turquoise sweater, decorated with a string of lapis beads, her cross tucked out of sight below the neckline. Her hair was tousled. She gave a weak smile at the word, but it was the perfect word. Tousled. She saw her face lighten as she smiled, the pain and fright lifting a little. She had not wanted that vision; she had had no touchstone at hand to take her into the past. It was a dream, a genuine dream. She had drifted off to sleep as the room grew dark, and that was dangerous. She could not let this happen again. She walked over to the window that looked out to the side of the house with its narrow strip of garden, aware suddenly that anyone out there in the dark could be looking in. She reached up to draw the curtains. Sitting down again she reached for a book and leaned back against the cushions. Somehow she had to distract herself.

Within seconds the book had slipped from her hand and she was asleep once more.

24

'I will attend the meeting with your ealdormen and thanes as usual.' Eadburh stood up as the men made to withdraw to the council chamber. She saw them glance at one another uneasily but no one argued, least of all Beorhtric himself.

It was as if, with her father gone and her brother now on the throne of Mercia, Eadburh felt the need to re-emphasise her position of power as queen. Her health restored, she had taken her place once more at her husband's side, dictating letters, signing charters, giving orders. She knew she was more deeply resented than ever for her failure to carry a son to term and she didn't care. She was queen and she would make sure that every man and woman in the country knew it. Her encounter with her husband's lover was never mentioned, but she knew him. He was one of the handsome young attendants who flocked to attend the king. Beorhtric lavished gifts on them, gave them jewellery and rich clothes, and sat with them often in the hall in the evenings, to hear the latest music and the poetry and laugh immoderately at the bawdy jokes and antics of the tumblers, and above all to get drunk.

She watched and she waited. She noticed now how Beorhtric could not keep his hands off the young men, how he slapped their backs, and how he embraced and slobbered over some of them. The disapproving glances of the priests, should any be present in the hall, did not escape her, and she saw the way one or two of them turned in her direction as if to see whether she condoned her husband's behaviour.

Her women sat around her, some openly enjoying the entertainment, some turning aside to occupy themselves with their spindles or their embroidery. She knew how much they still disliked her. She missed Hilde so much. She had sent several messengers to enquire after her and scour western Mercia and even the easternmost parts of Powys, but they returned with no news other than that Hilde had left Offa's court some weeks after arriving there. Anyone who knew or cared presumed she had returned to Wessex. They also brought news that Cynefryth had retired from her son's court to take up position as abbess at Cookham, one of the abbeys in her own gift, from where she would have oversight of the church in Bedford where Offa was buried. Eadburh's brother now ruled unopposed, but, one of the messengers said, it was thought he was ill. He had not appeared in the hall while the messenger was there. There was no word either of Ethelfled's fate, nor of Alfrida far away in the kingdom of East Anglia. She didn't care. There was no more she could do and she had no love for her mother or her brother. She had no love left in her heart for anyone save her handsome Welsh prince, ever bright in her memory. She thought of him every day, she dreamt about him, she ached for him in every bone of her body and, in her dreams, he was still alive.

And her daughter? She saw the little girl every day and she tried to care about her, but the small face looked back at her with indifference. The child loved her nurses and her playmates and shrank from Eadburh when she took her on her knee, perhaps sensing the coldness there, a coldness that was emphasised when Eadburh saw in the child's eyes and features a mirror image of her father.

Her dreams of Elisedd slowly became more and more real to her. When she woke in her empty bed she could feel his arms around her, hear his voice, smell the wild heather sweetness of his hair across her face, and in her dreams she was young again, young and free and happy, with a strong healthy body, unweakened by childbirth and sorrow. Surely he could not be dead, not when his spirit came to her so often and so passionately.

There was still no word from Hilde. Perhaps she was dead. She felt a flash of anger that the woman had failed in the second, so important, part of her mission and suddenly she knew what she must do. She summoned her husband's most trusted messenger, a man known for his discretion. 'You will go to King Cadell of Powys, saying I wish to set up diplomatic talks between him and my brother and my husband. As a start, I wish to find out what happened to his son, the Prince Elisedd who headed the delegation to my father some eight years ago.' Eight years. Was it so long since she had seen him, felt him touch her, felt the warmth of his body, his lips on hers? 'This matter is of the utmost delicacy and secrecy. There are to be no letters, only your private talk with King Cadell himself, and you will bring his response back to me in person and to me alone. These are the king's orders.' That last was an afterthought. 'No word must escape. I and I alone will take your reply direct to the king.'

She paused, her mind shying away, as it always did, from the memory of her father's words. *You should know. The King of Powys's son, Elisedd. He met with an accident and died.*

But in her dreams, Elisedd wasn't dead.

The substance of her dreams became more real every day. Supposing her father had lied and Elisedd was trying in her dreams to tell her so. If he had been murdered, there would have been war. No king would allow his son to be killed without redress.

As the man bowed and left the queen's bower she looked over her shoulder into the body of the chamber. Was she there, the woman who watched her from the shadows? The woman who spied on her, heard her words, perhaps witnessed her very dreams. The woman who might betray her. Before all else, she had to be disposed of.

'I need spells to rid me of a demon.' Nesta, back from her

plant-collecting in the forest, was sitting with her outside in the autumn sunlight. 'She haunts me day and night.'

Nesta looked up, her fingers busy with some careful stitching. She had established herb gardens in four of the royal palaces now, at Cheddar, at Corfe, at Wareham and at Winchester. At Eadburh's command, the woman reluctantly followed her each time the court moved across the kingdom, bringing with her boxes and bottles and pots and carefully wrapped seedlings. Everywhere she went she collected herbs and recipes for medicines, talking to the local wise women, scouring the hills and the heaths, the forests and fields for different ingredients, always learning, always consulting the ancient gods and the leechbooks and the books of the apothecaries and the monks, always listening to her own instincts and above all to the plants themselves. Her eyes darted towards the queen and then away again. Eadburh had grown harder and more bitter as the months progressed since her latest miscarriage. Nesta had hoped this child would go to term – there was every sign that all was well – but then it happened, the result of shock and fury had torn the child's frail life force asunder. She could guess the effect on Eadburh of walking in on her husband and his latest friend. She must have known this was his way, but even so, whatever had happened in the king's chamber had unseated not just the child, but Eadburh's mind.

'Well?' Eadburh's voice would brook no argument.

Nesta had seen the woman who followed the queen. She had invited her into their lives. She could not pretend she did not know to whom the queen was referring.

'Where does she come from? What is she?'

Nesta put down her stitching and stood up. 'She does not mean you harm.'

'So, you can see her?'

'I have watched over you for a long time, lady, and if I thought her a danger, I would have warned you. She is part of the strange pattern of Wyrd. She is a restless soul, come from another time.'

'I want her gone. She is a spy.'

'She only wants—'

'I don't care what she wants! I want her gone. You will banish her. You will bind her with charms and you will send her to the deepest vaults of Hell.'

'And you do not think to ask the bishop to perform such a ceremony for you?'

'No. I am asking you.' Eadburh froze. 'Is she here now? I can't always see her, but I feel her gaze on me.'

Nesta nodded. 'She is here.'

Bea felt herself gripped with panic. There was a buzzing in her ears. 'Wake up!' she muttered. 'Wake up, wake up, wake up! This is a dream. I am not there. I am here. At home. I do not want this!' She squeezed her eyes shut in her dream then opened them again. She was still there, hovering near the beech hedge in a sunny garden, half hidden from the two women, but still close enough to hear them talking.

'Make her go away!' Eadburh's voice had risen hysterically.

Nesta dropped her stitching into the basket at her feet and stepped towards the hedge.

'No, no, no!' Bea tried to retreat. She couldn't move. Nesta took several steps towards her and raised her hand and Bea felt the power from it like a bolt of electricity. She was paralysed. She couldn't breathe.

Bea woke with a start, her heart pounding, no longer in the sunny garden but back at home in the dark snug in the quiet Cathedral Close.

Staggering to her feet, she turned on the table lamp and glanced up at the picture of Jesus. He was looking particularly serene. 'I'm going to need your help with this one,' she whispered.

25

In the cottage on Offa's Ridge, Emma woke suddenly and lay staring up towards the darkened ceiling. Her heart was beating hard and her face was wet with tears. She listened, expecting to hear her father or Felix snoring, but there was nothing, only an almost tangible silence as though somewhere someone else was listening as intently as she was.

Their mother had rung last night, and it had been agreed that, instead of going back to London just before Easter, they could, if they both promised to revise hard, spend the rest of the holidays up here with their dad. Val would pick them up a couple of days before they were due back at school. Her alacrity at getting rid of them for a few more days had been laughable really, but her poor mother didn't have much of a life. Emma's thoughts strayed to her parents' relationship. Dad was either at home but working all hours of day and night and completely abstracted, or away doing research in some remote library or other, or on one of these writing breaks, while her mother was neither one thing nor the other. She couldn't go off and forge a new life for herself, but she couldn't really be happy with such a fogey either. Their marriage was rubbish really, Emma conceded to herself.

Why were they still together? She pondered this for a while. She had always assumed they loved each other and presumably at some level they still did. She would have to discuss it with Felix. Not that he would be any use. He never saw anything unless it was pointed out to him, preferably on a screen.

She sat up, her arms wrapped round her knees. This holiday had certainly been different. They had both been dreading it, wondering if they could possibly get out of it, but their mother had insisted. They would get some fresh air, she had pointed out. Well, they were getting that all right. She shivered as a draught stirred the curtains in the little bedroom. What with an ancient manuscript in a lost manor house, secret ciphers hidden in vellum pages, ghosts and people who actually lived in a cathedral, this was up there with the adventure stories she used to love so much when she was a child. And on top of that she had found someone who could help her with her night terrors and her weird visions. She hadn't mentioned it to Bea, but she had once tried to explain to their family doctor what happened. The man had heard her out, but then he had said that he would have to refer her to a child psychiatrist who might want to do tests to see if she had some form of epilepsy. She had backed off immediately, telling him she'd made it all up. It was obvious from his expression that she'd just confirmed what he'd thought all along. She had made him promise not to say anything to her mother – and reminded him about patient confidentiality, but she wasn't convinced he took any notice. She was probably in his eyes a child with an over-active imagination and no rights at all.

Tomorrow – no, today: she reached for her phone and found it was 2.33 a.m. – she would be meeting Bea again. They'd arranged to hook up at a coffee shop near the cathedral; not the one haunted by that dreadful spying woman, but one somewhere out in the town. Then Dad and Felix would head off to do their own blokey thing for the rest of the day while she and Bea returned to Marden Church. She shivered again. She was the one who had insisted that they go back, but now, in the darkness of her bedroom, she wasn't at all sure she wanted a second chance to meet St Ethelbert, king and martyr.

She was tempted to get up and go downstairs. Her mother often walked about the house in the middle of the night and she always said a 'nice cup of tea' would relax her and send her back to bed sleepy. That sounded illogical to Emma – everyone knew that tea was a stimulant and full of caffeine, but there you are. Her gaze drifted towards the door. She could make some tea then take it outside to sit on the terrace looking up at those amazing stars, and have a ciggy. Felix, snoring on his camp bed, would never wake up and it would be beautiful out there.

But the voice was out there.

She lay back on her pillow and pulled the duvet up to her chin. Perhaps she would try and go back to sleep instead. After all, there were plenty of nights left now before they had to go home. She began to count. Before she had reached number five she was asleep. And the dream returned.

The dean would want her to be certain. Sandra studied the rota with care. It was fortuitous that she had a couple of days off now, before Easter week when the cathedral would be busy, as it meant she could turn her attention fully to the problem of Beatrice Dalloway. She had seldom taken such an instinctive dislike to anyone or felt such an overwhelming suspicion, but she was after all, uniquely qualified to deal with the delusions of a ghost hunter and she was beginning to feel sure that she had been sent by God to investigate the situation and rescue the dear canon from his wife and her accomplices. In the unlikely event it turned out she was wrong, then she would quietly back off and leave Bea alone.

It had been complete luck that she had seen Bea that morning, emerging from the alleyway in Church Street. And there she was, yet again joining the Armstrong family in a coffee shop. Not the cathedral café, she noted. Presumably she had decided that was too public a place to discuss her nefarious deeds. Sandra didn't dare go in after them. Somehow she had to hang around long enough to follow them and see where they were going.

They were there for only about twenty minutes, then all four emerged into the narrow street and stood talking. Sandra moved closer. The narrow pedestrianised area was crowded. It was easy to blend in, and there were lots of little shops with interesting windows where she could hover amongst the crowds.

A group of students jostled past, enabling Sandra to move close enough to hear Bea's next words: '. . . we'll start at Marden, then we'll probably come back here. We'll see how it goes. Don't worry. I'll drop her back this afternoon.' Then Bea and the girl set off in the direction of the cathedral while Simon and his son headed towards High Town. For a moment Sandra was left standing there. If either couple had looked back, they would have seen her, but they didn't. She was smiling. So, they were still on the track of the martyr king. Turning away herself, she set off to collect her car.

Sandra pulled her car off onto the grass at the edge of the road and climbed out. She set off along the lane, passing empty barns and stock pens, on past the old vicarage and through weathered wrought-iron gates into the churchyard. The area immediately around the church was tarmacked, with newly mown grass bordering the graveyard itself. There was nowhere to hide. Although she hadn't seen any other vehicles in the vicinity, she took the precaution of climbing the bank on the edge of the path until she was among the ancient graves, where clumps of trees gave her shelter and she could creep nearer to the church. There was a car there, round the back, parked facing the river. Cautiously she moved closer. The car was empty and she realised she didn't know what kind of car Beatrice drove, but there was a good chance this was it. As anxious as she was to get inside the church, she could see no way of reaching the door without crossing the open expanse of the car park. She crouched there for several minutes, waiting and watching. The door was shut and all was silent. Taking a deep breath, she launched herself at last out of the bushes and across the tarmac at a run, opening the outer door as quietly as she could, then slipping silently inside the porch. She paused there in the darkness to get her breath back. There was an inner door and that too was shut. She listened, her ear pressed against the wood, then very gently she began to push it open.

26

Emma and Bea had walked slowly round the church before making their way into St Ethelbert's Room at the back and switching on the light. Bea felt Emma reaching for her hand and she grasped it reassuringly. She could feel nothing in this bleak, empty room. There was no sense that St Ethelbert, or anyone else, had left a shadow here. 'There is supposed to have been a ray of blinding light coming up from where he fell,' Emma whispered. 'I looked it up on the internet. And then the spring sprang from the ground.' She reached out to the pile of colourful leaflets someone had left on top of the wooden well cover. 'There he is.' She pointed at the picture. 'He's got very fetching boots.' She gave a small giggle.

'It's sad they don't make more of this place,' Bea said thoughtfully. 'I believe they do an annual pilgrimage from here to the cathedral, but it would be nice if there was some-thing for the pilgrims who come at other times. Perhaps we've caught it on a bad day, but a few flowers and perhaps a candle might be nice.' She paused for a few seconds, allowing the silence of the room to surround them. Outside in the church they heard a squeak from the door hinge.

'Someone else is coming,' Emma whispered.

'That's fine. We needn't talk to anyone if you don't want to.' Bea sighed. 'Do you sense there is anything actually in here, Emma?'

The girl shook her head.

'Where did you see your ghost?'

'Just outside this door. In the back of the church.'

'Shall we go and see?'

Emma nodded. They turned off the light and went back into the nave. There was no sign of anyone else there. Emma slipped into the back pew. 'It was here,' she whispered.

'Close your eyes and allow yourself to listen and feel,' Bea said. 'Wait quietly and see what happens. Don't be afraid. I'm here, right beside you.'

'Nothing.' It was a full five minutes later. 'Just a sort of warm feeling as if someone had put the heating on.'

Bea smiled. 'I surrounded us with light. A protective bubble. And I prayed.'

'And that made me feel warm?'

'And safe, hopefully.'

But they weren't safe. Not entirely. She could feel something there, an uneasy restlessness that was not there when they first came in, a sense that someone was there with them, listening. Emma had closed her eyes again, a small half smile on her face; Bea took the opportunity to look round slowly, scanning the pews, the corners behind them. At first the church seemed empty but there were places people could hide. The kitchen area, the stairs up to the gallery, the gallery itself, the columns, even the pulpit. Her eyes went back to the pulpit. Was that something on the steps? A piece of fabric with a buckle trailing from behind the stone? A raincoat belt?

She narrowed her eyes.

'Come on,' she whispered. 'Let's go and sit outside for a bit. It's chilly in here.'

There was a bench outside, looking out towards the river, and they sat there, side by side, near the door out of the wind. 'I didn't feel the king was there,' Bea said, 'but it may be that there is a thought form in the church. It would be strange if there wasn't when so many people have been thinking about him there for over a thousand years.' What she had sensed had not been a thought form, it had been a live person, and she had a strong suspicion she knew who it might be. Shelving her sudden irritation she turned back to Emma. 'So, you felt the warmth of my protection. The important thing is to be able to do that for yourself,' she said when they were settled. 'All you need is the ability to visualise. Picture yourself inside something safe. Traditionally people use a bubble, because that's transparent, so you can see out, and it's movable, it can stretch infinitely, enlarging your safe space, even enclosing the people with you if you need to, and depending on the way you see it, it's beautiful. A portable sanctuary into which no evil thing can stray. Try it.'

The church door stayed shut.

Emma was frowning, concentrating hard.

Bea watched her, her heart going out to the girl. She remembered teaching this to her daughter, Anna, when she admitted she was being bullied in school. In theory it shouldn't help at all, but somehow it did. It gave that feeling of safety and strength which sometimes was all that was needed to hide one's vulnerability and deflect the bullies' worst instincts.

'Don't try too hard,' she whispered. 'Just let it be there. Enjoy it. It's your space. Instantly there, instantly gone when you don't need it, like an umbrella.'

Emma giggled. 'I love the idea.'

'Go on practising. All the time. Use it when you're shopping if the crowds get too much. Use it at the dentist if you're scared. Use it at school if any difficult situations arise and above all use it if you feel there is something unseen threatening you.'

'The king wasn't threatening.'

'And that's fine too. You're safe in your bubble and you can still speak and see and feel as much as you want to, but when you're dealing with people from a different plane of existence, it's best to be safe. They're not always what they seem. We have lost the belief and the vocabulary in our present age to deal with these things, but they are as real now for some people as they were in medieval times.'

251

They both heard the latch on the church door click open.

Emma froze. Bea saw her eyes widen with terror and she put her finger to her lips and shook her head in reassurance. Standing up she took a few steps away from the bench. From there she could see the porch door open only a crack then hastily close again. 'Come on. We must go and find your dad,' she said loudly.

'You mean she followed us?' Emma was indignant as they climbed back into the car.

'If it's who I think it is.' It was hard to believe, and if it was Sandra, where was her car?

The empty Micra parked on the verge at the end of the lane answered that question.

'Is that hers?' Emma turned to peer at it as they drove past.

'I don't know what kind of car she has,' Bea negotiated the next bend and drove on, suppressing her indignation. What was Sandra's agenda exactly? Spying on her round the cathedral was one thing, but to go to the trouble of following them seemed beyond rational. She glanced across at Emma. 'Home?'

'It's funny, isn't it, but I do think of the cottage as home.'

'And you have extra revision to do.' Bea grinned cheerfully. She was not going to let Emma see how rattled she was by the thought that they were being followed. 'Practise your bubble. Everyone has their own energy field. See if you can see them.'

'You mean like an aura?'

Bea was concentrating on the narrow lane, slowing to cross the busy A49. 'Yes, the aura. You will find auras vary hugely. Different colours, configurations, constantly changing. With some people they are large, extending out a long way, and well defined, with others they are small and indistinct. You can learn a lot about how people feel about themselves and others, see how they interact with one another, you can see how people are feeling, their health, their mood. We all sense each other's auras instinctively unless we are singularly insensitive. Most people feel them – their personal space – but you can train yourself to see them clearly.'

'I bet Felix will laugh.'

'You don't tell Felix what you are doing. You keep it to yourself,' Bea said sternly. 'You don't tell anyone, especially school friends. The word aura reduces the vast majority of people to paroxysms of mirth. Save yourself the hassle. And anything you think you see by looking at someone's aura is private to them. You're in a privileged position, like a doctor or a priest, but you are not a doctor or a priest so you do nothing with the information you may or may not deduce, is that clear? You do not tell them what you have seen, and you do not tell anyone else.'

She had never tried to see Sandra's aura. No, that wasn't quite true. She hadn't been able to avoid sensing the woman's strange avid darkness, but now her reluctance to probe must change. The woman had violated her privacy again and again, so perhaps it was time to return the compliment. There was something more than nosiness in this obsession of hers and Bea had to find out what it was for all their sakes.

'What if you see someone has got cancer?'

'You're not a doctor, Emma, or a radiologist. Remember that. You are not in a position to diagnose illness. If someone tells you – really tells you – they're not feeling well, encourage them to see a doctor. That's all you can do. And,' she changed the focus of the subject abruptly, 'when you're confident you can do it, remember you can include someone else in your bubble to keep them safe, as I did in church.'

Emma leaned back in her seat and beamed. 'I'm going to enjoy this. The best lessons ever.'

The lane widened by a field gate and Bea pulled in and put on the handbrake. 'I'm sorry, I know this is exciting, but you will find it's not nearly as easy as it sounds. This all needs practice. The important bit for now is for you to work on your own "aura" and learn to strengthen it, turn it into a shield. You know when you're talking to someone and you feel they won't "let you in"? That's someone who does it naturally. They have put up barriers. You need to learn to do that. And at night you do it before you go to sleep.'

'To ward off nightmares?'

Bea nodded.

'I had the weirdest dream last night.'

'Oh?' Bea turned round to scan her face.

'I dreamt that Dad was dead.'

'But you knew he wasn't.'

Emma nodded. 'I got out of bed and went to stand on the landing to listen outside his door to make sure he was still breathing.'

'You didn't need to do that to know your dream was not about your father. Not your real father,' Bea said gently.

'I know. But I had to be sure.'

'Of course. Dreams can be so frighteningly real. So, do you know what the dream was actually about?'

'Everyone was running about and shouting and crying and I was there, listening.'

'Who was shouting?'

'People. Men. Rough big men with leather jackets and beards and,' she paused, replaying the memory, 'swords.'

'Anglo-Saxon men?'

'So it was to do with Dad's book?'

'Probably.' Bea made herself smile. Had Emma been there in Winchester? Could she have dreamed the same dream as she had? Heard the same messenger? Seen the same men, felt the same panic as news of the death of Offa, their king's greatest ally, spread around the court? She reined in her thoughts sternly. If Emma had been there, she would have seen Eadburh. 'Were there any women in your dream?' she asked after a moment.

'Only me.'

'Were you part of the scene or watching it like a film?'

'I was there. I was part of it. The messenger had come to me. I was wearing a lovely long red dress. I was the queen.'

After dropping Emma off at the cottage, Bea drove home in a thoughtful mood. She had studied for years on and off with different teachers to harness her own natural abilities and she was trying to teach Emma in a few hours. And Emma was all over the place. Would the girl remember what to do if she saw St Ethelbert again, or if the voice came back? And would she be able to resist the spirit of Eadburh invading her dreams? Somehow she and Emma had dreamt the same dream, watched the same scene, but she had been a witness, Emma, a participant. She hadn't had the chance to talk to Simon privately when she dropped Emma back at the cottage, but she had to do it. She had to tell him too what to do if there was another crisis. And in the meantime she had a crisis of her own to deal with. Sandra Bedford.

As she stopped at the gates into the cathedral grounds, waiting for the bollards to lower and allow her in so she could head for her parking space, she found she was repeatedly looking in her driving mirror to make sure there was no sign of Sandra behind her. What on earth was she going to do about the woman?

Heading towards her front door she fished her front door key out of her pocket and let herself in. 'Mark?' she could already tell he wasn't at home. When he was out there was always an undefinable sense of emptiness in the place, as though a part of her own soul was missing. However much she longed to be alone, she missed him when he wasn't there. She peered into his study and then the kitchen, to be sure, before heading up towards their bedroom. Pulling off her jacket and throwing it on the bed, she sat down next to it, strangely reluctant to go upstairs to her attic study.

Don't go, my child. Don't go. There is danger.

Danger up on Offa's Ridge. Danger not only for her, but for Emma as well.

She closed her eyes and took a deep breath. Listen to the old man. Whether the priest in the chantry was nothing but a memory in her head or yet another imprinted echo in the ether or an audible voicing of her own instincts, listen to his advice. But how could she? Now she had to worry about Emma as well as herself.

And it was with herself she should start.

Her own protection was patently less than satisfactory. Eadburh and her witch-woman Nesta could see her and were reacting to her and Eadburh was threatening her. She should not put herself in danger deliberately any more than she had

255

already until she had found out why her tried-and-tested methods were not working. That problem needed to be sorted at once. But her curiosity about Eadburh and her world was so strong. It was more than just part of her current undertaking to sort out Simon's cottage ghost and Emma's wildly uncontrolled talent, it was a personal quest.

She sat still, torn in two. She was obsessed and obsession was dangerous. The next instalment waited for her upstairs, the house was empty, there was nothing to stop her giving in to temptation, going up to her study, sitting down, closing her eyes and waiting for the curtain to rise. Nothing except the urgent advice of an ancient chantry priest.

Don't go, my child. Don't go. There is danger.

27

'This is very cloak and dagger!'

Simon agreed to meet Bea in the Co-op car park in Kington. He had left Felix and Emma at the cottage, supposedly revising, with the excuse he was coming down to pick up a takeaway.

'It has to be, I'm afraid. I am being followed by a woman from the cathedral who has made it her mission to uncover my satanic practices,' she explained as he climbed into the car beside her. 'You met her at the café there with me.'

'Oh Bea, I'm sorry. Emma mentioned you thought she had followed you both to the church. Is this our fault? Felix was such an idiot, sounding off like that.'

She gave a grim smile. 'Don't worry. She's been warned off. I'm not here to talk about her. I wanted a word without Emma overhearing us. How is she doing?'

'OK, I think. She is a bit hyper, but she's exhausted as well, so it's hard to judge. She's told us you've taught her how to protect herself against ghosts and being possessed, and how to see auras,' he said, keeping his expression and tone neutral.

So much for keeping things secret. 'Whatever you do, don't mock her, Simon. It's a real thing. Physicists need powerful machines to view human energy fields; some humans possess that ability naturally. End of. Trust your daughter. It's a wonderful thing to be able to do and it should be exciting and magical, that's the only word I have for it. But I need her to be careful. Not get carried away by the excitement because with it comes danger. She must not deliberately open herself to marauding spirits.'

Simon took a deep breath. 'Like the voice.'

'Like the voice.'

'Felix knows to watch her when I'm not there. She was asleep when I left.'

'Good. She needs rest as long as she doesn't have too many nightmares that make her scared to close her eyes.' She hesitated, wondering how to proceed. 'Simon, I'm intrigued by the story that's developing here,' she said cautiously, 'and I wanted to ask you about it. It's your focus on King Offa that's set these events in motion, that much seems to be obvious. We joked about you writing your own ghost when we first met, and we were being flippant, or we thought we were, but true words are often spoken in jest. Everything going on here involves Offa and his daughters and his sons-in-law. St Ethelbert—'

'Who was never his son-in-law. He was murdered before he actually got near his wife-to-be, poor lad. I don't think we'll ever know why. Legend has the field of possibilities pretty much covered.'

'And the King of Northumbria?'

'The husband of Ethelfled, the eldest daughter? They were violent times and his murder was probably locally plotted. Dynastic or to do with local politics rather than Offa. Offa wanted allies.'

'What happened to Ethelfled?'

'As far as I remember, she is never mentioned again in the record. My next book will be about Northumbria so I might know more when I've written my next bunch of ghosts.' He grinned. 'Poor woman. I rather hope she retired to a convent. That was the best hope for redundant women. As long as she wasn't pregnant and therefore the potential mother of a potential threat, she would probably have been OK. I think if she had been murdered too, we would have heard about it.' He sounded shockingly offhand.

'And then there was Eadburh.' Bea kept her voice neutral.

He laughed. 'Ah, now she was quite a player. Rather more feisty than her sisters, although Ethelbert's intended certainly raised two fingers at her father by escaping to the convent at Crowland and having herself walled up.'

'I need to know about Eadburh.' Bea wasn't interested at this moment in the sister in Crowland.

'She married the King of Wessex. Don't forget, I've already written my book about Wessex. I rented a cottage in the New Forest to write that one, but I was not haunted by Eadburh, something for which I am heartily glad.' He gave a theatrical shudder. 'You know we discussed the manuscript of the Anglo-Saxon Chronicle over at Coedmawr?'

She nodded.

'She is mentioned there. It's a local copy. Hereford. And history knows a lot more about Eadburh than about her sisters. She wasn't a lady to mess with. She—'

'No! Don't tell me any more!' Bea wasn't sure where the words had come from, but she genuinely didn't want to know the cold historical version. Not yet. Not until, not unless, she had heard it first from Eadburh in person.

Simon laughed. 'OK. Well, if you do want to find out I'll give you a copy of my Wessex book; the source of much of our information about her is King Alfred's biographer Asser, who was a gossipy old Welsh monk writing at the end of the ninth century, so both he and the chronicler at Coedmawr were writing pretty much within living memory of her.'

'Just one question.' Bea couldn't resist asking. 'She never married a son of the King of Powys, did she?'

'Good Lord, no! What makes you ask that? Why are you so interested in her all of a sudden?'

Bea shook her head. 'A dream.'

'Yours or Emma's?'

'Both.'

'Both?' He looked startled. 'You're both dreaming about her?'

She nodded. 'And that's why I'm worried. Eadburh is too strong a presence in this story.'

'Ah.' Simon looked at her thoughtfully. 'And you would be inclined to believe your and Emma's dreams rather than the historical record?'

'I'd rather Emma didn't dream about her at all, to be honest. She's too involved. Too open. Too exposed to danger.'

'Danger?'

'Not if we protect her, Simon.' She wished she hadn't used the word. 'I have told her how to keep safe, and if she has you and Felix to watch over her, she'll be all right.'

'That's a relief.' He frowned. 'And in your dreams, yours and hers, Eadburh married a Welsh prince?'

'No. At least I don't think so. Maybe. I don't know what happened. Yet.' She grimaced. 'Watch this space.'

'Well, let me know. There is a whole 'nother book in that theory.' He reached for the door handle. 'I must go and collect our fish and chips. You don't want to join us for supper?'

'Thank you, no. I must get back to Mark.'

'Does he approve of all this? Genuinely believe in it?' He bent down to look back into the car.

She sighed. 'Yes, he does. There is a ministry of deliverance within the Church. Ghosts and demons are a recognised problem.'

'Well, if I had to choose, I would categorise Eadburh as part of the demon department,' Simon said cheerfully. He stood up. 'Look after yourself. What was it my Scots grandmother used to say: "Frae' ghoulies and ghosties, and things that go bump in the night, the good Lord deliver us!"' He pushed the door closed.

She watched as he loped across the car park. 'You forgot the long-leggity beasties,' she whispered. 'But I always thought that meant spiders.'

Bea was sitting on the sofa in the snug, ostensibly watching TV but with the sound turned down. Mark was in his study working on a sermon. She knew he was worrying about her and about Emma. He had told her he had prayed for them both, but he had said it with an apologetic grin, as if expecting her to upbraid him for his interference.

Giving up the pretence of watching the screen, she turned it off and lay back, her eyes closed. Offa had told Eadburh that Elisedd was dead. Murdered, presumably like anyone else who got in his way. But if a Welsh prince had been murdered, surely there would have been repercussions. His father would have attacked Offa, dyke or no dyke. But then she remembered, he had. In the year 796, the year Offa died.

'Want a hot drink?' Mark appeared in the doorway, his pen still in his hand. He looked exhausted. She had learnt not to enquire about his cathedral work; it was all too complicated. When he had been a parish priest their life had involved the warp and weft of the parish and she had been a part of it, but here it was so different. It not only involved the cathedral and its work as a pastoral centre, but in his case it was his job to oversee the finances, a huge and never-ending burden. Raise money. Apply for grants. Supervise the budgets. And on top of all that her unsought conflict with Sandra was not helping. She scrambled to her feet and followed him through to the kitchen. 'Has she been at the dean again?'

He grinned. He didn't have to ask who she meant. 'Not as far as I know.'

'She followed me out to Marden. At least, I'm pretty sure it was her. While I was talking to Emma and trying to reassure her, there was someone creeping round the church, hiding in the pulpit! I don't know what kind of car she drives but there was a Micra parked up at the end of the lane so it wouldn't be spotted.'

Mark threw himself down into a kitchen chair. 'Do you want me to get her dismissed? Although, I'm not sure one can dismiss a volunteer. Perhaps on the grounds of age. But that doesn't really apply. Perhaps we could get her promoted to somewhere else.'

'Where is the furthest outpost of the Church?' Bea smiled. 'I don't think that would do it, in any case. She's obsessed.'

'She's jealous of you, Bea.'

'Jealous?'

'My spies tell me so. You are clever, talented, you have an interesting job, albeit no one quite knows what it is.' He grinned. 'And you are married to the most gifted and charismatic churchman ever. Oh, and it has been pointed out that you are also very beautiful.'

Bea let out a snort of laughter. 'Who says? But seriously, Mark, no one is supposed to know what my job is!'

'Don't forget, she showed the newspaper cuttings to the dean. That took some explaining, I can tell you. Luckily for you, he was deeply sympathetic. I have told him you used to teach full-time, which is perfectly true, and that since we moved to Hereford you've been doing some supply work, which is also true, and that now you're doing some mentoring, ditto. If the woman goes near the dean again, he will tell her in confidence that you're working with a disturbed child, which I think we can honestly say Emma is, and that if she is intrusive that will be seriously detrimental to the girl's stability. Also true.'

'Thank you, Mark.' It made her feel very guilty to think that he was lying for her. But then, as he said, it wasn't a lie. A sin of omission, perhaps, but not a lie.

'Hopefully, she will back off now.' Mark stood up and set about making hot chocolate for them both. He pushed a mug towards her. 'You saw Simon this evening?'

'He left Emma with Felix. He told me she is calm and very tired. I will see her again only if she wants to.'

'Do you think the ghosts are laid?'

'I think poor old St Ethelbert is a place memory. Emma is sensitive but she is also very imaginative. It's a pretty gory story when you think about it.'

'So she is not actually being haunted or possessed.'

Bea hesitated. 'Not by him anyway.'

'By Offa's daughter?'

She felt his thoughtful gaze on her and looked away. 'I'm not entirely sure what's going on. Let's wait and see if anything else happens. I've given her some tools to work with which should keep her safe. A few days after Easter she and Felix will be going home anyway. Term will start with all the terror of exams to keep her distracted.'

'Let's hope so.' Mark headed for the door, carrying his mug. 'Are you coming up?'

'Too much to think about; I'll never sleep. I'll follow you in a bit.' She knew he would be waiting, listening to see if she went up to her study, worrying. Making her way back into the snug, she flicked on the electric fire and curled up on the sofa. She was not going to allow herself to think about Eadburh, even though Simon's cryptic remark had intrigued her. Simon knew all about Eadburh, knew enough to make an off-the-cuff remark about her being a demon and knew enough to be quite shocked at the idea of her being married to a Welshman, an idea he had dismissed out of hand. Well, she had seen what Eadburh was capable of, if her interpretation of the killing of St Ethelbert's murderer was true. She was cold-blooded and calculating, a true daughter of her parents.

She took a sip from her chocolate. Perhaps it was time to think about the mysterious, attractive Elisedd instead. The man who so obesssed her; the man who had captured her heart and then turned it to stone. If he was real, and she truly believed he was, somewhere there must be a record of his life. And his death.

She cudgelled her memory, trying to think of the names in Simon's manuscript, names so complicated she had skipped over them as she read, the King of Powys, Cadell ap Brochfael, son of Brochfael ap Elisedd. Elisedd, pronounced Eleezeth, a family name.

Where was her iPad?

His name, if not common, appeared several times with different spellings given to various different princes and kings of a Wales that in the post-Roman era seemed to have been a confused, indistinct tangle of small kingdoms, some, according to one article, as small as fifteen miles across, remnants of the original tribal states. But Powys was one of the big ones. Powys had an ancient and well-established royal family with the advantage and disadvantage of a long border with Mercia and thus of being the near neighbour of Offa.

Cadell the king was there; the only son of his mentioned by name was Cyngen, but then she knew Elise was a younger son. Maybe he had not merited a record in history. Maybe he had died too soon. She stared down at the screen in her hands.

There seemed to be precious little known about the family. A sister. A famous grandson. But the name fitted, the name that someone, Eadburh herself, perhaps, was calling so frantically into the dark of a lonely mountain ridge on the borders of Wales and England.

The two kings were thought to have negotiated over the dyke. Even that wasn't certain. If Eadburh's Elisedd had gone to oversee the building of the part of the dyke that ran near what was still called Offa's Ridge, as a negotiator and ambassador, there was no known record of that either. And if, as a younger son who had suddenly become a threat to Offa's plans of domination, he was regarded as expendable, his murder, made to look like an accident, never made it into the historical record.

When Mark tiptoed downstairs an hour later, he found Bea asleep on the sofa, the iPad in her lap. He stood for a few minutes looking down at her fondly. 'So, where are you, my love?' he whispered. She didn't move. He leaned down and removed the iPad. He reached for the rug on the back of the chair and tucked it around her, gently, so as not to wake her, then he turned out all the lights and left her to sleep.

She was in the mead hall at Corfe and King Beorhtric was crying. His favourite had been found dead out in the latrines, lying awkwardly on the boards over the shit hole, his face contorted in agony, his leggings around his ankles. He had vomited copiously before he died. If he called out, no one had heard him, no one had missed him until the king himself had shouted for him to come and take his accustomed place beside him at the feast. The queen had been about to join her husband from the women's bower, with her ladies all round her and her little daughter who had been playing with her companions. As the king's scream of anguished denial echoed from the hall the women had looked at one another in consternation and Eadburh sent the wife of one of her husband's senior warriors to find out what had happened, herself waiting calmly by the fire, stooping to pick up her daughter's dolls.

There was nothing to be done. The man had obviously died

of poisoning. Queen Eadburh summoned the cooks; a search of the kitchens discovered rancid, rat-infested piles of food in the larders and the serf in charge of scrubbing the vessels was summarily executed by being buried head first in a vat of his own stale cooking fat.

Beorhtric was distraught at the loss of his closest friend, but Eadburh suggested they move on to spend Christmas at their favourite hall at Cheddar and he allowed himself to be distracted with plans for a spring offensive against the heathen Vikings should they choose to invade the southern shores of his kingdom again. She knew he would find another lover soon, and she knew that lover too would meet an unpleasant end. Three of them had died now. She saw people looking at her, she knew her husband's thanes whispered amongst themselves and glanced at her sideways, crossing themselves as she swept past them, but no one would ever know what had truly happened.

This time, Nesta had remained at Cheddar where her beloved herb gardens thrived in the gentle climate of the Summer Lands. After Christmas the court would make its way to Wareham and then to Wantage and then when spring came Eadburh would dictate that once again they wind their way back towards Cheddar. As Beorhtric amused himself hunting with his favourites, she supervised the treasury, planning to strike coins in her own name, oversaw the signing of charters and was present at the gatherings of the Witan, seemingly unaware of the looks of hatred cast in her direction. That her father had died did not seem to affect her influence. Her brother ruled now in his stead and when the devastating news came that her brother too was dead after only five months' reign, smitten by a wasting sickness, or as some said, in God's revenge for the sins of his father, she did not go to his funeral, nor did she acknowledge the new King of Mercia, a distant cousin of her father's, who meant nothing to her. She was far too busy watching with narrowed eyes as her husband lavished gold rings and silk shirts and embroidered tunics on the subject of his latest crush.

It was summer when, with Nesta beside her, she walked again through the gardens in the Summer Lands and they stopped near the lavender hedges to watch a mother cat suckling her kittens in the sun. 'I need more herbs.' Eadburh's order was peremptory as she reeled off her list. 'Bring them to me this evening.' She did not notice Nesta's arched eyebrow or the way the woman's shoulders squared.

'It is not the right time of the moon,' Nesta said, peaceably enough. 'As you know, the charms will not work if the plants are gathered in the wrong season.'

'Of course they will work. They always work,' Eadburh snapped. 'They are poison, are they not?'

Nesta took a few steps away from her and stood, her arms folded, gazing into the distance across the marshy levels towards the south. 'So, you plan another death?' she said after a moment.

'The king mocks me at his peril,' Eadburh replied.

'And you mock the sisters of Wyrd at yours, oh queen,' Nesta retorted.

'The priests teach us to despise the sisters of Wyrd and all their superstitious nonsense. God is not fooled by such children's stories.' Eadburh's eyes were glittering dangerously. 'You will do as I say.'

Nesta inclined her head graciously. 'As you wish.' She began to walk away towards the little herb house where she kept her baskets and her shears.

'Have I dismissed you?' Eadburh's voice behind her was like acid.

Nesta froze. She turned. 'You asked me to pick your herbs without delay. I was about to do so. Have you another request?'

'Yes. You will give me a potent herb to suppress the king's lust.'

Nesta appeared to consider the request for a few seconds then she bowed her head again. This time Eadburh did not call her back as she departed but she remained there, watching the woman's retreating back, a speculative look in her eyes.

'She will be sorry she questioned me.'

Bea looked round. She had seen no one else nearby.

'I was speaking to you, ghost of shadow and sunlight, rain and storm.' Eadburh was looking straight at her. 'Do you still imagine I cannot see you?' The woman did not seem afraid or angry at the sight of her, rather this time she was calculated; thoughtful.

Bea shrank back. She had intended to stay hidden, to peer round corners, to hide in the shadows, but her intention hadn't worked. Obviously she was there in plain view. She backed away, aware that she could feel the sunlight on her skin, the touch of the wind on her face; she could smell the beds of lavender and the dog roses and honeysuckle that scrambled over the hedges. Nesta was the other side of the garden now, a basket on her arm, cutting a sprig of flowers here, a branch of a shrub there, keeping her back resolutely towards her queen.

'I could banish you to Hell,' Eadburh went on conversationally, 'or I could use you, send you through the hall at night to my husband's side. And I could watch while you pour poison into his slack dribbling mouth as he paws his latest sodomite, and see you disappear as his warrior bodyguard flock round him to save his worthless life.'

'No.'

Bea found it a huge effort to speak out loud. The air would not enter her lungs, the wind, so gentle on her face, would not allow her to breathe. 'What you plan is evil.'

She saw Nesta straighten and turn to face them, she saw the basket dropping from her grasp to lie in the flower bed, the plants scattered, she heard Eadburh gasp. The sun had disappeared behind a cloud, its shadow racing across the garden bringing darkness. In seconds the scene had disappeared. She could see nothing. She couldn't breathe, she couldn't move.

'Bea! Bea, darling, it's all right! I'm here!'

Mark's arms were round her and he was holding her tightly. The light was on, and she was there, in the snug, on the sofa, gasping for air. She looked round frantically, expecting to see Eadburh there in the room, but everything was normal.

Almost everything.

On the rug near the fire lay a scattering of herbs.

28

'Don't touch them!' As Bea scrambled off the sofa, she saw Mark bending to pick up the discarded plants.

Mark straightened. 'Why not?'

'Because—' She hesitated. 'I think they're poisonous.'

He looked back down at the wilted greenery lying at his feet. 'I'm not going to eat them.'

'No, of course you're not. But even so. Please. Leave them. I'll get some gloves from the kitchen.'

'Bea.' Mark sat down on the armchair near the fire. 'What is going on?' He looked defeated. 'Where did they come from?'

She went back to the sofa and threw herself down, her legs curled under her like a child, pulling the rug around her shoulders with a shiver. 'I dreamt I was in a herb garden. I was watching a woman tell the herb-wife to gather poisonous herbs so she could kill her husband's lover.' She gave a deep sigh. 'Then you woke me up and there are the herbs, scattered from Nesta's basket.'

Mark closed his eyes and an expression of something like despair crossed his face. 'That can't happen.'

'It can, Mark. Things can travel between existences. I've seen it before. I'm going to find my herb book and see what they are. There is rue in there – I recognise that, it has such a distinctive smell.'

'But surely rue isn't poisonous.'

She looked down at the scatter of wilting leaves uncertainly. 'Perhaps I'm wrong. You go to bed, Mark. Leave this to me.' Suddenly she was determined. 'I will bag them up and leave them to check in the morning, then I will come up too.'

'You'd better take photos of them.' Mark stood up with a groan. He looked exhausted. 'In case they vanish back down the wormhole.' He walked over to the door, then he stopped and looked back. 'Do you have any idea what you're involved in, Bea?'

She grimaced. 'If I don't, nobody will. This is my area of expertise, Mark.' She wished she felt as confident as she sounded. 'I tried ringing Meryn a couple of evenings back. He's still lecturing in the States, and he hasn't returned my call. So,' she took a deep breath, 'I'm on my own. As long as,' she gave him a sad little smile, 'you've got my back, darling. You and Jesus.'

It had been Meryn who had taught her to use herbs as incense and for saining, the old Scots word for what the Native Americans called smudging. He had shown her how to look for the local plants and meditate with them, to study the traditions of the people with whom she was working. He had given her books on the Celtic lore of Wales, and he had talked of the Druids and their learning and the Physicians of Myddfai, but then he had moved on to the Anglo-Saxon leechbooks and the Nine Herb charm and the folklore of Herefordshire and the Marches and encouraged her to gather plants and dry them so she was ready for any emergency. And this was an emergency. She was strong. She could do this.

Labelled and sorted, the herbs gathered by Nesta fell into two distinct groups. Rue. Hops. Agrimony. All used by celibate medieval monks, according to her books, as remedies for lust. Perhaps something Saxon wives traditionally put in their unfaithful husbands' pottage. Then there were the poisons. Aconite and deadly nightshade and white bryony. Considering she had had only a few minutes to gather them, Nesta had known exactly where in her herb beds to find the plants she needed. In the case of the bryony she had snatched at it as it trailed with the honeysuckle over the hedge. No doubt, had there been time, she would have gathered more, dried, from her store of pots and jars. Bea sat at the kitchen table staring thoughtfully down at the collection. Those poisonous herbs had other names, according to her book. Wolfsbane, monkshood, mandrake. The words were resonant with threat. Nesta had picked them. The woman was a powerful . . . Bea found herself groping for the right word. A witch? An enchantress? A spaewife? What was the Anglo-Saxon equivalent? A plant-charmer? A cunning woman? Herbs and charms and amulets had been Nesta's business, just as they were Bea's, but the woman had had no time to empower these plants. Bea shivered. She should burn them, but still she sat unable to tear her eyes away from the wilting leaves.

Emma waited, holding her breath. Felix's gentle snore went on uninterrupted as she tiptoed across the living room. She looked back over her shoulder. His sleeping figure was a hump under the bedclothes in the corner of the shadowy room. Taking her jacket from the coat hooks behind the front door she slipped it on and then, holding her breath, she eased the door open. It was bitterly cold outside, for all it would soon be May, and still dark, though there was a faint light in the eastern sky. Under her hand she felt the hard ripple of ice on the gate as she pushed it open and headed up the lane towards the hill.

Climbing into bed the night before she had visualised the bubble of protection around herself exactly as Bea had taught her, then she had lain there, waiting. She wasn't sure what she had expected – figures battering the outside of her bubble perhaps, but nothing had happened. The bedroom had grown cold as she lay there, rigid, staring up at the ceiling. She didn't dare shut her eyes. She heard her father and Felix chatting quietly downstairs, then the sounds of them pulling out the bed for Felix and making it up. She distinctly heard her brother laughing quietly as Dad said something, then Simon's footsteps coming upstairs. The crack of light under the door disappeared as he switched off the landing light and she heard his bedroom door close, then the creak of floorboards as he wandered around the room getting ready for bed. In minutes the house was silent. It was too dark. She wanted to turn on her bedside light and she turned her head cautiously to look towards it. If she put out her arm, would it pierce her bubble of protection? What would Bea tell her to do? But she couldn't lie there in the total darkness, it was too scary. Cautiously she reached over and groped for the switch. As the fire downstairs died the house became colder. There were heaters in each room but they didn't seem to make any difference. She pulled the covers up even more tightly under her chin and very cautiously she closed her eyes.

In her dream it was nearly dawn. As she tiptoed downstairs all she could think about was the need to get out onto the ridge.

He was waiting for her on the edge of the wood, his horse tethered to a tree. Behind him the dawn was flooding across the sky, slowly spreading across the landscape far below, leaving a pattern of intense shadow and bright sunlit peaks. In the distance far away in the valley under the hill she could make out the outline of a tiny stone chapel hidden amongst the trees, spotlit by a sunbeam. Its very presence seemed to bless their meeting. Around them the air was loud with the songs of birds. She paused, looking at him, then she held out her arms. She saw the smile in his eyes as she ran towards him and heard the whicker of his horse as if it too recognised her, and then she was there, in his embrace, pressed against his chest and her lips were raised, seeking his. For a long moment they stood together looking out towards the distances. 'There, do you see that little church?' Elise was pointing into the distance with its pinpoints of sunlight striking a squat stone tower. 'One day you and I will go there together and we will find the priest and we will ask him to make us man and wife.' Gently he pulled her towards him and he kissed her again.

He led her through the edge of the wood towards the sheepfold and there he pulled her down onto the bed of bracken. Swathed in his cloak, they made love as the sunlight warmed the land and slowly the frost melted on the grass, unaware of the wandering sheep that peered through the entrance at them with mild astonishment before turning away to crop the grass on the hillside, or of the croaking of the raven as it flew high towards the west.

'Emma! Breakfast!' The voice from downstairs was an intrusion, an unwelcome interruption like the stone on the ground under her hip. 'I have to go,' she murmured, but already she was alone. As her eyes opened she saw that she was in her little bedroom at the cottage. She looked round, lost and confused. Her body felt strange. It felt warm and heavy and aroused. Her breasts were tingling and her lips felt sore and bitten. Her bedside light was on though outside the curtains it was daylight and she was, she realised, fully dressed. She sat up, running her hands through her hair and saw her thick padded jacket lying on the end of the bed. Reaching out towards it, she drew her hand away sharply. It was wet with melted ice.

'She looked a bit odd at breakfast. Strained. Tired, but otherwise OK.' Simon's voice message had been left at 10.04. Bea listened again. 'She didn't say anything to worry me. We were planning to drive over to Ludlow for the day. Then when I called her about half an hour ago there was no reply. I went up to her bedroom and there was this note saying she had gone out for a walk and we shouldn't worry. Not worry! Do you know where she might have gone?'

When Bea rang Emma's phone it went straight to messages.

Simon was waiting on the cottage steps when Bea drew in next to his car.

'You don't think she has gone out for an ordinary stroll?'

He shook his head. 'She knew we were all going out for the day together.'

'The important thing is she left you a message.'

'That's what Felix said.'

She could see the boy through the door, hunched over the computer, every inch of his body trying to convey the fact that he didn't care and wasn't upset.

'Can I see her note?' Bea could see Simon's hand shaking

as he reached into his pocket and brought out the crumpled sheet of paper. She took it and turned away from him, staring out across the hills, holding it tightly, trying to connect.

Behind her Simon sighed and threw himself down on one of the wrought-iron chairs by the little terrace table. He said nothing as Felix came outside and pulled out the chair opposite him. They sat there in silence, waiting.

Bea could feel the panic and the anger that was all Simon's. She was trying to probe further, feel Emma in the untidy pencil scrawl. The girl had responded to blind impulse, to some kind of imperative she didn't understand herself. Bea closed her eyes, concentrating. Waves of emotion were coming off the piece of paper: love and longing, loneliness, fear, regret, and over it all a deep enduring sense of loss. None of these were Emma's emotions. They belonged to someone else.

And then, suddenly, hope. Emma. Emma was back and she had thought of something, seen something, that had filled her with excitement and longing, something out there in the countryside below the ridge. It was something important, fateful. Not too far away. Something to do with the person whose emotions she had been feeling so intensely. The Emma who had walked out of the gate had been responsible enough to write a note, but powerless to ignore the longing that had filled her whole being.

Bea turned towards them. 'She's gone to find Elise,' she said, 'the man she should have married, the man she has been looking for for over a thousand years.'

'She. You mean the voice,' Felix put in. 'It. That woman, has possessed her and they're looking for this man together.'

'And you think this is Offa's daughter, Eadburh, don't you?' Simon looked at her hard.

She bit her lip. 'She is certainly hanging around.' Bea closed her eyes, conscious that she should be protecting them all with every means known to her. Not just the bubble she had demonstrated to Emma and which the girl had clearly forgotten or ignored, but with incense and prayers and incantations, and yes, with Mark. She needed Mark. 'I am going to set guards on this house and garden and then—'

'Stop it!' Simon lurched to his feet, pushing the chair out across the flagstones on the terrace. 'No more of this stupidity! If you hadn't encouraged her with all this crap, this wouldn't have happened!'

'Dad.' Felix looked up at him pleadingly. 'Bea is the only one who can help with all this.'

'Well, she hasn't helped so far, has she? She's made it worse!'

To Bea's horror, she saw there were tears in his eyes. She took a deep breath and ploughed on. 'Emma is dreaming about someone whose misery and loneliness has been written into the memory of time itself. I think she's getting flashbacks and nightmares and yes, beautiful dreams that are not her own and I have a sense of where she's gone.' She clutched the note to her chest. 'She had had a vision of a church tower, spotlit by the sun and this morning she remembered seeing it. Was that in her dreams or in reality? I don't know but I think Emma has gone to find that little church because she and Elisedd dreamed they would one day marry there. It's still there. It isn't far away. One can see it from the top of the ridge.'

'You mean you can scent her there, like a bloodhound. Is that another of your amazing gifts?' Simon was bristling with hostility.

Bea had lost his confidence and she couldn't blame him for that. She should have sensed what was going to happen. 'I'm going to go and look. I'll ring you if I spot something.'

She didn't wait for a reply. She knew where she was going. Eadburh and her prince had looked down on the tower of a little chapel as it emerged into the sunlight from the mist and he had promised one day to marry her there. Eadburh had remembered that moment. Remembered it and treasured it for the rest of her life.

She took the car.

The *clas* was now an isolated country church some three miles by car from the cottage, but probably far less via the footpath Emma would have followed, straight down towards the valley. She and Mark had been there together once a long time ago. It was a very special place and somehow she knew it fitted into this story. It still clearly displayed its Saxon origins in its low rounded doorway and heavy stone vaulted roof and above all in the ancient round tower. Pulling up onto the grass verge she climbed out of the car and stood looking up the path between the ancient yews. Had Hilde called there too? In her dream of Eadburh's hapless messenger, the yews were already ancient. It was an early stop on the obvious route into the Welsh hinterland.

There was a torn notice in the porch saying the church was open and that there was a service once a month; the door was an enormous lump of solid oak, bound by huge elaborate hinges that seemed as old as the tree from which the door had been hewn. She pushed it cautiously and peered in.

Emma was sitting in the front pew. She turned at the sound of the heavy latch. 'I knew you would come.'

'Are you OK?' Bea walked up the aisle and sat down beside her. The church was ice-cold and smelled of ancient hymn books and stone.

She nodded. 'I thought he might come to meet me here. He promised me that one day we would be married here.'

'Elise?'

Emma nodded and Bea saw the tears leaking down her cheeks. 'What's happening to me?'

'You let him in, sweetheart.'

'I didn't want to be protected against him.'

'I know. But I've got you now. You're safe.' The child's aura was thin and ragged, a pale shimmering veil, the colour of dust.

29

'Simon said he was taking her back to London. That I mustn't contact them again. I messed up so badly, Mark.'

They were sitting side by side in the snug. She had waited all afternoon for a phone call from Chris saying that Simon was demanding his money back, that he was suing her friend for having a haunted cottage; or from Simon himself, accusing her of some sort of child abuse. Her phone, lying there on the coffee table in front of them, had remained stubbornly silent.

'You should have called me.'

'I know you don't want to be interrupted when you're at work.'

'And you think this isn't part of my work?' Mark put his arm round her shoulders and pulled her gently against him. 'Was Emma OK, as far as you know?'

'Physically, yes. She was all over the place mentally. Will you go up there, please, Mark. He trusts you.'

When Mark rang him, Simon's phone went to voicemail.

Mark sighed. 'OK. I'll go up to the cottage.'

'I'll come with you—'

'No! I want you to stay here, and I want you to keep out of trouble.' He looked at her sternly. 'Please, darling. Don't go chasing Eadburh through the stratosphere. I need to know you're safe.'

She nodded slowly.

Mark stood up and was pulling on his jacket when there was a knock at the front door. Bea looked up, ragged. 'Not Sandra, please. I can't cope with her as well.'

It was Simon, with Emma and Felix behind him. Mark led them into the snug without a word.

'I'm sorry. I was unfair,' Simon said awkwardly. 'I tried to pack up to take the kids back to London but they wouldn't go.'

For a moment they all stood there in an uncomfortable circle then Emma flung herself into Bea's arms, sobbing.

'We had a family conference,' Felix announced as his father appeared to be incapable of further speech, 'and Em and I decided we didn't want to go to London. We think you two are probably her only hope. So there.' He glared at his father, then sat down on the armchair by the window, his hands folded neatly between his knees.

Mark looked at Simon. 'Is that what you think?'

'I don't care what Dad thinks!' Emma shouted through her tears. 'He doesn't understand.'

'No, I don't,' Simon said at last. 'But Emma seems to think Bea can help.' He looked from Mark to Emma and back. 'I don't know what else to do.'

Bea noticed he didn't look at her. 'I'm willing to help in every way I can,' she put in quietly.

'And she can help,' Felix put in from his chair by the window. 'None of this is her fault, Dad. The voice came to you. It was your book that escalated things; the manuscript we've been reading, the whole Anglo-Saxon thing has stirred it up and Bea's the only person who has a clue what's happening and how to deal with it. To blame her is ludicrous!'

It was nearly midnight when Bea slowly climbed the attic stairs to her room and went in, closing the door behind her. Simon and Felix had gone back to the cottage, leaving Emma behind. Mark had retreated to his study while Emma helped Bea peel potatoes. It had seemed a soothing, unthreatening way of defusing the day's events. The bangers and mash had gone down well, and Emma had retired to bed early without argument. Only when Mark too was asleep did Bea feel she could take the time to confront and attempt to unravel the day's events.

She stood for a while in the dark, staring out of the window across the dark oasis of the garden towards the loom of the city lights beyond the wall. Finally, she turned and lit a candle, then put the match to some charcoal under a gentle cleansing incense. The energies in the room were uneasy, a remnant of earlier experiences, not quite there but not completely gone either.

She sat and waited several minutes until she felt centred and calm then she looked deep into the heart of the candle flame and began to circle herself with light and the armour of prayer. Only when that was complete did she turn her full attention to Eadburh.

'Right,' she said softly. 'I'm ready for you. I want to hear the whole story. Go on, lady. Let's hear what happened next.'

The king's latest lover was dead. The royal hall was in uproar, the candles burned low and smoking, the high, elaborately carved rafters shadowed, echoing with whispers, the king's warriors aroused from their sleep on the benches round the walls. The queen wasn't there; she was in the nursery, bent over the sleeping figure of her little daughter, her face expressionless in the dusky chamber as the sound of shouting from the hall reached her across the courtyards and through the tapestry-hung walls. She was aware of the uneasy glances of the child's nurses as they huddled round the fire. No one approached her. They were all afraid of her.

Beorhtric did not come to her bed for several weeks, preferring to drink himself insensible with the men of his personal guard and amusing himself, so she had heard, with yet another favourite. When he came at last, pushing through the heavy curtains to their bed, Eadburh lay still, her eyes closed and gritted her teeth, waiting. He did not touch her. He threw himself down beside her, fully dressed, and lay there without moving, his eyes open in the darkness. 'It was you,' he said softly at last. 'You killed them.'

'How am I supposed to have done that?'

'You have devils and demons to serve you and do your bidding. Everyone knows it; everyone whispers that you are a sorceress. Everyone is afraid of you.'

He could not see her smile in the blackness of the bed hangings.

'Perhaps I am a sorceress. Or perhaps I am merely a wife who has been publicly insulted by the man who is supposed to honour her, the man who flouts the teaching of the Church.'

'Whatever you are, Wigfrith and the rest of my advisers have told me to be rid of you. Your father and your brother have gone to whatever hell is reserved for Offa and his family, and you will join him there if you do not leave my court.' His voice had grown louder until he was shouting. 'I will give you two choices. You may return to Mercia and beg its new king to protect you, or you may enter a convent and dedicate what is left of your worthless evil life to asking God's forgiveness for your crimes.' He sat up and swung his legs to the ground, standing up and turning to bend over her. 'Your choice, my queen. The third option is death.'

Flinging back the curtains, he grabbed his cloak and strode across the chamber to the door. The women who had been standing round the fire, listening in horror to every word, shrank back as he passed. As he disappeared into the night, they all turned as one to stare at the royal bed, exposed by the open curtains. After a moment, one of the queen's ladies tiptoed towards it and gently pulled them closed.

Eadburh sat up, drawing her bed gown around her. Her initial shock at his words had receded and she was thinking hard. Wigfrith, the senior royal thane at court and her husband's praefectus, had always been her enemy. He would never wish her anything other than death, but maybe this was her chance to escape from the life she had begun to think of as a prison. If she went back to Mercia she would find the new king. Coenwulf was a distant cousin, a strong ruler by all accounts, but unlikely to look favourably on Offa's daughter, especially if she had been banished from her husband's kingdom. He would still want to count Wessex an ally and friend. She had no desire whatsoever to enter a convent like her sister. Such a fate was unthinkable. But if she made it clear she was passing through, not planning to settle, then surely she would be safe. From Mercia she could travel on. To Powys.

Her thoughts, as so often when she was restless and unhappy, had flown back to Elisedd. Hilde had disappeared on her mission to find him; her next messenger had returned but with no information about Hilde or about the royal family of Powys.

No one seemed able to answer her question as to whether the youngest son lived or died. Surely, if he was dead someone somewhere would have known it. Someone would have told her. Someone would have demanded retribution.

But supposing her father had lied? Supposing he had told her Elisedd was dead to fool her, to force her to give up all hopes of the man she loved so passionately. Murder was second nature to him and to Cynefryth. One or other of them could have arranged to have him killed as easily as slaughtering an animal, but supposing her father had held back, worried about the construction of his precious dyke and the alliance it relied on. Supposing all this time Elisedd had been alive.

Alive. Was it possible? In her dreams he was too vivid and loving and real to be dead. And in her dreams he still loved her. In her dreams he was still here, waiting for her somewhere in the misty hills of his home.

She smiled to herself and lay back against the pillows, hugging the thought to her. That was what she would do. She would go to Powys and she would find him. But before she left she would have her revenge.

Beorhtric made no immediate move to carry out his threats, though he avoided her presence whenever he could. She was aware that she was being watched, that the court seethed with rumour and dislike and that the Witan were to a man against her, but no one dared to make a move. Not yet. So, ostensibly, neither did she. She was planning her journey with meticulous care. She had considerable wealth as queen and she was intent on making sure every penny of it went with her: money, jewels, furnishings, her daughter's small entourage of nurses and attendants, horses and mules. She felt sure Wigfrith guessed what she was up to. His intense, thoughtful gaze followed her whenever she was in the mead hall near him and she smiled to herself, sometimes catching his eye with deliberate hostility. She didn't care. Even Wigfrith must from time to time have felt a shiver of fear as that cold hard stare rested on his face.

It was not until a new young man arrived in court that matters came to a head. Worr was the son of one of the king's most senior ealdormen. The queen was performing her ceremonial role at a major feast, carrying the great auroch's horn with its decorated gold rim to the high table, presenting the drink to the king and then to Wigfrith, who met her gaze with defiant challenge, and then to Beorhtric's most senior guests in order of precedence. When she came to Worr, who sat beside the king in the seat of honour, closer even than the visiting dignitaries, she came to a halt, fixing him with her ice-cold gaze, then moved on without presenting the horn for him to sip. There was a sharp intake of breath from the watching crowd in the hall behind her.

Next day she was told that the king had commanded her removal from his court and from his kingdom. She was to leave before the next full moon.

The flagons of mead were carefully separated. One held poison for Worr, the other held a potion that would render the king impotent for the rest of his life. Both were strong and had been sweetened with extra honey and special magical charms to make them irresistible. Eadburh's household was packed and ready to leave. As was her right, she was taking her dowry and her morning gift with her, to be loaded onto the sumpter horses and ox carts that would take her belongings along the winding dusty roads into Mercia and then on into the Kingdom of Powys. These were enormous riches by any standards. No king or prince was going to turn her away.

The litter was waiting for her with the outriders already assembled when she gave the order for the manner in which the drinks were to be presented to the king, who had not emerged to see her off. 'A farewell gift,' she said, smiling, to the serf who took the tray, complete with two jewelled golden goblets. She was careful to instruct him that the king's was the larger and more splendid. The smaller, with its lethal dose, the one destined for his lover, was to be offered second. The serf was instructed to wait until the dust from her leaving had settled in the distance before he took her farewell gift to her husband's chamber. And with that she turned to climb into her litter. Behind her came a second litter with her daughter and the child's nurse, followed by her daughter's attendants and then the long train of wagons and pack animals strung out around the courtyard, with the escort, grudgingly lent by Beorhtric to see her safe across the border, drawn up outside the gates.

She had calculated that the king's potion would, before its more permanent incapacitating effects took hold, make him sleepy. He wouldn't notice when his lover, after drinking, slipped from the world. That shock would come later. She would like to have made the young man suffer agonies in his moment of death but it would be expedient to be well on her way before the unexplained death of yet another favourite was discovered.

As she turned to give one last backward glance at the king's hall, she smiled. Then she gave the order for the procession to start.

It was as the lead horse began to move off that she saw the tall figure of Wigfrith stride out of the doorway. There was a drawn sword in his hand.

'Stop!' he bellowed. 'Murder! The king has been murdered by that woman!'

Her shock was genuine; she wanted the boy to die, not her husband. His punishment was to have been far more subtle, more long-lasting.

She countermanded his order, shouting at the captain of the escort, insisting the cavalcade move off, but it was no use.

Wigfrith's barked commands were obeyed. Eadburh's litter was surrounded by the armed guard. She could do nothing but wait.

The serf who served the wine was sentenced to death. He had obeyed her instructions, he screamed, as the guard set on him, he had positioned himself outside the king's chamber, waiting for the dust to settle, but the king had seen him and, sniffing the delicious mulled wine, had snatched the nearest goblet and quaffed half of it before handing it on to his lover.

The serf was dragged away and immediately executed.

And Eadburh was still sitting in her litter, waiting, under guard. Wigfrith, standing implacably nearby, arms folded, holding the baying mob from the king's hall back with just the ferocious look in his eyes until they had calmed. At last he turned to the queen.

'That boy must have added poison to my husband's drink,' she said coldly. 'Why would I have wanted him dead? I'm leaving. He was nothing to me.'

No liquid remained from the poisoned goblet for them to test. The larger cup had fallen to the ground. Tasters were forced to drink the last dregs, left as it had rolled away but they did not die. Eadburh smiled. Their fate would be slow and probably unnoticed.

And still she waited. The summary court of her husband's ealdormen could find no proof. Wigfrith raised his hands at last in furious frustration and pronounced their verdict.

'As no proof of her culpability can be found, it is our deci-sion that the queen' – the word was heavy with sarcasm – 'shall continue on her journey out of Wessex forthwith. You will never return, madam. But the Witan of Wessex decrees that you be escorted not to Mercia, whose king is our friend and ally, and who will never countenance a murderer at his court. To ensure you are kept at a safe distance I am com-manding your escort to take you to our coast where you will board a ship at Hamwic and make sail for the kingdom of the Franks. No doubt they will know what to do with you. The king's child' – he turned to the escort that had clustered round the litter containing Eadburh's daughter and her nurse – 'will remain in Wessex.'

'No!' Eadburh screamed. 'No, you cannot take her away from me.'

'Why, madam? She belongs here with her father's loyal kin.' He did not wait to hear any more protests. Already the little girl's litter had been taken out of the procession and the leader of the queen's escort had spurred his horse forward.

The travellers were no longer heading north towards Mercia and Powys, they were on the road south towards the sea.

Bea was with her in the confines of the litter, feeling the thick fur of the rugs tucked around her, the bumpy motion of what was little more than a large chair inside a wooden frame, cushioned by coarsely stuffed bolsters. She watched Eadburh's face. Were those tears for her child genuine? She had never seemed to pay her much attention, seeing too much of her father in the child's features. In turn the little girl's affection had all been for her nurses and her playmates, and already Eadburh's tears had dried and were replaced by a calculated narrowing of the eyes. Her royal fortune was still there in her baggage train; Wigfrith had not dared confiscate her dowry and marriage portion. She was a rich woman, bound for the court of the Emperor Charlemagne, the most powerful ruler in the known world. The child would be safe, well cared for in Wessex, as the king's daughter. Almost at once, as she tried to make herself comfortable in the dusty confines of the royal litter, she had resigned herself to leaving the little girl behind. Once she had established herself at the emperor's court, she would persuade him to send for Eathswith. Until then the child would be perfectly happy where she was. She lay back against the cushions. All in all, it had not worked out badly.

But what happened to Nesta?

Bea put down the stone with calm deliberation and sat for a while in the peaceful candlelight. Eadburh had not seen her watching this time; her protective circle had kept her safe and invisible. No one in that terrifying horde of angry men had noticed her. She shivered in spite of herself, remembering the barely restrained hatred of the pressing crowds, the noise, the

284

nervousness of the horses, the placid indifference of the oxen harnessed to the baggage carts, Wigfrith's strength and authority. Did he become king next, she wondered. Simon would know. And through it all Eadburh had sat there with an expression of haughty indifference. Was she scared, under it all? Was she genuinely shocked that her plan had misfired so badly, too stunned by the sudden reversal of events to react? Bea thought not, but the scene had gone, closed down, once more locked in the distant past. She scrambled to her feet and went to stand at the window, looking out into the night. As the carts rumbled down the winding roads towards the port of Southampton only one heart-rending cry had escaped Eadburh's lips as the full realisation of where she was going finally dawned on her.

'Elise!'

30

The chantry priest was there in the corner of the chapel. It was early, morning prayer not long finished, and the cathedral was quiet, the great windows dimmed by the blanket of sullen cloud and veils of rain that hung over the city, the aisles and rows of wooden pews shadowy, only a few lights on as yet.

At the far end of the nave someone coughed, the sound echoing up into the vaults of the roof.

Bea was wearing a thick jacket against the early chill of the morning. She sat in her usual place, hidden in the corner of the chapel. There were no candles today and a thick rope had been hooked in place, dividing the altar from the body of the chapel, separating her from the old man on his chair. 'Should I tell them to take Emma away, back to London?' she whispered. 'Would that be best for her?'

His head was bent in prayer and he did not respond.

'Please, tell me what to do!' She spoke more loudly than she intended and was shocked to hear her words echo slightly off the stone walls and back down from the fan tracery above her head.

'That is your decision to make.'

'I need advice. Please.'

But he had gone.

Outside the chapel footsteps approached, echoing off the stone flags. They drew near and stopped.

'Please. I need you.'

But his corner was empty.

She sat for several minutes more, deep in thought, then she stood up and headed towards the entrance with a sigh.

Sandra had been attending morning prayer. When she saw Bea entering the chantry chapel she had felt a shiver of unease. Creeping close to the entrance she listened, holding her breath. There was someone in there with her. She could hear Bea's whispered voice echoing in the confined space. Stepping back, she waited in the shadows for Bea to leave the chapel, reach the main door and disappear out into the cold morning then she tiptoed forward, stood in the chapel doorway, peering in. It was empty and cold. There was no one there. So who had Beatrice been talking to? Who was she addressing when she had begged to be told what to do? It hadn't sounded like a prayer. It had been far too peremptory. She had been giving orders.

Sandra shuddered and stepped back. The atmosphere in the tiny chapel had turned suddenly sour. It was scary, evil. She tried to steady her breathing. Beatrice had taken something nasty in there with her – a demon. An evil spirit. She was sure of it.

What should she do? Who could she go to for help? She had spoken to the dean, she had spoken to Mark, but neither of them had seemed to take her seriously enough to do anything about it. There was only the bishop left and if he failed her it would be up to her.

She had to wait for a lull in visitors much later before she managed to speak to Heather Fawcett, who had been run off her feet in the cathedral shop. They carried their cups of coffee to the far side of the Chapter House garden and sat down out of the wind on one of the benches. The rain had stopped and sunlight was warming the garden.

'What do you think I should do?' Sandra leant forward anxiously after she had told Heather her story. Though she didn't know Heather well, she regarded her as a friend.

Heather took a thoughtful sip from her cup. 'Do you have to do anything?' she enquired mildly.

'Of course I do.'

'You said you had been to see the dean.'

'Yes.'

'Sandra, dear, what else can you do? You have to leave it up to him. He probably knows Beatrice far better than you do and if he isn't worried, I don't think you should be either.'

'But she was talking to an evil spirit! Here in the cathedral!' Sandra picked up her cup, gestured randomly with it, slopping coffee on the grass, and dropped it back down on the saucer. 'I can't stand by and watch. You know what she is, don't you?' She pulled the newspaper cuttings out of her bag. 'Look at this! I've always thought there was something odd about her.' She lowered her voice, leaning forward slightly. 'She's a strange woman. I can't think what a lovely man like the canon sees in her.'

Heather scanned the cuttings swiftly, then went back to contemplating the display of flowers in the border near their seats. 'If that's true, and to be honest I don't see what makes you think that's Bea in the photos, she seems to know what she is doing, so there would be nothing to worry about.'

'But I do worry. That's why I brought these with me. As the dean isn't interested, I thought I would speak to the bishop. Show them to him.'

Heather sighed. 'Can I suggest you leave it for now? And please, don't bother the bishop with this. You probably wouldn't get past his chaplain anyway. Don't do anything. It would be truly terrible to mention this to anyone when you don't really have anything to go on.'

'But the evil spirit—'

'I doubt there is an evil spirit anywhere in this cathedral, Sandra,' Heather cut her off sternly. 'This is a holy place.'

'But there was no one else in the chantry.' Sandra wasn't going to give up that easily. 'I told you! And when I went in there, there was the strangest atmosphere. You know when you walk into a room where two people have just had a row and you can sense it? Like that. It was electric.'

Heather brought her attention back to Sandra's face. 'It sounds to me as if you have magic powers yourself. Are you sure you're not the one who is practising mediumistic arts?'

Sandra stared at her, appalled. 'Don't even joke about it!'

'I wasn't joking. Most people don't sense things like that, dear.'

'But I don't. I'm not. I can't be!' Sandra looked as though she was about to cry.

'I know you think you've seen and heard things which at first glance seem strange, but they may not be,' Heather put in firmly. 'And it's not really our business, is it, to interfere with other people's affairs and perhaps beliefs. All you saw was the canon's wife praying. And if she spoke to God out loud, so do we all sometimes when we're upset and anxious. After all, that's what He's there for! And you should not have been listening.' She fixed Sandra with a fierce gaze.

Sandra coloured slightly. 'Perhaps you're right,' she said reluctantly.

Heather stood up. 'I know I'm right. Now, I must get back to the shop. We are very busy at the moment.'

Sandra watched her thread her way between the tables and disappear through the door. She had thought Heather would be a staunch ally. She turned her attention to the flower bed beside her and watched a bee foraging amongst the blooms. Perhaps Heather was right and she should leave it, but then, what was that adage: the only thing necessary for the triumph of evil is for good men to do nothing. Or women. It was going to be up to her to sort this out.

Bea had spent the morning with Emma; a brief lesson on chakras and energy points had given way to a trip into town to visit the shops. Bea had taken on board the extent of Emma's attention span, plus the need to go slowly with her lessons. She had also ascertained that Emma was no longer worrying about the ghost of King Ethelbert. 'No,' she had said airily when Bea enquired if he had appeared to her again. 'He belongs in his church. I know what to do now if he appears again, but he won't. Not to me. Eadburh doesn't even know he exists.'

Bea froze. 'What do you mean?'

'In my dream, we were carefree, young. Full of hopes. Father hadn't even thought about a husband for Alfrida!' The coquettish gleam in her eye filled Bea with misgivings. Was that Emma or someone else lurking in there?

'This is when you went to the little church to wait for him?'

Emma nodded, then she sighed. 'I'm talking rubbish, aren't I?'

'No, but you must be careful to keep a grip on reality.'

Emma giggled. 'Says you!' She was herself again.

Bea laughed. 'Point taken. So, we need some grounding. What about lunch?'

They agreed that Mark would drop Emma back at the cottage in the early afternoon on his way to visit the ailing priest in his hospice. Emma would practise all she had learnt so far and they would resume lessons the following day.

The moment they left, Bea went upstairs.

Nesta's herbs, still carefully stored, were lying on the shelf in her room where she had left them and she shook them out of their paper bags. They were wilting badly now. Still careful not to touch them, she reached for her touchstone and dropped it gently onto the pile. 'Where are you, Nesta?' she whispered. 'You and I must talk.'

For a long time nothing happened, then at last she sensed a change in the room, a slight movement of the air around her and in the distance she heard the deep echoing croak of a raven.

Nesta was sitting on a fallen tree on the edge of the forest. She was wrapped in a dark woollen cloak, the hood pulled up over her hair, and at her feet there was a bundle. At her girdle Bea could see the silver chain with the little crystal ball and the small sharp knife, a tiny leather wallet and a silver box suspended from a ring; the tools of her trade, all half hidden in the deep folds of her skirt.

'Did Eadburh not think to give you her protection and take you with her?' Bea asked.

The other woman smiled bleakly. 'She gave me not a second thought, nor did I expect her to. It was never in her nature to be generous. She would have been happy to let me die as the poisoner in her stead. I had the measure of that woman long ago and I was gone before the bane ever entered the mouth of the king.'

'You knew she would kill him?'

Slowly Nesta nodded. 'She did not mean that to happen, but she was a dealer in death. That was their destiny, hers to kill, his to die at her hand.'

'And you. Where did you go?'

'To Powys of course.'

Bea felt her attention sharpen. 'Why?'

'Was that not the seat of all her fears and woes and the place she left her heart? A man there turned her into a killer and I was curious to know how.'

'Surely it was her father who turned her into a killer. And her mother.'

Nesta raised her face to the sunlight as it began to filter through the boughs of the trees above her head and smiled. 'Whether it was in her blood or in her destiny, she learned her lesson well.'

'And when you reached Powys, did you find Elise alive?' Bea leaned forward eagerly. 'Did you tell him about her?'

Nesta closed her eyes against the sun and smiled. 'It was a long way to the kingdom of Powys. I had my own destiny to fulfil and first I had to avoid the men hunting me through the forests of Wessex and then on into the Forest of Dean between the Wye and the Severn rivers where I saw for the first time Offa's great dyke looming on the hilltops as I fled like a hind into the shadows of my friends the trees.'

'And you managed to escape,' Bea whispered confidently. 'You were a survivor.'

Nesta smiled. 'I had friends in the woods, I told you. The plants and trees, the elves and goblins, the fairies and sprites; I knew where to hide, I knew where to find shelter and warmth by the fires of the charcoal burners and the forest dwellers, I knew how to spin myself a cloak of green as I headed north following the star paths in the sky.'

'And you knew how to see me.'

Nesta glanced across at her. 'Were you trying to hide?'

'From Eadburh, yes.'

'But you failed. Your magic is faulty, full of holes. And she is powerful. You should beware.'

'Can you show me how to hide as I watch her?'

Nesta was thoughtful for a long moment. 'Why do you want to watch her?'

Bea hesitated. 'Her spirit is wandering the hillsides where she was happy with her prince. She calls for him endlessly, her voice echoing lonely and desolate, and I don't know how to help her.'

'Why should you be the one to help her?'

'Because that's my job. Because I can see the people others can't, the people who are trapped on this earth. Because I have always wanted to give peace to unhappy souls.'

'And that is why you live with a man of God and yet you hide from him and swathe the longings of your soul in dark cloaks of deception.'

Bea sat up, shocked. 'No!'

'No?'

Dark cloaks of deception. Bea recoiled at the words.

'People call you witch.' Nesta gave a rueful smile. 'That word I think implies evil and brings fear as much to your time as to mine.'

'So you know we are from different times.'

This time Nesta laughed out loud. 'My dear, I am from the place between time and eternity.'

'And you could help me. For the sake of Eadburh and for that young woman, Emma, up on the ridge where Eadburh and her prince made love. Please. Was it Emma's destiny to be drawn into this story? I think not. I need to teach her, and I don't know if I'm strong enough.'

'All you need is courage.' Nesta stood up slowly and bent to pick up her bundle. 'I am not a teacher, I thread my way between the stars. I will tell you if I found *y Tywysog* Elisedd when the time is right. God speed.' Bea watched her turn towards the shadows between the trees and in a few seconds she had disappeared. In the place where she had been sitting there was no trace of her, the grasses weren't flattened, there were no footprints in the dew.

When Bea awoke, someone had covered her with a rug. She lay still, unable to collect her thoughts. Then slowly it came back. She had gone into a meditation with the scattered plants from Nesta's basket. The woman had talked with her, a rational, informative dialogue, and then she had walked away into the forest.

She had fallen asleep on her cushion and dreamt, and Mark must have come up to look for her after his visit to the hospice. Slowly she sat up. It was still daylight outside the window. She scrambled to her feet and walked over to look out, still a little dazed. Her touchstone lay on the sill in a patch of warm sunlight. She looked down at it warily and then turned to look at the low table. The plants had gone, the empty paper bags lying where she had left them.

The house was empty, but there was a note on the kitchen table. *Hope you had a good sleep. I'll be back about 6 pm M x*

The plants were not in the compost box on the draining board, nor were they in the rubbish bin. There was no sign of them. Mark must have taken them. She felt a quick flash of anger. He had no right.

The text from Heather came as a complete surprise. Are you at home and alone? Must see you urgently.

The quiet tap at the side door only a few minutes after her reply was like something out of a spy movie. With a quick look back over her shoulder, Heather followed Bea into the kitchen and carefully closed the door behind them. 'It's Sandra Bedford.'

'Oh no.'

Bea's weary response seemed to be all Heather needed to know.

'So, she's spoken to you?'

'I think she's stalking me.'

'Oh yes.' Heather set her mouth grimly. 'She's stalking you all right. She appears to think you talk to demons! She's got the newspaper cuttings about that awful place you went to over on the border to chase out a poltergeist.'

'Oh God! Did she show them to you? I don't know what I've done to make her so determined to damage me.'

But she was being disingenuous there, Bea thought, ashamed. She knew all too well. She sat down at the table heavily and put her head in her hands. 'What can I do? She's already been to the dean.'

Heather sighed. 'She told me. Did he say anything to you?'

'No, but he had a word with Mark.'

'Bless him. He wouldn't want to believe anything bad about anyone anyway. So Mark knows? He's seen the cuttings?'

Bea nodded. 'I showed them to him when they first appeared.'

'So, what are we going to do?'

Bea smiled with relief. 'You don't know how much it cheers me up to know you're still on my side.'

Heather laughed. 'It's like being back at school! Sandra isn't a classic bully, she's the sneak who hides behind the lockers and then runs to the teacher pretending to be all innocence and only interested in the greater good!'

'So, what can I do?'

'Turn her into a toad?'

Bea opened her mouth to retort, then fell suddenly silent. 'You don't think I'm a witch too?'

Heather laughed again. She stood up and went to plug in Bea's kettle. 'I couldn't possibly comment,' she said. 'But if you are, you need to adopt a cloak of invisibility in future because she is out to get you. What we have to do is come up with a cunning plan.'

Bea watched as Heather made tea and reached for the mug gratefully as it was pushed across the table towards her.

'And that doesn't include turning her into a toad,' Heather added sternly, 'tempting though that might be.'

'You credit me with more talent than I have, alas,' Bea said with a rueful grin.

'Well, even if you can do such things, I expect there is a law against it by now. Animal welfare or something. So, we have the might of the Church on our side, in the shape of the dean and Chapter, but we also know they will never sack her for malfeasance or anything like that, so we are stuck with her.'

'Do I gather you don't like her either?'

'Let's say I've never warmed to her. Luckily I don't normally see much of her, but today she sought me out deliberately to warn me about you and ask me what she should do. Naturally I said do nothing and she didn't like that. I could see her little brain whirling with indignation and self-righteous zeal. So, you have to be careful. I wonder if she's capable of standing up at matins and denouncing you from the floor of the house.'

Bea gave a weary laugh. 'I think you're muddling the cathedral with the House of Commons.'

'She threatened to go to see the bishop. No, it's all right, I warned her off him as well.' Heather sat forward, resting her chin on her folded hands. Bea hesitated and Heather nodded. 'I won't do anything, Bea, unless you ask me to. I promise.'

'Even though you know it's true?'

She hadn't meant to say it.

Heather narrowed her eyes. 'You've been talking to demons in the cathedral?'

'No.' Or had she? Wasn't Eadburh close to the demonic? 'No, but I have been talking to, or perhaps praying with is a better way of putting it, the spirit of an old priest in the Stanbury Chapel. Sandra saw me, heard me speak out loud. That's what has given rise to all this. You know how discreet I try to be, but I've been helping a family whose daughter has been very disturbed. I brought her to the cathedral to pray and Sandra saw us together and followed us. She keeps asking me about what I was doing.'

There was a long moment of silence.

'Tricky,' Heather said at last.

'What am I going to do?'

'I suppose you could cast a tiny spell on Sandra. Something to shut her up.' Heather's eyes were twinkling.

People will call you a witch. Nesta's words echoed at the back of Bea's mind. *That word I think implies evil and brings fear as much to your time as to mine.*

'Only joking.' Heather noticed her expression. Her whisper got through and Bea smiled. 'I'm not into spells,' she said softly, 'but I know someone who is. I'll bear the idea in mind.'

31

Emma claimed to be too tired to do anything when Bea arrived to pick her up next morning. She reminded Bea of a Victorian heroine, flinging back her dishevelled blond hair, pressing her hand against her brow and throwing herself down in the chair nearest to the fire which was nothing but a bed of cold ash. Bea was quite pleased. She wanted the chance to talk to Simon alone and a walk seemed a good way of grabbing it without the possibility of being overheard.

Emma watched them leave out of the corner of her eye; as soon as they had disappeared up the lane she leapt to her feet.

'Duh?' Felix had been glued to his phone.

'I want to read Dad's book.' Emma had descended on the pile of manuscript that was now residing on the windowsill near his desk. She scooped it up and retired to the chair. 'Don't tell him, OK? I need to know what it is he was writing about that stirred everything up. I'm studying history, this counts as revision.'

'Whatever.' Felix shrugged his shoulders and went back to his phone, uninterested now that she appeared to be staying in one place.

Emma flipped through the pages. There was a marker about

halfway through and she turned to that bit, searching for the chapter heading, 'The Offa's Dyke Years'. Minutes later she was completely absorbed.

'How is Emma doing?' Bea pushed her hands into her pockets. In spite of the sunshine a lively breeze had got up and the air was sharp and ice-cold as they climbed higher up the lane.

'Better. Much more self-possessed. But she's exhausted. I think the whole thing has been a huge drain.'

She put her hand gently on his arm. 'Emma will be all right, Simon. This all takes a bit of getting used to, but now she has me to confide in I think it will be better. Up to now she has been hiding her experiences from everyone, but she's a strong young woman. She will learn to manage it.'

He gently removed his arm from her hand; she hadn't realised she was still holding it and felt herself colour with embarrassment. 'Sorry. I needed something solid to hold onto.' She stepped away from him and, staring off into the distance, she folded her arms. Then she turned to face him again. 'One of the reasons for coming up here this morning was that I want to distance myself from the cathedral. It makes sense to come here to the centre of the activities but for all sorts of other reasons I want to avoid taking Emma there; Ethelbert is an extra character in our lives we can do without at the moment.'

'His is a gruesome story.' He gave her a strangely intense look. 'And that dreadful woman who is following you around doesn't help matters.' He shoved his hands into his pockets. 'You should know that the kids and I are going over to Worcester to spend Easter Day with Val and her friends. I think it would be good to get away from here for a bit. If they want, I'll leave them there. They will be going back to school and exams soon anyway and by then Emma needs to have regained a bit of equilibrium.'

'Point taken. I'm sure she has all the tools she needs. After that it will be up to her.' She shivered. 'Perhaps we should turn back. If she doesn't want to talk to me today, I may as well go home.'

*

'Did you take the herbs from my room?' Bea had finally cornered Mark in his study.

He looked up from his desk, perplexed. 'What herbs?'

'The ones I had put into paper bags.'

'The ones you said were poisonous? No, I haven't touched them.'

She caught her breath. 'Are you sure?'

He nodded. 'Why?'

'I've mislaid them. I must have thrown them away. I meant to check what they were first.'

He gave her a long, studied look. He didn't believe that any more than she did. He gave a troubled sigh. 'Would you consider coming to church over Easter?' he said after a moment. 'You like the Tenebrae service, don't you, and it wouldn't be in the cathedral.'

Bea returned his gaze. 'Are you wheedling?'

He smiled boyishly. 'Yes, I suppose I am.'

'Then shouldn't you be asking me to come to the Easter Day service here, in front of the dean and the bishop and the whole congregation, so Sandra can see me and witness that I am not struck down by a bolt of lightning?'

'Yes, I suppose I should.'

'I will come to both of them. I'll make a point of it.' She saw the relief in his face and felt guilty. 'I'm so sorry I've been putting you into such an awkward position. I enjoy going to services, Mark. You know I do.'

That was the truth. Later, back in her own space upstairs, Bea stood looking out of her window down into the garden thinking about their conversation as she watched a blackbird perched on the edge of their little fountain, splashing happily in the spray. Her feelings about the Church of England were complex; she loved the beauty of the services, the music and the liturgy, the 1662 prayer book for its tradition and spirituality, the modern forms for their simplicity and modernity. And she appreciated other forms of worship too. Catholics and Methodists; synagogues and mosques and gurdwara. Each had its own truth and intense sincerity. But her own beliefs were tied up inextricably with her own experience, her inner knowledge that there was far more in heaven and earth than was addressed in an orthodox service of any belief. Her prayers were addressed to a non-denominational god and mediated through the spirit of a long-departed priest who sat in a tiny chapel in a Christian cathedral. Tricky.

She turned back towards the table in the centre of the room and picked up the small silk-wrapped bundle that contained her stone. Prince Elisedd. What had happened to him after he left Mercia? She was not going to ask Nesta, who was obviously inclined to play power games; she was going to go and find out for herself.

Cloud hung low over the mountains; the rocks were slick with rain and the grass tangled wet across her path. Bea looked round in panic, not recognising anything. Where was she? She could hear nothing but water. Rain poured down round her and the angry thundering of a river in spate was a background to the low rumble of thunder echoing around the countryside. A sudden fork of lightning lit up the endless emptiness of the scene.

'So, you think you don't need me?' The woman's voice in her ear was very close; she could feel breath on her neck. She froze, not daring to move. 'Who is that?'

'Do you have to ask?' Another shaft of lightning cracked like a whiplash amongst the rocks and for that split second she saw the face near her, staring past her into the distance. The rain on the woman's face turned the skin to the semblance of alabaster.

'Nesta?' she whispered. The word was lost in the cacophony of the elements.

'Welcome to the kingdom of the sons of Vortigern.' Nesta's voice was as harsh as the cry of the raven that seemed to follow her.

'Is this where Elisedd lives?' Bea struggled to make herself heard, her voice almost inaudible as she cried out into the rain. 'Where?' She didn't dare move. She felt she was perched on the edge of a precipice and a step would pitch her out into endless darkness. 'Is he still alive?'

'Are any of us still alive?' The reply was mocking. 'Are you not wandering in the place of the dead?'

'Stop it!' Suddenly Bea was angry. 'This is my vision! Why are you taunting me? I thought we were allies.'

She clutched at her collar, trying to find her cross. It wasn't there. In her rising panic she turned round, flailing out into the darkness. Then she heard a voice, a second voice, almost drowned out by the tumult of the elements.

'Bea? Bea!'

Her own name cut sharply across the raging noises in her head and Bea opened her eyes to total, shocking silence. She was out of breath and shaking as she looked blankly round the room, not recognising where she was. She heard herself give a little whimper. 'Are you all right, darling? Here. Give that to me.' Mark was kneeling on the floor beside her and took the stone out of her unresisting fingers. He looked down at it with distaste and put it down on the table, then he took Bea's hands in his. 'You're freezing. Come downstairs and let me get you something hot to drink.'

She found she was staring at him. She knew who he was, of course she did, and yet he seemed out of place.

Out of time.

She tried desperately to focus her thoughts, her gaze going past him, round the room, towards the window where a benevolent blue sky hung gently behind small white clouds.

'The storm has gone.' She heard her own voice, strangely flat and without resonance.

'Yes, my darling, the storm has gone.' After a moment's hesitation Mark put his arm round her shoulder and pulled her against him. He held her like that, close, until he began to feel some warmth coming back to her body.

'Where were you?' he asked at last.

She closed her eyes. 'The place of the dead,' she murmured.

His arms tightened round her. 'Christ be with us,' he whispered, 'Christ within us, Christ behind us, Christ before us.' He glanced round the room. Was there something there? An atmosphere, a lurking demonic presence? 'Can you stand up?' He spoke more loudly now. 'Let's go downstairs.'

'She isn't here.' Bea responded to his change of tone.

'She?'

'Nesta. She is there in the mountains. In the rain.' She straightened a little and he moved back so she could stand up. As she struggled to find her feet there was a small chink of metal as her cross fell at her feet. They both looked down at it. 'The chain broke.' She was staring at it blankly. 'That's why I couldn't find it.'

Mark stooped and picked it up. 'We'll find you a new chain,' he said. His mouth was dry.

She held out her hand to take it and stood looking down at it as it lay on her palm. She had not gone into her meditation seeking to see Nesta again. The woman had sneaked in under her radar and come between her and her goal, to find Elisedd. She felt a sudden visceral fear. Her quest was becoming dangerous; she had met someone who could with ease slip past her safeguards, someone who knew how to move between the worlds, who worshipped the ancient and powerful gods who had ruled this land long before Christianity arrived on the shores of Albion and who might even now be here in the room with them, watching. She looked up, unaware that Mark was watching as her gaze flitted from one corner of the room to another.

'What is it?' he asked gently. 'What are you looking for?'

'Nothing!' she jumped guiltily. 'I'm still feeling a bit shaky. You shouldn't have woken me like that, Mark!'

'Sweetheart, you were shouting.'

'Shouting?' Her gaze came back abruptly to his face. 'I wasn't!'

'Yes, you were. You sounded so frightened. What was I supposed to do? Stand and watch?'

She could feel her heart beginning to pound again, her breath struggling in her chest. Closing her fist around the cross, she swallowed hard. 'No. Thank you for being here.'

'Please stop this, Bea.'

'I don't think I can.' She gritted her teeth. 'This is something I have to finish, Mark. I have to find out where Emma fits in. Until I do that she might be in danger.' She saw his face and hastily rephrased her comment. 'From herself. She has run out into the countryside twice now, Mark. She is frantically looking for something, but she doesn't know what, or who she is looking for, and he isn't there any more.'

'So, she is looking for someone.'

'Yes, she's looking for someone.'

'And you know who.'

She nodded.

'And Simon knows what is happening?'

'Yes, we discussed it this morning.'

'And he's happy with this situation?'

'No, he's not happy, but the situation is as it is. He knows it's probably his own reading and research that has stirred up this swarm of bees—' She stopped abruptly. Bees. Somehow bees were central to this story.

'And how does my nun fit in?'

She had forgotten that Mark too was involved in this strange conundrum. 'I don't know.'

'Has she reappeared?'

'Not as far as I know.'

He sighed. It was his turn to walk over to the window and stare out as though seeking inspiration in the garden. 'What are you going to do?'

'I am going to do nothing for a bit while I think. My dream, my meditation, took me to a horrible place just now. The kingdom of the sons of Vortigern. I suppose it was somewhere in Wales, but it seemed more like some Arthur Rackham-type version of what hell would be. I don't want to go there again. I have grown over-confident and that leads to carelessness.' She gave a wan smile. 'I will come to you for help, Mark, I promise, and in the meantime, please, hold me in your prayers. I will follow you down, my love, but first I have to cleanse this room and light some incense.' She saw him hesitate, saw him frown, but he nodded slowly and turned back to the door.

'Don't be too long.'

She waited until he had closed the door and she heard the sound of his footsteps running down the stairs, then she slipped

303

the cross into the pocket of her jeans and turned to the shelf to retrieve what she needed.

Behind her the shape of a woman had coalesced out of the shadows. It was watching her, a faint smile on the drifting amorphous shape that was her face. Before Bea turned back with a dried bundle of rowan leaves and mugwort and a box of matches, the figure had gone.

32

Sandra was wandering round the aisles in Marks & Spencer, deep in thought. She had been there some time now, flicking through coat hangers, pushing at racks of jackets and skirts, feeling soft jumpers and trousers, going round and round in a half daze. She did not notice the figure some distance behind her keeping a suspicious watch on her activities. Pulling out a dress she held it against herself for a few moments, then shoved it back amongst the others. She hadn't even noticed that it was at least four sizes too big for her. When at last she gave up on her endless, pointless quest and headed for the doors, the store detective stood watching until she was out of sight in the crowded street outside. The woman was a troubled soul, no question about that. Exactly the sort of unhappy middle-aged loser who would find herself up before a magistrate for shoplifting without ever quite knowing why. She knew if the woman had shoved something into her bag it would have been without even realising what she had done. For once she was glad it hadn't happened. It would have been so needless a humiliation. She turned back into the shop and spotted a group of giggling teenagers. These were far more likely prey. They were the kind who thought nicking something was normal and easy and a laugh. Well, she was about to prove them wrong on every count.

Sandra wandered on down between the stalls of the street market, her empty shopping bag over her arm. Overhead she heard the ringing call of a gull as it flew low over the street, scanning the crowds below. She gave a rueful smile. Once that noise would have filled her with joy, reminding her of happy seaside holidays with her parents; nowadays, as a rueful neighbour had explained, all gulls needed to target a town was word to get out in the bird community that people were walking around eating chips. She stood lost in thought, studying a stall laden with joss sticks and candles, incense cones and statues of the laughing Buddha, until a woman laden with carrier bags in the jostling crowd pushed her out of the way.

By the time she turned back towards the cathedral, her mind was made up. There was only one thing she could do.

'She resigned?' Bea looked at Heather in astonishment. 'Why?'

'No idea. She loved her job. But we both know she has been very odd lately. On a bit of a quest. I told her she could come back any time and she would be very welcome. No.' She raised a hand as Bea opened her mouth to protest. 'I know this must be huge relief to you, but I wondered if perhaps she's not well. Maybe that's behind her weird behaviour. She has been looking very stressed and tired. It can't all be because she's witch-hunting you.' She gave a tight little smile. 'You didn't cast a spell on her, did you?'

'No, of course I didn't!' Bea's reply was sharper than she intended.

Heather looked at her thoughtfully. 'She has a flat in St James. As far as I know, she lives there alone. She's a widow or divorced, I'm not sure which, and I don't think she has any children. I always thought the cathedral was pretty much her whole life. I can't understand her going, especially now in the run-up to Easter and with her quest to thwart your evil plans in full swing. I'll look in on her in a day or two or so to make sure she's OK.'

Bea said nothing, pushing away her lurking feeling of guilt.

She was surprised though. She would have thought Sandra's quest would have led her to stay where she was, hiding behind the great Norman pillars, tiptoeing round the Chapter House garden, spying. Her guilt was followed swiftly by a huge wave of relief. She turned to Heather. 'Why don't I shout you a cup of tea? Are you in a hurry?' They had met by accident, both doing last-minute shopping.

Heather smiled. 'Why not? I have serious questions to ask you.'

She waited until they were seated in a quiet backstreet café.

'So, you looked a bit guilty when I told you Sandra had left.'

'And you know why. But I won't deny it's a weight off my mind to think she won't be tracking me round Herefordshire any more.'

'And you believe that, do you?'

'What do you mean?' Bea stared at her.

'You don't think she's left so she can pursue you full-time?'

Bea was speechless with horror. 'But what does she think she's going to see?' she retorted at last.

'You tell me.'

'Only me in a chapel praying. And working with a vulnerable child, which is something I shan't do again, or not in the cathedral anyway. That was a mistake, though I could be forgiven for thinking it was a safe space.'

'True.' There was a pause. 'Do be careful, Bea,' Heather said at last. 'I have an uncomfortable feeling about this. If I extrapolate from some passing remarks she made, I had begun to wonder if she fancied Mark; she definitely thinks she has a special rapport with him and she might, just might, be under the impression that he likes her.'

Bea's mouth dropped open.

'I know. I know,' Heather went on. 'It's not very credible, but I've met cases a bit like this before. You know yourself that gentlemen clergy, especially handsome gentlemen clergy, hold an irresistible fascination for the unmarried ladies in their congregations. Women have been known to come to blows over the honour of making them a sandwich. And this strikes me as being of a similar ilk. Only different in that it's infinitely more sinister.'

Bea was silent. Heather waited.

'You're serious, aren't you?' Bea said at last.

'Very.'

'You think I should be scared?'

'Be on the qui vive at the very least. Mark knows what's going on. He is an experienced clergyman who knows these things happen.' She smiled sympathetically. 'I'm sorry, I didn't mean to scare you.'

'You haven't!'

But that wasn't true. The malice she had seen in Sandra's eyes had shocked her deeply. The relief she had felt when Heather told her that the woman had resigned had shown her how worried she was. Something else struck her. Nesta knew about Sandra; the fact that Sandra thought her a witch. She shivered. Nesta was the one who really scared her. She was a powerful entity, far more skilled than Bea. And Bea didn't know whether she was friend or foe.

'Bea? You OK?'

Heather had noticed her abstraction.

'I'm fine.' Bea stood up. 'I must get on. I'm going with Mark to a Tenebrae service tonight.' She smiled. 'Pity Sandra won't be there to note the fact that I do go to church.'

They came home late after the service. It had been magical. Bea loved the theatricality of it, the silent meditation, the deep spirituality. As they drove back to Hereford neither spoke much, still immersed in the drama. The Close was silent, empty of people, the statue of Elgar with his bicycle in the corner of the grass a lonely presence in the shadows, the Precentor's House and the Chancellor's House, both in darkness, their own lit only by the half-moon of glass above the front door showing they had left the hall light on to welcome them home. Closing the door behind them, Mark kissed her on the cheek and whispered that he would see her later, before letting himself into his study. He was going to pray, she knew. He would probably sleep in there, stretching out on the sofa in the corner.

She lit a candle without turning on the light and sat down on her cushion in the flickering shadows. Her head was still full of the beauty of the Christian story, the drama and the tragedy that was all part of Easter; and she was exhausted. It was very late.

Without realising it was happening, she allowed her eyes to close.

But there was still no sign of Elisedd in her dream. Instead she found herself once more following in Eadburh's footsteps.

The Emperor Charlemagne's palace at Aachen was enormous. It was richly built and larger by far than any of the palaces in Mercia or Wessex, the clusters of buildings, linked by covered walkways, bewildering in their grandeur. Eadburh found herself lodged in one of the royal guest houses, ladies provided to wait on her, her vast treasures unloaded and stored in a warehouse nearby.

She had not enjoyed the voyage from Southampton even though the weather had been kind; the wind was from the northwest, gentle and steady, the long swell rolling in from the distant ocean. The ship that had brought her to the kingdom of the Franks, rowed by fifteen pairs of oarsmen, had been large enough to accommodate her and her baggage. Once unloaded on the dunes at Wissant her riches were reloaded onto wagons and her long journey continued north and east across the flat plains of northern Europe.

On the first night after her arrival at this, the emperor's favourite residence, she was invited to his mead hall, greeted as an honoured guest and, once the feasting was over, she found herself seated beside him. So, this was the man who had negotiated with her father for her sister's hand for his son, and who had toyed with the idea of marrying one of his daughters to her brother. She felt his keen gaze on her face as servants brought ewer and basin for the ceremonial hand wash and knelt with a soft towel as she dabbled her fingers in the scented water. She felt his eyes on her hands and was glad that she had worn her most beautiful rings and was adorned in the royal jewels of Wessex and Mercia. The king had provided a guard for the riches of her marriage portions and her dowry and she knew she came to his court as a wealthy and desirable widow. She did not know or care much whether he knew why she was a widow; the scandal of her life with Beorhtric was over.

She studied him surreptitiously. He was a tall man, powerful of build, wearing a golden coronet on his greying hair. Two large hairy dogs lounged at his feet, both watching her with lazy interest, and she felt his eyes too boring into hers. This was the most powerful ruler in the western world, crowned Emperor of the Romans by Pope Leo only two years before, after conquering all the German tribes, the man with whom her father had negotiated diplomatic treaties and alliances and who she now planned to ask for protection. She smiled and lowered her eyelids flirtatiously, waiting for him to speak. He leaned back in his chair with a smile. 'So, why has the Queen of Wessex come to see me?'

'I am newly widowed, sire.' She lowered her voice seductively. She had heard that this man could not resist a beautiful, powerful woman, and his wife of many years had died. His last wife, for he had had several, so she had heard, as well as countless mistresses.

'I came to you for protection, sire. I was surrounded by threats and dangers in my own country.'

'And your father and brother are dead.'

She tensed. 'Indeed, leaving me alone in the world but for a little daughter who has been taken from me.'

'But you have brought your marriage portion, I hear.'

She lowered her eyes again. 'I was allowed to take away what was my due when I told them I was coming to seek your help,' she said softly.

'Strange. I heard you were deported.' His gaze was steady. 'For unspeakable crimes.'

She tightened her jaw. 'The unspeakable crimes were not mine, sire.'

She dropped the pretence of coquettish weakness and met his eyes directly.

Behind them the hall was full of noise; the emperor's household had finished eating and the house slaves were clearing the tables away. A band of musicians were tuning their instruments. Fresh wine and ale and mead was brought in; the glass beaker at her elbow was refreshed with wine though she hadn't yet touched it. The roar of voices was growing louder and she wished she could speak to him somewhere quiet and private, but he made no move to end their public confrontation. Eyes were watching them and she became aware of several women, richly attired, who were standing nearby, ostensibly talking close to the great central hearth, taking enormous interest in what was going on on the dais nearby. The emperor held out a gold-rimmed drinking horn to a passing house servant and it was immediately refilled. He smiled thoughtfully. 'I like women of spirit; I admired your father greatly.'

'My father was a great king,' she replied with dignity.

'As was Beorhtric.' His voice grew sharp.

She nodded less enthusiastically.

'And you say your daughter has been kept from you by his successor, King Egbert.'

She bit her lip. 'Indeed, my lord.'

'Egbert who spent his days in exile under my protection.'

She tensed again. 'He is a fair man and a good king,' she conceded cautiously, 'but cruel to remove a child from her mother.'

'A child who could be married to a rival and carries with her the blood of her father.'

'If she came to me, sire, I could ensure that she made a suitable marriage with your approval,' she said carefully. 'Or she could enter a convent and give her life to God. I would trust you to ensure she was safe.'

She hoped her face showed all the love and desperation of a loving mother. She was beginning to tire of the endless scrutiny of those sharp eyes fixed so acutely on her face. They held a cold intelligence that chilled her.

'If she is indeed the daughter of her father.' His voice was suddenly harsh.

She looked down, genuinely stunned. 'Of course she's her father's daughter,' she said indignantly.

311

'Even though her father did not care for women?'

'He cared enough to come to my bed as a husband, sire.' She was blazing with anger. 'Why do you think I—?' She caught the words back in time. 'I can assure you that I was his true and loyal wife!'

To her amazement she saw his face light with amusement. 'I believe you, madam!' He quaffed the last of his wine with one swallow. 'And we will talk of this again soon. If I am to give you my protection, I will have to give some thought to your future position. Until then I trust you will be comfortable in the queen's guest hall.' He looked towards the gathered women by the hearth at last and beckoned. Two of them stepped forward. 'The lady Trude and the lady Waldrada served my late queen well. They will attend you.' Standing up, he stepped to the edge of the dais and gestured towards the musicians. At once they began to play. She was forgotten.

Eadburh dropped a dignified curtsy towards the emperor but he was striding away towards a group of his thanes. His dogs had risen with him, one on each side, huge animals with dark, intelligent eyes, half hidden by fringes of silky hair, and she felt their gaze follow her thoughtfully as she moved towards door. First one and then the other looked beyond her and she saw their focus sharpen. One growled in its throat. She turned and followed their gaze.

Bea shrank back but there was nowhere to hide. The noise of the great hall, the richly clothed and armoured men and women swathed in silks and velvets, the swirling shadows of a thousand candles, the smell of food, the smoke from the fires and the steady threatening gaze of the great dogs, one black and one fawn, pinned her where she was. Eadburh raised her right hand, pointing at Bea and she feared the woman was commanding the dogs to attack, but as one they seemed to consider and then dismiss her as of no importance and they turned away to follow the emperor across the hall. The women were approaching, but the sound was fading. The music lingered for a few seconds as an echo in the air and then all was silence.

Bea took a deep breath. She could taste the lingering smoke from the roasting meat on her lips, smell the reek of the hall. Her ears were ringing with the noise of lute and rebec, horn and trumpet. And now in her room all was silence broken only as the cathedral clock struck the quarter.

With a sigh, Simon stood up from the table and walked across to the door. He could hear Felix snoring softly in the corner, hunched in his sleeping bag with his back to the single lamp on Simon's desk. He had been asleep for hours. Simon glanced at his wristwatch. It was well after midnight. He eased the front door open, anxious not to disturb the boy, and slid outside into the cold night.

The clouds had drifted away to the north and the sky was ablaze with stars. He stood looking up, aware yet again that the view he was used to in London, the planets, a few of the brightest constellations at best, was outshone a thousand times over by the sheer number he could see here. The Milky Way was clearly visible, a great shawl sprawled overhead. It confused him. His usual signposts were harder to pick out. And this was the sky which the men and women of history had seen routinely. This was the vast storyboard with which they grew up as children and lived and beneath which they died before heading off into some vision of heaven above their heads. Unless they knew they were bound for hell.

He shivered. He ought to go back indoors to retrieve his jacket before he set off on a stroll up on the hill. His head was full of Welsh history and it seemed somehow appropriate that he walk beneath Welsh stars. Something was impelling him to turn westward, towards the vast distances lost in the darkness of the night. Forgetting the jacket, he made his way down to the gate and let himself out into the lane.

He had looked up Elisedd. It was a name that appeared several times in the story of the royal house of Powys, over several generations. The first to appear was Elisedd ap Gwylog who had reigned from about 725 for about twenty-five years. There was a famous monument known as Eliseg's Pillar at Valle Crucis near Llangollen which he promised himself he would visit. The pillar, all that was left of the great cross after which the valley and the abbey nearby took their name, had been inscribed with the family pedigree going back to Vortigern and Magnus Maximus. Quite a pedigree. It had been erected by his great-grandson Cyngen, who reigned from about 808 – too late to have been the king during Offa's time. Between Eliseg – a 'miscarving' of the name Elisedd, apparently – came two other kings, either of whom would have fought Offa – Brochfael ap Elisedd and Cadell ap Brochfael. Ap, he had already established, meant 'son of'. Both of those kings would have had sons and daughters, and both could and likely would have had a son called Elisedd after their illustrious ancestor. Eadburh's Elisedd, Emma's Elisedd, was obviously a younger son and as there seemed to be no record of him that Simon could discover in his first cursory scan of the internet, he had not inherited the kingdom or merited a mention in history. All that remained of this handsome young man was an echo on the lips of a lost woman wandering the hills for twelve hundred years.

He let himself through the gate at the end of the lane and walked out onto the hillside. The sky was overwhelming up here. So close. He stood staring up. He had been reading some of the Welsh legends about the constellations. The Milky Way was called Caer Arianrhod. The castle of the daughter of Dôn. Romantic. Recalling ancient stories, stories probably known by Elisedd and his lover. He found himself wishing that Bea was there with him. Last time they had stood here on this hillside they had had a frosty conversation. He regretted that now. All she had done was try and help him and Emma, and he had reacted with pig-headed obstinacy and refused to engage with her when, he had realised somewhat belatedly, she was genuinely troubled about the visions or dreams or whatever they were that Em was having. He walked on slowly, following the trackway through the grass, gorse bushes clearly visible in the starlight, their flowers luminous, the countryside opening up on either side of the ridge as though it was day.

He heard the horse coming from far away, its hooves drumming on the dry ground. He wasn't surprised. On a night like this it would be a joy to be out alone with the night. He stopped and turned round, trying to place the sound. And then he saw it, rider lying low on the animal's neck as it galloped flat out towards him. He wasn't sure if the man saw him but he seemed to be coming straight for him. Simon threw himself sideways behind some bushes as the horse passed within feet of him. He smelled the hot sweat, the tang of leather, he saw the rider, his cloak flying, leaning down, he saw the sword catch the starlight as it swung in his direction. The thunder of hooves, the rasping breath of the animal, the rattle of harness and then, as rapidly as it had appeared, it was gone. He climbed to his feet shakily and stared round. There was no sign of the rider. The night was silent again.

Had that actually happened?

He rubbed his elbow ruefully. If it hadn't, what was it? Had it been a ghost? He felt a raft of goose pimples run across his back. Suddenly his midnight walk didn't seem to be such a good idea any more. He turned back the way he had come as down in the lonely blackness of the woods below the ridge a fox let out an eerie warning bark. Maybe it would be a good thing to go out for the day to Worcester after all.

33

Simon waited until Tuesday morning to ring Bea.

'How did your weekend go?' she asked. 'Did Emma and Felix enjoy their Easter Egg hunt?'

'There wasn't one, thank God!' She heard the smile. 'Actually it wasn't too bad. We had a slap-up lunch and the kids seemed to enjoy it. And it was nice seeing Val so relaxed and happy. She is in her own comfort zone in a place like that. Big house. Lovely kitchen. Lovely city.'

'Good.' She ignored the wistful note in his voice. 'And has everything calmed down now with Emma?'

'She wants to see you. I said I would arrange something in the next couple of days. With Easter having been so late this year, they go back to school all too soon – from their point of view anyway.' There was a pause. 'I'd like a chat with you first. She heard the caution in his voice. 'Can we arrange to meet somewhere without her? What about lunch at that pub near Leominster? The kids are sitting down to their books today. Val put the fear of God into them about revision and holiday work.'

He was waiting for her outside the pub. After she parked her car on the village green and locked it, she stood still watching him. He was looking distracted, a faraway expression on his face.

'Penny for them!'

He jumped. 'I didn't hear you. Shall we sit outside?'

He went in to buy them drinks and came back with two shandies and a menu. 'I wanted to tell you in private, without Emma hearing, about something that happened to me.'

'Ah.'

'Yes. I think I owe you an apology.'

She listened to his account of the wild rider without comment, sipping slowly from her glass, her gaze fixed on his face. His expression was transparent as he explained what had happened and then went into more and more detail. The harness; the sword; the smell of horse; the heat coming from it in the cold of the night air.

'And the man in the saddle,' she said at last. 'Did you see his face?'

'Not really. It was dark. Wild and dark-haired Celt I would say, rather than helmeted and Saxon blond.' He grinned.

She had never told him about her own encounter with the horseman.

'It was Elisedd,' she said. 'I'm pretty sure of it. I saw him as well.'

She saw his face blanch. He drew his finger through the condensation running down the outside of his glass without seeming to see it, then at last he looked up. 'As it happens, I was researching Elisedd just before this happened. Trying to find out if he existed. Really existed. As a historical figure.'

'I did that too. I couldn't find him. Did you?'

He saw the sudden twitch of her lips as she suppressed a smile. He shook his head. 'I haven't found him as such, but it was obviously a family name. The kings of Powys supposedly traced their pedigree back several hundred years. Handily, it was all carved on a pillar near Llangollen. If he was a younger son, he wouldn't have necessarily been mentioned in any records.'

'Or on a pillar.'

'A pillar dedicated to his namesake, who was probably his great grandfather.'

It was her turn to grin. 'Perhaps he wanted to prove his existence to you.'

'Perhaps.'

'But you think he attacked you.'

'He was brandishing a sword. But to be fair, he rode straight past me. Perhaps he didn't know I was there. Perhaps I wasn't, in his world. If I had to choose, for preference I would opt for your theory that he was only an echo.' He sighed. 'It isn't just Em who needs your help, is it?' He stood up wearily, gathered up the menus and went in to order their food, leaving Bea lost in thought.

Their plates were delivered to the table as he talked on about his research into the royal family of Powys, about the shadowy details of early Welsh history that had opened up to him, about how the experience had suddenly altered his point of view of the history he was exploring. 'I have never been in any doubt that Offa was a violent, unprincipled man, but he was a man of his time. I considered his politics and his military strategy, but beyond exploring his daughters' marriages as part of his master plan, I had not really gone deeply into the human side of his machinations. They don't really have much place in a history book – there's too much speculation involved. But now, I'm not sure my approach is the right one.'

She pushed the remains of her salad aside and picking up her glass, turned on her seat to face away from him across the village green. He went on eating, watching her out of the corner of his eye.

'You know I told you I thought I was dreaming Eadburh's story,' she said at last. 'Elisedd is the missing segment. And this is the bit you can't put in your book, you're right. What if they are still searching for one another?'

He pushed his plate aside and leaned forward, his chin supported on his cupped hands. 'Go on.'

'That's it. That is my theory. He went home without his promised bride – if indeed she ever had been promised, which I doubt – and he died on his way home, either by accident or he was murdered. She was sent, much against her will, to Wessex to marry another. When Beorhtric died, at her hand, either deliberately or not, she seems to have been exiled to the court of Charlemagne.'

'That bit is true and it will be in my book. There isn't much in history about her fate but Bishop Asser, who wrote a biography of King Alfred in 893, that's about a hundred years after Offa's death, tells us what happened to her, or what he had heard happened to her. He was very biased, as you can imagine. He thought she was a thoroughly bad lot.'

She gave a wry smile. 'He wasn't entirely wrong. She did poison her husband.'

'Even Asser says that was a mistake. Which makes sense. To be a queen was about as good as it gets.'

'Until your husband dies.'

'So you wouldn't kill him, would you?' He thought for a moment. 'You said you were following her story. How far have you got?'

'After Beorhtric died she seems to have been deported. Sent to France. In my dream I saw her almost literally loaded into a sedan chair type thing after she was separated from her little girl, and sent on her way. But they didn't send her penniless. She had a huge train of ox-carts which I gathered were full of treasure. Her dowry, I think it was said, which she was allowed to take with her.'

'Who sent her? You said "they" sent her.'

'A chap called Wigfrith. One of Beorhtric's senior advisers, I assume. And his henchmen. They didn't use force, but I got the feeling that they would have if she had protested.'

'Wigfrith?' Simon murmured. He groped in his pocket for a notebook. 'My God, Bea! Then what?'

'She left Nesta, that was the herb-wife who had given her the poison for her husband's lover, to carry the can. But Nesta was too quick for them and vanished into the forest. The next bit was a bit blurry – I had sensations of travel by land and then by sea; I think she was seasick because she felt ill and I saw huge rollers going past the ship. It was rowed by dozens of men, the ship didn't seem to have had a sail, then they landed on a beach near a fishing village and reloaded her treasure on to new carts and then the story jumped to the palace of Charlemagne. A much larger palace than Offa's at Sutton, but the same sort of thing. Great halls with carved beams, decorated with swirls and figures and dragons and crowds of people – the same cooking smells from the bakehouse and kitchens, and smoke from huge open fires, but these buildings were joined by covered passages rather than open walkways, so it was much more like one great building.'

'And Charlemagne?' Simon whispered.

'And Charlemagne. He beckoned her over to sit with him and he knew exactly what had happened. She didn't think he would and was ready to lie about why she was there, but obviously the news had got there before she arrived. I should imagine he had a pretty efficient spy network. He mentioned the death of her husband.'

'What did he look like?' Simon had leant forward towards her. He was holding his breath.

'He was a large man, tall, but big in every way, with huge muscular arms and a thick neck, and he was wearing a coronet I suppose you would call it. A breastplate type thing with a heavy cloak trimmed with white fur. He had faded reddish hair – he wasn't a young man by any means – and was dripping with jewels. Rings on every finger. He spoke, they all speak – English – my English. At least, I understood everything they said. His voice was loud and confident and his eyes were blue and he was prepared to play with her a bit – tease her. But there was no question of his power. The hall was full of armed men. There were women there too, but mainly men.'

Simon was staring at her, speechless.

'Does that sound like him?' she prompted.

'I don't know,' he said at last, 'but there are descriptions I can check. I do know he was the most powerful man in the western world at the time. He had an empire that included most of modern France and Germany and Holland and parts of Italy, but it all fell apart eventually after his death and no one managed to even try to replicate his power till centuries later.'

'Don't tell me what happens in my story. Not yet.'

'I'm not sure anyone knows what happened to Eadburh,

apart from what Asser tells us, which was that at some point she disappears from history.' He sat back in his chair and stared at her. 'I can't believe I'm even listening to this, but after my experience with Elisedd, if it was Elisedd, I don't know what to think any more.'

'Don't put it in your book as gospel.'

'No. I won't,' he said with fervour. He sighed. 'How does Em fit into all this?'

Bea hesitated. 'I have my theories, but they don't necessarily fit into my experiences. I'm not sure exactly what it is that she has picked up, and I don't want to commit myself until we have done some more work together. I only hope she will allow me some time before she has to go back to school.' She paused. 'Has this ever happened at home, Simon? Does her mother know about these moments when she is distracted, or perhaps abstracted is a better word, somewhere else in her thoughts?'

'Don't all children do that to some extent?'

'Yes, but this would have been different, different enough for her to notice and have some concerns.'

'Val's never said anything to me. I think she would have told me if anything like this has happened in front of her. I . . .' He grimaced, 'I haven't mentioned any of this to her. Emma has begged me not to, and I think she's right. Val is not . . .' He hesitated again. '. . . not a particularly sensitive type. She is down to earth. A realist, like me. The trouble is, she even finds my fascination with history difficult to cope with.' He stopped abruptly.

'That must be very hard,' Bea said gently.

'Indeed. Most of the time we're fine. We cope. As you know, I do a lot of my writing in private places.'

'Where you can feel the spirit of the place,' she said with a smile. 'I remember you using that phrase when we first met.'

'Did I?'

'A Freudian slip perhaps.' She laughed. 'But I do see that you wouldn't want your wife to hear about Eadburh and Elisedd.'

'Completely off limits. Both the kids are well aware of their mother's trigger points and are circumspect with all the wisdom children have about these matters.' He hesitated. 'Val and I have a complex relationship, Bea. We need to be apart, but we need each other too.' He looked away as though considering what he had just said.

Bea nodded slowly, then tactfully changed the subject. 'Will you ask Em to ring me? I would like at least one more session with her before she goes home.'

'Of course.'

'And Simon, if you need help, let me know. I'm not convinced we are done with the royal family of Mercia yet.'

He nodded. 'I ought to go. I'm not super convinced they will stick to the revision plan if I'm not there. Felix doesn't seem to think he needs to revise at all, and only time will tell, but for Em the stress of these wretched A levels is not helping with this one bit, though she's bright enough. She should walk it, but this extra distraction worries me.'

'I'm sure she will cope.' Bea reached into her bag for her car keys. 'I'll come to you if Emma allows. I want to walk out onto the hill with her. Elisedd has appeared to us both up there. Let's see what happens. No.' She interrupted his objection before he voiced it. 'I won't let it upset her, I promise. If he should appear, I will know what to do.'

She didn't wait to say goodbye, heading for her car before he had even scrambled to his feet. He sat still, watching her pull out of her parking space and turn her car round. In a few seconds she had gone.

Thoughtfully he headed back into the pub and reappeared a few minutes later with a second glass of shandy. Then he pulled out his notebook again. He needed to get back to the kids, that was true, but first he had a lot of details to write down before he forgot them, and names to check. The kids would be all right on their own for a while yet. In fact, perhaps the longer he was away the better. They might actually get some work done.

34

'Dad's been altering his book.' Felix sat back and pointed at the screen. 'Take a look. See. He's using the review tools so one can see what he's changed.'

Emma peered over his shoulder. 'All this red bit?'

'Yeah.' He folded his arms. 'He's added in a bit about the kings of Powys. Quite a big bit.'

There was silence as she read, leaned forward to scroll down, then read on. 'Wow.'

'Quite. Wow. Do you think this stuff is kosher? I mean, it's quite a different style to the rest of his book.'

Finishing her scrutiny of the extract, she stood back. 'Some of that sounds a bit like guesswork. Maybe that's why it's in red. He's got to check it.'

'What do you make of this place, Em? Really.' Felix stood up and closed the laptop. They trailed into the kitchen. Felix opened the door of the fridge and brought out two cans of cider. 'You really are experiencing all this stuff? You're not making it up to get out of the exams or anything?'

'Get out of the exams?' she echoed. 'Hardly. They're impor-tant.'

'How does it feel when you do it?'

'It?'

'Well, what do you call it? Time travel.'

'I don't feel anything. I'm just there.'

'And you were a queen?'

For a moment she looked uncomfortable, then she grinned. 'What else, bro? I would hardly be a serf, would I!' Her grin faded. 'It was a bit scary, actually. I wasn't her and I wasn't me, but I was there and I felt lost. Trapped. I was looking out through her eyes so I must have been her. Mustn't I?'

He didn't reply immediately, thinking it through. 'What does Bea say?'

'She gave me all these exercises to practise being safe.'

'And have you done them?'

It was her turn to remain silent.

'Oh, Em!' He stood up and shoved his hands into the back pockets of his jeans, standing in front of the window much as his father did at home when he was about to deliver a lecture. 'What is the point of her taking all this trouble if you don't do it?'

'I don't want to be safe!' she snapped back. 'Don't you see? I want to know what happens. What it feels like to be a queen. It's exciting. It's like being the star of a fantasy movie all of my own. A queen has servants and soldiers and all those people in that great hall were watching me and I knew that if I clapped my hands they would jump!' For a second she was on the point of telling him about Elisedd making love to her. She stopped herself in time.

'I thought you were scared.'

'At the time, I was pumped, but later when I woke up I was scared. I didn't know where I was. Or when I was.'

'And you're still scared, aren't you?'

'I suppose so.'

'So, you don't want to do it again. Not deliberately.'

'I do, that's the point. But I want it to be on my terms.'

'Which brings us back to Bea.' Felix was staring at her reproachfully. 'She is the only one who can show you what to do and how to control this weird shit you're involved in. Get real, Em. You're messing with something really dangerous here.' He sounded very like their father. 'You mustn't try and do it on your own.'

'I wouldn't be on my own if you were here.'

'What! No! Oh no, Em. No way.'

'You wouldn't have to do anything except be here revising or whatever. I just don't want to wake up and find myself somewhere outside miles away. That would be scary. Please, Felix. I looked up sleepwalking and they say not to wake people, just make sure they are safe. That's all this would be. I'd only be dreaming.'

The look he gave her was one of extraordinarily mature compassion, combined with sheer frustration. 'As if you're going to take any notice of what I say anyway.'

She smiled sweetly. 'I knew you'd understand. And you have to swear not to tell Dad.'

'Not unless you've been carted off in a straitjacket.'

'I won't be. You go on. Read or whatever. I'll be upstairs in my bedroom.'

She didn't wait to hear any more arguments.

Back in the living room, Felix went over to his bag of books, discarded in the corner since the day they arrived and with a sigh began to sort through them. Perhaps it would be a good thing to give them a quick look. As he opened the first book he stared up at the ceiling uncomfortably, but there was no sound from upstairs.

As Bea walked into the cathedral, she found herself shivering. She peered into the shadows. Had Sandra done that to her? Made her nervous and afraid in this most beautiful and serene and safe of places. She had noticed the woman a couple of times now, hovering in the distance, watching, and she had succumbed to the temptation to break her own rules and study Sandra's aura. It had been as she'd expected, strangely jagged. There was anger there, and fear, and something else, something dark, lurking in the periphery of her energy field. Bea hadn't probed further but what she had seen disturbed her. She felt a wave of anger again now and dismissed it firmly. She was not going to let Sandra Bedford spoil her life.

She found the north quire aisle deserted. The organ was playing softly and there were quite a few people sitting in the nave enjoying the music. She sat for a long time in the little chapel allowing her agitation to settle. Slowly the peace of the place settled around her and she saw the familiar figure sitting in his accustomed seat, his head bowed, his cowl pulled low over his head, his hands folded in prayer.

'I ignored your advice,' she whispered. 'I'm sorry. Help me keep Emma safe.'

For a while nothing happened, then at last she saw him stir. Slowly he looked towards her and she thought she heard him sigh from deep within the shadow of his hood. 'It is too late.' The words drifted through the silence, barely more than a breath against the distant sound of the music. It was Bach. She recognised it. 'Come, Sweet Death', a funeral favourite in their last parish. Her momentary distraction was enough for her to lose him. When she refocused on the altar, he had gone.

Too late. He said it was too late. Standing up she made her way to the doorway and out across the echoing spaces of the transept, past the St Thomas shrine toward the north door that led out into the Close. Her heart was hammering anxiously, the peaceful moment dispersed. The organ had stopped playing.

Her phone rang as she reached the house. It was Anna. 'Hi, Mum. How are you?'

'I'm fine, sweetheart.' She let herself in through the front door and pushing it shut behind her, stood still in the hall. 'Any news?'

'I'm sorry Petra and I couldn't make it home for Easter. But we will be there for Christmas, I promise.'

'Christmas?' Bea felt a terrible pang of loss. That was months away.

'I know. I'm sorry. I'll try and get home for a quick break before that, but there is so much work to do. I was talking to Pet on the phone and she's had an idea. You and Dad need a puppy to replace us.'

Bea let out a gurgle of laughter. 'Well. That is a novel idea!'

'A good one?'

'Not at the moment, sweetheart. We're both frantically busy.'

'And you're not missing us?'

'Of course we are. But no puppy.'

She was still laughing as she pulled off her jacket and headed for the stairs. It was lovely that the girls were thinking about them, but it was true. She and Mark were frantically busy. And before she took on anything else, be it supply teaching or puppy walking, she had to help Emma. She paused, her foot on the bottom step. She wasn't treating Emma as a surrogate daughter, was she? She remembered Sandra accusing her of suffering from empty-nest syndrome and she shook her head. No. Emma was part of a far larger problem. The lost soul who was Eadburh.

Picking up her touchstone she managed to still her anxious thoughts at last as she sat, waiting. Emma was part of her job.

'Where are you?' she murmured. 'Emma?'

She could sense Felix watching, feel his anxiety as he kept looking up towards the beams in the ceiling above him. Upstairs. Emma was upstairs in her bedroom. But when Bea looked there was no one there. 'Where are you?' she murmured again.

Emma was standing on a hillside, looking west towards the setting sun, as the shadows lengthened across the valley at her feet. She was a young queen and he was somewhere out there, the man she loved. Her father had been lying when he told her that Elisedd was dead. She could feel him, sense him yearning as she was for their renewed embrace, dreaming of that time they had lain in one another's arms in the *hafod* on the hillside. Messengers had left the palaces of Wessex again and again to look for him and brought no news. Her prayers had received no answers. Dreaming another, older, Eadburh's dream, Emma looked down at herself and saw she was wearing her red silk dress. She was a girl again, the daughter of Offa, still the young maiden she had been when she first met Elise; her leather sandals were studded with gold that glittered momentarily as the sun finally slid below the rim of the hills.

She was beautiful, her hair flaxen, tearing out of its braids in the wind and she was free. With a joyous smile she stepped forward onto the track that led down the hillside towards the drovers' road through the valley. He would meet her, she was sure of it. Somewhere out there he knew she was coming.

In the distance she heard the lonely call of a curlew as night drew in across the land.

'Emma?'

Bea heard her own voice echoing through the landscape.

'Emma? Come back!'

But she wasn't Emma any more. She saw the girl throw a quick look back over her shoulder then she turned away and ran on, down the hill, her hair flying behind her, the silk of her dress blown against the body of a slim, young woman, Eadburh, a much younger Eadburh, who had taken over the body of a teenage girl.

'You can't call her back.' Nesta was there beside her, watching. 'Why do you not trust me?'

Bea felt her knuckles whiten as she clutched the stone in her hand. 'Because you scared me. You were in that terrible place.'

'You came where you were not wanted. You must wait for me to come to you.'

'I don't understand.'

'Then leave it to the sisters of Wyrd to allow things to fall as they may. You can trust them.'

'You talk of the Wyrd sisters in spite of the fact that Wessex and Mercia were long ago Christianised.'

Nesta smiled. 'I believe in one God and all gods, in fates and spirits and angels, as did so many of my countrymen and women. Why limit oneself to one when there are so many out there to guide and lead and, of course, mislead.' She smiled. 'It is up to us to make our own way through the maze. You do the same.' She put her head to one side. 'You live with a priest and yet you believe in following the paths through the other worlds.'

Bea gave a wry smile. 'But I can't follow Emma.'

'She has gone her own way. It is up to her which way she follows the enigma that is life. You have given her guidance. We must hope that is enough.'

'Tell me one thing. How come she sees Eadburh as a girl her own age and I see Eadburh as a grown woman?'

'Because a grown woman can dream she is a girl. Emma has left herself open and our queen has borrowed her body.'

Bea shivered. 'That in our world is called possession.'

'It happens. It is to be hoped the child will be strong enough to retrieve her own soul.'

'And your plants? Do you believe plants have a soul? Did you take them back into your world?'

'They are of my world. That was where they should die, to fall back into the soil of my time and live again in the cycle of all things.'

She supposed it was obvious when she thought about it. 'So, what of Eadburh in the court of Charlemagne? The Eadburh I see. Is she real? Does she have a soul? Who am I watching when I see her?'

Nesta smiled. 'You are watching a woman who was flattered that the king called her to his side, and she flirted with him and played with his affections, or she thought she did, but she had met her match.'

'So, what happened?'

There was no answer.

'Nesta?' Bea looked round but the woman had gone. The attic room was empty, her candle guttering as the flame burned low.

'Em?' Felix knocked on her door. 'Em, are you there?'

The cottage had suddenly felt very empty. He had grown used to hearing Emma move around in her room over the last days. The old beams creaked at every movement when people were upstairs, but he hadn't heard anything at all for a while now, he realised. She must be asleep.

He pushed open the door. She wasn't there.

'Shit!'

But he had been there, in the living room downstairs, for

hours. She couldn't have come down without him seeing her. Unless he had been asleep. He frowned with frustration, turning to run back down the stairs. The front door was still bolted on the inside. He went through the kitchen to the back door. That too was locked.

Shit. Shit. Shit.

He looked round wildly. She couldn't have climbed out through the window, surely. He raced back upstairs, but the windows were too small. There was no way she could have fitted, and if she had even tried, he would have heard her.

He retraced his steps downstairs and unbolting the front door went out to stare down the steps towards the lane. All was quiet. The sheep in the fields on the far side of the valley peacefully grazing, a buzzard slowly riding the thermals above, letting out the occasional desolate cry. Should he ring his father? Or the police? Or Bea? Felix was frantic. He had been left in charge. It was such a simple thing, to keep an eye on his sister, and he had failed.

He was sitting down on the low wall, turning his phone over and over in his hands, paralysed with indecision, when he heard the familiar sound of his father's car, the engine straining as he drove it up the steep narrow lane.

Simon parked and turned off the engine. 'Hi, Felix. Everything OK?' He turned to pull a shopping bag out of the boot. 'I've stocked up on some groceries and bought us pizza for tonight.' He paused, studying Felix's face for the first time. 'What's wrong?'

'Dad. It's Emma—'

'What about Emma?' The voice behind them made him leap out of his skin. She was standing in the doorway, staring out. Apart from dishevelled hair and a crumpled T-shirt she looked normal – perhaps a little sleepy. 'What have I done now?'

Felix leapt to his feet. 'Where were you? I looked everywhere!'

'What do you mean, where was I? I was asleep. I know I should have been revising but I was tired, OK?'

'You weren't in your room. I checked. I checked twice.'

'You can't have looked properly. I was there. Unless I was

in the loo.' She stepped outside onto the terrace and reached out. 'Let me take the shopping, Dad. That would be really nice, to have pizza. What kind did you get?'

As Simon turned back to the car to collect another bag of shopping she turned on Felix with a furious whisper. 'I told you to leave me alone! How dare you spy on me!'

'I'm sorry. I was frightened. You had disappeared.'

'I had done nothing of the sort! I was asleep in bed.'

'No, Em, you weren't.'

'What's the matter, you two?' Simon climbed the steps and put the second heavy bag down at his feet. The clank of bottles betrayed the contents. Lemonade and shandy for the kids, lager for himself. 'What is Emma supposed to have done?'

'I haven't done anything. He checked on me when I was asleep, and he seems to think I had gone out. Which I hadn't. If I went anywhere it was to the loo.' Emma was furious.

'Dad told me to keep an eye on you,' Felix protested.

'Well, he had no business to. I don't need anyone keeping an eye on me!' Emma turned back into the cottage with the groceries and disappeared through the far door towards the kitchen.

'She wasn't there, Dad. Honest.' Felix wore his wounded puppy expression which Simon from long experience immediately identified as guilt. He had obviously forgotten to keep an eye on anyone.

'Well, the main thing is she's here now and perfectly safe,' he said soothingly. 'So, may I suggest we forget it and have a nice evening together, OK?'

They trooped into the kitchen where Emma was stacking her father's purchases in the fridge. Simon registered her stormy expression with a long-suffering sigh. Felix sat down at the table and pulled out his phone. 'There's a text from Mum.'

'Is she OK?' Simon was stacking the drinks in the fridge.

'No!' Felix stood up, staring at the screen in his hand. 'No, she can't!'

'What?' Simon and Emma both stopped what they were doing.

'She says she's texted you both already. She wants us to go home. Tomorrow.'

'No. No we can't. Absolutely not!' Emma had visibly paled. 'Oh God, where's my phone!' She was groping in her pockets. Simon had found his:

I'm sorry about the change of plan, but it only means collecting them a few days earlier than expected. I find I have a meeting of my book group on Thursday and I don't want to miss it. It's a long drive, so we'll need to set off in good time. I'll pick the kids up at about ten, so make sure they're ready. It won't do them any harm to get them away from any distractions so they can get ready for school at home.

As he looked up, Emma snatched his phone. 'Let me see! What does she say?'

Simon looked at Felix. The boy appeared distraught. He was astonished at how upset he was himself. 'We can't go, Dad, not yet,' Felix said miserably.

'There's no way I'm leaving,' Emma announced. She dropped her father's phone on the table. 'It's out of the question. I have to see Bea again, for one thing. And there are other things I have to do. Ring Mum and tell her we're not going. It's not fair. Her stupid book group is hardly that important. She is always missing it at home if something better turns up. She's just bored with the Fords, that's all there is to it. If she wants to go, she can go without us. We can go later on the train.' She folded her arms.

Simon thought for a moment. 'It does seem a shame to cut your visit short. I'll ring her and see if we can sort this out.'

Picking up his phone, he walked out of the room. They followed him. No chance of a private conversation then. He sat down at the table by the fire, staring at the blank screen of his laptop as he waited for her to pick up. Her phone went to voicemail.

He put it down with a sigh. 'She's not there.'

'She's there all right. She's not taking your call because she doesn't want to argue,' Emma said furiously. 'I'm going to message her.' She had spotted her own phone on the arm of the chair by the hearth.

Don't come tomorrow, she typed. *We are not ready. Dad says he will put us on the train next week, so don't worry. Enjoy your book club! Em*

A few seconds later, Simon's phone rang. They all looked at each other.

'Val?' Simon took the call after three rings.

Emma and Felix could hear their mother's voice from the other end of the room. 'Tell Emma there is no choice in the matter, is that clear? I am coming to get them, and I expect you to make sure they are packed and ready.' She had hung up before Simon had the chance to speak.

'Tough,' Emma snorted. 'Because we won't be here.'

'You probably have to go, Em,' Simon said wearily. 'You know what your mother's like. If you don't do what she says, she'll never let you come and stay without her again and she'll make all our lives hell. It might be as well to get in some serious revision time at home before the exams anyway. Tell you what, I will make her promise to let you both come back here for a large chunk of the summer holidays, how about that?'

'She wants us to go with her to Provence for the summer holidays,' Felix put in gloomily.

'That's the first I've heard of it.' Simon looked across at him, shocked.

'I don't think you were invited.' His son looked embarrassed. 'She told the Fords you would be busy with your book and wouldn't be available.'

'The Fords have a farmhouse near Roussillon,' Emma put in. 'They showed us loads of pictures. It's very pretty.' Normally she would have been elated at the idea of going somewhere clearly so desirable, but it seemed Simon's little cottage in the Welsh borders had somehow gained precedence. 'I'm not going. I think she's behaving really badly. I'm not going in the summer and I'm not going back to London now. In fact, I might not go back at all. I can do my exams in Hereford or somewhere.'

'Ah, now, Em, that's not a good idea,' Simon put in hastily. 'Sweetheart, I know you're distracted, and I know Bea is helping you with everything that has happened here, but you can't just change schools like that.' Val was going to kill him.

Felix had obviously decided to adopt the role of peacemaker. 'Let's have a drink and think about cooking those pizzas,' he said quietly. 'We don't have to decide anything at this moment. I'm sure there's some way round this, but if Mum gets cross she won't shift, we all know that. We need to do some negotiating and that's easier on a full stomach.' To his relief, he saw both his father and his sister smile. His famous fondness for food was often a teasing point in the family, but on this occasion it was something to bring them together.

They trailed back into the kitchen and Felix dug in the fridge for a lager for his father and two cans of cider for him and Em. As he handed one to her, he saw her hands were shaking. He bit his lip. He didn't want to go home any more than she did, but he could tell this was a huge deal for her and one that was not going to be negotiable. He reached into his hip pocket and touched his phone. Should he ring Bea now or later?

35

The Kingdom of Wessex by Simon Armstrong.

Sandra pulled off the cardboard packaging and dropped it on the floor. It had been left with her upstairs neighbour while she was out. She turned the book over in her hands and looked at the picture of the author inside the back cover. Yes, that was him. It was a big book, heavy and serious looking, with footnotes on every page, but with lots of illustrations too. She had googled him several times but, to her intense frustration, short of telling her that he was married and had two children and lived in London, there was nothing of a personal nature in the information she could find, and that was all there was on the flyleaf as well. She already knew about the children, but the fact that he lived in London was interesting. And he was married. She sat down, the book on her knee, and considered the matter. The wife did not appear to be around, at least not when he was in the cathedral with the kids. Was it possible, she wondered, that there was something going on between Beatrice and him. If there was, it might explain the hold Beatrice had over the family.

She had a good idea where they were staying. She had laboriously looked through masses and masses of holiday lets in the area and researched them until she found one owned by someone called Christine. Isolated; beautiful; idyllic historic setting in the hills between Radnor Forest and Offa's Dyke.

She sat still for a long time, thinking, the book in her hands, and then she smiled. She stood up and put the book on the table. Tomorrow she would drive up to the isolated idyllic cottage and take a look.

'You have got to be joking!' Val had arrived before eight. 'I set off before dawn to get here early so we can get a good start, and you tell me Emma isn't here!' She looked from Simon to Felix and back, her face set with anger. 'Why isn't she here? Where is she?'

Simon was cursing to himself. He should have guessed Val might arrive early, and he most definitely should have guessed Emma might pull a stunt like this. 'I'm sorry, Val. I do know she was very unhappy about the change of plans, but I've no clue where she is.' He cast a pleading look at Felix, who shrugged moodily.

'I don't want to go back early either,' he said. 'Why on earth couldn't we stick to the arrangements and then go on the train? That way we could revise all the way back to London!' He kicked at his rucksack. He had packed it, Simon had noticed, but then there hadn't been much to pack. Emma's bedroom still had most of her possessions scattered round it. They had found the note on her pillow. *I'm not coming back until my mother has gone. Don't even think about looking for me.*

Val sighed theatrically. 'Well, be it on her own head. Get everything together, Felix. At least you've got some common sense. I'm not waiting for the stupid girl. She'll have to take the train on her own.'

'No. I'll stay and come back with her.' Felix looked completely distraught. 'Please, Mum.'

'Out of the question. You have your GCSEs to revise for. The last thing you need is to waste your time in this godforsaken place.'

'Val, darling.' Simon caught her wrist and pulled her towards him. 'Please, don't be cross. It's not really a big deal, is it, if she comes later? I'll put her on the train in Hereford. She's working well here. It's a good place to concentrate.' He kissed her gently. Glancing over her shoulder he caught Felix's eye. The boy gave his father a conspiratorial wink.

'I'll come with you, Mum. It would be nice to have some special time together, just you and me.' Felix was in diplomatic mode. 'If you make Emma come now, she'll be a pain all the way home, you know she will.'

Val sighed. She knew when she was beaten.

'Come and have a cup of coffee before you set off,' Simon cajoled her.

Sipping coffee outside on the terrace, she was forced to admit that the cottage was, far from being godforsaken, the possessor of the most beautiful view, and very cosy. It wasn't its fault it was small.

As Simon watched the car drive down the hill he thanked the gods of every pantheon that as they sat up there outside the cottage the sun had chosen to come out and flooded the unfolding mountainscape with beguiling golden light. The last thing he saw was his son looking back over his shoulder, and Felix's thumbs up as he waved out of the window. He was going to miss him. He turned and walked back in through the gate. Behind him a small red car had driven up the hill. It must have had to pull in to let Val drive by. He didn't bother to turn to look as he walked up the steep path to the cottage door. He was too busy wondering how long it would be before Emma showed up, and in the meantime he was going to have to ring Bea and tell her about the developments.

'I did wonder if she'd been in touch with you,' he said as he wandered round the kitchen, the phone to his ear. He looked forlornly at the three plates laid out on the table. Val may have stopped long enough for coffee, but poor Felix had not been given the chance to have some breakfast. No doubt he would persuade his mother to stop at the first motorway services they came to for a hearty fry-up. He had put the kettle on and was spooning coffee grounds into a jug when Bea picked up.

'I switched off my phone last night. I had things to do.' She sounded exhausted. 'Oh dear. I'm so sorry, Simon. But I can't say I'm surprised Emma didn't want to go. Do you want me to come over?'

'Wait till she shows up. I'll get her to ring you.'

Mark was reading the paper. He put it down as she ended the call. 'Trouble?'

She nodded. 'Simon's wife announced last night that she'd be taking the kids back to London this morning. Felix has gone with her, but Emma was absent when Val arrived, so she's gone without her. All does not seem to be well with the Armstrong family.'

Mark grimaced. He reached for the muesli and poured a large helping into his bowl. 'Hasn't Emma got exams coming up?'

'A levels. And Felix is sitting his GCSEs.'

'Stress all round then.'

'But not as much as one might have expected, at least as far as the exams are concerned. I was a bit worried, to be honest,' she paused thoughtfully. 'Well, I did wonder if Emma was going to cry off. She's been so disturbed by everything that's happened. Apparently she tried to ring me last night.' She reached for her phone again: three missed calls.

Mark poured out some muesli for her and added milk. 'Eat that, or you'll collapse.'

She gave him a fond smile. 'Thank you. Don't know what I'd do without you.'

He smiled. 'Do remember, Emma is not our daughter.'

'Oh Mark.' Bea gave him a fond smile. It wasn't the first time she had thought this man was telepathic. 'I know she's not ours. Of course I do. If there is anything personal in this at all, it's because I see myself in her when I was her age. One feels everything so acutely. One is so open. Vulnerable.' She leaned across and took his hand. 'I am being careful. I promise.'

Mark had a Chapter meeting and then he had calls to make on the far side of town, so she would have the whole day to herself.

She sat for a long time in silence, not climbing up to her study, but going into the bedroom and sitting down on the end of their bed. Not trying to contact Nesta. Not trying to eavesdrop on Eadburh. Just waiting to see what would happen. The clock in the tower struck the quarter, then the half hour and the sun shrugged itself behind a cloud. Rain drifted across the Close, soaking the walls of the cathedral, turning the stone dark. Outside, people had raised their umbrellas and were hurrying towards the lights of the shops.

The great Charlemagne was a generous man. She had her own guest house next to the hall of the princesses and the hot springs and she had servants to wait on her every whim. The king had given her gifts each time he had seen her. She smiled to herself, but this time it was one of his sons who bowed before her. A handsome man, far more her own age than his father, he had pressed a small book into her hand. It was a beautifully copied book of psalms, illustrated with coloured illuminations and capitalised in gold, the fine vellum of the pages stitched and bound in white silk.

She was enjoying the attention from the two men enormously, well aware that they were vying for her admiration. They had given her jewellery and silks, books, her own musician, a puppy sired by one of the king's two great dogs, and now this man, this the eldest son of the king, even more charming than his wily father, was suddenly paying her far more attention than before. She liked him. A lot. By her calculations he would make a good match and he obviously liked her. She was thoughtful as he raised her hand and brushed it with his lips. The question was, would the great Charlemagne see her as a good match for his son? He had held back when Offa suggested her brother as husband for his daughter, Bertha, and her sister, poor Ethelfled, had waited in vain to be betrothed to his son, Charles the Younger. He was notorious for dangling his offspring before prospective suitors and then snatching them away, keeping them waiting, keeping them always at a distance but still allowing them to hope for the ultimate prize. Of his three legitimate sons, Louis, Peppin and Charles, Louis was by far the best looking, the most important and now, here sitting at her hearth, the most charming, the most desirable and the most eligible. Now her father was dead she had to handle this situation herself. She had to play this cleverly, match the king move for move, but this man she could like. If she was clever, she could outsmart even the great emperor of the Franks at his own game and win the prize she sought.

The women's hall was warmed by the fire, and in the corner two young men, brothers from somewhere in the southern lands of Aquitaine, were singing together, their hands moving in unison over the strings of their instruments. It was a love song they sang. Sad and beautiful. She threw a quick look across at her suitor. They sat opposite one another, the gaming board between them, the pieces carved from stone, one set red agate, the other black tourmaline. She was winning. Her eyes sparkled as she saw his hand hover over the king. Perhaps it would be better to let him win. Behind them several of the ladies stood together watching them. It was the first time in a long while, she realised, that she was actually thinking about Hilde and Nesta. What had happened to them, she wondered? Both had been loyal, both ready to lay down their lives for her. She hoped Nesta had escaped the furore that must have followed the death of Beorhtric and her departure. Too many people would have guessed the poison came from her; too many people feared the cunning woman who was the queen's adviser and friend. Once they would all have gone to Nesta for her services, revered her for her healing skills and for her glimpses into the future, but increasingly they had abandoned her, frightened of her reputation of service to the hated queen. Without the protection of the queen they would all have turned on her and she would have paid with her life for her loyalty. Hilde, her friend of many years, had set off obediently, like so many others, at her request to find the prince she still dreamed of, and she had never returned. She would never now know what happened to either of them.

She glanced up at the man sitting opposite her and realised he was watching her. Could he read her thoughts? She profoundly hoped not. She smiled at him. No! She wouldn't let him win. Never. Reaching forward she whisked his piece off the board and set it aside. An expression of frustrated anger flashed across his face, then it was gone and his smile returned. He enjoyed a challenge, and this woman intrigued him more and more. 'Next time I shall win,' he said softly with a chuckle. 'I always do, in the end.' Behind them the attendant women clapped and laughed. The brothers finished their song. A servant brought a tray of drinks and they sat back watching as the new puppy played with a toy one of the boys who brought in wood to fill the baskets by the hearth had carved for it. It growled furiously, shaking its little head. She had called the dog Ava.

The summons to the king's presence came several days later. For the first time she followed his messenger up the broad staircase to his private quarters. As she entered, his entourage was waved away and withdrew to the far side of the chamber. She felt their eyes following her as she made her way towards him and took the chair beside him. It was far smaller than his. Carefully she arranged her skirts, aware that her attendants had remained in a group in the doorway. The atmosphere was tense and she began to feel nervous. Straightening her shoulders, she moved on the seat to face him. His eyes were narrowed and he was studying her intently. 'I have a question to ask, lady.'

He folded his arms and she found herself gazing down at his hand, counting his array of gold rings.

'I have it in mind to give you in marriage to my son, Louis.'

Her heart leapt but she schooled her face, careful not to react. She had come to know him well enough to suspect there would be a catch.

'Normally such matters would be discussed between your father and myself or in the case of your widowhood, your son or your brother, if you had one still living. It appears you have very few surviving male relations, madam.' She saw the trace of a smile behind his eyes.

She bit her lip and fluttered her eyelashes at him. 'Hardly my fault, sire.'

'And your female relations, such as there are, all appear to be in nunneries.'

'My daughter?' Her sangfroid almost deserted her.

'Is being raised by the Abbess of Wareham.'

Eadburh closed her eyes in relief.

'It may be that the Church is the best place for a woman without connections,' he went on, his tone thoughtful.

She frowned. Looking up, she saw that he was smiling again. He was playing with her.

'On the other hand, you have reigned as a queen and acquitted yourself well I gather, apart from the unfortunate error of killing your husband.' He fell silent, seemingly deep in thought, then he looked up again. 'Of course, I myself am without a wife.'

She froze.

He put his head on one side, seeming to consider. 'I am left with a quandary. You have a choice. Would you marry me and become Empress of the western world or would you marry my son?'

He closed his eyes, leaning back in his chair, waiting.

'Do you offer such a choice in good faith, sire?'

His eyes flew open. 'How would I not? Choose.'

'Then, sire, I would choose your son. You do me too much honour to offer me an empire.'

Too late she realised the mistake she had made. His look of fury lasted only a moment but there was no gainsaying her words.

'You have made the wrong choice.' He rose to his feet. Behind them everyone in the room stood to attention, watching and waiting. Had they heard the conversation? She thought they probably had, every word.

'Had you chosen me, I would have offered my son; but you show no discernment. You are not fit to rule an empire, nor the kingdoms I have apportioned to my sons. As I said, the Church is the best place for a woman with no connections. There they are prevented from meddling. So, to the Church you will go. The abbess of one of my most favoured foundations has recently died. You will take her place. You shall keep your dowry – to give to the abbey. Then you will make your peace with God. Perhaps you can explain to him how you came to poison the husband you were given in his presence.' He raised his hand and beckoned his attendants forward.

'Sire, you misunderstood me,' she cried frantically. 'I only chose your son because you did me too great an honour. I did not think myself worthy—'

'You thought me too old to be your spouse. So, don't be afraid. You will not have to lower yourself to accommodate an old man in your bed. You will leave Aachen today. Your belongings are already packed and loaded onto wagons. I do not wish to set eyes on you again.'

Her mouth fell open. 'So, you never intended to have me. You toyed with me!' She was furious.

He gave her a pitying smile. 'Had you chosen rightly I might have succumbed to your wiles. We will never know.' He turned away and swept out of the room, leaving her standing, stunned, as the men of his elite bodyguard surrounded her. They did not touch her, waiting patiently for her to move, but already her ladies were approaching, one with her cloak, one with her chest of jewels. A third carried the puppy. So, she would be allowed to take Ava with her to her fate. Holding her head high she stood while they wrapped the cloak around her and she stepped proudly from the dais onto the tiled floor, aware of everyone in the presence chamber holding their breath.

As she walked towards the door she looked back over her shoulder. 'And still you watch me,' she hissed at Bea. 'So, now you know my story and my fate. But be assured, your own destiny will be tied up with mine, as certainly as the sun and moon are linked in the heavens. And that will not go well for you.'

36

Sandra's drive up to the cottage on the ridge had done no more than confirm that it was the right place. She had glimpsed Simon Armstrong walking away from the gate as she went past and that was it. She drove on up the lane, turned round laboriously in the first gateway she came to and then drove slowly back. He had obviously gone back indoors; the front door was closed.

Letting herself back into her flat she sat down thoughtfully in front of the blank screen of the TV. She was increasingly sorry she had given up her job with the volunteers but on another level she was pleased to have the time to think. The cathedral was a distraction. It had an enormously powerful force field that clouded her thoughts.

'Witch!' she exploded. 'She's a witch!'

Yesterday she had covertly watched Bea walking across the Close and she had seen the swirling energies around the woman. They had masked her, enfolded her and protected her from prying eyes, Sandra's eyes. A deliberate shield.

Sandra clenched her fists in her lap. Mark Dalloway was obviously too generous a man to have recognised what his wife was and Heather too had been fooled. Sitting back, Sandra closed her eyes, forcing herself to relax. If she was going to fight this woman she would need every ounce of cunning she possessed. She would have to become once again the woman she used to be.

Standing up, she went over to the desk and pulled out the bottom drawer. Inside, under her file of cuttings, there was a large cardboard box. She lifted it out and set it down on the carpet. She sat and looked at it for a long time, then at last she leaned forward and lifted the lid.

Where were you?' Simon looked up as the door opened.

'I waited over there in the field until Mum had gone,' his daughter answered sheepishly. She scanned the room quickly. 'So, Felix has gone with her then?'

Simon nodded.

'Can I have some breakfast?'

He pushed the cereal box towards her and poured her a mug of coffee. 'So, are you going to explain?'

Emma gave an apologetic little smile. 'Why? You know why I couldn't go. I hoped Felix would stay, but it was up to him. He'll understand why I couldn't go too. It's important he gets his GCSEs.'

'And your exams don't matter?'

'They do if I want to go to uni. Which I will, I promise. But there is something else I have to sort out first. You must understand too, Dad. I know Mum won't. Not in a million years, so it was easier not to be here.'

'And leave me to deal with the flack.'

She gave him her most persuasive smile. 'You know how good you are at dealing with Mum. Text her and say I'm OK, then she needn't worry about me. Though' – she reached for the milk jug – 'I bet she hasn't given me a thought. She's got her beloved Felix back. That's all that matters.'

'Oh grow up, Em!' Simon sighed. 'You know that's rubbish. She loves you both.'

'And next you're going to say it's a mother and daughter thing. Well, it isn't. Bea has daughters and she knows how to talk to them.'

'How do you know? Have you ever met them?'

'No. But she must do. She knows how to talk to me.'

He sighed. 'I'll text your mum, and you text Bea. Let's see what she has to say about you skiving off.'

'I'm not skiving. I'll go back when I'm ready. On the train. If I'm late back to school, then you can tell them I was ill.' She gave him an angelic smile. 'That bit is true. I am definitely psychologically disturbed, aren't I? But I will go back for the exams, I promise.'

There was no point in arguing. He texted Val and then, picking up his mug of coffee, he went into the front room and sat down at his desk, leaving Emma to get in touch with Bea.

'Bea's coming to collect me in about an hour.' The whisper round the door was quiet, almost apologetic. He didn't look up. He was studying the blow-ups of the last page of the chronicle. There were a few words there he hadn't noticed before.

'So, when Felix said you weren't in your room when he went to look for you, where did you think you were?'

Bea and Emma were sitting on the hillside in the sun.

Emma thought for a moment. 'Up on the hills somewhere, but not here. The view was different.'

Bea had seen it too. She had watched with Nesta.

'And you say you were, or you felt you were, Eadburh?'

Emma nodded. 'I was wearing the long red dress. It was lovely. Softest silk, with a blue overtunic embroidered with beautiful patterns.'

Bea smiled. 'But not really something you would have worn to walk in the hills, either now or a thousand years ago.'

'Probably not.' Emma sighed. 'And I was wearing flat sandals with gold studs. So you think I was wearing what I saw myself in, not what Eadburh would have worn in real life?'

Bea was silent for a while, thinking. 'Or maybe Eadburh was wearing what she wore in her dreams. She obviously saw herself as young and beautiful.'

'No!' Emma leaned forward, hugging her knees. 'No, she WAS young and beautiful.'

Like you. Bea didn't point out the obvious. 'And in your dream she was completely alone?'

Emma nodded. 'No prince.' The two words were unbearably forlorn.

'And, more to the point, no attendants.'

'No.'

'No cloak, no belongings, no horse somewhere in the distance.'

Emma shook her head.

'So it was a dream, but it was such a vivid dream that when Felix looked for you, you weren't there. You had apported elsewhere. Then when the dream was over you reappeared in your bedroom.'

'Not possible. Even I can see that. He must have come upstairs when I was in the loo. I was half asleep and forgot I'd got up.'

'Or Eadburh borrowed you for a while, to feel again the joy of having a young woman's body.'

'If she had done that she would have organised there to be a young man's body around to feel as well,' Emma retorted. She gave a snort of laughter.

Bea hid a smile. 'I suspect that was what she was hoping. Which brings us back to the question, where was Elisedd? Your dad is trying to research him to find out who he was and what happened to him, but it's not easy.'

'And it doesn't matter. Eadburh met him. She fell in love with him; she made love to him. Why do we have to analyse everything? Why should it matter who he is? None of this will be believed by anyone else anyway. All we need to do is make it so I don't sleepwalk over a cliff, and don't see too many ghosts.'

She threw herself back on the grass, her arm over her eyes. 'Do you think I'm deranged?'

'No, of course I don't.'

'Everyone else will.'

'Not if you keep all this to yourself. That part is in your hands. You will have to tell your dad and, above all, Felix to keep it to themselves.'

'Felix will already have told Mum.'

Bea grimaced. 'Well, if he has, you must ask him not to say any more. Do you remember what I was telling you about respecting the privacy of anyone whose aura you see and how you can't tell them if you see illness there?'

'Or their future.'

Bea sighed. 'Or their future. Not that that will happen. We are not fortune tellers.'

Emma sat up again. 'If I was, I wouldn't have to bother with exams. I could make my living with a crystal ball.'

'I shall ignore that remark. I'm being serious, Emma. You must keep all this private. What is happening here is so complex. Dreams within dreams. People drifting backwards and forwards through time and space. It's like nothing I've experienced before. All I can do is keep you safe. Or at least teach you how to keep yourself safe, and one way of doing that would probably be to go back to London and school and try and forget everything that has happened here. Or if you can't forget it – which, being realistic, you probably never will – at least keep your distance.'

Emma frowned, resting her chin on her knees. 'Do we know what happened to Eadburh in real life?'

Bea was staring away into the distance. The horizon had grown hazy. 'No, I don't think we do. Your father told me she disappears from history.'

'But she wants us to know what happened, so he can put it in his book.'

'Do you think that's what this is all about? She wants people to know the end of her story?'

Emma nodded slowly. 'Doesn't that make sense?'

Bea didn't answer. Lost in thought, she gazed down the hill, where the view had disappeared.

'Simon! Are you completely out of your mind!' Val's voice shrieked out of the phone at him. He didn't try and argue. Clearly Felix had spilt the beans and there would be no chance to explain to her until she had got it off her chest. 'If you don't bring Emma home now, today, I am calling the police.

You have clearly been consorting with a madwoman. I suppose you've been having an affair with her?' She didn't wait to see if he was going to answer. 'Put Emma on. This minute. I've been trying to ring her but she isn't answering.'

When at last she ran out of breath he had worked out what he was going to say. 'Can I speak now? Bea is a highly trained counsellor, and incidentally no, I've not been having an affair with her or anyone else. She is happily married and in case you hadn't noticed I love you, you stupid woman! Heaven knows, I would hardly have hung around this long if I didn't!' He paused and took a deep breath. 'Emma has been having a lot of problems, Val, not only here, but over some considerable time, and she had to have help. We were extremely lucky that Bea was here when she was needed, otherwise all this could have come to a head in school. The pressure Em has been under has been colossal and the worry of exams has increased the stress tenfold. I'm amazed the school hasn't said anything to us, because according to Em they have noticed something was very wrong.'

There was a heavy silence at the other end of the phone. 'They did say something, actually.' Val sounded chastened. 'I assumed it was because of the exams and would resolve once the pressure was off. It did before, when she was taking her GCSEs.' Her tone reverted to one of indignation, rather than worry. 'Felix is walking it and Emma seemed to as well. She is such a bright girl. It's so unlike her to get flustered.'

'Flustered?'

The tone of Simon's voice clearly annoyed her. 'Yes, flustered! What was I supposed to think?'

'Perhaps if you had discussed it with me, I would have had a chance to think.'

'How could I discuss it with you when you're never here? If you are here, you have your head in your books!'

'Val—'

'No, Simon, this is clearly your fault. You have to bring her home. I've spoken to the doctor and he wants to see her as soon as she's back. He's going to put her on tranquillisers so she can get down to her studies.'

'No.'

'What do you mean no?'

'I mean no. I am not bringing her home. At least not until she's ready to come back voluntarily, and you are not going to medicate the poor child. Absolutely not.'

He was interrupted by a small gasp from the doorway. Distracted by their shouting match, he hadn't heard Bea and Emma come back from their walk. One look at Emma's face was enough to make him switch off the phone and throw it down on the table. 'Darling, I'm sorry you heard that. You mustn't worry. I am not going to let anything happen.'

'Felix told her.'

'I'm afraid he must have done.'

He saw Emma's face crumple. She looked from Bea to her father in despair then pushed between them and ran up the stairs to her bedroom. They heard the door slam followed by an outburst of impassioned sobbing.

Bea walked towards the kitchen door without a word. Simon followed her. 'I'm sorry you heard that as well. Val can be a bloody cow sometimes. However much I love the woman, she still manages to infuriate me! I'm afraid our relationship can be a bit tempestuous. It appears the school had spoken to her, but she decided not to tell me or to do anything about it.'

Bea pulled out a chair and threw herself down at the kitchen table. She put her head in her hands. 'I'm so sorry.'

'This is absolutely not your fault.'

'But I haven't helped. I should have done something more.'

Simon sat down opposite her. 'I suppose I'm going to have to drive her back to London.'

'I'm not sure that's a good idea.' She looked up at him wearily. 'I'm not a psychologist, Simon, but as a former teacher myself and the mother of two daughters, my advice would be to let everything calm down. When is her first exam?'

He thought for a moment, then shook his head. 'I'm not sure when they start. How bad a father does that make me?'

'A hard-working father, no worse than some, better than a lot. Can I make a suggestion? Would it be a bad thing to ring Emma's head teacher and talk it over? In broad brushstrokes, without too much detail. If they have already raised the subject, then they know there's something worrying her. And you must tell Emma that there is always the option of sitting the exams later. It's not the end of the world if she postpones them. She needs to know that.'

'It's funny, you know. I've been schooling myself to cope when the subject of boys raises its ugly head, but this . . .'

'This is boys, Simon. Only this particular boy is a Welsh prince who lived twelve hundred years ago. And Emma is feeling the pain and longing and excitement of another young woman who had her dream snatched away, which is unfair, but that's the way it has always been. It happened in the past and happens all the time now. We have to find a way of mediating that pain and helping Emma deal with it. You have three teenagers, not two, to deal with. The fact that one of them is a Saxon princess is just an added complication.' She gave a wry smile.

'And what about the older Eadburh, the one you see?'

'In my version, after her exile from Wessex she was offered marriage to his son by Charlemagne, who seems to have been furious when she said yes.'

'Ah, I remember that story. He offered her a choice, didn't he? Catch twenty-two. And she made the wrong one.'

'Of course you know what happened from the history books. So that bit is true.'

'I can quote from Asser. "*He did however give her a convent of nuns in which, having put aside the clothing of the secular world and taken up that of nuns, she discharged the office of abbess, but—*"'

'Stop! Don't tell me!'

He grinned. 'You still don't want to know what happened?'

'No. Not yet. I want to see it for myself. I am trying, Simon, to find out why she yearned – yearns – back to her younger self. Or was that younger self so traumatised by what happened that it somehow split from the rest of her? We read so glibly of the horrors of history, but if one thinks, really thinks, of the things that happened, the things people witnessed, the things that made them helpless victims of events and compare that with what we do for people today if we are in a position

351

to help, what with PTSD, with schizophrenia, with multiple personality disorder, all kinds of trauma, with all these things diagnosed and heavily medicated today, then think of that one woman. Her whole family were dead. Her father was, one assumes, a controlling and arrogant tyrant, probably capable of genocide and maybe an abuser, her mother was a murderess, her sisters disappeared and I don't know if she ever found out what happened to them. She was forced to abort her lover's child, and her daughter, the only child she was able to carry full term, was taken from her. Her husband turned out to be gay, and flaunted the fact in front of her. She was guilty of murdering some of his lovers, and at the very least of the manslaughter of her husband, she was exiled, she was offered the world on a plate by an emperor then he snatched it away and locked her in a convent. Perhaps all that was left were her dreams of that love affair, long ago, as a teenage girl with Elisedd, dreams that are now anchored to a real teenage girl, Emma.'

'And the object of all this teenage angst rides fast and furiously past our door up here. So, he's still looking for her?'

'Perhaps he is. And she's still calling for him. A thousand or so years of lost love and yearning.'

There was a long silence.

'This is what I do, Simon. Try to comfort lost souls who stay anchored to this earth by unfinished business, so that they can move on to another stage of their journey.'

A sound in the doorway made them both look round. Emma was standing there, her eyes red from crying, her hair dishevelled. 'It's what I should be doing as well. One doesn't need to do exams to do what you do.' She came over and threw herself down on the chair between them.

Simon opened his mouth to protest, but Bea shook her head at him sharply.

'As it happens, I did do exams, Em,' she said gently. 'I have a degree in English and a diploma as a teacher, and I have attended dozens of courses in healing and spiritual development, and on top of all that, I have years of life experience. It's that experience you need before you can help other people. If you really want to help the dead move on, that's a wonderful thing to do, but it's not something you can do without study. I can help you channel your abilities and teach you how to begin, but you have to do the other things as well. Maybe not a degree, you would have to decide about that later, but there will be study involved and I'm sorry, there are no short cuts.' She reached out to put her hand over Emma's. 'Your dad wants to help you and your mum does too in her own way. We have to make this work between us, so you can deal with all this and help Eadburh.'

She pushed back her chair and stood up. 'I'm going home now. There are things I have to do there. Your dad and you need to discuss all this calmly and carefully, then I want you to have some supper – it's important you eat, remember what I told you? To ground yourself properly and then get some rest. And you must protect yourself.'

Mark was waiting in the kitchen, sitting silently at the empty table as she walked in.

'What? What's happened?' She stopped abruptly.

'Mrs Armstrong rang me.'

'Mrs?'

'Emma's mother.'

'Oh God!' Bea sat down. She was exhausted and this was the last thing she needed.

'And Sandra came over earlier,' he went on. 'She was looking for you. If you ask me, she's completely lost it!'

'Mark!'

'She was ranting on about needing to save your soul by destroying your powers and she was the only person capable of rendering you harmless.'

Bea closed her eyes.

'And docile.'

Her eyes flew open. 'Docile!'

Mark grinned. 'If it wasn't all so serious, I would be laughing. She is not, you will be glad to hear, going to have to confront you to perform this miracle, but she seems to be convinced that such things are possible from a distance.' His smile faded.

'I've got a very bad feeling about it. I hope you have the skills to save yourself from this scale of psychic onslaught, my darling. She assured me that she respects me and wants to save me from the witchcraft that enfolds me. She can do this by taking action against you. Oh, and she's fixed her sights on Emma as well, as your sorcerer's apprentice.'

Bea shivered. 'Oh Mark.'

'And on top of that Val Armstrong is threatening us with the police, social services, the bishop and the *Daily Mail*.' He sighed. 'She rang me from her car. So, how was your day?'

A smile hovered for a second on her lips. It didn't last. 'You obviously know about Emma refusing to go home, which means that she is, at least for now, still part of my problem, the more so if these threats are real.'

'Well, don't go chucking any psychic slings and arrows about yet. Perhaps a nice cup of tea first?' He managed a weary grin. Standing up, he bent and kissed the top of her head. 'I'm going to pray.'

She sat without moving for a long time after she heard his study door close, then she headed for the stairs.

'I need your help.'

Nesta was there, still in the shadow of the woods, her hair drifting free of her hood in the summer breeze.

Bea realised she hadn't ever seen her wearing anything on her head, unlike every other woman of her period, apart from the hood of her cloak. The wild locks, deep copper, streaked with white, seemed to be a symbol of her freedom.

'You were right about me being considered a witch. It seems I have enemies on every side.'

She was turning her stone over and over in her hands as she sat before her candle. 'I have been threatened with what my husband calls a psychic onslaught.'

Nesta gave a snort of derision.

'What should I do?'

'You know what to do. And your priestly husband has surrounded you with the power of his prayers. I can see the love of God all around you.'

Bea found she was smiling. 'He's a good man.'

'He is a powerful man. Don't be afraid to ask him for help.'

'And does his love mean I'm safe from this person?'

Nesta was less distinct now, her shape almost invisible as darkness fell round her. 'We shall see.'

Was that what she had said? Bea leaned forward, clutching the stone more tightly. 'Nesta? Wait!'

But the candle flame was flickering. Bea leaned forward anxiously. Already it had gone out. The room was dark and very faintly she smelt the autumnal aroma of woodsmoke. Nesta had vanished.

37

Emma lay listening to the sound of her father snoring in the room next door. He had been asleep for at least an hour and still she didn't dare try to close her eyes and see what had happened to Eadburh in case somehow he knew that she was deliberately defying him. He had made her promise not to go out, and she wasn't going out. She was in bed, under the duvet, clutching her pillow tightly as a child would hold on to a teddy bear in order to stay safe. But she wanted to know – she needed to know – what happened next in Eadburh's dream of her youth. Had it ever really happened, this story of teenage love and loss, or was it wishful thinking by a woman who had been snatched from her lover and sent away in a whirlwind of misery and loss and who, incarcerated in a convent in the kingdom of the Franks, had once again lost everything?

In Emma's dream, Eadburh's memories too had turned sour. The scarlet dress was bedraggled now, the hem torn, the silk muddied. A kindly woman had given her a rough woollen cloak and she hugged it round herself as she walked on. She was near the summer seat of the kings of Powys, trudging northwards along the track up a broad fertile valley. Once or twice on her long journey she had seen signs of her father's great dyke, running across the top of a distant hill, far off to the east, then the woodland would close in and she would lose all sense of direction, following the muddy ruts of farmers' wagons on their way towards a distant market, until after a long weary climb she would once again find herself on a shoulder of hillside with long views towards distant, higher, ever wilder mountains.

The track was following the river now. The water was broad, with shallow pebble beaches, glittering in the sunlight as it wound through a wide saucer of countryside surrounded by low hills. Over to her left, she saw it, a hill fort on one of the lower hills, surrounded by palisades rising above the surrounding meadows, a gold-and-crimson banner flying from its tallest building. She stood still, her heart thudding in her chest. Was this it at last, the *caer* of the kings?

They wouldn't let her in. The guards at the gatehouse stared at her in disdain. They made as if to run at her, clapping their hands, making shooing noises. They laughed, then one of them raised his sword and smacked the blade with the flat of his hand. His meaning was all too clear.

She turned and walked away. Behind her she could hear the noise of a busy community. She could hear the sounds she had grown used to in the royal palaces of her father. Shouts and laughter, music from somewhere in a great hall, the whinny of a horse and the clatter of hooves on stone, the ring of a hammer on iron from a forge somewhere on the far side of the encampment, the clacking sound of shuttles and beams and the rattle of loom weights from the weaving sheds, the singing of a woman and the shouts of children. Wisps of smoke rose from behind the walls and she smelt roasting meat on the wind, torturing her empty stomach.

When she heard the cry of hounds and the beat of hooves behind her, she did not even try to move out of the way. She was too tired. She turned to face the horsemen and as they drew close she felt her legs give way beneath her.

When she woke she was lying on a palette bed, covered by a soft chequered blanket. An old woman was sitting beside her, spinning. When she saw Eadburh's eyelids flicker she put down her spindle and stood up.

It turned out that it was the blacksmith's grandmother who had taken her in and tended her. Much later, fed with scraps of roast venison and bread and sheep's milk, her feet bathed and soothed with ointment, her dress brushed and sponged, Eadburh found herself in the presence of the wife of one of King Cadell's *teulu*. It appeared the old woman who had looked after her had recognised the silk of her gown and noticed the gold of her rings as she washed Eadburh's filthy hands, and seen the gold and garnet necklace hidden beneath the torn shift, and realising this lost young woman was of high birth, had gone in search of one of the queen's ladies.

Now that she was at last inside the palace of the King of Powys, Eadburh's courage almost failed her. Her voice was hoarse and her strength seemed to have deserted her, but she managed two words. 'Prince Elisedd?'

The woman's smile vanished, to be replaced by an expression of puzzled suspicion. 'He's not here.'

'But, *mae'n fyw?* He is alive?' Eadburh felt herself struggle with the words of the Welsh language. *'Nid yw wedi marw?* He isn't dead?'

The woman seemed confused by the question. She smiled a little sadly. 'Why do you want to see him?'

Eadburh nearly replied, nearly said, because I love him, felt herself ready to throw herself on her knees before this woman and beg, but she managed to restrain herself. 'Because he and I knew each other once, long ago. We were friends and I need to give him greetings.'

Long ago. The woman stared at this child-woman who looked no more than seventeen. 'Then I will call for his brother to speak with you. Wait here.'

And that was it. She swept away, leaving Eadburh standing there in the middle of the floor. People went on about their business all round her; they were talking, laughing, hurrying here and there. By the fire a young woman began to strum her harp and quietly she began to sing. Her song was of love and loss and irretrievably sad and as she sang Eadburh felt her eyes fill with tears.

Prince Cyngen, when he came to find her, was a much older version of his brother, tall, weathered, his hair already greying. He was followed by several older men, some were armed, some wearing loose long gowns trimmed with fur. He bowed gravely to Eadburh and asked her who she was. She told him the truth, straightening her back, squaring her shoulders, meeting him eye to eye.

He didn't seem surprised. 'Elisedd told us about the girl he met when King Offa called a conference about the building of the dyke. He spoke of her often.' Unlike the woman standing nearby, watching, he did not seem to see the disparity between their ages. He was a man in his forties, she a slip of a girl.

She tried to keep her gaze steady. 'Is he alive?'

Prince Cyngen hesitated then he nodded. 'He is alive.'

'Where is he?'

'Not far from here. He retired from the world. He is one of the canons at the *clas* of St Tysilio at Meifod.' He gave her a look of gentle sympathy. 'He gave his life to God many years ago. He will not wish to see you, Princess.'

She stood as if struck by a stone, unable to breathe, unable to think.

'He's a monk!' When the words exploded out of her mouth at last she had forgotten where she was. She felt the hot tears well up. 'No! No, it can't be. It can't!'

She was aware that the prince bowed to her again. He beckoned forward the blacksmith's wife and with a gesture ordered her to take the girl to the guest house, then turning, led his followers away. His last words to her were, '*Mae'n ddrwg gen i*, I'm sorry.'

All round her the crowds went on as if nothing had happened. If they had cast a curious look towards the stranger talking to their prince, they soon lost interest. Only the harpist played quietly on, the words of her song weaving through the noise, fading to echoes that blended with the wind.

*

In her little cottage bedroom, Emma stirred and moaned in her sleep. Her pillow was soaked with tears, her dream within a dream a cruel nightmare of love and loss.

As the echoes of the harp faded, Eadburh awoke with a start. She had never gone to look for Elisedd, not as a girl and not as a grown woman. Her plan had been thwarted from the start, and now she realised bitterly that even if her dream was true and he was still alive, Elisedd would have rejected her. An older man, a man of God, what use had he for that slip of a girl who didn't even look like the princess of his dreams, never mind the reality of the older woman who lay here now in her convent bed. She grimaced as she tried to straighten her legs, stiff and cramped from the cold in spite of her covers. As abbess, she was entitled to a comfortable suite of rooms near the nuns' dormitory with her own fire, but even so, as the cold winds howled around the convent walls she huddled down again under the coverings. She had had the dream before and probably she would have it again.

Outside her narrow window she could hear the bell calling the sisters to matins. She had excused herself from getting up for this service. She was ill. Her throat was raw. In her dream it had been summer. The people had been kind to her. Had she gone to find him? She didn't think so. And yet she had come so close.

She closed her eyes and another tear trickled out from beneath her lids. If she called one of the lay sisters they would bring her a honey tincture for her throat and another blanket, and even a hot stone to put by her feet.

Her thoughts drifted back to her daughter. Was the little girl happy in her new home? She would have her nurses and her playmates with her, she would live in comfort in a convent at Wareham and God-willing, she would be safe there and her life would be contented. Would she ever think about her mother? Eadburh doubted it. As queen she had had little input in the child's life beyond giving her birth. That, she realised with sudden brutal honesty, was probably lucky for the little girl.

The soreness in her throat was growing worse. If only Nesta

were here. The herb-wife was skilled in concocting remedies for every ailment; she would have administered some potion to soothe the pain. It was a long time since she had thought about her. Nesta had been the one who brought about her downfall. If she hadn't made that poisoned drink, everything would have been different. Had she been caught and killed by the king's guard? Eadburh nestled deeper into her pillows and in a rare moment of compassion she found herself hoping that Nesta had somehow survived.

A log fell from the firedogs into the hearth and the sudden flame lit the carved stone corbels supporting the ceiling above her bed. The sound had made her open her eyes and she saw a woman standing near her, not Nesta, but the witch woman from another time. How was it she could find her way even here over the sea and into the holy house of God? Sitting up and pushing off her covers, she made the sign of the cross.

But the woman had already gone.

Bea was cold and stiff and she was clutching her little cross at her throat. With a groan she reached across for the switch on the lamp on the side table. The candle had gone out a long time ago, leaving not even a trace of the smell of wax in the air. She had dreamed Eadburh's dream with her of the girl in the scarlet silk dress who had had Emma's face and then awoken with Eadburh in the convent cell with its silk-covered pillows, soft rugs and fine linen sheets. 'Oh God!' She buried her face in her hands. 'What's happening to us?' She looked at her watch. It was two in the morning. She couldn't ring Simon to see if Emma was all right at this hour; please God, they would both be asleep.

Climbing to her feet she opened the door and, trying to move as silently as possible so as not to wake Mark, she began to creep downstairs. She passed their bedroom, its door half open in the dark. There was no reassuring shape in the bed; it was empty. There was a lamp on in his study. She could see the faint line of light round the door. Cautiously she pushed it open. He was kneeling at his little prayer desk in the corner. Looking up, he smiled. 'What time is it?'

'Late. Have you been praying all this time?'

He nodded. 'I had a lot of prayers to say.' Standing up with a groan, he stretched. 'Shall we make a hot drink?' Putting his arm around her shoulders as they made their way into the kitchen, he went over to draw the curtains against the darkness outside in the garden. 'I hope you haven't had any interference from the most powerful exorcist in England.' It was meant to sound like a joke but somehow it didn't come out that way.

She ducked away from his arm and went over to the kettle. 'I'm hoping I don't need exorcising. But I am prepared. I haven't sensed anybody poking round.' She had been much too busy watching an abbess in her faraway convent to worry about Sandra and her attempts to interfere. 'Did she give you any idea how she had come by these amazing powers?'

Mark sat down at the table. He yawned deeply. 'Nope. I've no idea.'

'And she didn't tell you how she was going to manage this exorcism?'

'Absolutely not.' His smile didn't quite reach his eyes.

She sighed. 'It's too late for coffee. Do you want a hot chocolate? I think we've got enough milk.' Stooping, she opened the fridge. 'Oh dear God!' She slammed the door shut.

'What? What is it?' Mark was on his feet in a second. 'What's in there?'

Pushing her out of the way, he pulled open the door. Staring in, he shook his head. 'What is it? What did you see?'

She peered over his shoulder. 'It was on the shelf. A rat.'

'No. No, there's nothing here. Sweetheart—'

'It's OK. I let my defences down. I'm so tired.' She turned away, rubbing her arms with a shiver. 'I know what's going on. There's nothing there. She's testing me. I won't be caught again.' She gave a brief, bitter laugh. 'That's the way to deal with this sort of thing. Laugh it off.' Her eyes widened. 'Oh Mark. If that was Sandra, she knows what she's doing! What on earth is going on? Who is she?'

Mark closed his eyes. He murmured a short prayer and made the sign of the cross then he reached in for the milk.

'Whatever fiendish powers she may have acquired, I'm not letting her come between me and my bedtime drink.'

She gave a wobbly smile. 'I should think not. Quite right.'

Reaching for an empty saucepan, he sighed. 'I've never blessed a fridge before. Do we gather that that was some kind of psychic attack?' He poured the milk into the pan.

As they sat down at the table he reached across and put his hands over hers. 'Shall we recite Patrick's breastplate together?' It was the special prayer that never failed to wrap her in a feeling of warmth and protection. As Mark closed his eyes and prayed out loud, she felt the words spiralling round the kitchen, sealing them with God's love. Whoever, whatever, had been prowling the shadows had withdrawn into the dark.

In her bed in the cottage Emma stirred again. She was asleep in the guest house of the king's hill fort of Caer Mathrafal and tomorrow she would ride to the *clas* of St Tysilio to find out if the senior canon, the king's son, *Abad* Elisedd would see her. She moved back and forth restlessly in her sleep, her tears dry now, a smile on her lips. She was in a dream within a dream, a dream treasured by a man and a woman of their younger days, and a dream in the sleep of a young girl, lost in the past. Twelve hundred years of time spun and twined around her, and the wind and rain and sunlight of a millennium of seasons.

Simon crept downstairs and opened the front door with infinite care, not wanting to disturb Emma. Something had awoken him and he had lain quite still staring up at the ceiling in the dark and not for the first time. Each time he had started awake, he had heard his daughter in the next room, tossing and turning, and occasionally she had cried out in her sleep. She seemed to be quiet now and he squinted at his wristwatch. It was nearly morning. Easing himself into his jeans and sweater, he had tiptoed to his bedroom door.

A glimmer of light on the horizon showed where dawn would soon come and he stood for a while letting his eyes get used to the dark. Quietly closing the front door behind him, he crossed the terrace and ran down the steps to the lane.

The dawn chorus rose at him like a wave from the woods below the ridge and he found himself smiling involuntarily at the beauty of the sound as he walked slowly along the track. The air was bitterly cold and the stars were a glittering carpet only now fading slowly as the light grew stronger.

He had come outside to think. The peaceful retreat he had selected to finish writing his book had proved to be a whited sepulchre and he didn't know what on earth to do. Emma was his first concern, of course; she was here and he had to make decisions about her today. And then there was Val. And Felix. And the book. And Bea. He was puffing slightly when he reached the high point of the ridge and stood staring out towards the valleys that still lay in darkness. Behind him the light on the eastern horizon was growing stronger.

Part of him was wondering if he would hear the thunder of hooves, but the hillside was deserted. Only the sound of the birds filled the air. The foundations of his existence had been shaken. From certainty and a quiet smug comfort with his position in an academic world he had taken for granted, he had been tossed into a frantic questioning of the historicity of his view of everything he had written and was going to write.

'Dad.' Emma's voice behind him made him jump out of his skin. She had followed him up the track. She was wearing joggers and her red cagoule, her hair wild on her shoulders. 'I'm sorry. I didn't mean to give you a fright. I couldn't sleep either.'

He put his arm round her. 'I was trying to decide what to do.'

'I'm not going back to London.'

He didn't reply. The birdsong was fading now as the light grew stronger. He glanced at his watch. 'Shall we go out for breakfast?'

She nodded. 'I must see Bea.'

'Later. First you and I need to talk, Em. Very seriously.'

He saw the set of her jaw and felt his heart sink.

By the time they had retraced their steps down the track towards the cottage the woodland chorus had stopped and instead he could hear the echoing cry of a curlew as the sun appeared over the ridge of the distant hills. He knew enough about the legends of the ancient gods to know the sound presaged disaster.

38

'Her phone is still switched off.' Simon had tried to call Bea a couple of times.

Emma's shoulders slumped. 'I tried as well. I need to see her.'

'I know, sweetheart, but you can't expect her to be at your beck and call every day. I've left a message. I'm sure she will get back to us as soon as she can.'

'What about Mum?'

'I've left her a message too.' He didn't tell her that he had got through to Val again, endured ten minutes of ear-bashing and eventually hung up. 'I think we will discuss the situation a little bit more here before we bring Mum into the conversation again.'

He watched as Emma stood up and walked agitatedly back and forth across the room a couple of times, then she sat down in front of him again. 'You mustn't laugh.'

'You know I'm not going to laugh about anything you say.'

'I've got this horrible feeling that there is someone following me.'

'Not King Ethelbert?'

She let out an uncomfortable snort of laughter. 'No, not the king. Not Eadburh, nor her prince. Someone, something, nasty. I don't know what. I'm scared, Dad. Really scared.'

He felt his heart lurch with love for this difficult, pig-headed but oh so vulnerable child of his. Why could she not have left all this alone? 'All I can do is ring Bea again. Leave her another message. I'll tell her it's urgent.'

'Thanks.' She gave a shaky smile. 'Actually, I think I might go upstairs to lie down. I'm feeling a bit sick.'

He followed her up ten minutes later, a cup of tea in his hands. 'I thought this might make you feel a bit better.'

She was lying on the bed, still fully dressed, the duvet pulled over her. Her face was very pale and she was shivering. 'Has Bea rung you back yet?'

'As soon as she does, I'll tell you. I promise.'

'Thanks for the tea.' She attempted a grin. 'I'll be OK after I've had a sleep.'

He stood for a second or two looking down at her, then he nodded. 'Good idea. Sleep well, sweetheart.' He tiptoed out of the room and shut the door quietly behind him.

She lay for a long time, gazing up at the ceiling. All she wanted was to close her eyes and be with Eadburh again, to mount one of the king's beautiful horses and feel the sleek muscles of the animal between her legs. She would ride up the valley to find Elisedd. He couldn't have become a monk. It wasn't possible. And even if he had, she could win him back. He had only gone into the Church because he thought he'd lost her. He had loved her once. He would love her again. As her eyes closed, she slipped her hand inside her shirt and gently began to stroke her breasts as he had done all those years ago. Why would he want to reject her? All she had to do was go to him.

The knock at the door took Bea by surprise. She had awoken late to find a note from Mark saying he had gone to early communion and was then driving over to the hospice to visit his friend who had taken a turn for the worse. The note ended: *If you need me, ring and I will come.* She had smiled, kissed the note and slipped it into her hip pocket, then she had walked into the kitchen to make coffee. Only ten minutes later she heard the knock. A sudden warning prickle of unease at the back of her neck brought her up short.

At first she didn't recognise the woman standing outside on the step. She was well dressed, dyed red hair pinned back in a neat chignon. 'Mrs Dalloway?' The voice was cold and hard. But familiar.

'Sandra?' Bea froze.

'May I come in?'

'I don't think so.' Bea folded her arms, every layer of protection in place. 'I didn't recognise you.'

Sandra smiled. 'But you saw my little gift? In your fridge?'

'I saw it.' Bea was conscious of a grey miasma coiling its way round Sandra's shoulders. The woman's aura was alive with contradictory colours. Angry red flashes of light, green and yellow flickers, pulsing shades of dirty maroon and above all that heavy dark grey entity that clasped her in a cloak of evil.

'I think, Mrs Dalloway, that you would be advised to let me come in.'

'So why am I suddenly Mrs Dalloway, Sandra? Have you forgotten my name?' Bea's hand crept up to her cross and she clutched it tightly. Sandra had invited something in. She had opened herself up to something vicious that was feeding on her soul.

'Because I am no longer your friend, Mrs Dalloway.'

'I see. Well, I'm sorry to hear that, but then I can't let you in. I'm sure you understand.' She looked the woman in the eye. 'You could be anybody, in that disguise of yours.'

The venom in her visitor's expression was fleeting but unmistakable. It was alien and all too powerful. 'I'll be back, Mrs Dalloway.'

'And I'll be waiting for you.' Bea folded her arms again. She caught the sudden flicker of uncertainty in the woman's eyes and she smiled. 'Goodbye, Sandra,' she murmured.

Sandra hesitated, then she visibly squared her shoulders, her antagonism back in place. 'I'll see you soon and next time I won't knock on the door, I shall be in the heart of your evil doings.'

Bea watched as the woman turned to let herself out of the little wrought-iron gate and, leaving it open behind her, walked away across the Close, an almost visible cloud of malice trailing behind her. She did not go near the cathedral, Bea noticed, but veered away to walk past the west door, towards the gates of the Close and on out into the street, as if the creature clinging to her soul had been repelled by the presence of a sacred space.

'Christ be with me, Christ within me . . .' Bea's whispered words circled her with their blessing and protection.

Closing the front door, she leaned against it for several seconds, allowing her pulse rate to steady, then she went back to find the phone. This was far more serious than anything she had anticipated and there was only one person she could think of who could advise her.

'Meryn? I need your advice.'

'I don't think you do, Bea.' The line to California was so clear it sounded as though he was in the room with her. It must be, she suddenly realised, the early hours of the morning for him.

'I'm sorry. Did I wake you?'

He laughed. 'You know better than that. I was expecting your call.'

Why wasn't she surprised? 'I may have met my match.'

'Bea, you were my best pupil. There is nothing I can do that you can't. You must have confidence in yourself. And you are far more than a match for this one.'

Bea paused. 'So, you know what's happening?'

'I have a fair idea. Multi-dimensional phenomena are what we are discussing here at the institute, and yours is a splendid example.'

'And this woman?'

'Is an amateur. The ones you've got to watch are in the past, my dear. They have had more than a thousand years' experience.'

'Eadburh. She is very scary. And Nesta.'

'As to that, you have to make your own judgements, Bea. I can't do it for you.'

Bea bit her lip. 'There is so much going on. Layer upon layer.'

'And you can cope with it. But you must keep especial watch over the child. I'm right? There is a child involved?'

Ah, she felt her lips twitch into a smile, so he didn't know quite everything. 'Yes. There is. Emma. She's seventeen.'

'A dangerous age. Very vulnerable. Very open. Probably far too eager. She must be safeguarded.' That word the social services loved to use.

Bea was chewing her lips. 'How? Her parents are a part of the problem.'

Both of them in two such different ways.

'That is beyond my scope. You will have to deal with this yourself. Are you still married to that splendid clergyman?'

'You know I am.'

'Then you are not alone. Don't be afraid to ask his help. This may not be his acknowledged speciality, but his job makes it such and he has a strong and very genuine energy field. He will be there to guard you, Bea.'

It was what Mark had said.

'When are you coming home?'

'In the autumn. I've spent too long in the States. I need some good Welsh rain to refresh me. You and I will have some master classes then, and you can tell me all about how you coped with this situation. Just remember, be strong and have faith in God and in yourself, Bea.'

'And you will watch over me?' It was a frantic plea, but he had gone. The line was dead.

She sat staring down at the phone in her hands and it was only then she realised there was a list of messages, two from Emma, one from Heather; three from Simon, increasingly urgent in tone. Simon first. She pressed the button and waited for him to pick up.

'Would you like me to come over?'

'She's asleep for now but she wants to see you so badly. She's in quite a state.'

'I'm on my way.' She had a quick look at Heather's message. Before going to see Emma, there was something else she had to deal with. She had to find out how Sandra had become so powerful. All this could not have come out of the blue.

Heather picked up the phone at once. 'Are you OK, Bea? I've been thinking about you.'

'I need Sandra's address.'

There was a long pause, then Heather replied. 'Can I ask why you want it?'

'Things have escalated. She seems to have become mixed up in something extraordinarily stupid; I'm not sure she even realises what she's done, but I have to try and fix it before any more harm is done. I have to go and see her.'

'No, Bea. You mustn't go near her.' Heather hesitated, then she went on resolutely, 'Besides, you know I can't give you her address, even if I wanted to. It's confidential information. I'm sorry. Is there anything I can do?'

'I doubt it.' Bea thought for a moment. 'Well, yes, perhaps there is. Could you go and see her for me?'

When the call was over, Heather sat for a long time looking out of the window at her garden. It was a place of peace and love, somewhere she felt very close to her late husband. And safe. 'Help me with this, my darling, please,' she murmured, then with a heavy sigh she rose to her feet and reached for her jacket. Whatever her misgivings, this was something that had to be done face to face and at once.

Sandra was obviously not expecting a visitor. She stared at Heather in astonishment when she saw her on the doorstep, her hostility obvious. To Heather's amazement, she saw Sandra had dyed her hair. She was wearing scarlet lipstick.

'I have to talk to you.' Heather marched past her into the hall before Sandra could object. 'I need to know what's going on with Bea.'

'What do you mean?' Sandra's expression morphed from surprised to crafty then to casually bland. She looked away, refusing to meet Heather's gaze.

'I think you know.' Heather headed into the woman's sitting room and stopped in the doorway, appalled. The room was a mess. A half-drunk cup of tea stood on the table, milky scum floating on the surface of the liquid, books and papers were scattered on the chairs and on the floor, a pencil, broken in two, lay on the table beside Sandra's phone. There was a large box lying on the floor, its lid beside it on the carpet. Inside Heather glimpsed more books and papers, a strange wand-like stick, two packs of cards with exotic medieval pictures on the boxes, a small crystal ball and a plastic bag with what looked like a large dead mouse in it. She stared at it, her mouth open.

Sandra's eyes narrowed. She perched on the edge of one of the chairs, leaned over to replace the lid on the box and then to Heather's horror she burst into laughter. 'So, you under-estimated me as well! All you saw was goody two shoes Sandra, who wouldn't say boo to a goose. I tried to warn people, Heather, I begged for help, asked what I should do, and nobody listened! Nobody cared! And I kept thinking about that child, that girl, Emma.' She took a deep breath. 'And then I realised that it was the girl herself who was evil. But she was untrained. She needed a teacher and then I saw what was going on. She had a teacher and that teacher was here, amongst us, in the heart of the Church.'

'Whoa!' Heather sat down opposite her, balancing uncom-fortably on the very edge of the chair. 'Slow down, Sandra, please.' She was eyeing the box uneasily.

'Isn't that what you wanted? To know what was happening? I spoke to you, Heather. I warned you, but you were just like the others, you took no notice, so now it's up to me. I am the only one who can deal with this.'

'Deal with what?' Heather was fighting the urge to stand up and run out of the house.

Sandra was still avoiding her gaze. She looked down at the box on the floor and her gaze was almost caressing. 'I had given all that up. I had even come to think that what I was doing was wrong. That was why I came to join the volunteers. I thought I would be safe in the cathedral, but I see now that I was being told to bide my time, that something would happen that only I could deal with and that when the time came, the rot I had to root out was here at the heart of the cathedral itself.'

Heather froze. 'What do you mean?'

'Bea Dalloway, of course.'

'And what exactly', Heather interrupted, 'do you think Bea has done?'

'You know perfectly well. I told you. I told the dean. It was you who talked me out of going to the bishop. She and the child are possessed by demons.'

'Sandra!' Heather was trying desperately to keep calm. 'You know that's rubbish. Whatever you think you've seen, you are wrong. Bea is a decent God-fearing woman. She is married to the Canon Treasurer, for goodness' sake!'

Sandra nodded. 'That's what is so horrifying.' She climbed wearily to her feet and walked over to the table. She picked up a magazine that was lying there, folded open at the small ads page at the back. One of the advertisements had been ringed in red ink. She pushed it towards Heather, who took it and studied it with increasing disbelief.

Madame Soozie. Your fortune told. Your cards read.
If you need to settle scores from the distant past
and prevent evil following you into the future
I can solve your problems today.

At the bottom of the advert there was a mobile number.

Heather looked up. 'Madame Soozie?' she whispered.

Sandra nodded. 'That's me. Sandra Susan. I needed a professional name.'

Heather stared at her, speechless.

'That's an old magazine. I haven't done it for years. Something happened and I thought it was my fault and I backed off, but I see now that it was merely the playing out of destiny.' Sandra sat down again, leaned back in her chair and sighed. 'I needed the rest anyway. One's powers sometimes get depleted after too much psychic work. But now I'm ready to take on the greatest challenge of my life. Beatrice Dalloway and the girl Emma are, as I keep telling everyone, possessed by fearsome demons. I have sensed them and seen them and I have felt their power. It's up to me now. I have to deal with

373

the situation. And I can.' She looked up and met Heather's gaze at last. 'You do see that, don't you.'

'No, I don't see it. I don't see it at all.' Heather swallowed hard. 'All I know is that Mark and Bea are concerned for your welfare. You are letting this,' she paused, looking back at the box on the floor, 'this obsession, get inside your head. There are people you can talk to, Sandra. Kind, wise people who can help you.'

Sandra nodded slowly. 'But when I asked for help, they didn't, did they? And now I can see that's because you would all rather believe Beatrice than me.' She gave a small bitter laugh. 'The demons are clever.' She stood up. 'Please go away, Heather. I would hate you to get involved in all this. You are a good person. You are not part of it. Leave me to sort it all out.' She moved towards Heather, standing over her menacingly, far too close in the small room.

Heather scrambled to her feet and backed towards the door. 'Sandra—'

Sandra smiled. 'No. The time for talking is over. Please go.' The house was suddenly incredibly cold.

With every ounce of dignity she could muster, Heather turned and walked out of the room. She couldn't wait to get out of there, but on the front doorstep she turned. 'Are you sure—?'

'I'm sure.' Sandra was right on her heels and Heather flinched. The final words Sandra shouted after her as she hurried away down the pavement left her reeling with shock.

'I fled.' Heather followed Mark into his study and threw herself down on the sofa. 'Oh God, Mark. That woman is evil! There is no other word for it. I'm sorry. I don't think I helped at all. All I've done is warn her that Bea is on to her. Where is Bea?' Her hands were actually shaking.

'She's gone up to see Emma.' Mark pulled his chair away from his desk and spun it round to sit down opposite her. 'Tell me exactly what happened.'

Heather described her visit. She swallowed hard, shuddering. 'She used to be a professional psychic, for God's sake!'

Mark sighed. 'I'm not all that surprised. I thought at first she was probably a typical nosy parker, but Bea was beginning to sense the power. That woman knows what she is doing.'

'As I left, she shouted something after me, Mark.' To her embarrassment Heather felt a tear roll down her cheek. 'She said that when Emma and Bea next dream about the past the demons that possess them will win and they will be stuck in the past forever and only she could have saved them, but maybe it would be better if they were trapped there and burned at the stake as the witches they had become. That was the only way to destroy demons.'

Mark sighed. 'I don't know much about the Anglo-Saxons but I don't think witch burning was one of their hobbies. Shall we say a prayer together, Heather, and then I will ring Bea and warn her what's going on.'

After Heather left he headed out into the hall, then stopped in his tracks. There was something moving round in the kitchen. He heard the scrape of a chair leg on the tiles, then the rustle of paper and a door softly closing. He crept towards the door and listened. Silence. The kitchen was empty. He tiptoed round the room, and paused by the fridge. Taking a deep breath he opened the door. For a split second he thought there was something in there. The slightest movement, a pair of eyes, the whisk of a tail disappearing between the packages and pots, but then it had gone. The fridge was neat and tidy and empty of wildlife. He made the sign of the cross and closed the door firmly. What was it Bea had done to scare the woman away? She had laughed.

'She's still asleep.' Simon had waited for Bea, sitting on the wall outside in the hazy spring sunlight. 'What are we going to do?'

Bea had been planning her strategy as she drove over. 'I think we should wake her and talk. Have you spoken to her mother today?'

He grimaced. 'Not usefully, no.'

She sat down beside him and let out a sigh. 'Oh dear.'

'Indeed. I think, I hope, I have made her realise how catastrophic it would be to escalate all this beyond the family.'

Bea looked up at the bedroom window. She didn't dare tell him how far the situation had already escalated. 'Can I go up and wake her?'

He nodded. 'If you think that's a good idea. I'll wait here.'

The room was shadowed, the curtains half drawn and Emma was lying across the bed. She had pushed the duvet onto the floor. 'Em?' Bea sat down on the edge of the bed and put her hand on Emma's arm. 'Em, wake up.'

Emma made a small grunting noise and moved away fretfully.

'Em, can you hear me?'

'Go away!'

In her dream, Emma looked back over her shoulder at the four horsemen who were escorting Eadburh along the riverbank. The water rippled and glittered in the sunlight over the stony shallows they passed. One of the king's bodyguard had ridden up beside her and pointed ahead. She could see the squat stone-built tower of the little church now, and the cluster of thatched buildings round it in a loop of the river.

As they rode through the gates and into the central yard she slid from the horse and looked round. 'Ask where he is,' she commanded.

The warrior nearest her dismounted and handed his reins to his companion. He shouted across at a young man in a homespun robe who was sweeping up the wisps of hay blown from the newly built stack in the corner. The air was full of the sweetness of its scent.

They waited while he scurried away. Eadburh looked round at the tidy buildings, the solid little church with its stone walls, arched windows and door and heather-thatched roof. The place seemed deserted.

When the young man returned, she felt her heart sink. She could tell from his face that Elisedd would not see her. He spoke to the man beside her in soft courteous tones, keeping his eyes shyly on the ground, knotting his fingers together nervously. She could make out some of the words. 'The lady cannot be who she says she is.' He bit his lips frantically, his face red with embarrassment. 'The lady would be many summers older than this young person. Princess Eadburh is a queen now, with children of her own, living far away.'

Emma gave a cry of anger. 'I'm not! I'm who I say I am. I am Eadburh. I have to see him.' She dodged past the outstretched hand of the armed man beside her, heading for the door in the largest of the buildings from where she could see several faces peering at the scene. He was there, wearing a simple dark long woollen tunic. She could see him. She recognised him. 'Elise!'

They caught her before she reached him.

'Elise! I'm Eadburh! I have looked for you for so long; I have searched for you—'

As he gazed at her, she saw the recognition in his eyes, the hunger and then the denial and disbelief. 'No. No, you can't be. I would know you.' He crossed himself. 'You cannot be her. You are an imposter. A shape-changer. A cunning woman. A witch!' He stared at her eyes for a second more then he turned away, ducked back inside the building and the door closed with a bang.

She stood there, distraught, unable to move, and then at last fell to her knees in the cobbled yard. 'Elise!' she called again. She buried her face in her hands, sobbing. 'You have to talk to me. You have to.'

They surrounded her, the brothers of the monastery, the king's escort, the farmworkers, and now several women appeared, sisters from the community and lay women. Someone helped her to her feet, someone else guided her across the cobbles back to the horses and she felt herself lifted onto the saddle. All around her they were talking and whispering and making the sign against the evil eye, and over and over again she heard the word 'witch'.

She couldn't fight them all. Slumped helplessly forward over the horse's withers, not even reaching for the reins, she let them lead the animal back the way they had come, leaving the *clas* and Elisedd behind them.

When she saw Bea waiting for her, she slid from the saddle in tears and threw herself into her arms. 'He didn't recognise me,' she cried. 'He didn't want to see me.'

Bea rocked her gently. 'Wake up, sweetheart. Wake up. You've had a bad dream, that's all. Everything will be all right.' She looked up as Simon appeared in the doorway.

'What's happened?' He gazed down in horror at his daughter as she sat up in bed, her face sodden with tears.

'She's all right. She had a nightmare. Give us a few minutes.'

He backed away unhappily and slowly retraced his steps downstairs.

She had surrounded them with the circle of protection, whispered the prayer, taken off her cross and fastened it round Emma's neck. In her bag downstairs she had herbs to burn to cleanse the place, crystals to place around the cottage as Meryn had taught her. And she had his support, she knew that, whatever he had said about her coping alone.

It was a long time before Emma stopped sniffing and groped for a tissue. 'I'm sorry.'

'There is nothing to be sorry for.'

'I was so sure he would recognise me.' She was still half in the dream.

'He would have expected to see a middle-aged woman, the same age as himself, and instead he saw a beautiful young lady in a scarlet dress.'

Emma stared at her. 'How do you know what he saw?'

'Because I'm looking at her now.'

'But the dress?'

'You told me about the dress before, remember?'

'Was I really there? In the monastery?'

Bea gave a small shrug. 'I think you might have been.'

'He was very handsome. But so old. His hair was going grey.'

Bea smiled sadly. 'He wasn't a young man any more, certainly. And you gave him a real shock. He didn't know where you had come from.'

'They thought I was a witch.'

'The more so if you have now disappeared right in front of their eyes. Sweetheart, you can't, you mustn't try and go back. You do know that, don't you?' Better to say it now straight away. Make sure she understood the danger. 'This is an important part of your training. You have to learn when to say no, this is not right. This is not something I should do.'

'But it was exciting!'

'It made you very miserable.'

'Only because he didn't understand. If I can explain to him—'

'But you can't explain, Emma.' She caught both Emma's hands in hers and pulled the girl to face her. 'Don't you understand? You can't explain this to anyone, then or now. Even we don't understand what's happening here. This has to be kept a secret.'

Emma held her gaze and Bea saw the defiance there, but then slowly it faded. The girl gave a reluctant shrug. 'I suppose so.'

'Good. Because it's vitally important you remember this. Now, we need to go downstairs and speak to your dad. Come down as soon as you've washed your face.'

Somehow she managed to persuade Simon to wait calmly; they made tea and sat at the kitchen table until at last Emma appeared. She was very pale, but sat down with them without protest.

'My darling, we have to decide what we are going to do over the next week or so.' Simon pushed a mug of tea towards her. 'Decisions have to be made about school and exams. They are vital too, Emma, you are too intelligent not to realise that, and you have to speak to your mother because she is very anxious.'

Val was not answering the phone so Emma rang Felix instead.

'Hi, Sis. Are you prepared for the onslaught?' He sounded quite cheery.

'I can't get through to her.'

'Ah.' There was a significant pause. 'You don't know, then?'

'What?'

'I thought she'd spoken to Dad. She's on her way to you. She was incandescent, I believe the word is, after she spoke to him earlier, so she leapt into the car and she's on her way. She said it would take three and a half hours at this

379

time of day, and I bet she doesn't stop unless it's to top up with coffee every half hour. She's coming to collect you and bring you back, and to be honest, Sis, you'd better come otherwise it will be awful for Dad and probably Bea too. She seems to have it in her head that Bea is some kind of Satanic abuser.'

Emma handed the phone to her father. 'You'd better speak to him.' Tears were pouring down her cheeks again.

Bea reached over to put her hand on the girl's shoulder. 'It'll be OK,' she whispered.

Emma shook her head. 'It won't.'

They watched as Simon stood up and put the phone to his ear. As he listened to his son's impassioned plea, he walked through the sitting room to stand outside on the terrace, looking across the valley.

When the call ended, he sat down on the wall without a word, deep in thought.

'Can I come and stay with you?' Emma whispered to Bea.

'No, sweetheart, I don't think so. Not at this point.' Even without Simon's confirmation of the way it had gone, Bea had gathered the gist of the conversation. 'We have to agree to whatever your mum and dad decide is best for now. Until your exams are over. It may be we can arrange something for the summer holidays.' They had followed Simon outside.

'I hate my mother!' Emma's anguished cry pierced her father's introspection.

He looked up. 'She means well, Em. She's worried about your future. It's very hard for her to understand what has been going on. To be honest, it's hard for everyone to understand.' He glanced at Bea.

Bea exhaled sharply. 'Even me. We can put all this on hold, Emma. It's up to you. You can stop all this happening, now, and you would find that much easier to do if you went back to London, I promise you.'

'But I can't leave him. I have to explain. I have to make him understand.'

'Him?' Simon's fists were clenched on his knees, his knuckles white. 'Who is this him?'

'Elisedd, of course.'

'And you expect your mother to understand that? That you are besotted with a twelve-hundred-year-old man!'

Emma smiled. 'Don't be silly, Dad.'

Simon looked at Bea in despair. 'You have to talk some sense into her.'

'No! She doesn't,' Emma retorted. 'Don't you understand, Dad, this is real. I'm not making it up! I'm talking about a real person.'

'And you have to respect that person's wishes,' Bea put in sternly. 'And he does not want to see you, Emma. Not at the moment, perhaps never. And you are bound by your honour as a healer and a traveller between the worlds to respect that.'

Emma looked at her, stunned. 'A healer? Me?'

'Yes, a healer. You may not choose to use your gifts of healing, but that's what this is all about. You are not toying with the affections of some boy from school, you are dealing with very real adult pain and anguish, pain so dreadful it has lasted many lifetimes, and you have to respect that. If you can't do that, you and I are finished. I can't teach you any more.'

There was a long silence. Emma walked away from them and stood staring out across the valley as her father had done earlier. 'I'm sorry,' she said at last.

It was grudging but Bea thought it was sincere. 'So am I. We will get there, Emma. But not now, OK?' She hated herself for speaking so sharply but it seemed to be the only way to get through to her.

Emma nodded. She couldn't trust herself to speak.

39

They used to come to this forest sometimes when she was a child, Bea and her mother and her father. It had been a wild, special place, full of magic; a place where she could imagine fairies and elves and all kinds of woodland sprites and trees that whispered and talked high above her head as she hid amongst the bushes playing hide and seek with her father, while her mother found a clearing where she could spread out the rug and unpack the picnic basket.

Bea pulled into the car park and peered through the windscreen. There were a few other cars there, but not many, and the woodland tracks leading off into the distance were empty of people. She opened the door and stepped out. Only a few minutes' walk along the track and she was out of sight of the cars and alone in a forest that had been there since the days of Offa, probably centuries before him. This would have been the kind of place Nesta was born and brought up, the place she would have learned her magic. She stopped and looked round. A narrow path led off to her right, winding off amongst the bushes. A huge branch had fallen from one of the oak trees in the winter gales and lay across the clearing in front of her. She paused and then quietly she sat down on it and waited. The birds came first, a nuthatch peering at her with beady eyes from the trunk of an ash tree, a thrush calling from the top of a tree, and then a robin, head to one side, hopping closer, wondering if she had brought crumbs. Nesta was standing by the trunk of the oak, half in shadow as she waited, swathed in a shawl the colour of lichen.

'I need to talk to you,' Bea said quietly. 'I knew you would be here.'

Nesta moved towards her and sat down on the branch beside her. Her weight did not register as she moved closer, the unfurling leaves motionless in the still air. Close to she had an uncomfortably powerful energy field, cool and green and nebulous.

'You never told me. In your wanderings, did you ever find Elisedd?'

Nesta smiled. 'Eadburh was not the only one to dream. In his heart, at night when he was not at his prayers, sometimes *Abad* Elisedd dared to wonder where she was and if she was still alive. He heard stories from time to time, even from the seclusion of the prayer desk. He heard of the murder of Beorhtric from the lay brothers who had it from a pedlar; he heard of her exile from a pilgrim come to the shrine of St Tysilio from far away Canterbury. And then came a mendicant friar who brought the bones of a selection of saints to sell to the abbot, with a story about her death. Elisedd did not believe that the bones of a sheep had somehow transformed into the sacred relics of a holy man, but he could not dismiss the possibility that Eadburh was dead. How would he ever know the truth?' There was a long pause. 'My own wanderings took me to the *clas* as the spring sunlight filtered across the land and the shadows of the mountains shortened, and I made my confession to the *Abad* Elisedd. As I knelt before him, I let slip that once I had known the daughter of Offa and that in my dreams I saw her, now an abbess, safe in a convent in the northern forests of the empire. I may have hinted that she too had yearned for her only love, whom she believed dead, murdered by her father.'

'So, you told him?'

'As I left, he gave me a tiny gold enamelled cross, such as the metalworkers of Offa made. I wondered if it had been hers. And I wondered if he had understood me, but I had interfered enough with the plans of the sisters of Wyrd. It was not for me to say more. If he followed the meandering paths of my reminiscence, that would be up to him. I asked for his blessing and I left the *clas* to return to the forests of my own land.'

'But you had told him she was still alive!'

'I had made my confession after the fashion of the Christians, that was all.' She was staring away again into the deep green shadows of the forest.

Bea was afraid the enigma that was Nesta was going to fade into the shadows again. 'I need your advice; your help. There is so much going on. Eadburh and Elisedd haunt me. And Emma is at risk.'

'Eadburh and Elisedd need no help from you. Their time is past, their story written.'

'Yet Emma has become involved.' Bea sighed. 'It's hard to understand what is happening. I dream the story of Eadburh; as she lives her life, it unfolds before me. Emma dreams Eadburh's dreams of still being a young girl in love.'

Nesta nodded slowly. 'You are all weavers of dreams. Emma has the beautiful ripe body of a girl. What woman would not want to borrow that for her dreams as she sees herself wasting away in the lonely confines of a convent cell?'

A gentle breeze blew through the glade and the new leaves overhead seemed to whisper agreement.

'We all may wish for younger bodies.' Bea heard the wistful note in her own voice. 'But we don't go out to hijack someone else's. I am very afraid for Emma. And there is more. You warned me about her once, a woman, an erstwhile colleague of my husband's, who seems to have set out to destroy me. Somehow she's become involved in all this, but now she's threatening Emma too. We have to stop her.'

Nesta turned to look at her for the first time. 'And how can we do that?'

'I expected you to know.' Bea spoke more forcefully than she had intended. 'You have the knowledge.'

'You have taught the child that time is but a plaited rope, looped and knotted as the fates dictate. You have shown her what to do. It's up to her if she makes use of your advice. Maybe she wants to sleep with a prince. She has already done so in her dreams. Dreams are powerful.' Nesta's voice was soft, almost indistinguishable against the breathing of the forest. 'Eadburh's voice is seductive. Impossible to resist. The child would need to be very strong to push it away to go back to her schoolbooks.' Sunlight was filtering through the branches overhead, casting mottled shadows over Nesta's face. The silver streaks in her hair beneath her shawl caught the gleam of the setting sun and as though sensing the touch of the light she pulled the shawl closer. 'But this other woman,' she paused thoughtfully, 'becomes ever more powerful through her mission to destroy you. She invited evil in and she plays with fire without even realising how near to the abyss she walks.'

Bea shivered. 'Sandra. I don't know how she has suddenly transformed into this awful mirror image of herself. She scares me.'

Again she saw Nesta glance towards her. This time her look was withering. 'You have to be strong. You are the only one who can deal with her and to do so you will have to abandon caution and hesitation. You are not yet fully committed to your path. If you want to walk with the power of a wise woman, you have to have the courage to face demons.'

Bea drew in a shuddering breath. 'I'm not sure I have that kind of strength.' She looked down at the ground. When she was a child her father had once told her there were dragons in this forest. She had been scared then and she was scared now. Taking a deep breath, she looked back towards Nesta.

The log where the woman had been seated beside Bea was empty. The moss and leaves showed no sign that there had been anyone there.

'Nesta?' Bea scrambled to her feet. 'Nesta? Please. I haven't finished. I need you!'

But the moment of magic had passed. The sound of her raised voice had scared the birds. The robin flew off, its alarm notes cutting through the silence followed by the sound of wings high up in the canopy of the trees.. A large black bird had flown up from the tree and circled out over the forest. Crow? Raven? The messenger of a witch spying on her or a warning from the gods of the forest that she needed to be on guard and that she wasn't alone in her battle to save Emma's soul. She took a step forward. She could hear voices in the distance, a child shouting, a parent calling.

Thoughtfully she sat down again. Nesta was right. She had to be strong.

After Heather left, Sandra had gone back into her house, slamming the door behind her and decisively drawing the bolt before she returned to the sitting room.

Heather Fawcett was an unmitigated busybody. Sandra smiled grimly. She, Sandra, would deal with her later, but for now she was a nonentity in the great scheme of things. She bent to pick the box up off the floor and, putting it on her coffee table, once more removed the lid.

Sitting down, she leaned over her box of treasures, angry with herself for leaving it lying open for anyone to see. Thoughtfully she picked up the bag that contained the desiccated body of the rat and she smiled. She had enjoyed that exercise, one she remembered from her days of studying with an American wizard whose devotion to the dark side in his online lessons made him immensely popular with legions of followers. It was gratifying to think it had worked even on someone as experienced as Bea obviously was. She put the bag aside.

The crystal ball was cold in her hands and she weighed it thoughtfully, dropping it from one hand to the other as she tried to think what her strategy should be. Did she want to save Bea and the child or leave them to their fate? She had a choice as to what to do, however much she disliked Bea as a person and resented the fact that the woman was dragging the canon into her evil world – did she want to free her from whoever, whatever, it was that had entwined her in its wicked coils, or did she want to be rid of her? Perhaps she should allow fate to decide for her.

Sweeping all the papers and pencils aside, she made herself comfortable and, balancing the ball on the table, began to study the small muddy swirls in the crystal, forcing her gaze out of focus, not letting herself blink, waiting for the pictures to appear. She was expecting to see Ethelbert the king. Surely it was the evil swirling around him and his murderer she was dealing with here. But this was someone else, somewhere else. Another time. This wasn't about Bea. This was about her. Her own past lives. She leaned forward, avidly watching the scene unfold.

She watched as the cavalcade containing the murdering Queen of Wessex finally turned the bend out of sight on the forest track. She, Sandra, had been there, one of the crowd, jeering and shaking their fists, baying for the woman's blood. The scene changed. There was another target now for their fury. She heard the name as a whisper. They were hunting for the herb-wife, Nesta, who had made the poison that killed the king. It was the women now, their menfolk outmanoeuvred, who gathered in an angry swarm and turned away from the palace courtyard, streaming up the hill to the herb gardens and the still room where the poison had been concocted.

The hut was empty. Only the herbs hanging rustling in the draught were still there. The table was bare, the shelves cleared, the witch had gone. She had disappeared into the forest.

Backing away, Sandra looked round, no longer part of the scene, a mere bystander as the women set light to the hut. Now they were trashing the garden, angrily pulling up the lovingly cultivated herbs, stamping on them, hurling them into the fire.

And still she watched.

The scene changed again. She was a maid in the palace at Aachen, waiting on the Queen of Wessex as she flirted with the emperor, carrying water, emptying chamber pots, washing clothes, a maid who is never noticed, cowering against the wall as Eadburh swept past with a curse for the servants who dared to stray into her path.

This had been her destiny, she realised, in a dozen previous lives, in a hundred meditations, in a thousand dreams: to stand by the village pond as another screaming old woman was thrown into muddy waters to sink or swim, to laugh as the hangman's noose tightened and the victim's legs kicked help-lessly as they died, to watch at the foot of the scaffold for a head to roll, to knit by the guillotine, always to watch others dragged away to their doom. It was her destiny to follow and jeer and laugh and then impotently to wander away.

Well, not this time. Now she was ready. She drew her hands over the crystal as if to wipe out its memory and, reaching for the silk scarf she kept in the box, she draped it over the ball. She felt a sudden shiver of real fear. This was not a game. It had never been a game. In this lifetime she had real power over real people. The power of life and death.

Her plan was simple. She needed to speak to Emma. Negotiating the narrow lanes up to the cottage, Sandra drove on past it, parking at the top on the sheep-cropped grass beyond the cattle grid. Walking back down the lane between high shaded banks laced with violets and primroses, she crept along the hedgerow towards the gate. Quietly unlatching it she tiptoed up the steps and stood for several seconds on the terrace, then, taking a deep breath, she raised her fist and banged on the front door.

There was an interval of several seconds before she heard footsteps inside. The door was opened by Simon himself. He did not look happy; even less so when he saw who it was. He spoke before she could say why she had come. 'I'm sorry, this is not a good time for visitors. I'm expecting someone.'

Sandra felt a surge of anger. 'I haven't come all this way on a whim. I need to talk to you.'

'Why? To explain all the damage you're doing to Bea?'

Sandra took a step forward. 'Bea is a dangerous woman and I want, I need, to help your daughter.' She put out her hand as though to push him back so she could enter the house.

He didn't budge. 'No. I'm sorry. I don't want you here. I'm expecting my wife at any moment.'

'I will go, but not before I've explained.' She spoke through gritted teeth. 'You don't understand what is happening.'

Behind them a car pulled into the layby outside the cottage and parked beside Simon's old Volvo. He groaned. 'Please. Go. Now. I told you, I do not want you here.'

'Dad?' Emma had appeared behind him. 'Is that Mum's car?' She spotted Sandra and stared at her. 'What are you doing here?'

Sandra clenched her fists. 'Your wife should listen to what I have to say as well.'

The force with which Val slammed the door of her car after she climbed out spoke volumes. She opened the gate and ran up the steps onto the terrace and only then seemed to see the stranger standing by the door. She stopped in her tracks.

'Mrs Armstrong? I am sorry to intrude but there are things you ought to know about what your daughter has been doing.' Sandra was oblivious to the family tensions around her. 'You need to listen to me. I don't think your husband understands what is happening to him. He is blinded by Bea's charisma and now there is an added problem and he can't see the danger of what has been going on.'

Emma pushed past her father. 'What is going on is absolutely none of your business!' she shouted. 'You've been following me, and we should call the police! You're nothing but a vicious stalker!'

'Em!'

Simon put his hand on Emma's shoulder but she shook him off. 'No. Everyone is too scared of her to tell her what an appalling person she is. A busybody. A spy. A vicious, jealous interfering—' Words failed Emma and she burst into tears.

'That's enough!' Val walked past her husband and Sandra and pushed Emma back towards the door. 'Go inside. I have no idea what is going on here, but I'm beginning to under-stand. This lady' – she threw a withering glance at Sandra – 'appears to have a very good idea of the situation, but I gather it has nothing to do with her, so I think we can deal with this ourselves, thank you.' She glared at Sandra. 'I suggest you leave us to our own affairs.'

Sandra held her ground. 'I didn't come all this way up here to be sent away. I'm not the one in the wrong here,' she stated stoutly. 'I'm coming in. That child will lie to you, and your husband is besotted with the woman who is grooming your daughter!'

The silence that followed this statement was broken only by the call of a buzzard riding the thermals above the valley. Sandra took the chance to walk inside and sit down by the empty hearth.

Even Val was left speechless by this. She turned to Simon, who also appeared dumbstruck. 'Call the police!' she hissed at him. She followed Sandra inside and stood looking down at her.

'Val. Let's all calm down.' Simon shouted after them as Emma pushed past him and ran upstairs to her bedroom. The whole house shook with the force of the door banging behind her and they heard the sound of her sobs through the ceiling.

'Now see what you've done!' Val spat the words, whether at Sandra or Simon or both wasn't clear. 'All right, if you're so keen to tell me what you think is happening, let's hear it, then perhaps you will leave us in peace.' She sat down opposite Sandra, perching on the edge of the chair, her arms folded.

'No, Val.' Simon tried his best.

'Shut up!'

He sat down at his writing table and put his head in his hands.

'Well, I'm waiting.' Val looked at the woman opposite her. Sandra smiled. This was her chance.

40

Sandra spoke without interruption for several minutes, all too aware of Mrs Armstrong's eyes fixed unblinkingly on her face. Val's expression was forbidding. When at last Sandra fell silent, there was a long pause. Simon raised his head to look from one woman to the other.

'Thank you.' Val spoke very quietly. 'Leave this with me.'

Sandra looked perplexed. 'But I have to help you deal with this.'

'I don't see how, or why you need to involve yourself further in our affairs.' Val stood up. 'I would like you to go now so that my husband and I can talk. Please' – for the first time her voice rose slightly – 'leave us alone.'

'But—'

'No. Nothing else. Speak to no one, follow no one. Leave us all in peace!'

'You don't believe me!' Sandra was outraged.

'I believe you are perfectly sincere, Mrs Bedford. But I don't believe our family is any of your business. Whether or not there is a problem here, it's for Emma's parents to address, not a complete stranger.'

She moved forward to stand over Sandra's chair. There was

no mistaking her body language. Sandra stood up and shuffled unwillingly towards the door. 'I did tell you that the bishop and the dean—'

'Yes, you told us.'

Simon moved at last. He walked over to the front door and pulled it open. 'Time to go, Sandra. Thank you for your help, but my wife is right. This is for us to sort out now. Please do not take this any further. And don't come here again.'

'But Bea—' Sandra was already outside on the terrace.

'Leave Bea alone.' Simon closed the door with a bang and leaned against it, his eyes closed.

'What a ghastly woman.' Val threw herself back down into her chair. 'Mad as a box of frogs! I hope and pray that's the last we see of her, although I doubt it will be. I can recognise the type a mile away: a self-righteous busybody of the worst kind.' She gave an exaggeratedly loud sigh, then she looked over at Simon. 'Please tell me you don't believe any of this utter and complete nonsense. I have never heard such drivel. When Felix told me what had been going on, I couldn't believe my ears. Ghosts, apparitions, possession. And now black magic and witchcraft, exorcisms and God knows what! You have obviously all lost your senses.'

With a quick look up at the ceiling where Emma's sobs had fallen silent at last, Simon pushed himself away from the door. 'Come into the kitchen. We can talk better in there.'

Following his look, Val stood up. 'Coffee. I've been driving for nearly four hours.'

'And you must be exhausted.'

'I'm taking Emma back, you do know that, don't you?'

He nodded.

'Does she?'

'I think so. Val, you've got to—'

'I've got to nothing. You listen to me.' She sat down at the kitchen table, white with fatigue. He switched on the kettle and reached for the coffee pot. It was no use arguing until she had had her say.

'This woman, Bea, is at the root of all this. That much is obvious. I cannot think how you allowed her to get such a hold over Emma. That dreadful Sandra person seems to be right as far as that goes. This is clearly a case of some sort of grooming. No, nothing to do with sex. I know it's not that.'

Simon bit his lip and waited.

'It sounds as though Bea is thoroughly unhinged. I rang her husband and warned him off. He must be out of his mind with worry, but then all religion is verging on the insane, in my opinion. I should imagine the atmosphere in a cathedral is beyond unhealthy and thoroughly incestuous. Bloody hell, Simon! What on earth have you got yourself mixed up in?'

She paused and Simon took his chance. 'Finished?' he enquired mildly. He pushed the mug of coffee across the table towards her.

'No. Not by a long chalk!' She glared at him.

'Any chance I can get a word in edgeways at this stage?'

'Why not. Let's hear your excuses. I trust she's wrong about you being in love with this woman.'

'I don't need to make excuses, Val. And no, I am not in love with anyone except you, and that's tricky at times, believe me! I may not have handled all this as well as I should, but we have been experiencing an extraordinary, unprecedented series of events and you screaming scorn and derision at what has happened here does not help the situation. Emma needs sympathy and understanding. She needs help and advice and she has been getting that from Bea. I doubt very much if you know anyone who can do what Bea has been doing to help her, but if you do, then by all means wheel them in.'

Val gave a snort of disgust. 'I will find someone in London. And I'm taking Emma back today.'

Simon frowned. 'I don't think you're fit to drive anywhere today, Val. You can't do that journey twice in one day. At least stay the night and take her tomorrow. Then we will all have the chance to talk this over first. Calmly,' he added as he saw Val draw breath.

To his surprise, she subsided. She took another sip of coffee. 'I'm not sleeping here.'

'Well, I'm sure you will be able to find somewhere in a B & B. Or you can go to a hotel in Hereford.'

'Leaving Emma here to disappear again?'

'I'm not keeping her here against her wishes, Val. You can take her with you. If she'll go.'

Abruptly Val pushed back her chair and stood up. Simon stayed where he was as she disappeared into the sitting room and he heard her steps as she climbed the stairs.

It was five minutes before she reappeared. She had washed her face and combed her hair. 'She's fast asleep,' she said.

'Let's leave her then. At least for a bit. Felix must have told you how stressed the poor girl has been. Please, Val, let's have something to eat together and talk quietly. If we take the time to discuss this situation, however oddly it strikes you, perhaps we can sort out a solution between us.'

'Are you going to suggest we invite the charismatic Bea to join us?'

The remark was deliberately waspish. Simon flinched but didn't rise to the bait. 'I don't think so. She has done her best and she is there if Emma needs her.'

In the forest, Bea was sitting on the fallen log, deep in thought. Her attention had moved from Nesta to Emma and Eadburh, and now she was thinking about Sandra. Why hadn't she realised what a serious player Sandra was? Nesta had warned her and she had ignored the warning. It was obvious now. The woman was transparent, her motivation clear, her malice tangible in an aura that she had dragged after her through incarnation after incarnation. She was an observer, her self-appointed job was to incite others to violence and to mockery, to get enjoyment from watching others' pain. In life after life she had been dismissed and ignored, a watcher not an instigator, but somewhere along the way she had learned lessons and now she had become dangerous.

Bea closed her eyes, trying to set her thoughts in order, trying to summon the strength she needed. But the need for sleep was powerful. Sitting above her in the tree canopy the robin cocked its head to one side, bright-eyed, then seeing no sign of crumbs, it flew away. In the convent, the soul that would one day emerge as Sandra Bedford had brought the abbess a pot of new tapers, bowed deeply, and left, closing the door behind her. Bea dozed once more.

The lamp in the corner of Eadburh's chamber was burning low and the room was almost dark. The building was silent. There were no shuffling steps outside in the long corridor, no noises from the cloister below her window, no creak of the wind on the shutters. She had heard the great bell in the tower strike three times to signal lauds. The nuns would be in church. She rose stiffly from her bed and pulling her heavy fur-lined cloak around her shoulders went over to the table. It was perhaps the benefit of being abbess she most appreciated in winter, the fact that her chamber was situated over the warming room, while the sisters had to freeze in their cells at night, waiting for the rare moments when they could go into the room down there to thaw their cold hands and feet. She groped on her table for a taper and held it to the wicks in the beeswax of the bronze lamp on the prayer desk. The walls of the chamber were visible now.

The knock at her door was barely audible. She frowned. No one would normally dare to interrupt her sleep. She had made it clear she did not attend lauds. The abbey ran smoothly under her guidance. It was wealthy, well organised and a place she could feel safe. The system was efficient and her household officers and servants well trained. A disturbance in the early hours of the morning was unheard of.

Clutching her cloak more closely round her shoulders, she moved across to the door and pulled it open. One of the sisters who helped run the guest house was standing there with a candle in her hand, a tall figure barely visible behind her in the shadows.

'Mother Abbess,' she stammered. 'I'm sorry, but your visitor insisted.'

'How dare you!' Eadburh shivered as the icy draught blew down the long passage, making the woman's candle flicker. Behind her the flames on her lamp flared and smoked.

'It was I who dared.' The man stepped forward. 'I have travelled hundreds of miles to see the lady abbess. You may leave, Sister.' He turned to the nun with a little bow. 'And you will make no mention to anyone of my visit. Your abbess and I have important matters to discuss in private.'

The sister bowed her head obediently and turned away. She moved silently out of sight around the corner and the shadows followed her, leaving the man standing in the darkness of the passage.

Eadburh was staring at his face, unable to see it clearly in the light of the lamps, but remembering the voice so well. Her heart performed a frightened, incredulous leap in her chest. 'You?'

He stepped inside the room and closed the door silently behind him. 'Me.' He put his arms around her and pulled her close. As she raised her lips to his, she managed only one word. 'Elise.'

'Are you all right, my dear?' The voice at her shoulder made Bea jump. Her awakening was so sudden and so outrageous she couldn't at first work out where she was.

'Sorry, I didn't mean to startle you, only you've been sitting there a while and what with it getting dark I thought I would check.'

Bea stared round, bewildered. The stone walls of one of Charlemagne's newest and best-endowed convents with its state-of-the-art buildings and fabulous frescoes in the latest Byzantine style, lit by bronze tripod lamps and beeswax candles, had vanished and she found herself sitting in a lonely clearing in the forest. The only similarity was the encircling darkness.

They had met again, Eadburh and Elisedd. He had taken her into his arms. And then, as they were about to kiss, the scene had disappeared and they had vanished into the shadows.

She looked up at the old man, confused. 'I must have fallen asleep.' She scrambled to her feet.

'But you're all right?' The elderly man at her side was genuinely concerned. There was an equally elderly golden retriever at his side and both looked worried as they surveyed her. Rain was beginning to fall; she could hear it patter on the leaf litter around her feet. 'I'm sure it's safe out here,' he went on, but it's lonely in the dark.' He gave such a sweet smile her heart warmed to him. Somehow she dragged her attention back to the present. 'That's kind of you. I must have been more tired than I realised. I've got a car nearby.'

He stood back. 'Then I'll leave you to it. I'm sorry to have disturbed you.' With a click of his fingers to the dog, he walked off down the ride. She stared after him then, with a little shiver, she turned back the way she had come. Nesta had vanished into the trees long since and Eadburh and Elisedd? She found she was smiling. So, he had found her. Was it true? Was there to be a happy ending after all to the story? If that old man hadn't woken her, she might have discovered the answer to that question. She might have witnessed their reunion.

Hers was the only car left in the car park. She made her way across to it and climbed in, instinctively locking the doors against the night before she inserted the key in the ignition. It was late and she felt exposed and vulnerable and very alone and she needed to go home. To Mark. To her study in the attic. To the story.

Picking up the note on the kitchen table, Bea read it with a rueful smile. *Back soon. Love you, M xxx*

Walking over to the sink she picked an empty glass off the draining board and filled it from the tap. Sipping slowly she looked out of the window at the garden. It was dark out there but it had stopped raining. With a sigh of exhaustion she opened the back door. Sitting down on the bench, huddled in her coat, she closed her eyes and listened for a while to the gentle trickle of the little fountain.

The abbess's lodgings were impressive. She had her own sleeping cell above the warming room, but there were other offices from where she ran the abbey with the help of her officials and it was there that she kept Ava, who had grown into a magnificent animal. Her long dark golden fur glossy from brushing, she stood level with her mistress's hips. No one dared to query the abbess having a dog; on the contrary, many abbeys kept hunting animals and many a particular favourite managed to make its way into an abbot's quarters. The first time she saw the guest, the dog Ava had growled and snarled at him and from then on she was banished from Eadburh's presence and left in the care of the guest house almoner, who liked dogs.

The guest house was on the far side of the compound run by two lay brothers and three lay sisters who answered to her chamberlain. When Eadburh announced to him that her visitor would be lodged in the room next to hers, eyebrows were raised. 'He brings messages from my cousin, the King of Mercia. He is an envoy and emissary from his father the King of Powys. It is only right that he have access to me at all times.'

It was after the bell had rung for lauds that he came to her each night, unpinning her veil, lifting the gold chain of her cross over her head and dropping it on her prayer desk, before pulling the gown from her shoulders. The silk shift slid easily from her body, still slim and youthful, and he took her into his arms and then into bed.

He had laughed when he saw the shift. 'So, my lady abbess dresses like an empress under her habit, where no one can see; she does not espouse the rules of the Order and wear rough clothing next to her skin.'

She smiled. 'I wear black.'

'Because it suits you.' He stroked her bare shoulder.

'I want to come back with you,' she whispered. 'Back to your hills to see the dragons you promised me when we were young. I want to see the shrine of the hares.'

He buried his face between her breasts. 'We will live our dream, I promise. We will walk the hills together and watch the sun set in the mists.'

Pushing him away at last she sat up, suddenly businesslike. 'We will leave as soon as the weather improves.' She was looking past him towards the windows. Behind the shutters the snow was falling heavily. 'I will give orders for my dowry to be loaded into wagons and we will leave as soon as the roads are passable.'

'Will the great Emperor Charles allow it?'

She frowned. 'It is none of the emperor's business. I will take only what is rightfully mine.'

'And does that include the emperor's dog?'

She smiled. 'He gave Ava to me when she was a tiny puppy; she loves me and she will grow to tolerate you, my prince. If I love you, she will love you too. And we need her. There will be wolves and bears on the roads and footpads and wild boar in the forests. Ava is the best of guards.'

'Then she will be our entourage. You forget, although I am still my father's son, and a prince of royal blood, I gave up the royal estate when I became a monk. I didn't bring an escort. I travelled alone as a pilgrim. I didn't know if I would be able to find you.' He had told her how he had thought her gone forever and she had told him how, long ago, her father had claimed her prince had died. She did not mention the baby that had never existed save in the lonely longing of her dreams. Why taunt him with more stories of what might have been?

He had dreamed of her often, he told her, murmuring his story, his lips on her hair, and sometimes in his dream he had seen her as a girl of eighteen again, but as she looked at him he had seen the gaze of someone else's eyes and he had been filled with fear. He smiled as he pulled her close.

It was the story told by a strange woman of the forest who had come to see him one day, seeking his blessing, and telling him that his Eadburh might still be alive, that had led him to dream again of the golden girl he had loved and lost and led him to leave his own monastery in Meifod and follow her trail to find her here at last in the verdant fields and forests of the empire.

'So, you followed your dream.' She smiled, bending over him to kiss him again. Her hair, scented with rosemary and lavender, slipped from its heavy coils, veiling his face. They had both forgotten their vows to God; their only promises now were for one another. He knew she was bewitching him all over again. He surrendered willingly.

It was proving easy to make plans. As soon as spring unlocked the roads and tracks they would set out for a convent some miles away on a visit to the abbess there, then on towards the next religious house, and the next, heading always southwest towards the coast and the distant shores of Albion. Their needs would be few. She guessed she might have to abandon her dowry lest word of her imminent departure reach the emperor. She would say the wagons were loaded with gifts for the other houses of the order on her progress. It didn't matter to her what she had to leave behind. She would be with Elise. The icy months of January and February passed and March arrived in a blast of rain and wind that at last unlocked the ice. The lovers watched as the snow banks began to melt and the days grew imperceptibly longer.

Eadburh could barely contain her excitement as she sat in the chapel, hearing the services as each day passed, living only for the evenings when her visitor could make his way secretly into her chamber and they could lie in one another's arms.

They planned to leave in the third week of Lent in order to reach a neighbouring convent in time for Holy Week. Eadburh allowed the younger sisters to pack a travelling trunk and she realised they would have to take an escort of lay brothers from the farm. The abbess making an official visit with her honoured guest could do no less. No matter. They would send the men home when they reached their first destination. She let it be known that after Easter her guest would go on alone towards his distant home. There was no hint that she planned to go with him.

Weeks after the first thaw and only days before they planned to leave they were lying in one another's arms after making gentle, lingering love, whispering sleepy plans for their future as the firelight died and the room grew dark when the sound of loud persistent knocking echoed through the convent buildings.

They lay there, listening, frozen with horror at the sound of shouting, the clash of swords, the splintering of doors, and then the hurried tramp of feet through the stone passages of the buildings. There was nowhere to hide. Within minutes the abbess's door burst inwards and the room filled with men. Ignoring her, they dragged Elisedd from her bed.

He flailed out wildly, looking round desperately for something

400

to use as a weapon. His fist closed around a candlestick, but it was struck from his hand and as he was hauled away down the passage and out of her sight she screamed his name once.

'By the order of the emperor!' their commander sneered as Eadburh was dragged from the sheets and held, half-naked and sobbing with fear, to stand before him. 'One of the servants here reported to the sisters her suspicions that you had a lover and they made sure the emperor came to hear of it. He has had you watched. You have betrayed your vows, and shamed your name and that of this convent, and you have dishonoured God. The emperor commands that your lover pay for his sacrilege with his life. As for you, my orders are that you be thrown into the fields. You came here as a queen. You will die naked in the snow. Should you survive the winter blast, you can live as a penniless beggar, grovelling in the backstreets of some lonely city. Do not go crying to the emperor. He will not allow you into his presence. His orders were clear. "She is to be thrown out like the whore she is!"'

She glimpsed the shocked faces of the nuns, brought from their prayers by the commotion and the cold triumphant face of one of her servants, a face strangely familiar, as she was dragged from her chamber, her shift torn from her shoulders, her feet bare, scrabbling wildly on the stone flags as she was pulled helplessly through the long passages and out across the courtyard. There was no sign of Elisedd or of the armed men who had wrestled him away, no sounds of shouting. As her own screams died away, she heard for a brief moment the anguished howl of a dog, swiftly cut short, then the convent fell eerily silent. The men who had seized her hauled her towards the entrance to be pushed out into the slush of the thawing fields.

Behind her, the gates were slammed and she heard the bolts drawn across. As she lay face down in the snow where they had thrown her there was no sound now except for the wail of the icy wind across the plains and her own broken-hearted sobs.

'Bea? Wake up, sweetheart.'

The arms into which she snuggled were Mark's. She turned

back to see the figure of Eadburh lying in the mud, wearing nothing but her torn shift, her legs and feet bare, her arms scrabbling in the snow at the field's edge, then darkness closed in over the scene and she was sitting on the bench in the garden with Mark beside her.

'Don't cry. It was a dream.'

'Someone betrayed her. They told Charlemagne that she had a lover and he was furious, or jealous or both, and poor Elisedd was murdered and she was thrown out of the convent to die a beggar.' Bea clung to him. Mark was wearing his cassock, she realised, with his silver pectoral cross on its black cord around his neck. He must have come straight from church. 'What time is it?' she snuffled.

'After midnight. I've been at the hospice.'

She pulled away from him and looked up at his face. 'Oh, Mark. Was it your friend?'

He nodded. 'He died a couple of hours ago.'

'I'm so sorry.'

'He was at peace with the world and ready to move on to the next where he would be out of his pain. A brave man.' He eased her out of his arms and stood up. 'Are you all right now?' He held out his hand.

She nodded. 'It was a very bad dream.' This was not the time to pour out the horrors of Eadburh's story. Stiffly she stood up. The garden was cold and very dark as they went back into the kitchen and closed the door on the night and on the anguish of Eadburh lying broken in the melting snow. Bea took a couple of tumblers out of the cupboard and poured him a small shot of whisky, then one for herself.

'Do you want to talk about Eadburh?' Mark sat down at the table. Under the bright strip light she could see the strain and exhaustion in his eyes.

'Not now. She's waited twelve hundred years to tell her story. She can wait a little longer.'

'Thank you,' he whispered. He took a sip from his glass. 'I think I might go up to bed. We'll talk about it all tomorrow, I promise.'

When Bea tiptoed into their bedroom twenty minutes later,

he was fast asleep. She stood looking down at him then she dropped a gentle kiss on his forehead and crept out of the room. She would sleep in Anna's room. If she had more nightmares, she didn't want to wake him.

41

The cottage was incredibly quiet without the children or Val. Simon had waved the car off down the lane the next morning. To his astonishment, Emma had in the end made no fuss about going back to London. She said she had slept well and, though pale and strained, had collected her gear and climbed into the car beside her mother with barely a word.

Val had stayed the night in the end after sharing supper with her husband and her daughter, and after Emma had gone up to bed she and Simon had talked long and late over a bottle of wine. As always with Val's tempestuous rages, her fury had exhausted itself, and in the end she had conceded the cottage was rather nice, that he was doing his best with Em and that she was very proud of him. The Fords, she said, had copies of all his books. When Simon had tentatively offered to sleep in the blow-up bed downstairs so she could have his room, she had told him not to bother, then had snuggled in beside him. Result! He smiled at the memory.

He walked back indoors and stood looking down at his worktable. Almost on cue, his phone rang. It was Jane Luxton. 'I've news about the chronicle,' she said. 'I've arranged to take some of the photos the experts have sent me over to give to

Kate and Phil, and it occurred to me you might like to meet me there.'

He didn't need asking twice. By midday he was bumping slowly up the hidden drive and parking beside Jane's car in front of the main door to the house. Jane had brought a folder of beautiful high-definition photos which she spread out on Kate and Phil's kitchen table. 'Look at this, Simon. We sent the chronicle to the Bodleian Library where they have all sorts of specialist infra-red cameras and things that can show up old inks.'

'There is masses more than we could see before.' Simon marvelled at the detail; Felix's efforts, brilliant as they'd been with the resources available, could not compare with this. He leaned closer. 'I wish Felix was here. He would love to see this.'

'He can see them when he comes back next holidays,' Kate said comfortably. 'Poor old Felix. When do the dreaded exams start?'

'May thirteenth.' Simon leaned closer to the table. Blown up this large, he could see the characters easily. 'This is fascinating. This shows the details about that last Welsh raid in 1055. So, they did know who it was who was on their way to attack Hereford. Gruffydd, the King of Gwynedd and Powys was accompanied by the outlawed King of East Anglia.' He leaned closer. 'With an army of Vikings from Ireland, for goodness' sake, coming to attack the Earl of Hereford. What a mixture!' The next photo showed the last page of the chronicle, the final, panicked scratch of the pen and then nothing more. 'It did not end well for the minster or the priory. We can almost see it before our eyes. Those poor guys. It must have been so utterly terrifying. Monks had no way of defending themselves presumably, no way of knowing exactly when the end of the world, in the form of that army of men with swords and spears, was going to appear over the horizon.'

They gazed at the photos in silence for a while. Simon was thinking how pleased he was that Emma wasn't there. With her imagination she would have been poleaxed by the words of the ancient monk, sitting scribbling at his desk, clinging to his pen as the only thing he knew how to do, the only thing he could know what to do.

'Simon?' Kate had leaned across and put her hand over his. 'Are you OK?'

He grimaced. 'I was thinking about my kids. We are made so vulnerable through them.' He nodded ruefully towards her protruding stomach. 'Until they come along, we only have ourselves to look out for, but once they're there, we are hostage to our love for them.'

'But this man was a monk, Simon,' Jane reminded him briskly. 'No kids.'

'His community would have been his family and as dear to him perhaps as children,' Kate retorted. Her hand strayed to her bump. Her baby was due any day now. 'I know it might have been quite different. Perhaps they all bickered and fought and hated each other, like a real family, but I don't see it somehow. Not if he stayed at his desk to the last. And how do we know he was ancient?'

'Perhaps because of his skill,' Simon said. He had shrugged off the moment of weakness and was back in didactic mode. 'It takes years of practice.'

'And perhaps because the younger monks and lay brothers, if they had any sense at all, would have gathered up the monastery treasure and headed for the hills at high speed. No one in their right mind would have stayed there, writing their diary and waiting to be massacred, unless they were incapable of moving,' Phil put in. 'Either way, we will never know. Apart from those scribbles there is no way of finding out what happened.'

Simon caught Kate's eye and realised she was thinking exactly what he was thinking: unless, like Emma, they had the gift of seeing the past in graphic recall, with all its love and longing, its horror and squalor and hatred and, who knew, at the end, the terror and pain of its death.

'That's enough winding ourselves up for now,' Kate said firmly. 'The past is the past and must stay there. I'm going to make us all some good twenty-first-century coffee.'

*

That morning Bea had stirred when Mark put his head round the door to check where she was before he went out. She was fast asleep, her face serene. He hesitated and then quietly closed the door again without waking her.

Staggering to her feet, Eadburh dragged herself back across the field to the convent entrance gates and beat on the high oak doors with her fists. No one came and there was no sound from inside. Slowly the sound of her frantic calls grew more feeble and at last she subsided onto her knees, too exhausted to move. She heard the chapel bell ring out for lauds. Snow began to fall again; the only sound was the sighing of the wind in the trees across the fields and the soft patter of its flakes. She could no longer feel her fingers or her toes. No one was coming to her aid. Somehow she managed to climb to her feet. Looking round now that it was growing light, she saw buildings in the distance and remembered the byres and barns of the abbey farm where she would at least find shelter from the snow and perhaps warmth from the huddled beasts. Somehow she managed to shuffle one foot in front of the other and grope her way along the wall and it was there in the cowshed that the dairymaid found her as she brought in her pail and her stool as the first cocks crowed and the convent bell rang out in the distance, for the daybreak office of prime.

When she regained consciousness, Eadburh was in the farmhouse, wrapped in blankets. She had friends, it appeared, amongst the farmworkers. The king's men were searching for her, she was told. The convent was in uproar, the sub prioress had assumed command, forbidden anyone to mention her name and threatened her with death, as ordered by the emperor, should she be found on the home estates. It was only a matter of time before they came here. She had been lucky. A second brief fall of spring snow had covered the footsteps that led from her desperate flight from the gates to the barn and those of the men who had come to carry her back to the warmth of the fire. They gave her a gown and a rough woollen cloak with a pair of worn shoes; they fed her

407

some potage. Her desperate questions about the man who had been with her were met with shrugs and shaken heads.

It was full daylight when the boy who had collected the milk for the convent kitchens returned with the empty pitchers. He squatted before the fire and with a quick worried look at Eadburh as she sat huddled on a stool nearby, he told them what had happened.

The abbess's friend, he cast another fearful glance in her direction as he stammered over the word, had been dragged out to the shambles behind the cookhouse and there he had been tied down and the slaughterer had castrated him like a hog before his body was thrown out into the pig pens.

Eadburh's screams were so loud that the farmer's wife ran to her and put her hand over the abbess's mouth. 'No, no, no. Please, you will have us all killed.' She clutched Eadburh's head to her bosom, trying to stifle her cries. 'Please, Mother Abbess, please, be quiet! You are not supposed to be here. You can't be found or you will be killed as well.'

Eadburh was shaking all over, her grief and rage overwhelming. 'No, no, no!' She cried again and again, rocking backwards and forwards. 'No, no. no. This can't happen. It can't. I won't let it. Elise, my love!' She wrapped her arms around herself and her rocking grew more frantic. 'I can't lose you now. Elise! Elise!'

One by one the men crept away, dragging the milk boy with them. They would not betray her, but this was women's business. If they were shocked at what had happened, they kept their faces impassive. Best to go out to tend the beasts.

It was a long time before Eadburh stopped sobbing, too exhausted by her grief to do more than cradle her head in her arms as the firelight died. The farmer's wife crept to the door and looked out. Her husband and the other men were nowhere to be seen. The convent farm was deserted and quiet. With a sigh she looked back at her uninvited guest, no more than a humped shadow in the flickering light of the dying fire. She didn't know what to do. 'You have to go,' she whispered at last. 'I can't hide you here. They will find you. Is there no one who can help you?'

Eadburh had few friends within the convent walls. She shook her head. 'Better I die here.'

'Not for me,' the woman replied tartly. 'If you are found here, we will all die!'

In the end they sent one of the farm boys with a message for Sister Ermintrude, the nun who had charge of Ava.

It was much later that one of the slave girls from the dairy crept back across the yard with a secret message. The mother abbess must leave. The slave girl, Cwen, would go with her and guide her up into the forests where she would be safe. Her only chance was to leave Francia as soon as possible. If she was caught by the emperor's men she could expect no mercy. His rage at the betrayal of his trust knew no bounds. From the bundle in her arms Cwen produced a grey shawl from Sister Ermintrude's own cell and a few silver pennies, stolen no doubt from convent treasury, all the nun could extract without being seen. There would be ructions when the shortfall was discovered when the chamberlain did her accounts at the end of the month. Eadburh took the bundle from the girl, and then let it fall to the floor, still shaken by sobs. She had no desire to run anywhere, no will to live. If Elisedd was dead, then so was she.

Cwen bent to retrieve the bundled cloak and the pouch of coins. 'Please, lady, we must go now,' she murmured timidly. She looked desperately across at the farmer's wife who was standing uncomfortably by the fire, watching. 'If they are searching the estates, they will find you.'

'Go!' the older woman sprang into life. If the lady abbess was found under her roof now after all this, her family would pay dearly. She seized Eadburh by the arm and pushed her towards the doorway, where she checked to see no one was around before giving her unwelcome visitor a final shove to send her on her way.

Outside the day was grey and the wind was bitterly cold. As the door slammed behind Eadburh and the girl with her they heard the bar fall into place. They were locked out.

For a moment neither woman moved. The girl Cwen stared round, still clutching the bundle. She was panting with fear.

Seeing the abbess's indecision, she grabbed her by the hand and began to drag her towards the woods that bordered the farm. Eadburh followed, barely aware of what was happening or where she was, only slowly realising as she ran how cold it was out there and that the hand that clutched hers so desperately was as cold as her own. Her head was bare to the elements. She had no coif, no veil, no hood. The farmer's wife's gown was hugely too big for her, and she tripped as it slipped from the knotted belt that was holding it in place. The woollen shawl she had been given was already wet through. Her hair was wild and tangled. The shoes she had been given leaked and within minutes she was shuddering with cold all over.

When at last they were in the shelter of the trees she staggered to a stop and leaned against the trunk of one of the tall beeches that marked the border of the abbey's land. She was gasping for breath and it took her several seconds to see her young companion was doubled over, clutching her side. 'You have a stitch?' she asked, for the first time seeming to be aware of what was happening or that there was someone with her. 'Breathe slowly; it will pass.' She looked back across the field. Already the snow was melting from the strips and furrows, leaving lines of puddles that reflected the cold light of day.

It took them a while to get their breath back. All the time Cwen was staring nervously around them. 'We must go on. They will won't stop searching until they are sure you've gone.'

'No.' Eadburh was still looking back towards the dark silhouette of the church with its community of huddled buildings against the night sky. 'I have to go back for him. I can't leave him there.'

'You cannot go back, lady.' The girl's eyes widened with horror. 'They will kill you!'

'I have to find him. Supposing he's still alive!' Eadburh stepped away from the trees, her arms outstretched, her shawl falling to the icy ground.

'No!' Dropping the bundle, the girl grabbed her wrist again. 'Did you not hear the boy? The man is dead! His body was thrown into the midden!'

Eadburh closed her eyes. Hot tears began to stream once more down her ice-cold cheeks. Slowly she sank to her knees beneath the tree and she gave herself once more over to her grief.

'Please!' Cwen watched her for a while, not sure what to do in the face of such overwhelming sorrow, before retrieving the abbess's sodden shawl and wrapping it around the woman's shoulders. 'Please. We have to go. We can't stay here. They will find us.' The girl's teeth were chattering; her fingers brushed Eadburh's cheek as she pulled the shawl closer with sudden tenderness.

Eadburh sighed heavily and looked up. The girl, dressed only in a tunic and thin ragged overdress was shivering violently. The bundle she had carried was lying at her feet. 'Unwrap that cloak and wrap it round you. It will be easier than carrying it,' she said at last.

Cwen's eyes widened. 'But the cloak was for you, lady.'

'And I give it to you.' Eadburh gave a bitter smile. 'I have a warm gown and a woollen shawl. I have no need of it.' Was it altruism or the miserable longing for death that overwhelmed her? She did not give the matter any thought as she watched the girl shake out the heavy cloak and wrap it round herself with a look of amazed joy.

In the distance they heard the tolling of the abbey bell, barely audible now above the quiet whisper of the fir trees.

Cwen turned towards the field where pale evening sunlight was reflecting off the mud and her face filled with horror. 'They're coming!' In the distance three men had appeared, on foot, standing near them at the edge of the field. 'If they have dogs, we are lost.'

Eadburh took a deep breath at the mention of dogs with a sudden desperate yearning for her beloved Ava. She offered up a silent prayer that Ermintrude would look after her. Surely the emperor would not act vindictively against one of his own beloved animals. There was no movement from the men. They appeared to be scanning the fields. And there was no sound of barking, so they didn't have hunting dogs with them. The shock of the sight of them spurred Eadburh into action. Climbing stiffly to her feet she nodded. 'We must go.'

Holding hands, they began to run, heading deeper into the

trees, following a steep narrow path that wound into the dark heart of the forest.

They had thought themselves well clear of pursuit as it grew dark, when the sound of barking far behind them brought them to a halt. Terrified, Eadburh looked round desperately for somewhere to hide.

'We need to cross water, to break the scent,' Cwen whispered. Her already pale face was white. 'I can hear it nearby.' They scrambled up the path and over some rocks to gaze down at a cascading waterfall, the water a white streak against the black rocks of the valley that opened up below them.

Somehow they scrambled across and threaded their way once more into the undergrowth.

Still the barking grew closer. Eadburh glanced behind her, waiting to hear the shouts of the men, but the forest fell quiet again, as though the hounds had paused to pick up the scent anew. Hardly daring to breathe, she and Cwen huddled together in the shelter of a covert of thorn, waiting. They could hear the crashing of broken branches and the rustle of leaves as the pursuit drew nearer, and then it was upon them, a tawny animal, bursting into the glade with a yelp of joy. It was Ava, her fur smeared with blood, her ears torn, and tangled with brambles. She flew to her mistress and threw herself at her feet, too exhausted even to wag her tail. Eadburh sank to her knees in tears and put her arms round the dog's neck. It was a moment before she looked up anxiously. 'Has she been followed? Has she led them to us?'

They listened, but the forest was quiet. Eadburh kissed the animal's silky head. 'She was calling to us to stop and wait for her.'

They found a hollow in the rocks out of the wind, huddling together to rest with the dog between them for warmth as at last night fell. There was nothing to do, nowhere to go in the long cold hours of darkness until daylight began to show once again in the east.

Somewhere deep in her dream, Bea had heard the bedroom door close. Slowly she opened her eyes and looked round. It was daylight and she was in her daughter's bedroom. The dog in her arms was an old stuffed toy that Anna had left on her bed when she went off to college and which Bea was too soft-hearted to put away. She sat up, looking at the worn, much-loved creature in her arms and felt tears trickling down her cheeks. Tears for Elisedd, brutally killed on the orders of Charlemagne, and the woman he loved thrown out into the snow to die, finding true love from a loyal dog. She shivered. The reality of that dream, the cold and hunger and fear as the two women had made their way up through the dense fir forests was still with her, even as she made her way to the bathroom and turned on the shower to thaw the cold from her own bones.

After two mugs of coffee and some toast she began to feel more human. She checked her phone but there was no message from Simon. Did that mean that Emma had gone back to London with her mother? No doubt she would hear eventually. Propping her own little Ava on the shelf between the pots of jam and marmalade that Mark loved with his toast, she sat back to think. Mark was obviously out and she had no idea when she would see him next, so there was nothing to stop her going back to bed. She resisted the thought sharply. No more of Eadburh and her misery. Not now. She reached for her phone instead and called Heather.

They walked together down towards Castle Green. 'I assumed Mark would have told you what happened when I went to see Sandra. I was so rattled after I left her, I came straight over to see you. You weren't there so I told him. I'm sorry. Perhaps I shouldn't have, but you had said he knew.'

'He never had the chance to tell me. He was very late back last night.' They stopped beneath the lime trees to watch some children playing with a ball.

A little boy, slightly bigger than the others, retrieved it from the edge of the grass and ran off with it, jeering, leaving the little ones in tears. Moments later, two women detached themselves from the group of adults gossiping nearby and set off in pursuit of the ball and a peace settlement. The interlude had given Bea the chance to think. 'Can Sandra be convinced to stand back now and leave things to me? What did she say to you?'

Heather sighed. 'Let me tell you what happened.'

They walked slowly across the grass as Heather talked, and stopped at last on the footbridge across the river, standing side by side looking down into the water. 'Sandra is not going to give up on this,' Heather said as she finished her story. 'I never had a hope of convincing her.'

'Couldn't you persuade her to come back to the cathedral?'

Heather looked at her incredulously. 'You don't really mean that?'

'I would rather she was somewhere we can keep an eye on her. Emma has almost certainly gone home now, to concentrate on her exams, so there's nothing here for Sandra to anguish about any more. I know she won't forget this, and she will probably be watching me forever, but I can but hope she'll grow bored and think of someone else to persecute.'

She didn't really believe it herself and, judging by Heather's expression as they turned to walk back, neither did she.

42

For the first couple of days Val stayed at home, afraid to go out and leave Emma alone, then at last she had begun to resume her usual routine, shopping, coffee with friends, hours of what her daughter considered to be vacuous gossip on the phone. Two more days and Em and Felix would be back at school and then it wouldn't be long before the exams began. As the door closed behind her mother, Emma ran up the stairs to her brother's room. Felix was seated at his desk.

'She's gone to meet someone at Peter Jones.'

Felix grinned. 'Then you've got a few hours of peace. She's been like the angel of doom hanging over you, hasn't she!'

Emma cast her eyes towards the ceiling. 'She's driving me nuts!'

'Never mind. Once the exams are over, she'll let up.'

'And drag us down to Provence! Doesn't it occur to her we might not want to go with her?'

'I don't think we've got an option. You could've played your hand better, Em. Then she might have let you go back to Dad for the summer. I'm afraid all that ghost stuff has freaked her out good and proper. Anyway, Provence will be cool.'

Emma glared at him. 'I thought you'd be on my side.'

'I am. But I don't see what I can do about it. Stop flopping about and acting all wounded and dramatic and do some revision like she wants, then she might be in a better mood.'

'Dramatic!' Emma echoed, but the sigh she gave as she flounced out of her brother's bedroom would have done credit to the stage of the Old Vic. She headed for her own room, then at the top of the stairs, she paused, thought for a second and then crept down towards her father's study.

The room was at the back of the house, looking out onto their small walled garden. It was a room she loved, book-lined, peaceful and still. Very still. He did not encourage his family to come in here, so it managed to avoid the noise and bickering and somehow preserved its atmosphere of scholarly calm. It smelled slightly musty after being shut up for several weeks. She breathed in deeply. She loved the smell of old books. A curtain of pink clematis hung across the window, making the room shadowy, but she was reluctant to turn on the lights. She had always liked it like this. Sometimes when she was smaller, when her father was out she would come and sit in here on her own, feeling close to him. She had that feeling now, though this time the feeling was mixed with guilt. She looked round, then went to stand in front of the wall of bookshelves. There were huge gaps left by books he had taken with him to the cottage but somewhere amongst those that were left was the one he had quoted to Bea. Asser's *Life of King Alfred*, the book that mentioned what had happened to Eadburh in the end. When she had asked him about it, she thought he was making excuses not to tell her when he said he had left it behind. It was with his books on Wessex, he said, and so it had been missed out when he had been piling the boxes of books into the back of his car.

The silence of the room was soothing as she stood before the shelves running her eye along each one. The books were well organised now she came to study them. Northumberland took up a whole section. History, geography, maps, a box file labelled tourist leaflets; then she found the books on Wessex. Wiltshire, Sussex, Winchester, her eye scanned the shelves. History, geography, leaflets again. She went back to the history

416

section, more carefully this time, and there it was, a slim black paperback, hard to see between its neighbours on the shelf in the shadowy room. *Alfred the Great*. No author on the spine. She pulled it out. A Penguin Classic. *Asser's Life of King Alfred and Other Contemporary Sources*. She clutched it to her chest and turned for the door. Opening it, she listened. There was no sound. Felix had stayed in his room.

Since coming back to London she had had no dreams, perhaps because she had meticulously followed Bea's instructions for surrounding herself with light and protecting herself before she went to sleep. Somehow, here in Kensington she was more in control, far abler to resist the urge to find out what happened. Perhaps Eadburh's own dreams were blocked by this place. Quietly shutting her bedroom door, she went to sit at her desk and, switching on the lamp, she checked her bubble of protection was in place and opened the book.

It was easy to find the relevant passage. It was one of the many her father had marked with little yellow stickies.

There was in Mercia in fairly recent times a certain vigorous king called Offa.

She read on and turned the page.

There were only two paragraphs covering Eadburh's life, describing her exile to the court of King Charlemagne, his indignation at her choice of potential husband between him and his son, her banishment to a convent as its abbess, her reckless living, her welcoming of men to her bed, and the king's discovery of her and her ejection from the convent. She was at the end before she knew it. Too late to backpedal and pretend she hadn't read it.

. . . begging every day, she died a miserable death in Pavia.

'No!' Emma let out a cry of denial. 'No. He's got it wrong. It wasn't like that!'

Asser made her out to be a horrible person; he implied that she deserved to die in poverty and misery. He had actually met people who saw her begging in Pavia, with only a single slave boy for company. Emma frowned. If she had a slave, surely she can't have been that poor? And where the hell was Pavia?

Mopping her tears, she switched on her laptop. Northern Italy. On the pilgrim route to Rome. It was a famous place. She ought to know where it was. That was something else she would have to study. Geography.

So how had Eadburh reached Pavia? She went back to the book. A note in the back said no one knew which convent she had been abbess of. Was it in France or Italy, she wondered miserably, or Germany somewhere? She wasn't sure how big Charlemagne's empire was. That was something else she ought to know if she was going to study history at uni one day.

By the time Felix had put his head round the door to suggest it was time for lunch she had mugged up on the Carolingian Empire and Renaissance, the early Medieval Church, and had speed-read an overview of the Anglo-Saxons – not written by her father, but well-thumbed, from his library.

Felix eyed her cautiously. When he had opened her door he had found her hard at work at her desk. Somehow that wasn't what he had expected. He watched as she dug out a couple of ready meals from the freezer and stuck them in the microwave. 'How's the revision going?'

'OK.' She went over to the wine rack.

'Mum will go ballistic if we open a bottle of wine,' he said cautiously.

She gave a grim smile. 'She won't notice. Do you want a glass?' She took his silence for acquiescence and poured. 'Do you know where Pavia is?'

'In Italy.'

She looked up astonished. 'How on earth do you know that?'

'General knowledge. Why d'you want to know?'

'It came up in my history notes.'

He hauled himself up to sit on the table with his feet on a chair. 'Have you heard from Bea since you came home?'

She narrowed her eyes suspiciously. Why had the mention of Pavia made him think of Bea? 'No. I haven't. I expect she and Dad have forgotten I existed.'

'I doubt that.' Felix spoke with feeling. He reached for the bottle and topped up his glass. 'Do you think Dad and Bea have something going?'

She stared at him, astonished. 'No! Of course not. What on earth makes you say that?'

'He fancies her. I've seen him looking at her. She's quite attractive for an older woman, you've got to give her that.'

'You mean because she's over twenty!' Emma punched him on the shoulder. 'I do think Dad and Bea have become friends, though. He hasn't got many real friends, has he? He has lots of colleagues, but that's not the same.' She paused thoughtfully. 'I wouldn't be surprised if he isn't quite a lonely person, deep down. But he wouldn't. No, of course he wouldn't. He loves Mum.' Noting Felix's sceptical expression, she added, 'No, he does. I think they really do love each other deep down. Otherwise they'd have got divorced years ago. Mum's got a temper, we all know that, but he knows how to wait until it's over. Anyway, Bea's happily married.'

He conceded the point with a slight nod. 'It's all so weird. Dad was the one that conjured up the ghost by writing about her, then you and Bea ended up haunted by her. Three people!'

Emma grimaced. 'She wants her story told. Asser lied about her.'

'Asser?'

'A monk who wrote history.'

'Like Kate and Phil's chronicle.'

'Which all ties in. Perhaps a moment comes when lots of right moments collide and the truth has to come out and it's Dad's job to reveal all.' She gave a rueful smile.

'"The truth is out there",' he quoted in a hollow voice. 'But he can't tell anyone how he knows. He's a real historian. He can't quote ghosts!' He paused. 'What a bummer!'

'Eadburh doesn't know she's a ghost,' Emma put in quietly.

'No, but we do.' The microwave pinged and, putting his glass down, he slid off the table. 'It's all fascinating, isn't it? Maybe we should both demand to go back to Dad for the summer. Mum can bugger off to Provence on her own. She'd enjoy it much more without us, and seriously, even if they still love each other, she and Dad need time apart. We both know they do. I think they've got it worked out, the way they do things. He goes away for a few months then when they get back together they're all lovey-dovey again!' Reaching for an oven glove, he pulled their meals out of the microwave and put them on the table. 'Don't do any more ghosty stuff, Em, please,' he added quietly as he spooned the food onto their plates. 'Mum would freak out, and we want her on side. You've only got to forget it for a few weeks while we do these wretched exams, then she'll be in a much better mood and we can start our campaign to persuade her to let us go back.'

In Eadburh's dream she was young again and pretty and at her father's court and riding up into the hills for a secret meeting with her lover. In the dream they were not spied on or followed and the sun was shining. The prince's black stallion and her white palfrey nuzzled one another in the shade of an old oak tree while their riders lay on a woven checked rug within the walls of the sheepfold on the edge of the woods, high on the Welsh side of the ever-deepening dyke being dug across the hills. Overhead the buzzards circled ever higher, calling to one another; some days they were joined by kites and once by a great golden eagle from the distant mountain crags.

Emma woke up, stretched and smiled. Through her open window she could hear a robin singing in the garden as it grew light. The noise of morning traffic from their narrow road, a rat run to the West End, was building already. She could ignore that, because the rest of the dream was coming back.

She sat up. Her protection hadn't worked. Or was it that reading about Eadburh had somehow broken the circle and allowed the memories in. She had woken, not in her lover's arms, but in a cave somewhere in a dark forest, huddled with a skinny girl and a dog as the rain poured down outside, the noise of the traffic somehow morphing into the sound of water on rock. She reached for her phone. It was just after 6 a.m. Too early to call Dad. Instead she began a text.

Miss you. Would love to come back after the exams. Any news of Eadburh—

She deleted the word and replaced it with Bea.

I hate London. Mum is being a pain. I had a nightmare again
last night.

She paused, her thumbs poised over the screen. A nightmare? Part of her dream had been delicious, erotic, exciting.
Not something she could tell her dad. Leave it as nightmare.
She finished with three xs and pressed send before she could
change her mind.

She wanted to ask him about Asser's version of events and
the horrible old man's obvious bias against Eadburh. About
Pavia and why Eadburh would have chosen to go there. And
what happened to the lover she was caught with in the convent.

Emma's thoughts skidded to a halt and between one moment
and the next she knew what had happened. The lover was
described by Asser as a man 'of her own race'. He was from
Britain. Would Asser, or his gossiping informants, have known
whether he was Anglo-Saxon or Celt? Would they have cared
or even guessed that he was a prince in disguise? Somehow
she knew it for certain. Eadburh's last wild wonderful moments
in the convent had been with the man she loved above all
others, and Charlemagne had had him murdered.

Val came downstairs half an hour later to find her daughter
sitting in the kitchen sipping a mug of coffee. Emma jumped
guiltily. 'I've been revising. I needed something to keep me awake.'

Val put her arm round her and gave her a kiss on the top
of her head. 'Don't get too tired, darling. Shall I make you
some breakfast?'

Emma nodded. 'That would be nice. Then I must get back
to my notes. Would Dad mind if I borrowed a few books from
his study? There's stuff there that fits in with my history.'

'Of course he wouldn't mind.' Val was relieved that Emma
was working. It never occurred to her that the syllabus Emma
was following at school was unlikely to include the Anglo-
Saxon kingdoms that formed the core of her husband's research
and that were now the focus of her daughter's full attention.

*

421

'Simon!'

Bea had answered the knock on the door with extreme caution. She did not really expect Sandra to return, but there was always that chance.

'Can I come in? I've something to show you. Sorry. I should have rung first.'

She showed him into the snug. 'Mark is out at a Chapter meeting.'

'You can tell him about this later. I've just been up Coedmawr. Your librarian lady, Jane, has some amazing photos of the ancient chronicle now. Fresh angles with far more information, and I was so excited I had to tell someone.' He gave a sheepish grin.

'It must be quiet without Emma and Felix.'

'It is. Partly a relief, but partly not.' He heaved a deep sigh.

'Have you heard from Emma?'

He nodded. 'She asked after you.' There was no point in mentioning the nightmare, so he changed the subject. 'Sandra Bedford turned up while Val was there,' he said. 'Amongst the various poisons she dripped in my wife's ear was the possibility that you and I might be having an affair.'

Bea stared at him incredulously. To his relief he saw her smile. 'She really is a piece of work, isn't she? I suppose she assumes a man and a woman can't be friends. Or perhaps it's wishful thinking. I am fairly reliably informed that she fancies Mark. I trust your wife didn't believe her.'

'No. She didn't.' Probably because she thought him too boring to have the energy for an affair. Simon kept the thought to himself. He reached into his pocket for his phone. 'Let's forget about Sandra Bedford. Let me show you these new photos. Jane is making me a set of prints for my records, but in the meantime this will give you an idea. Take a look – it mentions Eadburh.'

Bea glanced at him sharply. 'What does it say?'

He pushed the phone towards her but she shook her head. 'You know I can't read Anglo-Saxon. Tell me.'

'It seems to confirm she died in Pavia. The chronicler echoes, or prefigures, the disgust at her behaviour that we see in Asser.

But then he adds something. Look.' He scrolled the screen and enlarged it. *'Some say her lover was a Welshman.* He uses the word, just like that. And that's interesting because Asser calls him a man from her own country, and he would know Eadburh was Mercian. On the other hand, Asser himself was Welsh and he may not have wanted to admit her lover was a fellow Welshman. Anyway, our chronicler here goes on to say, *and Charlemagne spared his life,'* he glanced up, *'because, he said, no mortal man could avoid her . . .'* He hesitated, frowning. 'This word is wiles, I think. *No mortal man could avoid her wiles.* The next bit is hard to read in every sense: *He ordered that the man be castrated then he turned him out into the snow to live or die according to the will of God.'*

Bea sat down abruptly. 'Oh no.'

Simon slipped the phone back into his pocket and sat down facing her. 'It's a nasty outcome. A touch of Heloise and Abelard.'

'You mustn't tell Emma.'

'No. But what if she dreams it?'

'We must hope she doesn't. If Eadburh never learnt the truth, if that is the truth, then we can only be happy for her that she had some more time with him before it ended so badly.' She sighed. 'Actually, I know some of this, Simon. I've had more dreams since I saw you. I meant to try to stop myself, like Emma, but it's hard to stop wanting to know what happened.' She gave him a quick look and was relieved to see he appeared interested rather than sceptical. 'I dreamed her lover was Elisedd, but it's good to have it confirmed. Eadburh thinks, thought, he was killed after they dragged him from her bed. She was thrown out into the snow and escaped with a slave girl called Cwen and Ava, the dog Charlemagne gave her.'

He laughed. 'How I wish I could use this stuff in my book. So, how did she reach Pavia?'

'I don't know.'

'You haven't got there yet?'

She smiled. 'I'm trying to resist, but the story is frighteningly compelling.'

He stood up. 'I suppose I must get back to my own story. The politics of Mercia seems very dull without Offa and his family.'

423

'So who became king after Offa's son?'

'A chap called Coenwulf. A descendant of one of the great King Penda's brothers, so, I suppose, Offa's distant cousin.'

'And how would he have regarded Eadburh?'

'With horror, I should imagine. I think we can probably assume she would not have been welcomed back to Mercia even if she had survived, and she would not have dared to go back to Wessex, so where could she have gone? Perhaps that's where Pavia comes in. She had no reason to go back to Britain.'

'Wouldn't she have looked for her daughter?'

'I have tried to look the daughter up. There is no mention of what happened to her as far as I can see. I think we must hope that the best outcome for her, if she ever existed, would have been in a happy convent as a happy nun.'

Bea made a face. 'You're probably right. What a sad time.'

'To them, God was real. He would have been there for them at the end.'

'But he's not real for you?'

'Ah. Sorry. I forgot I was talking to a clergy wife who lives within spitting distance of a cathedral.'

'What an unfortunate choice of words!' She grinned.

He put his hands together and bowed. 'Time to go.'

'Keep me in the loop, Simon, please. I care greatly about Emma. I haven't tried to contact her. I really think it's better if I keep my distance for now, but I'm there if she needs me.'

'Oh my goodness, that reminds me!' He turned back from the door, reaching into his pocket. 'Another reason for coming to see you. Emma asked me to give you this before she left.' It was a small envelope. Inside was Bea's cross. 'She said to tell you she thought you might need it more than she does now she's back in London. If she does need one, she'll buy one herself.'

After he had gone she closed the door with an unexpected pang of loss. Their parting seemed almost final. She looked down at the cross in her hand and sighed.

*

424

Simon was cursing himself as he drove away from Hereford. How could he have handled that conversation worse? He wanted to stay in touch with Bea. He wanted to know she was there at the end of the phone, that she would come if he needed her.

He walked up to the cottage and stood on the terrace looking into the distance. The afternoon had turned hazy; the sheep had fallen silent and for once there were no great birds circling in the sky. It was as if time was standing still.

And then he heard it, in the distance. The voice calling.

Elise.

Elisedd.

43

Cwen carried a knife in her belt and flint and steel in her pouch, and she found them shelter in a cave out of the wind and rain where they made beds of dead leaves. Ava seemed to know they needed game. After feeding herself, she caught them rabbits and hares and even a squirrel. Cwen cooked them over the fire, scraping the skins clean and saving them. As the season turned they ate the young leaves of hawthorn and gathered herbs to make into potage, improvising a cooking dish from a hollow stone. Eadburh was very ill at the beginning and they both thought she would die; but she improved and slowly grew stronger as she became accustomed to the hard way of life.

And they talked.

'Where was your home, Cwen?'

'My mother was captured by the king's armies when I was a child.' The girl had startlingly blue eyes and a ragged lock of blond hair that escaped routinely from her head-rag to trail across her face.

'And your mother is a slave at the abbey?' Eadburh reached forward to brush the hair out of the girl's eyes.

'I don't know. I haven't seen her since I was brought there to work in the kitchens.'

Eadburh saw the wistful sadness in the girl's face; until now, she'd never thought of her as a person, merely a servant. Cwen had saved her life, there was no doubt about that. The girl was resourceful and loyal and could read the countryside round them, finding food and following the stars. At first they headed north, anywhere to put more distance between them and the convent, but it was up to Eadburh now to decide where they should go. One thing was sure, they had to leave the territories of the emperor. She had no way of knowing how far they extended or what lay ahead of them. All they knew was that there was a long, long journey ahead.

There was a choice to be made. If they made their way towards the west she would be in Charles's territories until she reached the coast of the Northern Sea where she could try to find a boat to take them across to Kent or East Anglia or even Northumbria. She allowed herself a brief moment of hope. In either of the latter two kingdoms she might find herself near one of her sisters, if they still lived. Kent was the most dangerous. There she would be among allies of Wessex who might still be her enemies. Supposing, having reached the shores of Britannia, she headed back overland towards Mercia? But she was not wanted there, and her dream of the mountains of Powys was gone. There was no one there for her now. Her beloved, the hero of her dreams, was dead. As long as she didn't allow herself to think about Elisedd, didn't dwell on those few treasured hours beneath her blankets, didn't let herself remember that by coming to find her, his only love, Elisedd had lost his life, she could carry on, if not for her own sake then for the sake of this girl at her side.

With renewed bitter resolve she looked up at the sun. Every step westward would remind her of Elisedd and the journey he had made to find her. The other choice was to walk east, towards countries she did not know, to places she had never heard of, until they came to the empire's end.

'The sisters of Wyrd have decided for us.' She smiled at Cwen. 'We will head for the rising sun.'

Each time they heard travellers on the road below them in the valley, Cwen went down alone and made the decision from the safety of her hiding place in the trees as to whether or not they would prove generous to a beggar girl in rags. On the whole she chose well and they were kind. As the weather grew slowly warmer so the meagre pile of possessions they amassed in their bundles grew. She came back with food and old shoes, shawls and a torn but blessedly clean shift, once a small cooking pot complete with stew to reheat over their fire; and best of all she gathered information. As far as she knew, she reported back, no one was looking for them now. She and the mother abbess had joined the legions of nameless outlaws and beggars who roamed the country without home or master.

Slowly they moved on, avoiding towns and villages. Eadburh didn't know where she was going or what she wanted. Life went on as they lived hand to mouth, both glad each evening that they had managed to survive another day.

Then as summer tipped over into autumn, Cwen came back to Eadburh with news. 'There is a group of pilgrims on the road, men and women of God. They say we can join them. I told them we had been robbed and lost everything and they said we could become part of their number. I came to fetch you.'

After that, life was much better. They shared food and companionship and lodgings with men and women on the pilgrim road, heading for Rome, aiming to cross the high pass over the Alps into Lombardy before the early snows came. Each one had their story, the reason they had embarked on a pilgrimage and each night they regaled one another with tales of regret and penance and promises broken or kept. Cwen told of the loss of her mother and the hardship she had endured until a convent took her in. She was on pilgrimage, she said, to thank God for saving her life. Eadburh told something approaching the truth. She had been, inadvertently, the cause of her husband's death and lived in permanent regret and sorrow at his loss. The dog had been, she said, a gift from the man who wanted her to be his wife, but she had refused, knowing she did not deserve happiness. Instead, she said, she had resolved to beg forgiveness at the shrine of St Peter for what she had done.

The group joined other pilgrim bands and then split off again as people elected to follow different routes; it lost some members as they dropped by the wayside, others decided to stay longer at one place or another. As each new face appeared, Eadburh shrank back and drew her hood across her face in case she was recognised, but there was never any glimmer of recognition and gradually she grew less afraid.

Then, as the pilgrims rested for several days at an abbey guest house in the gentle foothills of a river valley, lined with vineyards, came her first shock. Cwen came to her and with tears in her eyes begged for release. 'I want to stay here. I feel at home here and the novice mistress said I could take the veil.' She looked pleadingly at Eadburh, who was astonished at the devastation she felt. She and Cwen had grown close over the long months of their journey and somehow she had envisaged them being together forever, but, in a strange moment of altruism such as she had never experienced before, she found she couldn't bring herself to refuse. The girl had stayed with her of her own free will, had served her faithfully, saved her life on numerous occasions, and for once she felt the need to be kind, to put someone else first. And besides, she still had her faithful Ava, plodding beside her mile after mile on the long roads south.

Autumn drew on and the pilgrims' pace increased. Snow comes early to the high Alpine passes and more and more often they were warned that they should hurry if they wanted to cross the great mountains before winter set in. Their route took them past Besançon, then on south, towards Pontarlier, around the great lake Lemmanus to Vevey then along the old Roman Road over the pass beneath Mont Blanc. Now in early autumn it was bitterly cold at night and they huddled together for warmth as they reached each pilgrim halt on the route, following the trail through the southern foothills of the Alps towards Vercelli on the Lombardy Plain where it was still warm and bountiful autumn.

It was when they reached the town of Pavia that, in her loneliness, Eadburh confided in the abbess of the convent to which the hostelry was attached, claiming once more in half-truths and elaborate inventions and evasions that she would be going back to find her sister in East Anglia once she had completed her pilgrimage to the shrines of St Peter and St Paul. She had acquired a slave boy now, Theoderic, who carried her bundle and her scrip and cloak and groomed Ava, whom he adored. She finally began to feel safe, despite the horrifying discovery that, for all the great distance they had travelled, she was still within the empire of Charlemagne, who was amongst his many titles, King of the Lombards. Thankfully, he ruled through others; no one in Pavia could possibly know of her existence. She moved into more gracious accommodation, thanks to the abbess, and wore richer clothes, gifts from the generosity of the abbey treasure chests, and at last dared to allow herself to enjoy life a little. When she dreamed of Elisedd it was to wake with tears in her eyes, but tears could not touch her heart. That had been sealed away with some deep inner core of her soul, together with the memories of their nights of love in the privacy of the abbess's rooms in a Frankish convent, and the horror of their violent parting. Sealed there too were her dreams of the misty hills of the Welsh kingdom he would never see again and the wasted, empty years in Wessex when she could have been at his side in Powys.

The day of Emma's first exam, the school rang Val to ask if Emma was ill. 'She's not here. I'm so sorry, but I'm afraid she's missed her first English paper.'

The headmistress had seen it all before. 'Nerves,' she said. 'Please don't be too anxious. She can resit.'

Neither Felix nor Simon had any idea where she was. For the last few days she had seemed to be working hard, had made no complaint and, Simon assured Val, had not been in touch with him. He rang Bea at once, guessing Emma would have been heading for Hereford, but she had heard nothing either.

When Emma had not returned by that evening, Val rang the police.

Had Sandra managed to worm her way into Emma's head? Bea sat thinking hard after Simon's frantic call. Or was it Eadburh? Always Eadburh. Had Emma remembered to protect herself or had she allowed her dreams back in? Cautiously, carefully, she put out feelers, trying to find some trace of the girl out there, but there was nothing. All she could do was try to protect Emma from afar, surround her with light and send prayers.

Eadburh had been seen in Pavia. That much Bea knew from Asser. But she didn't know by whom she had been seen or what had happened next. Perhaps now, in search of Emma, she had more reason than ever to follow the story on from there. It was with a feeling of sick dread that she made her way upstairs to the attic and picked up her stone.

It had been bad luck beyond measure. After all the time Eadburh had spent in Pavia as the friend and protégée of the abbess, one day in late spring the following year, as she walked towards the river with Theo in attendance, she was seen by a party of pilgrims heading towards the bridge on their way to Rome. Their party had originated in Winchester and two amongst them had spent time at the court of Beorhtric and seen his queen. One of them was a woman who had moved on to work as a maid in the abbey in Frankia. Her look of incredulity, followed by a shout of recognition and then her jeers of mockery and disgust, were eagerly taken up by the mob. People did not bother to ask questions; they threw stones, they swore at Eadburh and spat, they cornered her and tore at her clothes until she feared for her life.

As her dream darkened and faded and Bea began to wake she saw, for one confused instant, the figure of Sandra Bedford standing on the covered bridge over the River Ticino. She was at the forefront of the mob, a stone in her hand, a look of smug enjoyment on her face. As Bea watched she hurled the stone towards Eadburh, then stood back, leaning with her elbow on the balustrade to watch the fun. It was a moment later that, slowly, as though feeling Bea's horrified gaze, she looked round and the women eyed one another in astonished recognition.

*

Bea opened her eyes and looked round frantically. Her heart was pounding with fright. She scrambled to her feet, visualising herself surrounded by light, alone, calm, quiet and she reached for her cross, once more back around her neck. 'Christ be with me, Christ within me . . .' She had seen Sandra, on a bridge in the centre of Pavia. How she knew it was Pavia she wasn't sure, she had never to her knowledge been there, but that was where Sandra had been standing.

Running downstairs, Bea found her iPad. It took only seconds to find the place. The Ponte Coperto, in the centre of the historic city, on the road from Pavia to Genoa, a bridge built on Roman foundations. She took a deep breath. This wasn't someone who occasionally dabbled in crystals and Tarot cards. This was a woman who could worm her way inside other people's minds. And if she could attack Bea like this, she would be more than capable of finding her way into Emma's head.

What would Meryn do? Filled with resolve, Bea wrapped up her stone and went over to her jars of dried herbs. He had told her she was strong enough to cope with this. She didn't know where Emma was, but she could deal with Sandra. And she would start by cleansing the house.

The smoke of ancient incense, rowan and juniper, mugwort, vervain, nettle, chamomile and lavender circled gently up to the highest corners of the ceilings, cleansing, raising the vibrations so no lower entities could thrive – and Sandra was possessed by a lower entity if ever there was one.

She knew Mark would wrinkle his nose when he came in – saining was a step too far in his book, nearer to magic than some of the other things she did – but sometimes the old ways were best. In any case, the Church still used frankincense. Not Mark perhaps, but some High Church clergy did, and she always thought how lovely it was, a nod to ancient beliefs, cleansing, carrying prayer up to heaven on its fragrant, protective smoke.

The house felt cleansed and safe after she had carried her little bowl of smoking herbs – and, yes, she had added a grain or two of frankincense – round every room. She had a shower, then walked across the Close to the cathedral to pray. Her chantry priest wasn't there, but she sensed he was listening. Like Meryn, he expected her to be strong.

Sandra had been sitting at home beside the open window that looked out onto her small untidy garden. The bridge over the river had puzzled her. That sudden split-second memory of herself there in a strange world, part of the mob, filled with anger and vicious enjoyment, watching a woman dressed as a nun and a boy in ragged trousers and a loose woollen shirt, being pelted with rocks, shouted at, threatened with death, was visceral, a moment of intense enjoyment. The woman had been a queen. She had seen her before. She had been at her court and seen her kill her husband. Then she had seen her with her lover. And now she was watching the woman face retribution.

It was then, feeling herself watched in turn, she had swung round to find herself face to face with Beatrice. And then everything was gone. In a flash. The river, the bridge, the people on the bridge all stationary, frozen in time, then vanished, switched off, a glimpse into another world visible for a split second, then extinguished.

On the table in front of her was her pack of Tarot cards. She had a list of names in her hand and had been gazing thoughtfully at them, waiting for one name to jump out at her.

Beatrice. Emma. Eadburh.

Eadburh. Princess of Mercia. Queen of Wessex. How did she even know that name? But somehow she was part of this.

Beatrice was a genuine opponent. A challenge. Someone to fight, to defeat; to grind beneath her heel. This Eadburh was dangerous, greedy for energy, a soul prowling the darker corners of the universe in search of unfulfilled desires. And Emma. It was Emma who was truly interesting. Ostensibly a victim in need of rescue and reassurance, there was something ambivalent about Emma. Emma was all over the place and completely inconsistent. She had two sides to her, two distinct personalities. One was a schoolgirl on the verge of adulthood, and the other was a scheming, vicious woman.

Eadburh.

Cutting the pack, Sandra lifted the top card and, leaning back in her chair, turned it to face her. She smiled. So, Emma could wait; she would think some more about the conundrum that was Emma and her alter ego, Eadburh. The card was clear. Beatrice was her immediate concern. An enemy worthy of her complete attention. An enemy who needed to be dealt with now.

She returned the card to the pack, cut once again and began to deal out the top three.

She looked at the line of cards in front of her.

A powerful woman; false hope; the end of a journey.

She gathered the cards back into the pack and wrapped them up thoughtfully.

The woman on the bridge was Eadburh, she realised. Perhaps it was better to assume that she was her main opponent. She shivered as she felt the air around her growing cold and suddenly she could no longer visualise the river. Everything around her had blurred. Someone was spying on her, interfering with her sight. She stood up and pushed the cards into the drawer of the table. She was an old hand at this. She knew what she had to do. Surround herself with protection and then from a position of strength attack with every ounce of power she possessed. First she should put running water between herself and her enemy until she was ready to strike. Was that what the bridge had signified? She had been standing on another bridge over another river. She didn't know where that one had been, but there was a river, here in town.

Leaning over the stone balustrade she stood looking down into the Wye, staring at the water as it flowed beneath her then slowly she began to walk across, putting the great sweep of the river between herself and the cathedral with its Close. Immediately she felt better. Safer. To launch an attack on Beatrice she would have to cross back, hurl a curse then retreat across the water again. She was good at curses. She'd had a stock of them once and she could remember every one.

She stood still for a while, running through the options. She should have thought of grabbing something when she visited Beatrice's house, a link, but she had felt too intimidated by the surroundings, the large house, the railings, the elegant front door, its position so near the cathedral, the power of the Church echoing off every brick. Still, this was good practice for her. Making her mind up, she recrossed the bridge, walking quickly and, picturing Beatrice standing in front of her open door, she closed her eyes and sent a vicious thought form in her direction, a thought form to match the occasion, a thought form that fitted the era of Offa and Ethelbert. It was a flaming spear, dipped in poison, humming with evil. Her message on its way, she stood waiting, as if expecting to hear the woman scream. Then, satisfied it would find its mark, she turned and hastened back across the water towards the safety of the far bank.

On her windy hillside, Nesta smiled. Just this once she would interfere. She would deflect the curse. Beatrice was open. Vulnerable. She had to be warned.

At the snap of Nesta's fingers the spear veered then turned and sped back whence it had come.

'Make up your mind, woman!' a furious voice shouted as a car slammed on its brakes in front of her. Her heart thudding with fright, Sandra stepped out of its way onto the pavement and clung to the parapet, her head spinning. Something was terribly wrong. Her ears were drumming and she could feel herself bathed in sweat.

'Are you all right, my love?' A woman passer-by stopped beside her. 'He had no business shouting like that.'

'I'm fine.' Sandra managed a smile. 'My fault. I wasn't looking.'

And she wasn't expecting the spear to be hurled right back. Beatrice had been ready for her; she was obviously going to be more of a challenge than she had expected. And her riposte had been far from churchy. Which was worrying. Sandra had never done anything quite like this before; and certainly never had a reply to any threats she had made, in kind. This had all the hallmarks of a practitioner of skill and strength.

*

Smiling, Nesta watched Sandra with satisfaction. The woman was like a child playing with toys. No doubt Beatrice could have dealt with the curse, but a curse was something she understood and it had been a reflex action to intercept elfshot in any form and hurl it back.

In central Pavia, the woman who had started the riot had staggered back from the parapet of the bridge clutching her side. She screamed as blood seeped out between her fingers. Around her, the crowd swarmed closer, their attention shifting from their original victim, their bloodlust roused. As they closed round her, suddenly the mob halted in its tracks, thwarted. The woman who had screamed had disappeared.

It was several minutes before Sandra felt strong enough to move on. The traffic lights had changed. Her would-be rescuer had walked on towards Hereford Cathedral, leaving her alone beside the swiftly running water.

Bea had gone to sit in the garden at home. She had not expected to see Nesta there. Behind the woman she could see the wild hillside and beyond it the forest.

'It was I who told Elisedd to go to the kingdom of the Franks,' Nesta said, the wind catching her words and whipping them away like so many dead leaves. 'I told him if he loved her he should follow her, and he paid with his manhood.'

'Did he survive? Did either of them ever return to Britain?' Bea reached out towards her and felt with her own fingers the cold wind that tore at the woman's cloak.

Nesta said nothing for a while then she smiled, ignoring Bea's question. 'The enemy you have made in your own time grows more daring. She thinks she can throw flaming spears at you to frighten you away.'

'Flaming spears!' Bea repeated the words in astonishment.

'She has read books and studies cards with pictures that tell her what to do and she flails in the halls of the elves like a trapped moth.'

'Sandra?' Bea whispered.

'You need to swat her away.'

'Swat!' Bea echoed, unable to prevent herself from repeating Nesta's words like an echo.

'She travels through time, trailing previous lives behind her, always the same person, incapable of redemption.' Nesta folded her arms. 'But in this story it was she who pushed Eadburh back towards her destiny. The sisters of Wyrd were working through her.'

Fleeing back to the hostelry, Eadburh threw herself on the abbess's mercy. The woman told her she could no longer stay but, good Christian that she was, she did not turn her out in rags. She told the sobbing woman who knelt before her to leave the hostelry, leave Lombardy and follow the long route back over the mountains and across the empire and across the northern sea to Britannia where in expiation of her sins she should go to a shrine somewhere in one of those cold distant kingdoms and remain there, an enclosed anchorite, until she died.

Eadburh froze with horror at the abbess's words, visions of her sister rising up before her eyes, but by the time she had packed her belongings into a bundle and once more gathered up her scrip and staff to join a party of pilgrims on the return journey from Rome on the Via Francigena, she was more optimistic. She had her slave, Theo, with her still, and she had Ava and where else was there for her to go?

She had much to fear, going once more into the heart of Charlemagne's territories, but if she managed it and headed across the sea to the northern parts of Britannia, far away from Wessex, she would surely find shelter and solace there. She could look for her sister Ethelfled in Northumbria, and if she was still alive find succour there. Of one thing she was certain, she would not join Alfrida in Crowland Abbey in the bleak, lonely fens where as far as she knew her happy, carefree sister was immured by her own choice, forever, giving her life to God. No way was Eadburh going to obey that part of the abbess's injunction. Ever.

Slowly Bea became aware of the trickle of water from the fountain. The garden was very quiet. So, Eadburh had not died in misery and rags in Pavia. The people who had reported that news back to Asser so long after the event had succumbed to wishful thinking. The former queen had set off once more on the long walk home.

And Emma? Once more she tried to reach out, to find her, but there was nothing but a wall of silence.

She sat still, thinking hard. What had happened next to Eadburh? Had she made it back to Britannia or had she fallen somewhere unknown and unnoticed by the wayside? Whatever had happened to her, she had not in the end drawn enough attention for her demise to be mentioned in the chronicles. If she had been captured and murdered or executed there would have been a record. Asser in his malicious account of her life could not have resisted mentioning that.

With a sigh, she leant back on the bench and sat with unfocused eyes, waiting for the past to open up to her again.

'Bea!' Mark's voice from the kitchen brought her back to reality with a jolt.

'Do you want some tea?' He was filling the kettle. 'You'll never guess who I was speaking to just now. Jane Luxton came over. She was wondering if the budget could stretch a few million to buy the Coedmawr Chronicle for the cathedral library.' One look at her face told him something was wrong. 'What's happened?'

She told him about Emma. 'It was her first exam. The school got in touch with them and told them she never arrived.'

'Oh no.' He pulled out a chair and sat down at the table. 'That poor child. She must be so distressed and confused. To skip her exams is terrible. I take it this is wretched Eadburh again?'

'I would guess so. Simon thinks Emma will try to come here. I promised him I would ring at once if I hear anything. He's waiting at the cottage in case she turns up there.'

'Is she still looking for Elisedd?'

Bea sat down opposite him. 'It seems that Elisedd was murdered by Charlemagne. But Em is lost in a world of dreams and ghosts. I don't know what she's thinking.'

'What's Eadburh thinking?'

Bea gave an exhausted smile. 'Last time I looked she was heading back to Britannia, once more afraid for her life. She didn't die at Pavia as the chronicle said, but who knows what happened to her on the way back.' She sighed. 'I don't suppose the cathedral can afford to buy the chronicle?'

He laughed wryly. 'As if! I told Jane the only option might be crowdfunding. She told me the people who own it have just had their baby, by the way. A little boy.' He leaned forward on his elbows. 'That's not somewhere Emma might go, is it? Coedmawr?'

Bea shook her head. 'I don't think so. Whenever she rushed off somewhere, it was to find Elise. She has this vision of a handsome, lusty prince.'

'And where would this handsome lusty prince be when he wasn't on Offa's Ridge?'

She never got to answer the question.

'I've had a text from Emma!' Simon's voice was taut with anxiety as she picked up the phone. 'She's on her way to North Wales. She wants you and me to meet her tomorrow at Eliseg's Pillar.'

44

Simon had checked the history of the pillar. 'I don't think it was the seat of the kings,' he said to Bea as they drove north. 'I've seen so many pictures of it. It was originally a stone cross, placed on a Bronze Age burial mound. Not a palace. If the palace was anywhere, it was on top of the hill nearby. Castell Dinas Bran.'

They had left his car in the Close and Bea was driving as he sat beside her, his phone in his hand. His eyes kept flicking towards it.

'I'm sure she'll ring,' she said at last.

'It's still switched off. I don't know what she was thinking. To walk out on the day of her first exam.'

'Maybe she was more stressed about them than we suspected and this has nothing to do with Eadburh.'

'That's what the headmistress said. Not about Eadburh – we haven't mentioned any of that to her obviously – but about exams. She knew Emma hadn't done enough revision.' She heard him sigh. 'The head said we mustn't worry too much. She can always resit. It happens a lot, apparently. The strain is too much for some kids. When they realise the world doesn't fall apart because they haven't turned up, they relax a bit.'

Except that wasn't what had happened to Emma. They both thought it, although neither voiced their fears.

It took them almost two hours to drive to Llangollen. The Pillar of Eliseg turned out to be a short walk along the main road from the beautiful ruins of the Abbey of Valle Crucis. It stood on the edge of a field, a broken stone shaft on top of a steep mound. The carved inscription had long ago worn away, and the family tree of the kings of Powys had only been rescued by a transcription copied down in the seventeenth century. The mound itself had, it was thought, been the resting place of families who might have been their ancestors going back as far as the Bronze Age. They stood side by side in front of the notice board. 'It was once a great Celtic cross,' Simon murmured. 'The cross from which the valley and the abbey take their name.'

There was no sign of Emma, and her phone was still switched off.

The Cadw ticket office for the abbey was open. Simon went in. He showed them Emma's photo on his phone.

'She was here. Yesterday. Asking about the history of the cross, looking for the palace of the kings of Powys,' he said as he climbed back into the car. 'The man in there was very helpful. Luckily he was a history buff. He said after the Romans left at the beginning of the fifth century, the kings of Powys probably lived in Castell Dinas Bran, the Iron Age fort on the hill up there.' He pointed vaguely behind them. 'But at the date Emma is looking for, the main seat of the kings was at a place called Mathrafal, which is near Meifod, about twenty miles from here. She had a rucksack with her and was wearing boots. He got the impression she was hiking.'

'She was going to walk there?' Bea had reached into the back of her car for the road atlas lying on the back seat.

'He gave her some leaflets.' Simon reached for his phone. 'She's still not picking up. She must know we'd be frantic.'

'Perhaps she doesn't want to be found. Not yet.' Bea sighed. 'She doesn't know the full story. That Elisedd died far away. Perhaps in her mind they are still young and in love. Oh, poor Emma! You'd better ring Val and let her know what we're doing.'

Simon studied the OS map in his hands. His informant had inked a red cross on the place for him. 'He reckoned it's about forty minutes' drive from here. He said there are actually two castles there, of different dates, both hard to find.'

They found the first castle on a tump in a field. It was a beautiful site, surrounded by ancient trees on a bend of the River Vyrnwy. There was no sign of Emma there and no one to ask. Simon had found the castle on his phone. 'This is the wrong date. After our period.' He sat down on a fallen tree. 'Who are we kidding? She could be anywhere. Why didn't she wait for us by the pillar? She asked us to go there!'

'Your expert from Cadw said there was a second castle round here, Simon.' Bea put her hand on his shoulder. 'Let's go and find the other one. We can't give up yet.'

The Mathrafal Castle they wanted, the seat of the ancient kings of Powys, had originated as another Iron Age fort, this one in the centre of a wood only minutes away from the first, but it too was deserted. Without any idea of where to go next, they retreated to the nearest village. Meifod was only a mile away and it was there, outside the church, that at last they met someone who had seen Emma. The woman had greeted them with a smile as they made their way towards the church door. She was middle-aged, wearing a tweed skirt and water-proof jacket, a pair of secateurs in her hand, gardening gloves tucked under her arm.

'It was early this morning,' she said as Simon showed her the photo. 'She told me she had walked all the way from Llangollen yesterday. She spent the night at a B & B on the outskirts of the village. She said she came here because it was the burial place of the ancient kings.' She looked from Simon to Bea anxiously. 'It never occurred to me there was anything wrong. She seemed fine: confident, a bit intense perhaps, but not unhappy.'

'Where is she now?' Simon's mouth had gone dry.

'I don't know. She asked me if I knew where the burial place was. To be honest, I don't know much about it. She went into the church to look for a guidebook, and I went home. She had gone when I came back after lunch. Look' – she felt in her pocket for a notebook – 'I'll give you the number of the B & B where she was staying. It belongs to a friend of mine. It might be worth you speaking to her. Your daughter might have told her where she was headed. I'm so sorry I can't help any more. I hope you find her.'

As the woman left them to themselves, they stood by the door of the church, helplessly staring round. 'I've found something about this church.' Simon was staring at the phone in his hand. 'It was an ancient ecclesiastical centre, a *clas*, founded by a saint in the sixth century, and is traditionally the burial place of the kings whose seat was at Mathrafal.' He looked up triumphantly.

'So, is this the place where she saw Elisedd in her dream,' Bea murmured. 'He was an abbot here. Although she said there was a river nearby.'

'There seems to be a stream down here.' Simon wandered off the path a little way. 'And the river can't be far. Oh Bea. What are we going to do? Where is she?'

'Simon, we've so nearly found her and we know she's safe.' She tried to reassure him. 'She's being sensible and her detective work seems to be pretty good. Why don't you ring that number?'

Ten minutes later they were parked in the driveway of the B & B. The owner appeared at the door. 'I was bit surprised she was on her own, I must admit; she seemed so young, but she was very composed and we get so many walkers up here, I didn't think it suspicious.' She seemed anxious. 'I asked her to have supper with us as she was on her own and she chatted quite normally. She told us her brother was doing his exams and she was on a trip to research some material for her degree.'

Simon snorted. 'Degree! She's seventeen!'

'I didn't ask her age.' The woman stood her ground. 'She talked about her research and my husband got some local history books out for her to look at. She was going up to the church today to see the burial ground. It's huge, with some lovely old trees, and there's an ancient cross which is now inside the church.'

'Did she say where she was going after she had been there?'

'Mathrafal. It's only up the road. We told her there was nothing to see.'

'We've already checked there,' Simon said despondently.

'Is there any chance she said she was coming back here tonight?' Bea put in.

'I'm afraid not. She didn't say where she was going after that. I hope you find her.' Her last words echoed those of her neighbour.

'At least she's safe, we know where she is and we know what she's doing,' Bea said as they climbed back into the car. She's being sensible and staying in proper accommodation. You'd better ring Val again, Simon. She'll be going out of her mind back in London.'

'And she'll come rushing up here or tell the police.'

'Then you must reassure her. See if you can persuade her to stay with Felix. After all, he needs her too.' She engaged gear and headed back down the gravel drive. 'Now, I'm driving back to the church. I'm going to have a go at connecting with her. See if I can learn anything that way. I have tried, but ironically I've trained her too well. She's protecting herself, but you never know, in the church she might have let her guard down a bit. It's worth a try. Why don't you go into the pub and get us both a drink and a sandwich and I'll join you there.'

The girl was open, easy prey. Sandra smiled as she sat with the cards before her on the table.

'Emma? Can you see me? I've come to find you. Where are you?'

Closing her eyes, Sandra emptied her mind, allowing the scene to appear. It was wild country, with a track winding through desolate hills down towards a shallow river valley and there was a church there, more than a church, a community of buildings, stone-built, roofed with thatch, a broad river nearby. She noted the cross on the roof of the church, the busy community of men and women coming and going about their work, a monk wandering between them on his way to church or into one of the other buildings. There were old yew trees in the churchyard, signs that it was an ancient holy site.

The girl was moving forward, but she was still frightened, not sure of her welcome, creeping closer under cover of the trees.

Sandra probed gently. 'Who are you looking for?'

The girl was startled, looking round. 'Elisedd. I'm looking for Elisedd. Bea? Is that you?'

So, she was accustomed to Beatrice being there beside her in her head.

'Of course.' Sandra smiled. 'I want to help you, Emma.'

'You don't sound like Bea.' The girl was raising a boundary wall. She was suspicious and she had been well taught.

'I'm your friend, Emma. I can take you to Elisedd.'

'Why are you calling me Emma?' Now she was bristling with indignation.

'What should I call you?'

'Eadburh.' She pronounced it Edba. 'I've come to look for him. I've travelled so very far to find him.'

'Then let's go in together.' Without even realising she had done it, Sandra held out her hand over the cards.

Emma flinched. 'Don't touch me!'

'I won't touch you.' Sandra withdrew her hand. 'Is Elisedd in the church?'

'Elisedd is dead!'

Sandra felt a prickle of fear. 'What makes you think he's dead?'

Emma whirled round. 'Because I killed him! Because I have brought him nothing but misery! Because I have spent a hundred lifetimes looking for him to beg his forgiveness. His death was my fault and mine alone. I need you to go. You're not Bea. Why are you interfering? Why are you spying on me? You are not wanted here.' Her eyes were boring into Sandra's skull. The transition had happened. Emma had gone. The eyes were blue. Eadburh's eyes.

In Hereford Sandra groaned with frustration after her initial shout of triumph. She sighed. Then she drew back, turning sharply away. She shuffled the cards together in front of her.

445

When she opened her eyes again, Eadburh was still there. She was dressed in a long gown, with a mantle of black wool, a white scarf around her hair, a carved wooden cross hanging on a cord around her neck. A nun.

A nun with a knife in her hand and vicious fury on her face. She was no longer a girl of seventeen, she was a woman in her fifties, strong, experienced, tired of life and very angry.

45

Bea was seated towards the back of St Tysilio's church in
Meifod, beside a pillar in the darkest corner she could find.
She was watching Eadburh as she boarded a small trading
vessel anchored off the fishing port of Wissant. Still accompanied by the boy Theo and by her great dog, she was with a
band of pilgrims, most of whom had made the long arduous
journey to Rome and were now returning home, following
the ancient pilgrim route, the Iter Francorum, so named, her
companions had told her, by an ancient bishop called Wilibald
who had written about his own journey a hundred years
before. She had joined them at a pilgrim hostel in the town
of Besançon. No one had recognised her, no one had bothered
her unduly and now, so many exhausting miles later, she was
within sight of the sea. She had decided that after they made
landfall she would continue to travel with the group as far as
their destination, which was Canterbury. Once there, she would
work out where to go next. She had no wish to go back to
Wessex or to Mercia. She had thought often about Wessex on
her long journey west, and about her little daughter, but the
child would be much older now, no doubt having been fed
innumerable lies about her mother, and perhaps resigned to

a life in God's house. The risk of being recognised if she went in search of her daughter was too great. The remaining choices were stark; she had already discounted journeying to find her sister Alfrida at Crowland in the far away Fens, or travelling north in the hope that Ethelfled was still alive. If she was, she too would no doubt be an abbess, probably in some remote abbey on a rugged coast facing across a hostile sea. Perhaps some of her travelling companions were planning to go further once they had visited the shrine of St Augustine and she could go with them. Life on the road as a pilgrim was not unpleasant. Thieves and footpads tended to leave them alone, knowing they would be unlikely to be wealthy, on foot as they were, and for the most part dressed in near rags. They were cordial to one another and she had even forged a cautious friendship with one or two other women in the party.

There was one choice left. To make her way in disguise across the kingdom of Mercia, avoiding the court, avoiding anyone who might have a remote memory of King Offa's daughter, travelling on towards the western stars that still called her incessantly. To Powys. To the land Elisedd had loved so much, to see if she could find his ghost.

Bea watched their journey across the choppy sea, their landfall beneath the white cliffs and the last leg of their journey towards the cathedral, disjointed scenes from Eadburh's dreams. She saw her walk with her friend, Freda, up the aisle of the cathedral, followed by Theo and Ava, still there in her wake, and give thanks before the shrine of St Augustine at the end of the journey for God's protection and deliverance before she and Freda hugged and kissed goodbye. How strange, Bea found herself thinking. She had seen Eadburh show so few signs of emotion or genuine fondness for any other human being. Elisedd had been the one exception. It was as though her passion for him had sucked her dry. And yet in the last months she had grown fond of Cwen, and Theo and now of Freda, and more than all of them she loved her dog.

The pilgrimage to Canterbury accomplished, she joined another group of travellers heading west, who were happy to give her a lift on the back of their ox-cart until she found herself at last in Wareham, the final resting place of her murdered husband, Beorhtric.

For a whole day she hesitated outside the abbey, overwhelmed with unexpected remorse, then at last, wrapping her face in her veil, she went to kneel before his tomb. He had been generous to her in his way and allowed her to become his queen. She had not intended to kill him. Once more a man had died because of her. Once more she needed to do penance for his soul. Spending two days in prayer beside his stone-built catafalque, she walked at last with downcast eyes out of the abbey and resumed her journey with Theo and Ava, north now, through a landscape she still carried in her head from the days she had progressed around the kingdom of Wessex as its queen, heading towards Mercia.

It was on the road to Hereford that she found herself with a band of men and women, many of them blind, heading towards the shrine of St Ethelbert. Healing springs had sprung up, she learned, in the places where his head had rested on its way to its tomb. This time her prayers were heartfelt. She knelt and prayed with the others for the miracle of sight, that in exchange for the punishment she had exacted on the martyr's murderer she might be permitted to see again the man she loved.

That night one of their number let out a cry of joy as he found suddenly that he could see, and that same night as she lay in the dark, an anonymous, penitent, guest in the hostel at St Guthlac's Priory, she fell asleep at last and dreamed of Elisedd.

Elisedd, maimed and delirious, had lain for a long time between life and death in a priory, deep in the heart of the mountains and forests of the Ardennes. He was brought back to life and hope by the ministrations of the almoner and his medical knowledge, and of the prior with his deep compassion. Emperor Charlemagne, it appeared, had after all spared his life if not his manhood, aware perhaps in some part of himself that it would have been hard for any human man to resist the wiles of Eadburh, the witch Queen of Wessex.

Elisedd blamed himself for what had happened. If he had stayed at home she would not have been tempted away from her vows, she would have been still abbess of a rich and beautiful monastic estate and she would have been content if not happy without him. He vowed to spend the rest of his life in penance for his weakness in giving in to his lust, and for his inability to save her. What had become of her he didn't know, but he doubted she still lived.

He heard once from a gossiping lay brother a rumour that she had survived the first winter that had almost killed him and that she had been seen far away in the kingdom of Lombardy somewhere south of a great range of snow-capped mountains; she had been in great distress and poverty, he was told, but after weeks of intense hope the prior's enquiries confirmed that she had died there at last of starvation and despair. And so the legend of Eadburh's fate was reinforced as it moved from mouth to mouth and telling to telling.

He spent the following winter in prayer for her soul and in studying the books that Charlemagne had donated to the monastic library. When spring came, Elisedd set off to return to his own land in Powys where, he vowed, he would retire to his *clas* at Meifod and spend the rest of his life in prayer.

Opening her front door, Sandra found Heather standing on the step.

'You can't keep away, can you,' she said nastily. 'What do you want now?'

Heather pushed past her. She walked straight through into the living room and stood looking down at the table, strewn with Tarot cards. There was a book on Anglo-Saxon magic lying open beside them and she spun round. 'You have to stop this!'

'What I do is none of your business, Heather. None at all.'

'It is when it is my friends you're hurting.'

'Friends!' Sandra's voice shot up an octave. 'Not the kind of friends I would like to have. But, if you must know, I'm trying to help them. To do that I had to find out who or what was possessing them.'

Heather stared at her. She was fervently wishing she hadn't come. 'And did you find out?' she hazarded cautiously.

'Oh yes.' Sandra clenched her teeth. 'It's a woman called Eadburh. She's some kind of uber-powerful witch.'

She was, she had to admit, still traumatised by the vicious fury of the woman who had confronted her, knife in hand. She shuddered. It had taken all her resolve to throw a protective shield between her and the virago who had turned on her when she held out her hand to Emma, silly little Emma. She glared at Heather, who was staring down at the Tarot cards with a look of extreme disgust.

'Please stop doing this,' Heather repeated firmly. 'It's dangerous.'

'No chance. It's not dangerous; it's interesting. I'm not stopping. No one believed me when I warned them what was happening. They probably "prayed" for me' – her voice assumed a note of sarcasm as she uttered the word – 'which obviously had no effect whatsoever. I am going my own way now and I realise that is the real me. I was good at what I did. I can make a difference, whereas you, what are you?' She couldn't contain the bile. 'A goody-goody who sits in the cathedral and asks God to make something exciting happen because it sure as hell has never happened up to now, and when God listens and sends you a full-on case of possession to watch, all you do is whimper and come to me and beg me to stop. Well, I'm not going to. I want to see what happens. I watched this girl Emma change into a vicious murdering woman and when she does it again, I want to be there to see it happen.'

'Sandra! Emma is not a murderer. She's a child!'

'That's the point. She's not a child. Not when she's possessed. You don't understand how this works.'

'All right. You tell me.' Heather was clutching her coat around her as though her life depended on it. She didn't even recognise this woman any more.

'It works when people like you interfere. She will kill you and she will kill Beatrice.'

'No. That's not true.'

'How do you know? Do you know anything at all about it?'

Heather hesitated. She wanted very badly to turn and run out of the house. She wasn't even sure why she had come. She took a deep breath. 'No. I don't. You had better explain it to me.'

'I'm not going to explain anything. But I will show you how powerful I am. Every bit as powerful as the witch woman in the past who thinks she can defeat me. You came to me for help, and you are going to get help. But not in the way you ever dreamed!'

Heather turned and began to walk towards the door. 'I pity you, Sandra. And I shall pray for you. And I shall ask Mark and the dean – everyone – to pray for you.'

Sandra stood where she was, watching as Heather, summoning every ounce of courage she could, walked down the passage and out onto the street.

With a satisfied smile, Sandra sat down again. She was deep in thought. Finally, she shuffled through her Tarot pack until she found the card she wanted. Temperance. A good manager. Normally placid and likeable. But reversed. She reached out to turn the card upside down. Failure to understand. Conflict of interest. Discord.

'So, Heather. I have added you to my list. You are going to regret trying to thwart me,' she murmured.

She didn't notice at first the card that fell, face up, on the carpet at her feet. The High Priestess. When she did, she stared at it thoughtfully and pushed it back into the pack.

From the shadows Nesta, ever watchful, smiled. Time for her to step forward and put an end to this woman's nonsense.

'Bea?' Simon whispered. He was standing next to her in the nave of the church dedicated to Elisedd's sixth-century ancestor, St Tysilio. 'Are you asleep?'

She gave him a weary smile. 'I was in the past. Here. Eadburh headed back here in the end.'

'So she found him.'

'I don't know. If she found him, why is she still calling his name?'

They were silent for a while, then he sighed. 'I've ordered food. We should go back to the pub and eat something.'

Bea reached for her mobile. Still nothing from Emma. She nodded. She was sick with fear but they had to eat. 'Afterwards, I will come back to the church.'

In her dream, Bea was still in the church at Meifod, but it was not the church they had explored, it was a tiny stone building with rounded doorways and a small tower surmounted by a beaten metal cross, on the far side of a broad cloister garden. Beyond that lay the yard farmed by the other buildings of the community. Eadburh was there, confronting the abbot, who was listening ashen-faced as she shouted her demands. 'He's here. I know he's here.' She turned and shouted up into the vault of the roof. 'Elise! Where are you?' She swung back to face him. 'I know he's here. I have prayed and my prayers were answered. My love is here. Why are you are hiding him from me?'

'Lady, I promise you he is not here. Elisedd, our father in Christ, left here two years since to go on a pilgrimage and he never returned. Please, you must believe me.' He was looking at her, anguished. 'I cannot help you.'

'No. He's here. He must be here. I've crossed the world to find him.' Tears were beginning to pour down her cheeks.

'He never returned,' he repeated, his voice broken. 'We heard he was killed on the orders of the Emperor Charlemagne.' He dropped his gaze, visibly embarrassed.

So, he too knew the story. She shrank away from him. 'And that is why you hide him. Even now, after all my travails, you dare to keep him from me. Tell him.' She threw down her staff, watching as it rolled away with a rattling sound over the floor tiles. 'Tell him I'm here. Let him decide.'

The old man let out a deep sigh. Behind him, one or two of the other monks had appeared, anxiously watching. One of them tiptoed away to return with two of the younger lay brothers. 'Please leave our church. This is the house of God. No one tells lies here, Lady Eadburh. He is not here. He never returned from his . . .' He hesitated over the word, 'pilgrimage.'

'Please, lady.' Another man, this time not in holy orders,

his head untonsured, stepped forward. 'Please, lady, let me take you to our guest house. You can refresh yourself and rest. Father Abbot speaks the truth. Our beloved *Abad* Elisedd has not returned. If he had, you would be informed, I promise you.'

She looked wildly from one to the other, then let out an anguished scream of frustration. 'I don't believe you. A pox on you all! A curse on this place! I will not rest until you give him up!' She spun round and stamped back towards the door, and out into the sunlight, leaving the men crossing themselves in horror.

'So, are you still watching?' Eadburh was looking straight at Bea. 'You who haunt me and follow me half across the world with your evil eye. A pox on you as well. And you!' She was looking at someone behind Bea. Someone who was wearing modern clothes. Someone who was smiling in utter triumph. Sandra. Bea let out a cry of fear. Her wall of protection wasn't working. She could see no way out. She could feel the mud of the track beneath her feet, smell the dung of the cows in the byre, see the men and women approaching across the cloister garth, one of two of them clutching pitchforks to threaten the intruders.

Slowly Eadburh began to laugh. The sound was chillingly bitter.

Bea groped for her cross. 'Christ be with me, Christ within me.' The sun had disappeared and the sky was growing black. She could hear the wind in the trees on the hillside. And now another man, the reeve from the abbey farm, was approaching them with a sword in his hand. 'Get you gone!' He was shouting at Eadburh. 'We offered hospitality. We offered you food and rest and you reply with curses. You are truly Offa of Mercia's daughter.' The man's words were laden with scorn and hatred. 'I remember the story well. You flouted God's law; you are a murderer and a witch. How dare you come here to this peaceful sacred house of God and sully it with your curses. You and your women.' His angry gaze took in Bea and then behind her, Sandra.

Bea froze. Desperately she was trying to break the trance

that was holding her there, but she was trapped, unable to move.

She could hear Sandra laughing. 'So, I have you where I wanted you,' she crowed, ignoring Eadburh. 'Beatrice, your powers are nothing compared to mine!' Bea felt a band of pain tightening round her head. Why was this woman turning everything into some weird competition between them? Throughout her training she had been taught that revenge was out of the question. She must not fight back. She must call on her protectors. Call on the name of Jesus. And where in God's name was Nesta?

More men were appearing out of the barn. The pitchforks were pointing directly at them and they were coming closer.

'You wouldn't dare touch me,' Eadburh screamed. 'I am Queen of Wessex. The king of your country would dismantle this place stone by stone if you laid a finger on a royal head, and the armies of my kinsman King Ceonwulf would destroy you all without a second thought.'

They hesitated, looking at each other. Bea could feel the first drops of rain. The wind was cold, from the north. 'In the name of Jesus Christ!' she called out. 'Please, stop.'

They didn't hear her. They were no longer looking at her. They were coming closer to Eadburh. Then the abbot was there beside the reeve. 'Hold back!' he called. 'Don't harm the queen, nor her followers.'

So he too could see Bea and Sandra.

'Open the gates. Let them depart in peace.' His was the voice of authority. The men lowered their pitchforks and the man with the sword stood still. Eadburh turned towards the gate. Her face was stony, her eyes like flint. She walked past the two women from another time without glancing at either of them and set off up the track towards the woods.

The scene changed. Bea and Sandra were outside on the track as well. The gates had closed and the night was all around them. Bea turned towards Sandra, who was close to her now, her eyes slits of malice, and suddenly she knew what to do. A mirror. She needed a mirror. She had a mirror. In her bag. In her hand. Somehow she managed to hold it up, let Sandra see her own face as with a final shaft of light the sun set behind the hill.

Sandra let out a scream. And then she was gone.

Mark's mobile was ringing again. He picked it up eagerly, desperate to hear from Bea, but it was Heather. With a sigh he rejected the call. He would call her back later.

The phone rang again. This time it was Simon. 'Mark? We're in trouble. I'm driving Bea home. She's been taken ill. I'm heading back to Hereford now.'

46

Emma knew she should not take lifts from strangers. Every girl in the world must know that by now; she had had it drummed into her since she was about four, but the old man with two huge black-wrapped rolls of hay in the back of his ancient pickup had a kind face. He drew up a few yards in front of her, his indicator blinking. 'Are you going up to the farm?' he asked as he leaned across and wound down the window.

The first part of her journey had been easy. She had bought her train ticket online several days before leaving, using the details from her mother's credit card, memorised one evening when Val had gone up to bed with a headache, leaving her handbag on the table in the kitchen. By the time the school had rung Val, Emma had been well on her way to Wales. She had carefully planned every stage of her journey and knew she would have to walk once she got to the station the other end, but that didn't matter. That way, her journey would feel more like a pilgrimage. She would start at Eliseg's Pillar.

Ringing her father had been part of her plan. From her study of the map it had seemed a good place to meet. Iconic. Central. Near the royal palace at Dinas Bran. Then he could take her home to the cottage. She hadn't thought it through. She was in the wrong place. The distances were far greater than she had expected. And there was no trace of Elisedd.

At first it was fun; a great adventure. She had worn her boots and had her rucksack with her. Stocking up with sandwiches and water from a shop near the station at Llangollen, she was on her way. She had her phone but she kept it switched off. She had no intention of letting Felix track her down. It never occurred to her that her mother might call the police. She only wished she hadn't rung her father. It had been too soon. She wasn't ready.

She knew where to go next. The man at Valle Crucis had been helpful. She was lucky enough to pick up a bus for part of the way, but otherwise, she walked. Her feet were covered in blisters by the time she arrived at Meifod.

Elisedd wasn't at the church of St Tysilio. He had never returned there. A kind woman had directed her to a B & B and there with the help of her host she had found a book that mentioned Mathrafal as the seat of the kings of Powys.

He wasn't there either.

She was almost in tears, exhausted and hungry, when the pickup pulled in beside her. 'Yes,' she replied. 'I'd love a lift.'

'Hop in then.' The driver pushed the door open. 'Chuck your rucksack in there. Don't mind the dogs.'

The footwell was full of rubbish and the seat was covered in notebooks and leaflets and sheets of old instructions covered in oily finger marks. She manoeuvred her way in beside him.

He gave her a quick glance as he engaged gear. 'You look just about done in. I reckon my wife can find you something to eat.'

'Thank you.'

'So, where were you really going?'

The tears came at last. 'I don't know. I was going to meet someone, but he wasn't there.'

'Boyfriend, is it?' He turned off the road and they bumped up a track for some half a mile before pulling up outside a long low stone-built house covered in ivy. He climbed out and went round to the side to pull her rucksack out as the dogs raced away round the back of the house.

'What's going on, Dai?' A woman appeared at the door. Small and plump, with a rosy-faced smile, she was wearing an apron and her hands were covered in flour. 'Who is this?'

'Young lady in need of some TLC, Annie.' The old man smiled kindly. 'I reckon she's had a bit of a disappointment. A cup of tea wouldn't come amiss. I'll leave you to it while I go and feed the dogs.'

Emma followed Annie into her kitchen and sat down at the large scrubbed table watching miserably as the woman rolled out the dough from her mixing bowl, cut it into rounds and put them deftly onto the greased bakestone on top of the old black range. Annie washed her hands and filled the kettle, sliding it onto the hotplate. 'So,' she sat down. 'Do you want to tell me what's happened, *cariad?* How can we help?'

Her kindness was the last straw. Emma burst into tears again. She poured out her story, or most of it. She didn't tell Annie that her parents would be looking for her frantically, she didn't mention the missed exams and she didn't mention the fact that her boyfriend had died 1200 years ago. None of that made sense, even to her. All she knew was that she had to find him.

'What made you think he'd be at Meifod?'

By now Annie had poured the tea and, retrieving the hot Welsh cakes straight from the griddle, sugared and buttered a couple, put them on a plate and pushed it in front of Emma. The kitchen was full of the sweet, spicy smell.

'That was where he came from originally.'

'And he agreed to meet you there?'

Emma sipped her tea gratefully and reached out to her plate. 'Yes. No. We planned it long ago. He didn't know I was coming today. It was a surprise.'

'Have you rung him?'

Emma shook her head. She groped for a believable excuse. 'My battery is flat.'

'Then you plug your phone in right now and charge it up.' The woman climbed to her feet. 'We may look a bit old fashioned here, but we do know about mobile telephones. Our son made sure we had all the technology – and sometimes we even know how to use it.' She smiled.

Emma could hardly refuse. She produced her phone and the charging cable from her rucksack, ignoring all the missed calls that flashed up as she plugged it in. 'He used to tell me all about his land of Wales and how beautiful it was. He said one day he would take me to see a place where there were dragons and the shrine of a saint who loved hares.'

'Ah.' The old lady nodded gravely. 'I'm not sure I can help you with dragons. One never knows where they will be found these days, if at all. They're quite rare you know.' She gave another gentle smile. 'But the shrine to the patron saint of hares, there I can help you. That's not too far away.'

Emma felt a huge surge of hope. 'Do you think he might be there? We talked about it so often. The King of Powys who gave the princess the land for the shrine was an ancestor of his.'

'My goodness. Proper Welsh he is then, this boyfriend of yours.' She pushed the plate in Emma's direction. 'Well, you finish up your tea and have another of those Welsh cakes and I'll get Dai to drive you up there and see if the boy's there. How about that?'

'Mum!' Felix burst into the sitting room where his mother was sitting alone, staring into space. 'Emma's just popped up on my phone.' He held it out to her.

'Oh thank God!' Val burst into tears. 'Where is she?'

'Exactly where Dad rang from. A place called Meifod. I've looked it up. It's in what was Montgomeryshire. That's in Wales,' he added. 'It's an hour and forty minutes from Hereford, I checked.'

'Did you speak to her?'

He shook his head. 'She's switched it off again. She must have plugged it in to charge it up.'

'When your father rang me, he said a local woman had seen her there, in the church, but by the time he got there, she had gone.'

'Well, she hasn't gone far then. I'm going to look up the

coordinates, then I'll know exactly. She'll be OK, Mum.' He sat down on the arm of the sofa, touched by the extent of his mother's distress. Up to now she had been mostly angry, but now he could see the strain this whole thing was having on her.

'You're so good, Felix. If you hadn't known how to track her phone we wouldn't know where she was.'

'Are you going to tell the police?' A small part of him felt a bit guilty at spying on his sister; but the other part was furious with her for being so bloody selfish.

His mother nodded. 'I must. They've been looking for her all over the country. Your dad said someone had seen her in Llangollen and I told them that, but since then, nothing. I have to tell them we think we know where she is.'

'And you'll call them off?' He had been horrified when she had first involved the police. None of what was happening to Emma would be explainable in their terms. Or anyone else's.

'I will when your father finds her. Did you ring him back to tell him you'd heard from her phone?'

'I tried, but his phone is off too. They may just be out of reach of a signal up there. There are some quite remote areas. I looked it up.'

She gave a little moan. 'I don't know what to do, Felix.'

'Leave it, Mum.' Her helplessness made him feel very responsible. 'I've messaged him. He'll ring as soon as he gets the text. I'm sure everything will be OK. Em is sensible. She won't do anything silly.'

Apart from running away, missing her exams and trying to find a man who died over a thousand years ago. He kept those thoughts to himself.

Val was blowing her nose hard, pretending not to cry. She looked up at him, her eyes shiny with tears. 'I'm so sorry, Felix. I forgot to ask. How did the exams go today?'

He gave a theatrical shrug. 'Not bad. I think I did OK.'

Dai dropped Emma off in the village of Llangynog, at the foot of the Berwyn Mountains. They were outside an Edwardian house with a carved B & B sign hanging by the gate. He had shown her where the shrine to the patron saint of hares was on her map. It was still a couple of miles away, he said, in a little church up a long deep valley, but she had the impression that unless he knew she was safe, he wasn't going to leave her on her own, so as he drove away she waved goodbye and began to climb the front steps to the front door of the house. Within seconds he was out of sight. Immediately she stopped, ran back down the steps and hurried back up the main street. She was heading for the trail he had pointed out to her.

Mark had the front door open before Simon had even pulled the car up opposite the gate. Between them, he and Simon managed to extricate Bea and carry her in and through into the snug where they laid her carefully on the sofa.

'Shut the front door, Simon,' Mark whispered urgently. 'That wretched woman Sandra's probably out there somewhere. I really don't want her barging in.' He took Bea's hand in his and rubbed it gently. 'Sweetheart? Bea? Wake up.'

'She was muttering something about Sandra in the car. It sounded as though she had followed us there, I couldn't make it out and I didn't want to stop.' Having slammed the front door and slid the chain in place for good measure, Simon went over to peer out of the window. 'I can't see anyone. Do you want me to go out and look?'

Mark shook his head. 'Let's keep all the doors locked.' He bent to kiss Bea's forehead. 'Bea, please wake up.'

'Should we call a doctor?' Simon was still standing by the window.

'Not yet. Let's see how she is when she's warmed up. She's so cold.'

'The car wasn't cold.' Simon was chewing his lip in anguish.

'What about Emma? I'm sorry. I should have asked at once.' Mark glanced up at him.

'You have more pressing things to worry about.' Simon stared helplessly at Bea. She looked so pale and so vulnerable lying there on the sofa, he felt a sudden terrible pang of anguish. He turned away. 'Em visited the church at Meifod yesterday evening and spent the night in a B & B nearby. Since then, as far as we know, there's been no sign of her.'

'So, how did this happen?' Mark gestured down at his wife.

'Bea was in the church. I'd gone to the pub across the road from the church to organise some sandwiches for us and ask them if they'd seen Emma. Bea and I had a bite to eat and a cup of coffee, then she said there was something else she needed to check in the church. There's an ancient cross in there that's rather special. She went over ahead of me and she was sitting in a pew when I went in. I thought she had fallen asleep, but then she sat bolt upright and let out a cry. I don't know if it was surprise or pain, or what. I grabbed her arm and, and' – he swallowed hard trying to find the words – 'it was as if she was in a different place, with different people. She was looking straight past me, talking, but so fast and so softly I couldn't hear her. And she looked afraid. So terribly afraid. I didn't know what to do, but I had to get her out of there. I tried to wake her, and I managed to get her back to the car and pushed her into the passenger seat, then I realised I would have to get the keys off her to drive. I assumed they were in her bag and opened it. She'd been clutching it on her knees and she let out a shriek and I thought she was trying to stop me looking inside it, but she started rummaging around in it frantically and she pulled out a little make-up mirror. She held it out in front of her, pointing away from herself at something, someone I couldn't see.' He took a deep, shuddering breath. 'Someone screamed, someone else, Mark, someone who wasn't there, couldn't see, the most awful agonised sound, and then Bea fainted.'

It was two hours before Bea awoke. She stretched and groaned. 'Mark? What time is it?' She was looking around her in a panic, completely disorientated. And then she remembered. The drive up through the Welsh Marches, the search for Eliseg's Pillar and for Mathrafal and finally the church at Meifod. 'Simon? Where's Simon?'

'He had a text from Felix.' Mark knelt by the sofa and brushed her hair back from her forehead with a gentle hand. 'He's driven back to Meifod. Emma's phone has been switched back on and Felix tracked it down to a farm a mile or so outside the village.'

'He'll be exhausted. We've been driving all day.'

'I tried to dissuade him, but he insisted. He's a good man.'

She pushed away the rug he had tucked over her and sat up groggily. 'Thank God Emma's all right. Sandra was there, Mark, at Meifod. In the church. Somehow she was there in the past with Eadburh. She was vicious. Like nothing I've ever seen. I didn't know what to do. I had to think of something to ward her off.'

'And that was why you held up the mirror. Simon told me.'

'I did? A real mirror?'

'A real mirror. It was in your bag. He told me he was looking for your car keys and you grabbed it and held it up. He said someone screamed.'

'And he heard it? It was Sandra. Sandra screamed. The mirror reflected her evil back at her, like some awful basilisk.' She lay back, exhausted. 'Oh Mark, it's all such a muddle.'

'I didn't try to wake you when Simon left,' he said firmly. 'I thought it better if you slept.' He grabbed his phone as it rang again. 'Heather. She's rung several times.'

'Did she leave a message?' Bea held out her hand. 'Let me speak to her.'

Mark stood up and, passing over the phone, walked over to the fireplace. He leaned his elbow on the mantelpiece, staring down into the empty hearth.

Bea listened for a few seconds. 'Come over, Heather. Now. Please.'

She lay back, exhausted. 'She went to see Sandra again. We need to hear what she has to say.'

Mark went through to the living room and over to the front window. Outside the Close was dark save for the street lamps dotted between the trees. The cathedral was closed. The scent of new-mown grass drifted in through the window. He turned round to find Bea had followed him. 'I hope Simon finds Emma soon. The poor man is beside himself with worry.'

When Simon drew up outside the farmhouse he saw every light in the place was on. Climbing out of the car he walked towards the front door. It flew open and an elderly woman appeared. She stared at him in confusion. 'Who are you?'

'I'm sorry. I am looking for my daughter, Emma. I understood she was here earlier this afternoon.'

'Well she's not here now!' the woman cried, shaking her head. 'Why won't anyone believe us? We told the police all we knew. Why on earth would we hurt her? Dai has gone with them to show them where he dropped her. That was hours ago, and he hasn't come home.' The woman broke down in tears. 'They searched the house and the barns. Everything.'

Simon stared at her, aghast. 'I'm so sorry. I didn't realise the police had been called.' He followed her indoors. 'My son told us he had tracked Emma's mobile signal here, which was why I came as soon as I could.'

He stood where he was as the woman turned away and went to sit down at the kitchen table, her head in her hands. 'We would never hurt her. Why would we?' she repeated brokenly. 'I gave her a cup of tea and some of my Welsh cakes.'

Simon followed her, reaching for his phone. 'You said your husband – is it your husband? – dropped her off somewhere?'

'Llangynog. She wanted to go to Pennant Melangell to see the shrine. He thought it was a bit late to drive her up to the church, so he dropped her outside a B & B. He couldn't remember the name of it, so the police said they would drive him there to talk to the owner. That was hours ago.'

'A shrine?' Simon was perplexed. 'What shrine?'

'She said she had arranged to meet her boyfriend there.' The woman looked up at him pleadingly. 'We were trying to help. We didn't think she should be wandering around on her own, a pretty girl like that. Dai would never lay a finger on her.' Suddenly she was angry. 'I could see what that police sergeant was thinking, but we've got granddaughters her age!'

The word boyfriend was echoing round Simon's brain. Did she have a real boyfriend, or were they talking about Elisedd? 'I'm so sorry.' He knew he kept repeating himself. 'I suppose it's the police's job to believe the worst of people. Perhaps I'd better follow them and see what's happening. Where is this shrine?'

She repeated the instructions and he typed them into his phone. 'I'll make sure someone gets in touch with you and lets you know what's happening,' he said as he walked out to the car. 'And again, I'm so so sorry about this. You were only being kind.'

Tucking his phone into the cup-rest between the seats he allowed the satnav to guide him along the dark winding road. Halfway to Llangynog he pulled into the hedge and called Felix. 'Yeah, Mum called the police,' the boy said. 'They were questioning her about social media and stuff. Perhaps they thought the old man was impersonating someone. I didn't know they'd rushed over there. Oh God, that's awful. Those poor people.'

'As far as the police were concerned she's a seventeen-year-old girl who's been missing for two days,' Simon said. 'Now they've been told she's trying to meet up with a mysterious boyfriend and was last heard of in a remote farmhouse with two elderly people who probably looked a bit sinister. They were trying to do what's best for her. Have you managed to track where she is now?'

'No. Her phone is still off, Dad. I'll ring you the second she pings up again.'

'OK. I'm going to head for this shrine. I don't know what else to do.' Simon stared out of the windscreen at the silhouette of the mountains, impenetrably black against the blackness of the sky, and wound down the window. The car flooded with the scents of deep country, flowers, hay, a faint aroma of sheep and above all the immensity of silence. Without the car lights on it felt as if he was in the middle of nowhere. It was the middle of the night, he was completely exhausted, and he had no idea where Emma was.

47

When Sandra woke it was dark. She was lying on the floor at home in her own front room, alone, with a splitting headache and ribs that felt so bruised she couldn't breathe.

For several minutes she lay there wondering what had happened. That flash of light, blinding, a lightning flash, had flung her backwards against a stone wall. She remembered feeling as though her head would burst and an agonising pain in her chest, then nothing.

It was several minutes before, clutching her chest, she staggered to her feet. She could see her phone lying on the far side of the table. If she could just reach it, she could call for help. She winced again as a sharp pain sliced through her ribs, leaving her gasping.

She had been in this incredible place, an ancient monastery, watching Emma pleading with the monks. No, it wasn't Emma. It was a vicious, hard woman who knew her stuff. Eadburh. Bea had been there too. Watching. Always bloody watching. And someone else. Another woman, in the shadows.

She reached out for the phone and grabbed it. She was feeling dizzy; the room was spinning. She sat down, trying to catch her breath and, both elbows planted on the table, brought the phone up close to her face, squinting at the little screen, trying to find her contacts. There must be someone she could call

She remembered now. She had looked away from Eadburh to find Beatrice watching her. Beatrice who had been distracted, who hadn't even seen her, Beatrice who had been open to the entire scene. That had been her chance. She had gathered all her strength and hurled a curse towards her. She had seen Bea struggle and stagger, and then there was a man there with her. Simon. The author. Emma's father. He caught Bea and pulled her away, away from the past, away from the scene, saving her from, from what? The next thing she remembered was the flash of light, a blinding reflection, the slam as she hit the wall, and then nothing.

Somewhere Emma had taken a wrong turning. She had made a last-minute decision to follow the signpost towards the trail rather than stick to the road along the bottom of the valley and found herself climbing up through fields and then woodland as she headed west above the course of the river. It was growing ever darker as she walked and she found it hard to see where she was going through the trees. Deep down she was beginning to feel frightened. She was exhausted and lost and hungry. Now was the time to call her dad. Before the last streaks of red had faded from the sky she sat down at the foot of an oak tree and turned on her phone.

There was no reception. Almost crying with frustration, she stared at the screen in despair. Leaning back against the trunk of the tree she closed her eyes and felt the hot tears begin to slide down her cheeks.

It was some time later later she remembered she had food. Annie had wrapped up some Welsh cakes and put them in a bag for her to take with her. She felt in her rucksack for the package, still slightly warm from Annie's stove, and she began to eat. The food helped her think more clearly. She needed to find a signal for her phone then she would be able to find where she was in relation to the path. Standing up, she turned on the phone's torch and flicked it round the trees. She mustn't use it for too long in case she ran down the battery again, but there was enough to find her way upwards towards the higher ground where there would be a signal. She spotted a path almost at once, narrow, but definitely a path, winding through the trees out of sight. With a renewed sense of hope, she set off and found that almost at once it started to climb.

Then, somewhere in the distance, she heard a wolf howl.

Bea was sitting up in bed. Mark had insisted on walking Heather home and, finally acknowledging her exhaustion, Bea had climbed upstairs. But she couldn't sleep. Sitting up again she pulled a throw round her shoulders and she went back carefully over their conversation. It seemed that Heather had gone to see Sandra and found her with her Tarot cards. According to Heather, the woman had completely lost it and virtually threw her out. After Heather left, they assumed, Sandra had returned to her cards and travelled, not to Pavia this time, but to Meifod. How had she done that? Where had she learnt all this vicious stuff, the Dark Arts? Bea shivered. Sandra was more than a professional psychic. She was the real thing. Whatever that meant. She had obviously seen the danger at some point in her past and sought refuge in the cathedral, but even that had failed to save her.

Bea lay back against the pillows. If only she didn't feel so tired. She had depleted her reserves these last few days; psychic work uses a lot of energy at the best of times and she had been using hers constantly. Add to that the driving and the stress and the worry, and she was almost at the end of her tether. But somehow she had to find enough energy to go back into the fight. She wasn't sure now who she was fighting against, Eadburh or Sandra, but what she was doing, above all else, was trying to save Emma.

She needed help, she realised that now. She had been stupid to try and handle all this alone. She sighed as she climbed out of bed. However stupid it might appear, she couldn't lie here, doing nothing, she had to see if she could find Nesta in her wanderings across the universe. Nesta would know what to do. She had spotted the problem long ago. Surely she would at least dispense some of her enigmatic advice.

At the top of the attic stairs she paused and listened. The house was very silent. Pulling her dressing gown around her more tightly, she went into her room. It smelled faintly of herbs and beeswax candles. She could see the light from the street lamps behind the rooftops reflected on the ceiling and in the distance she heard the chime of the cathedral clock, echoed faintly a few seconds later by the clock from the Buttermarket in High Town. The sounds reassured her. Time was where it should be.

Lighting a new candle, she sat down on her cushion and, out of habit, reached for her touchstone. It felt warm and receptive, reassuring. Closing her eyes she centred herself, careful with her circle of protection. Sandra was not going to sneak under her guard again. Here, in her study, surrounded by all she held sacred, she was doubly protected and this time she was expecting trouble. Slowly she sank into the silence, waiting.

Theo and Ava had been hiding in the shelter of the woods until Eadburh returned. Alerted by the quiet growl in Ava's throat, they spotted the young monk as he crept out of the gate and set off hesitatingly towards them, along the track. He was carrying a horn lantern and a staff, much like Eadburh's own, but he was not striding out confidently, he was obviously nervous, looking round, peering into the shadows. They had heard the bell ringing for vespers some time ago. Soon it would be full dark. Eadburh had hoped so desperately to be ensconced, if not in the arms of her beloved, then at least in the small guest hall by now; had not God himself taught holy men and women to entertain the weary traveller without question? As it was, she and Theo were still there, huddled together with the dog under the trees. Her resolve had gone. She was tired and miserable and, for the first time, without hope.

'Hello!' he was calling quietly. 'Are you there, my lady?'

She stepped out of the shadows of the undergrowth. 'I'm here.'

He turned towards her with obvious relief, then immediately

ushered her back into the cover of the bushes. 'Father Abbot and his sons in Christ did not tell you the truth, my lady. They did what they thought best, but I know *Tywysog* Elisedd would have wanted you to know what happened to him.' He broke off, suddenly realising she was no longer alone. There behind her was a young man and a large tawny dog. He stepped back, afraid.

'They won't hurt you!' she said wearily. 'This is my servant and my dog. So, you know where Elisedd is? He is still alive?' Her whisper floated through the trees of the coppice around them. She felt a rush of hope.

'He came back to Meifod, but he was greatly troubled. He would not take up his place here again for all he was so much loved by all the brothers. He held many private talks with the Father Abbot.'

'And how do you know this?'

'Because the prince told me himself.' She saw the young man's cheeks colour slightly in the dim light from the lantern. 'I looked after his needs when he went into retreat in a private cell in the woods near here. I brought him food every day and sometimes he would sit and talk to me. It was not a confession – for that he went to Father Abbot – but he needed to talk, I think, to understand himself what had happened. He believed you dead, and he told me he blamed himself for your death. He could never be easy in his conscience for causing you so much distress. He told me what they did to him.' There was a long pause.

'What who did to him?' She felt herself grow tense.

'The emperor's men.' He looked at her, his eyes troubled. 'They spared his life, on the direct orders of the emperor of the Franks, but . . .' The young man fell silent, unable to go on. He blushed even more deeply.

'I know what they did.' Eadburh bit back a sob. She had prayed it wasn't true.

'They spared his life so he could dedicate it to God,' he went on eventually, 'and, after much thought and prayer here, he told me he was going to walk up into the Berwyn Mountains to visit the shrine of the Blessed Lady Melangell. He said he had promised you that one day he would take you there. He told me he would make offerings at the shrine and seek counsel from the mother abbess there, then he would go into seclusion for the rest of his days somewhere over there in the heart of the mountains.'

Eadburh let out a little cry of pain. 'When was this?' she could barely frame the words.

'Two years since.'

'While I was still living a life of comfort and safety in Pavia. God forgive me.' She was silent for a while as an owl hooted close beside them in the depths of the rapidly darkening wood. 'I must try and find him. Can you tell me where to go?'

The young man nodded gravely. 'I will guide you there, lady. He thought you dead, but in my heart I swore to God that if ever I saw you I would try and unite you. It would ease his guilt and his grief. The shrine is a day's walk from here, perhaps less. There's a pilgrim path. It leads from our St Tysilio's shrine here to the shrine of St Melangell, which is on land given to the holy saint by an ancestor of our prince.' He studied her more closely and she saw concern in his eyes as he noticed she was shivering. 'The night is growing cold, my lady. I will guide you and your servant to a barn nearby where you will be safe and sheltered. I will bring you food and blankets, then at first light I will return to show you the way.'

Eadburh lay shivering, wrapped in the rugs he had brought them. He had produced bread and cheese and oatcakes and a flagon of ewe's milk too, which she had shared with Theo and Ava. Even snuggled against Ava's warm back she was unable to sleep for the cold, and she heard the bell ring for prime as the daylight began to flood slowly across the broad valley.

Sometime later he reappeared, two scrips slung across his shoulders, a second staff in his hand. He smiled as he sat down beside her and began to unroll a linen napkin to reveal a breakfast of spiced meat and bread. This time he had brought a leather bottle of mead. 'To fortify us on our long walk, lady,' he said cheerfully.

'Will you not be in trouble with the abbot if you're absent

472

all day?' Eadburh commented as they gathered up their belongings. Each took a rug to drape over their shoulders in the chill of the early morning mist.

'I will confess all to him when I return, and I will gladly do penance if he requires it.'

The young man led the way confidently, following an almost invisible path, seeming to know which way to go even without the help of the sun, which was still lost in the morning haze.

She followed him blindly, sometimes lagging behind, sometimes catching him up to walk at his side, Ava always at her heels, Theo a little way behind, her thoughts fixed on Elisedd and the fact that before the sun went down she was going to see him again. This man had been a part of her life since she had first set eyes on him all those years ago at her father's court in Sutton, when the great dyke was under construction with its ditches and ramparts and high wooden palisade, already breached in many places. Now here she was deep in the kingdom of Powys, in the land of dragons and magical hares, coming closer to him every moment as they walked along the river valley, ever deeper into the wild hills. She was going more slowly now on the steep stony tracks. Every now and then the young men ahead of her were pausing to wait for her as she plodded on, her shoes worn into holes, her feet dusty and sore even before they had started their journey. Above them the sky slowly cleared and the sun beat down. Two ravens were circling high above the wooded hills, their croaking calls echoing from the cliffs above the valley.

'Dad, I've had a ping from Emma's phone.'

Simon was dozing in the car outside the little church of St Melangell, at the end of the long single-tracked road that led from Llangynog when he answered his phone.

'Felix?' He sat up and groaned. He was cold and stiff. There was a house nearby, he could make out the outline of it in the dark, but when he had knocked a couple of hours before there had been no one there. It was some kind of religious retreat house, as far as he could make out, and he had hoped against hope that Emma would be there, but the house was in darkness, the church was locked, the car park empty and the valley was silent. 'Where is she?'

'Not far from you. Up on the hillside. I just spoke to her. She's cold and lost, but she's OK. Phone her now. She knows you're quite close.' He clicked off and Simon was left staring at his blank screen.

'God bless you, Felix,' he murmured.

'Dad?' Emma sounded tearful. 'I'm lost. My battery is low.'

'I'm not far away, sweetheart. Don't worry. I'm beside the church, down in the valley.'

'There are wolves here.' Her voice was very faint. 'I'm scared.'

'Listen, Em. Save your battery. I'm going to hang up. Leave your phone on so Felix can track you. I'm coming to find you.'

Felix answered at once. 'I'll give you her coordinates, Dad. It's wild moorland as far as I can make out. You might need to alert mountain rescue or the police or someone.'

Simon was outside the car now, gazing up where the high sides of the valley rose above him, black against the stars. 'Which direction?'

He heard a muttering and distant click of a keyboard as Felix consulted his laptop and he pictured the boy at home in his London bedroom. 'Can you contact the police and tell them where she is, Felix? I can't hang around. I have to try to find her. I'm not sure I'll be much use in the dark, but she's so scared up there alone.'

She had said there were wolves. He felt a rush of panic in his throat. There were no lights anywhere. Were there wolves in these mountains? He had heard they were thinking of reintroducing them back into parts of Scotland, but not in Wales, surely? Or was she back in the past in one of her dream states? He went round to the back of the car and pulled out his walking boots, first aid kit and his waterproof jacket. He was about to close the boot when his phone rang. 'Mr Armstrong? This is the police. We have your daughter's location from your son. Please, stay where you are. If you get lost as well, it won't help anyone. The mountain rescue team are on their way. If you're in touch with Emma, please tell her to stay exactly where she is and then cut the call so she doesn't waste her battery, but tell her to leave the phone switched on so we can track her. That will help us find her more quickly.'

Simon stood there, staring up at the sky. A swathe of stars was visible above his head, but the mountainous sides of the narrow valley were impenetrably black around him. He kept hoping to hear a car or better still a helicopter, but the night was totally silent. He found his torch in the glove pocket of the car and with its powerful beam he found a signboard at the edge of the car park with a map of the valley. He scanned it with an ever-increasing sense of panic at the size of the vast mountain range around them. Eventually he switched off the torch and made his way under the lychgate into the church-yard. He could see the church in the starlight. It was a long low building with a small square tower. All round him were gravestones, old and shining in the damp. He found himself wondering if they were slate. According to the maps he'd studied there were old slate quarries all round these mountains. Cliffs, quarries, mineshafts. Disused mines up on the moors. Don't think about it. Emma was safe. She had promised she would stay put.

He was standing under an ancient yew tree. Somewhere an owl called, a sharp, unexpectedly loud sound in the silence. Its mate hooted in the distance and he realised he could feel the hairs on the back of his neck stirring. He could smell the resinous tang of the yew, and the fresh cold sweetness of the mountain air. Why was no one coming? Surely the police would be on their way by now? He checked his phone. The battery was still 60 per cent. Resolutely he pushed it into his pocket. If there was news, someone would call him. He wandered further up the narrow path towards the church porch. Perhaps he should pray. Say a prayer to St Melangell herself. He found he had closed his eyes, squeezing them tight shut as he used to when he was a little boy. His mother used to tell him to say his prayers at night when he was frightened of the dark. He gave an inward groan. He had had no concept then, in his cosy little bedroom with red and blue zoo animals on the curtains, of just how empty and lonely and scary the real dark could be. He surveyed the silent churchyard. 'Please, please, look after my little girl. Keep her safe. She was coming to find you, to pray at your shrine. Tomorrow we'll come together and bring flowers, offerings. We'll give thanks if you keep her safe tonight.' He took a deep breath, trying to contain his despair. Here he was, trying to bribe a saint. But surely she would understand. She had been a compassionate woman, keeping the hare safe, away from a king and his hunting dogs. She was brave and kind and obviously beautiful as the king had wanted to marry her on the spot. It was when he had failed to lure her away from God that he had given her this whole valley. He pulled out his phone and stared at the screen. It was still dark. There had been no missed calls.

Sandra sat staring at the table in front of her. An ambulance had come in the end and the two women had sat with her on her own sofa for ten minutes, making her breathe slowly. 'You're all right, Sandy,' they kept saying. 'It's a panic attack. Relax. Breathe. You're not hurt.'

Not hurt! When she had been knocked across the room by the force of the psychic blast. She could still feel the bruises. But they had found nothing. No bruises. No injuries. One of them had made her a cup of tea in her own kitchen and they had treated her as if she was senile, holding her hand and talking to her as if she was demented. Then they had had a call-out to a real case, someone who was genuinely hurt, and they left, telling her to remember to breathe and to go and see her doctor if it happened again.

She groaned. The parting shot from one of them had been, 'It must have been a bad dream, love.' She wasn't supposed to hear the next comment, made to the other paramedic as they crossed the pavement back to their ambulance: 'Either that or her imagination. What an imagination! As if!'

Imagination. As if! Was that it? She pulled up her jumper and stared down at her own front. They were right. Their delicate probing had found no damaged ribs, no bruising, no scars, and there weren't any. She was completely unhurt. She realised there were tears running down her cheeks. They were right. She hadn't interacted with Beatrice or with Emma at all. Everything was a sham, a make-believe. A dream. This whole Tarot thing and the psychic powers she had assumed she had, the curses, were a load of hooey, a pretence to make her feel good and in control of her life. None of it was real. In the past she had enjoyed having power over people, frightening them, glorying in their gratitude when she pretended to do things for them in the psychic realms, and she loved it when they paid her without question for her services.

She had believed it. She had genuinely believed it was real.

And those two calm confident women in their green uniforms had told her it was all a dream.

She looked down at her spread of cards, still lying neatly arranged on the table and with a howl of anger she swept them onto the floor. Her life had been no more than a scene from a film. *Alice in Wonderland*. When the Queen of Hearts and all the other characters at the tea party changed and dissolved and fluttered around Alice's head, nothing but playing cards.

48

Dad had spoken to her. And Felix. They knew where she was. Rescuers were on their way. All she had to do was wait. Emma stared round in the dark, her eyes wide, trying to make out the details of her surroundings. There were gorse bushes up here, their flowers blazing gold, even in the dark, smelling of warm coconut and sugar. Again she heard a wolf howling in the distance. Further away now. She bit her lip, trying to hold back her tears. She wanted to run away, hide in some cranny in the rocks but there was nowhere. The moor seemed to spread out before her eternally, rising gently towards the summit of the mountain, a clear silhouette against the stars and she didn't dare move. Her phone battery was down to 12 per cent and she didn't want to turn on the torch. Without it, she couldn't make out the path and any moment the phone was going to die. Overhead the stars blazed down over the high moors and she could hear a curlew in the distance, its eerie call echoing across the heather in the dark. She heard a movement behind her and she spun round, her heart thudding, poised to run. There was a man standing only feet from her. She stared at him, frozen with fear, trying to make out his shape, but he didn't move, he didn't make a sound and she realised at last it was an old thorn tree, twisted and tortured by the wind into the shape of a human torso.

'Elisedd,' she whispered. 'Where are you? Please, help me.'

Her tears were scalding on her cheeks, her hands freezing cold as she brushed them away. 'Please, Elisedd. You said we would come here together.' She drew in a deep breath, trembling. 'Please.' There were demons in these hills, giants and trolls, spirits flitting across the moorland towards her. She could feel her panic building.

A few minutes later she saw another figure near her. Not a tree this time, a woman, moving towards her, drifting across the ground in the starlight. She felt a stab of visceral fear. She had expected her rescuers to have torches but the woman was coming straight towards her without hesitation, surefooted in the darkness.

'Emma?' The wind was rising now and Emma could hardly hear what the woman was saying. 'Don't be afraid. I'm here to help you. Rescuers are on their way. You must stay still. Nothing can harm you. There are no wolves here. No demons. Here, take this.' The woman had long, silver-streaked hair and a dark scarf over her head and round her shoulders. She held out her hand and pressed something into Emma's cold fist. 'Your angels are watching over you, child.'

'And Elisedd?' Emma stammered. 'Where's Elisedd!' But the woman had gone and now she could hear shouting in the distance and the excited barking of a dog and see the light of several powerful torch beams far away below her down to her left, emerging from the trees.

When Simon's phone rang he was leaning against the stone wall of the church, staring out into the darkness while listening to the dawn chorus, the sound pouring from the trees around the church, from the blackbird in the yew tree and the robin in the thorn and a thousand other birds from the depths of the woods on the slopes of the hills.

'Mr Armstrong? This is the police. Your daughter has been found. She is safe and well. They will be taking her down the hill to Llangynog if you would like to meet them in the car park there.'

She didn't want to go to hospital.

'Take me to the church, Dad. Please. After all that, I have to go there.'

'Emma!'

'No. I mean it.' Her voice was hoarse and she was still shaking with cold, wrapped in a space blanket in the back of the car.

One of the mountain rescue team had been a doctor and had given her a quick check-up, squatting by the car door with her stethoscope, listening to her chest, taking her pulse. 'We can't make her go to hospital,' she said as she stood up again. She looked at Simon with a weary smile. 'She's been very lucky. She's uninjured and she's not hypothermic. All she needs is to get warm and have some hot food and rest with her dad there to look after her.' The doctor herself looked worn out.

Simon felt a pang of guilt. 'I am so sorry you were all dragged out like this.' He glanced back at Emma, whose eyes had closed as she leaned back in the seat, shivering.

'It's our job.' The doctor was packing her gear back into her bag. 'We're very happy to help. Things could have been an awful lot worse. Your daughter didn't do it deliberately. She seems confused and distressed, but she was sensible. She stayed where we could find her. She's told us, she didn't realise how long it would take to walk to the church or how quickly the darkness can fall in the mountains. But she's safe now, that's the main thing.'

Early in the morning though it was, they were taken in by the lady who ran the B & B where Dai had dropped Emma off all those hours before. 'I was too worried about the girl to sleep much and I saw the mountain rescue people heading into the car park so I had to come and see she was all right. Come you in and welcome. Emma can have a warm bath and I will make you both a nice cooked breakfast, then she can have a sleep upstairs. You can go up to the church later.' The woman, whose name was Helen Jones, directed Simon where to park his car and then ushered them up the steps to her house.

She sat Simon down by the fire in her dining room then took Emma upstairs, ran a bath for her and provided her with a pile of fluffy towels. 'Now shout if you want anything.' Simon heard her strict instructions floating down the stairs as he huddled close to the fire. He could smell the scented bath oil and he smiled.

'The police came yesterday looking for her,' she explained when she came back downstairs. 'Poor old Dai was distraught about what happened. I'll give him a ring now and let him know Emma is safe. He'll be so thankful.' She gave Simon a searching look. 'You look as though you could do with a hot bath as well.'

He smiled. 'That's a kind thought, but I'll be fine. All I needed was to find her safe.'

She nodded. 'Well, I'll leave you to ring your wife while I cook breakfast. I'll run up and check Emma is all right. We don't want her falling asleep in the bath. I've a bedroom made up upstairs, so once she's eaten something she can go up to bed for a couple of hours.'

Simon was swept away on the tide of her kindness.

With a smile he picked up his phone. Val was so relieved at the news she forgot to be furious. He could hear her voice trembling. He cut short her stammered demand to speak to Emma. 'She's still in the bath. No, it's not too hot. The doctor told us what to do. She's fine. Tell Felix he saved his sister's life,' he added before he ended the call. He was fending off waves of exhaustion himself and he hoped he could stay awake long enough to eat breakfast.

It was not until after lunch, rested and revived, that Simon drove Emma towards the little church. In daylight he stared up at the precipitous sides of the valley rising above them with increasing horror as they drove slowly down the winding single-tracked road. The mountains were utterly beautiful but deadly, he could see that now. Outcrops of slate, high cliffs, old quarries, at least one still operational as far as he could see, thick forestry and wild woodland on the sides of the valley and behind, the high peaks of the moorland, with disused mineshafts lost in the heather, rising in austere beauty under a clear blue sky.

There were no other cars parked outside the church and Simon stood back as they climbed out. 'Do you want to go in alone?'

Emma nodded. 'Thanks, Dad. But before I do' – she groped in her pocket – 'I want to show you something.'

He looked down at the little cross in her hand. It was obviously gold, intricately engraved and set with garnets and it was bent, damaged, engrained with dirt. 'That lady I told you about? She gave it to me.' Emma looked at him and bit her lip. 'It's very old, isn't it?'

Simon caught his breath. He picked it up off her palm and held it up to the sunlight. 'Yes,' he murmured. 'I would say so.'

He put the cross back in her hand and she slipped it into her jeans pocket. Then she grinned at him. 'If it's Anglo-Saxon, it's probably worth millions.'

He smiled back. 'Well thousands, perhaps. What makes you think it's Anglo-Saxon?'

'Duh!' It was the reply her brother would have made. She had bounced back as though nothing untoward had happened, revived, Simon thought to himself, like a drooping flower put into fresh water.

He watched as she walked away from him, through the lychgate under the yew tree that had sheltered him the night before, up the path and into the church.

Sandra crept into the cathedral, holding her breath, peering round her apprehensively as though she expected to be zapped from on high. Tiptoeing, she made her way to the back of the nave and sat down. She still loved this place, she realised. And it was still here for her, whatever she had done. She leant back, staring fixedly in front of her up towards the great gilt crown hanging above the crossing beneath the tower. Her mind was a blank; she had no idea what to do next. Everything had fallen apart. She had had complete and utter faith in herself and her own judgement. Certainty. It had stayed with her unwaveringly ever since she had walked away from the church. But she had upset and perhaps nearly killed people she respected and looked up to and in trying to do the right thing she had exposed them all deliberately and intentionally to the most terrible danger. Weird, unbelievable danger.

She would stay for evensong, then she would go home. Perhaps God would speak to her during the service. Reassure her. Tell her how she could make it all better.

Eadburh was exhausted but with gritted teeth she walked on in the young man's shadow. He strode ahead with an easy confident stride, glancing round every now and then to make sure she was still behind him. 'We'll be there before dusk.' He gazed up at the sun, westering now into the mist. Soon it would have disappeared behind those high dark hills.

'Not much further.' They had turned into a steep valley following the gentle course of a winding river, treading the damp meadowland. 'The shrine is up ahead,' he confirmed at last. 'Do you see the hares in the field over there? It's as if they know they're safe here. The sisters allow no coursing dogs in this valley. It is a sanctuary for the creatures.' He cast a worried look at Ava, who had stopped at Eadburh's heels. The dog showed no sign of wanting to chase anything.

Eadburh stopped, leaning on her staff, and gazed round. She had loved hunting in her youth and had watched the death of so many animals with equanimity, but here she could accept the peace and tranquillity of the sacred space and feel it wrap around her and she felt strangely certain that Ava understood and felt the same.

She said nothing as their guide moved on, his calm demeanour seeming to transmit itself to the creatures who watched them from the gently swaying grasses, their enormous eyes fixed on the visitors without fear.

They were welcomed by the small community of nuns who cared for the shrine and shown to the guest house. Now she was so close to finding him, Eadburh was reluctant to ask for Elisedd. It would only confirm what she already knew, deep inside herself. There was no point. He wasn't here. It had all been in vain.

It was late evening when at last they went into the shrine and Eadburh knelt before the statue of the saint. She had no money to give and could only present a posy of flowers to leave at the feet of the statue and light a candle to carry her prayers to heaven.

Later, as she sat in the abbess's presence, she found herself unable to ask the question she had been nurturing in her heart for so many years and she sat without words. It was the abbess who broached the subject. 'Your companion told me you seek *Tywysog* Elisedd ap Cadell, my dear,' she said. Her voice was gentle and spoke of long acceptance of her role. 'I fear I have sad news. He died of a fever soon after he came to us, surrendering his soul to God with gratitude and acceptance. I spoke to him before he died and heard his confession and the message that he left for you, should you have survived your own trials and find your way here one day.' She gave a serene smile. 'He said if you came, he would know it, even in Heaven, and he would bless you with all his might and with all his love and when eventually you join him in paradise he will be waiting to guide you as he promised into the gentle mountains where the snow-white hares of winter roam.'

Eadburh couldn't speak. For a long time she sat without moving then at last she stood up. 'Can I see his grave?'

The abbess nodded. 'Of course. It isn't here at the shrine. He died as a hermit up in the mountains he loved and asked to be buried there. I will send one of the sisters to show you where he lies.' She stood up and came over to put her arms around Eadburh's shoulders. 'I know this is not what you hoped, my dear, but comfort yourself with the thought that few people have been loved so much and so consistently. Whatever you do now, you keep him there in your heart forever.'

Elisedd was buried on a plateau high above the river valley. Leaving Ava with Theo in the guest house, Eadburh followed a young sister up the hillside. There was no stone on his grave, no wooden cross. No one would ever know where the Prince of Powys lay, save the sisters of the shrine and now the woman he had loved and lost. The nun who had guided her here crept away, leaving her alone to mourn him in privacy as she threw herself down on her knees beside his resting place. When at last she stood up it was to look out across the immense distances towards the setting sun and let out a cry of despair.

'Elise!'

Simon opened the door and tiptoed into the church. It was long and narrow, the roof heavily beamed, and at once he saw the hares everywhere, small tokens and models and sculptures. At first he couldn't see Emma, then he realised she was up beside the shrine itself, beyond the altar. Reconstructed from broken fragments that had been scattered at the Reformation, this little place of sanctity was the most peaceful, sacred space he had ever been in. The church was empty except for the two of them. Quietly he walked up the aisle to where Emma was kneeling. She had lit a candle.

'Did she find him?' Simon asked quietly.

'No. She was too late.'

'Is that why she still calls for him?'

Emma nodded. 'She was never reconciled to his loss.'

He sat down on one of the seats nearby. 'What happened to her?'

'I don't know. What was there left for her? Perhaps she stayed here and died near him. Perhaps they buried her with him.'

'That would be a lovely ending to such a sad story.'

Emma stood up and came to sit beside him. 'But then, if she had done that, she would have found him, wouldn't she? She would have joined him in paradise.'

'Perhaps she wasn't allowed? She was a cold-blooded murderer, after all.' He could have bitten his tongue. If he could have taken back the words he would have done so, but it was too late. He glanced at her sideways and to his surprise saw she was nodding.

'Perhaps you're right. Just because that's a neat romantic ending we would all love so much, it doesn't make it right, does it. I suppose she is at best in purgatory. Did the Anglo-Saxons believe in purgatory?'

'I'm not sure I know. I suppose so. They were good Christians by this time.'

'Then perhaps you should light a candle for her too, Dad. Every candle must help her journey onwards towards the light.'

Simon didn't argue. He stood up and reached up to the basket on the windowsill for a tea light and a lighter. He touched the flame to the wick and bowed his head. 'God bless you, Eadburh,' he whispered, 'and may you rest in peace.'

They bought a guidebook and some postcards and Simon found her a little statue of a hare, leaving the money in the box provided, and then at last, reluctantly, they wandered outside. 'It's a long drive back to the cottage,' he said as they climbed back into the car. 'We'll find somewhere nice for supper and then you can sleep on the way.'

He gave her a quick look as she was fastening her seat belt. She was thoughtful. As he reached forward to start the engine he wondered if she was thinking, as he was, that this was not the end of the story. Eadburh was not at rest.

49

Bea was looking out of the window. Across the grass of the Close the cathedral was a huge black silhouette crouching against the clear dawn sky. At this hour there were no people about. She had crept out of bed without waking Mark and headed down to the kitchen. Only then did she check her phone. There was a text from Simon: Emma safe. We are back at the cottage. Will phone you tomorrow.

The text had been sent just before midnight.

'Thank God,' she whispered. 'Thank you, Nesta.'

She had watched Eadburh, her Eadburh, weary from her long walk across the empire of Charlemagne and then on across the kingdoms of England and across Offa's Dyke into Powys, standing at last on the hillside high above the little stone church, heard her cry of distress echo down the centuries, seen Nesta, leaning on a tall staff, her hair blowing in the wind, standing behind her. She had watched as Eadburh stood up, her eyes blind with tears, and reached out to the woman. Briefly they stood there together, hands clasped, then Nesta had left her and walked alone up the mountainside and across the moorland, her skirts dragging in the heather. There was another younger, more naïve Eadburh there now, the version of Eadburh from the woman's own dreams, Emma, lost there in the twenty-first century in the darkness of the mountains, who was, without knowing it, looking towards the distant grave.

Nesta approached the girl and put her arm around her shoulders and Bea, watching from unimaginable distances, saw the woman press something into the girl's hand. From the safety of the future she saw the wolves prowling the high moors, knew there were wild boar in the remote forests on the steep hillsides, saw a herd of wild cattle plodding slowly along the shadowy valley floor. None of them came near the girl. Only a lone hare stood up amongst the tall grasses and watched over her with huge unblinking eyes.

'Bea?' Mark's voice made her jump. 'You were up early.'

She smiled. 'I was thinking.'

'Any news of Emma?'

'Simon texted me. She's safe. He's taken her back to the cottage.'

Mark came to stand beside her. 'Thank God for that!' he said fervently. He stood silently for a while beside her, looking out into the garden. 'I wonder what they'll do,' he said at last. 'Will she go back to finish her exams, d'you think?'

'He said he would phone me later.'

'Good . . . I'm off to morning service. I'll be back for break-fast.' He bent to drop a kiss on the top of her head. 'I'm so glad he found her.'

She turned to him with a smile. 'Scrambled eggs for brekkie?'

He laughed. 'That would be perfect.'

When he came back later, he had news. 'Sandra was at the service. You are not going to believe this. She admitted that she had dabbled in the occult, but she knew now it wasn't real. She confessed, more or less, there and then, that she realised it had all been her imagination. So, she has decided to go on a pilgrimage. She said it would give her a chance to rethink her life and to make up for the awful things she might have done.'

Bea had been stirring the eggs. She spooned the mixture onto their plates and put toast and coffee on the table before she sat down opposite him. 'You have got to be joking!'

'No. She cornered me and I was all set to give her a not-too-gentle ticking off when she burst into tears and begged my forgiveness. What else could I do? It was then she blurted out her news.'

'So, where is she going on this pilgrimage?'

'The Camino.'

'She stared at him. 'In Spain?' She was incredulous.

He nodded. 'She came to evensong last night, apparently, and had some kind of revelation. She said she thought about it all night and then looked it all up on the internet. She's going to fly out to France and join a group there, and do the whole thing, over the Pyrenees, along northern Spain, and walk the whole way, with the last bit to St Iago de Compostela barefoot.'

Bea sat back in her chair. Words had failed her.

'I told her I thought she was being extremely brave and that it would be a wonderful thing to do.' He grinned as he picked up his knife and fork. 'And do you know, I almost envy her.'

But it was real. What she did was real. She had real power. And what about what she did to me?

Bea wanted to say it out loud, but somehow she prevented herself. She had, after all, done the unforgivable and retaliated. She thought guiltily about her little mirror, the instinctive gesture she had barely been conscious of making. Was that retaliation? Or did it count as self-defence?

'So, what happened to make her see the light?'

Mark gave a rueful smile. 'Apparently it was a paramedic.'

Mark drove Bea up to the cottage that afternoon. Emma, white as a sheet, with great dark rings under her eyes, seemed over-whelmed with exhaustion. Bea followed her out into the garden at the back of the cottage while Mark and Simon sat out in front on the terrace.

'It must have been very frightening, all alone on that hillside in the dark.' Bea went straight to the point.

Emma nodded. She sat down on the wooden bench under the apple tree, leaving room for Bea beside her, then she groped at the back of her neck to unfasten the gold chain she wore there. 'Look at this. Dad went and bought me a chain this morning.'

Bea looked down at the little cross in her outstretched hand. She could feel an ice-cold halo emanating from the gold. 'That was what Nesta gave you?'

Emma looked at her, astonished. 'How did you know that?'

'I saw her. She was there for you, to keep you safe.'

Emma swallowed hard. She closed her fist over the little ornament, letting the chain dangle through her fingers. 'And you were watching over me too.' She turned towards Bea and clutched her hand tightly. 'This little cross feels weird. It's holding me there, close to them.'

'Then why have you kept it on?'

'Because I want to. Because I don't dare take it off. It's to protect me, to save me from her.'

'From Eadburh?'

Emma nodded. 'She screamed when she knew he was dead.'

Bea nodded. 'I heard her, sweetheart.' No one could forget that level of despair, echoing down the centuries.

'If she knew I had made love to him, she would kill me.'

Bea looked at her sternly. 'But you were her, Emma. You were not yourself. You and she were woven into a dream together; it was never a reality. You dreamt her dream and she dreamt yours.'

'And if I dream it again?'

'I don't think you will.'

Emma's gaze was so full of doubt, Bea felt a shiver run down her spine. She reached down and took the cross out of Emma's hand. She had an eerie feeling she had seen this cross before. In another dream she had seen Elisedd give it to Nesta. She would never know for sure. None of this made sense, but for Emma it was a treasured amulet to keep her safe and that was all that mattered. She kissed it with a silent prayer then reached out to fasten it back round Emma's neck. 'Take it off when you want to. Don't feel trapped by it. Appreciate its blessing.'

Emma reached up to touch it. 'I slept in the car on the way home last night, but the moment we were here I felt more and more cold. I slept with it in my hand. It kept me safe. It's strange though. Out here, in the garden, in the sun, it's worse.' She bit her lip. 'I wanted you to tell me what's wrong. I've never liked it out here at the back. I've never been able to sit under this tree. On the terrace it's fine and the house is fine, but here?'

Here, where Bea had seen the figure of Eadburh, a shadow under this very tree on that first day she had come up here alone to find out why Simon thought his holiday home was haunted.

And suddenly she knew why. She looked at Emma, still seated on the bench beside her, and she nodded. 'But you know why too, Emma. This is your dream. Tell me what is wrong out here. This is an important lesson for you. Close your eyes. Let the story come.'

'You will be here? You won't let me go?'

'I'll be here.'

Eadburh left the convent of St Melangell as the winter snows receded, the hares began to lose their white winter coats and the first brush of spring touched the high mountains of Pennant. She kissed the abbess goodbye and with sturdy shoes and staff and a new leather scrip stitched for her by one of the novice nuns she set off for the south. She was alone this time but for her beloved Ava. Theo had returned with the young monk to Meifod before the snows had set in and planned to become a novice there. She needed no one with her as she headed back towards the court of the King of Mercia. She seemed to be guided every step of the way. He was at Sutton, a larger palace by far now, so she had heard, than in her father's day, with rich stone buildings and verdant fields and it was her plan to demand her right as a Queen of Wessex and Princess of Mercia to a place at his table.

Perhaps she had always meant to turn off her path and head for the high ridge where she and Elisedd had trysted under the summer skies. Last time she had come here on horseback; this time it was as a penitent on foot. She was very tired as she toiled up the long track and stood at last on the summit of the ridge, gazing down across the hazy distances the way

491

she had come from the heart of the kingdom of Powys. She had met no dragons, but she had seen the shrine of the hares as he had promised. She stood for a long time watching as the sun moved lower in the sky and settled into a crimson haze. Slowly the light faded, until there was nothing left but a narrow line of dull red cloud along the far horizon and all at once it was gone.

She turned and made her way in the dark towards the sheepfold where they had made love. There, behind the wall, she found a pile of dry leaves, blown by the wind. Rolling herself in her cloak she lay down with Ava beside her, cuddled up close as the icy rain started to fall. In her dream as she slept Eadburh was once more in the warmth of Elisedd's embrace. The dog woke, and feeling her mistress had grown cold, snuggled up more closely as far away a wolf began to howl.

When the shepherds came to gather in the sheep before the autumn storms arrived they found their bones, stripped of flesh by the creatures of the night, and they buried what was left of the woman and her dog where they lay.

The shepherds did not return to the *hafod*. Nor did anyone.

For generation after generation the story remained potent of the ghost of the woman on the hill who cried for her lover and of the great dog who ran at her side. Time passed. Anglo-Saxon and Celtic rulers were replaced by Normans. Welsh princes and English kings disputed the borderlands as again and again this Marcher country changed allegiance. Plantagenet, Lancaster, York. A man called Owain Glyndŵr, descendant of the Welsh princes, tried and failed to take back his country. The Tudors came and Welsh blood again ruled over the ridge but by now the legend was forgotten. There was no one there to hear the woman's cries. Three hundred years later men came and seeing the heaped stones of the fallen walls built a farmhouse for a new generation of hill folk.

They too heard the sad call of the woman, carried echoing on the wind. They attributed it to the *tylwyth teg*, the fairies of Wales, and left offerings of milk and bread to ensure their benisons. The offerings were always gone by morning. In March shepherds would watch the hares boxing and on moonlit nights in summer they would see, sometimes, a lonely hare staring up at the sky and they would shiver, but they would never harm her. The hare had always been a magical creature. She was sacred to the Celts . . . Their sheepdogs would not go near the wall where Eadburh and Ava lay.

The farmhouse fell into ruins in its turn and then a Victorian collector of oddities came and fell in love with the site and built himself a cottage there. He pressed ferns into a book and wrote poetry and he heard the cries on the wind and shivered and went away. No one by then remembered the story of the lonely lady of the hares who was Offa's daughter.

'So, she's buried here?' Emma stood up slowly and looked round her.

Bea nodded. 'I believe she is.'

'What shall we do?'

'Perhaps we could set up some kind of memorial to show that she and Elisedd are not forgotten. To show them we have understood their joy in this place and their pain at being separated and we could pray that their spirits can now be released to join one another in the light.'

'Their two lonely graves were high on separate hills.' Emma gave a sad smile. 'It would be nice to mark this place somehow, you're right. And say prayers to allow them to rest in peace together at last. Then the cottage won't be haunted any more.'

'I think it's a lovely idea.' Bea put her arm round Emma's shoulders. 'Let's go and talk it over with your dad and Mark.'

And Chris, she thought privately. What would she say to a memorial in the back garden? Would that go down well with her holiday visitors? It seemed strange to think of anyone else staying here in the cottage Emma had referred to as home, but when his six months were up, if not before, Simon would be going back to London. That had to happen for Emma's sake. Once she was back amongst her friends, and refocused on her own life, she would slowly be able to distance herself from all this. But she was right, here, before they left, there had to be some final closure for that troubled spirit and the first thing she, Bea, could do was return her touchstone to the flower bed. This time it would stay here, invisible beneath the mats of wild thyme and saxifrage.

Sandra did not waste any time. She rented out her flat, immaculately cleaned, with fresh flowers on the table, booked her trip online and packed her bags, but not before she had disposed of her Tarot cards buried in the bottom of the rubbish bag and quietly slipped her crystal ball into the swiftly flowing waters of the River Wye.

'It was all in my head,' she said before Heather could enquire. 'I was ill. I hurt myself quite badly and I thought Bea had done it with a bolt of lightning. As if she could hurt me. An ambulance came and they explained I was having panic attacks.'

Heather stared at her, aghast. 'Why didn't you call me?'

'I did. Your phone was off.'

Heather closed her eyes. She had blocked the number. 'And you've given up all that psychic stuff?'

Sandra nodded. 'It's not real. It never existed. I was making it up. I've been to the doctor and he sent me straight to a counsellor who made me see it was all to make me feel important. It was because I was lonely. I'll get a job when I come back from Spain.'

Heather nodded slowly. 'And you'll come back to us at the cathedral?'

'I might do,' she said. 'I'll send you a postcard when I get to Compostela. Look after yourself, Heather.'

Kate and Phil asked Mark to christen their baby; their chronicle was to be sold the following year and they had promised donations in remembrance of St Ethelbert and St Melangell. Simon was going to write the official description.

When his mother had left for Provence, reluctantly accepting that her children would not be going on this particular holiday, Felix had caught the train to spend the summer with his father and his sister. His results when they were published were exemplary and he planned to return to school in the autumn to study for his A levels, so Val was in a good mood when she returned from France.

Emma enrolled at a sixth form college in London to take her exams and prepare for university and Simon was going back with them at the end of the holidays to finish the edits of his book in his own study at home, overlooking the quiet Kensington courtyard.

It was at the end of August that they set the statue of a young woman with a hare in her arms and with a dog sitting at her feet, carved by a sculptor friend of Kate and Phil's, in a shallow alcove in the stone wall at the back of the garden. Mark held a little service of dedication and of blessing for the spirits of Eadburh and Elisedd. Emma planted a rowan tree nearby.

'You're going to miss them terribly,' Mark said to Bea after they left the cottage. The Armstrong family were driving back to London the following morning.

She nodded sadly. 'I will. But in a way I'm glad. That little service at the statue was lovely. There was a real sense of closure.'

'And nothing there to frighten off Christine's paying guests. Did you notice, already there's some moss growing on her feet. The statue might have been there for years.'

She smiled. 'The new people move in next week.'

'And I trust Christine has promised not to call you if they hear anything untoward.'

'They won't hear anything untoward, Mark. We both know that. Offa's daughter is finally at rest.'

She had seen the figure of the woman standing at the end of the garden watching them. At her feet sat the great golden dog, and there in the distance Bea saw the figure of the prince striding across the fields towards them, his arms outstretched, his cloak blowing behind him in the wind. The two figures approached one another and embraced, then as she watched they turned and walked away together across the hillside, followed by the dog. In seconds they were out of sight.

Author's Note

This story owes its original inspiration to my dog walks on the Offa's Dyke footpath. Several times a week I set off for two or three miles on part of the national trail that follows – more or less – the line of the original dyke. I often found myself wondering about Offa and why he built or dug the dyke. To answer the question I headed to the visitor centre in Kington and subsequently immersed myself in the history books. And thus this novel was born.

The Anglo-Saxons had always fascinated me, living as I had for many years near to Sutton Hoo (as witnessed in my novel, *River of Destiny*), but I was now drawn in by another thread of their history: Offa of Mercia, his family and his neighbour, the neighbour he was at such pains to keep at arms' length. All Offa's daughters had novel-worthy lives, but Eadburh especially intrigued me. There is very little mention of her, but what there is is startling. All we know is that she witnessed some charters, married Beorhtric and killed him. She appears in the Anglo-Saxon Chronicle and in Asser's history. Asser had nothing good to say about her. He tells us she was last seen in Pavia. But supposing she didn't die in Pavia? That magic word 'supposing' is the key to the novel.

I knew very little about the kings of Powys or the early kingdoms of what we now call Wales and not enough, after reading up as much as I could find, to provide a protagonist who would fill in both the Welsh side of the story and the gaps in Eadburh's recorded life and give a motivation for her character and her actions, so I gave her Elisedd. This is a novel and the story of Eadburh and Elisedd is fiction. I was filling in spaces where history falls silent, but I hope I have given them a credible story.

Charlemagne of course is all too well documented. But there is one thing about him which doesn't seem to appear in the history books. The legend goes that he had a passion for the hunting, herding dogs which we call Briards, or Bergers de Brie. My own beloved Dizzy, long gone to the great dog playground in the sky, reminded me with a ghostly nudge to my hand, as she often does to let me know she has actually gone nowhere and is still in charge, that a Briard must play a part in my novel, and so Ava was born.

Because my modern story is set in the kingdoms of Mercia and Powys I have used real places throughout the story. Offa's Ridge and the cottage are fictional, as is Coedmawr. I am sorry to say its Chronicle too is totally imaginary. Hereford, Marden, Meifod and Llangynog with the magical little church of St Melangell are all real. There has been no Canon Treasurer at Hereford Cathedral for many years and there is no Treasurer's House in the Close. As I realised the cathedral was becoming more and more a central character in the story I was tempted to invent a diocese. But how could I? It had to be Hereford. The cathedral is the most wonderful building, nestling in the centre of the town in an elbow of the River Wye. Not one of the huge Gothic cathedrals, it is older, smaller, stouter, with fat Norman pillars rather than fluted columns. It has a very special atmosphere.

For a real place I needed extra help. I would like to thank The Revd Canon Chris Pullen, Chancellor of the Cathedral (and Deliverance Adviser), for his enthusiastic support and patient answers to my endless questions about life in the Close, deliverance, and the running of a cathedral. Thank you as well to Dr Rosemary Firman, the cathedral librarian, for fascinating insights into ancient manuscripts (and wistful suggestions that only crowdfunding would possibly secure my imaginary chronicle for the cathedral library). Also thanks to Sheila Childs for her invaluable knowledge of the inner workings of the cathedral and its inhabitants and to the various guides and helpers who are absolutely nothing like Sandra. So many people helped generously with advice and suggestions and no one seemed fazed at the thought of ghostly goings on. Mark Townsend, sometime vicar in Herefordshire and now priest at large, who combines his Christianity with magic and mystery, gave me some very useful ideas and advice as did the enthusiastic guide (sadly I never found out your name) in Lichfield Cathedral who showed me their angel and the St Chad gospels.

I would also like to mention the many healers and spiritual teachers who have shared with me their learning and experience of other worlds, in friendship and courses and books, over many years. The knowledge I have gained from them has emerged in most of my novels. I feel I should at this point say, 'please don't try this at home unless you know what you are doing'. My particular thanks go to Sue Percival whose friendship and wisdom I have valued for almost 40 years. She helped me so generously during her last illness with information for this book. Sadly she was no longer with us by the time I had finished it, but we hoped that one day, somewhere, she would find a way to read it.

A final word of thanks goes as always to Kim Young, to Sophie Burks and my wonderful team at HarperCollins, plus my editors Susan Opie and Anne O'Brien and my brilliant agent Isobel Dixon with Sian Ellis-Martin, and to my son Jonathan for his constant support.

The writing of this book coincided with the first Covid Lockdown in 2020. That put the kibosh on one or two of my carefully planned research trips – hopefully you didn't notice. And who knows if GCSEs and A levels will still exist by the time the book is published, but, if not, I am sure everyone will always remember them and the stress they caused.